The gap between the Rathi soldiers and the elves closed to a few yards. Tents were burning all along the north side of the camp. Behind the smoke and flames, the elves hurled salvoes of spears. Their snakefang tips were keen, and though they didn't always pierce Rathi armor, they did find enough chinks to inflict casualties on the advancing infantry. When the soldiers slowed under the hail of spears, the fire caught up to them. The lead ranks wavered and began to fall back. Moggs were already scampering through the camp, hooting in alarm.

"Why are they retreating? I ordered no withdrawal!" Crovax shouted.

"Men can't fight in a fire," Nasser said. "We must abandon the camp!"

"Give up the camp to rebels? Never!"

He spurred forward, trampling men and moggs who got in his way. A wave of fire was inundating the tents and had almost reached the center of camp. Soldiers staked in the square for punishment screamed for help as the flames advanced. Some of their comrades tried to reach them, but the conflagration rapidly engulfed the area, turning the square into an enormous funeral pyre.

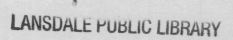

A World Of Magic

NEMESIS

MASQUERADE CYCLE · BOOK II

Paul B. Thompson

Dedication

For Jen Lee

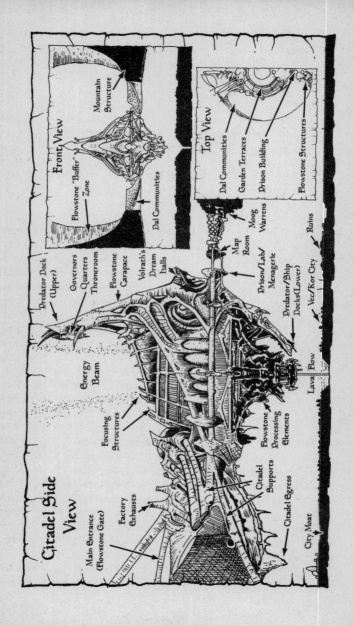

Citadel Side View

Main Entrance (Flowstone Gate)

Factory Exhausts

Citadel Egress

Citadel Supports

City Moat

Lava Flow

Flowstone Processing Elements

Focusing Structures

Energy Beam

Predator Dock (Upper)

Governors Quarters Throneroom

Flowstone Carapace

Volrath's Dream halls

Map Room

Prison/Lab/ Menagerie

Predator/Ship Docks (Lower)

Vec/Kor City

Ruins

Moog Warrens

Front View

Mountain Structure

Flowstone "Buffer" Zone

Dal Communities

Top View

Dal Communities

Garden Terraces

Prison Building

Flowstone Structures

OVERTURE
Lens

The ever-gray sky of Rath darkened from pearl to slate before the agent moved. He'd spent a day and a night in his hiding place, molded into a crevice between two large trees. His hooded shroud took on the color and texture of bark, and the special unguent on his hands and face had the same mimetic properties. While he was hidden, elves of the village had passed within arm's length of him. He could have struck them down with impunity, but such were not his orders. He had a specific target, and his new masters did not tolerate deviation.

As shadows lengthened in the Skyshroud Forest, the agent stirred his stiff, aching limbs. His legs burned with the sensation of a thousand needles pricking his skin, but with his altered senses he was able to block out the discomfort, just as he disregarded any feelings of hunger, fear, or remorse.

Villagers went about their evening tasks. Greenish light from their foxfire lamps filtered down, and for a moment the agent froze, startled by his own faint shadow on the black water beneath the trees. He craned his hooded head and saw the tree dwellers pass unconcernedly over him, scaling their vine ladders and bridges with practiced ease.

The large tree house in the center of the settlement was his target. The village had been denuded of warriors by the recent

1

attack on the Stronghold, but a lone elderly elf in snakeskin armor leaned against the doorway of the target's home.

Don't underestimate him, his master's voice whispered inside his head. *What strength elves lose in age, they make up for in skill.*

He gave the old guard wide berth, circling under the plank porch to the far side of the tree. The enormous swamp elm, a living pillar twenty feet wide, ran straight through the center of the house. On the trunks of their tree houses the elves cultivated a special type of gray-green lichen. It looked harmless, but when pressed, it exuded an oil that made the tree too slippery to climb. Under ordinary circumstances it was meant to keep out hostile merfolk and large predatory snakes.

Beneath his chameleon shroud, the agent wore two pairs of black cloth pads. One set had finger loops for his hands, the other, large bands to fit around his knees. The pads exuded a sticky substance developed in the evincar's own laboratory. His master assured him it would defeat the elves' lichen.

He sprang onto the trunk and stuck there like a wasp on a smear of honey. He raised his right hand and knee and heaved them upward. The pads adhered to the tree without a wobble. Soon his head was brushing the underside of the porch. The climbing pads worked just as well on smooth boards, and in moments he was on the porch.

The house was still—as it should be, for its master was away fighting the evincar. The target's shuttered window betrayed a hint of foxfire within. Was she still awake?

He inserted a finger between the shutter slats. The kidney-shaped room beyond was hewn from the living tree. There was a bed of boughs at the far end of the room, away from the only door. The target lay in the bed covered by a dappled green animal skin. By the door, a carved image of an angel held an open foxfire lamp.

The shutters were locked with a simple hook, which easily yielded to his knife blade. They swung out, and he lifted a lean leg over the sill. The figure in bed never stirred. Once in the room, he closed the shutters and went to the door. It was barred with a carved wooden beam as thick as his arm. Such primitive safety measures were useless against an agent of the evincar.

He crept to the bed, removing the sticky pads from his hands as he went. The agent knelt beside the bed and studied the face of his target. She was the one, all right. How many days had he looked into her eyes and felt love? How many days did it take the evincar's minions to condition such feelings out of him?

With a sudden motion, he yanked his knife from its sheath. It wavered for a moment in the lamplight as the deepest vestiges of his old self struggled with his new loyalties. He could not . . . resist. The blade slid quietly into the nest of soft boughs. He took out the vial provided by the overlords and used the knife tip to pierce the wax seal on the stopper.

One drop is sufficient.

He was supposed to pour a single drop in the eye or on the lips, but he saw something that made him change his method. A feather headdress hung from a peg above the target's bed. Silently, he plucked a single blue feather from the stylish array. Not so long ago he'd worn feathers like this.

He dipped the feather into the vial and gently pulled it out. Clear liquid clung to the tip. It smelled fresh, like a field of newly mown grass.

He brought the feather to the sleeping girl's mouth. For a reason no one will ever know, she sensed his nearness and awoke just as the elixir touched her lips.

Her eyes opened wide. The agent dropped the vial and feather and reached for his knife.

She must not scream.

No sound came from her slightly parted lips. She was dead. At the exact moment the deadly potion touched her livid lips, her life was extinguished. Her eyes, still soft with sleep, stared sightlessly at her killer. Without a shudder, he closed them.

His mission was only half done. He quickly set about finding something to hide the body in. An emerald snake hide would give him away in the dark, so he cast about for a more suitable wrap. He found a brown homespun blanket, trade goods from some Dal weaver, and flung aside the animal skin. The girl's linen shift might rustle, so he stripped it off. In death, her naked body resembled one of the evincar's statues, her pale skin translucent in the failing foxfire. The agent swallowed three times, trying to dislodge a strange lump in his throat.

Noise outside—shouts and the clamor of a crowd. Startled,

he flung the blanket over the body. A gentle knock on the door thundered through the small room.

"Avila? Are you awake?" said a female voice. "Did you hear the cries? Your father returns! He'll be here shortly!"

The agent hurried to the window. His knife and the open vial of death elixir were still in the girl's bed. There was no time to retrieve them; his arms were full.

"Avila? Avila, are you all right?"

When no one answered, the woman's tread could be heard rapidly retreating. She called, "Firanu! Firanu, come quickly! Something's amiss with Avila!"

No time for stealth now. He burst through the shutters onto the porch. He ran toward the high bridge platform. Pursuers would expect him to descend to a boat, not climb higher in the trees. As he rounded the curve of the great tree, he came face to face with the elderly guard, no doubt Firanu. He was armed with a barbed snake-fang spear.

"Stand where you are, or I'll kill you," the old elf said. The agent stopped so suddenly that the blanket around his prize slipped down, revealing his burden's lolling head.

"Avila!"

The agent leaped and kicked the spear from Firanu's hand. Before the elderly elf could go for his knife, the agent lowered his head and butted him squarely in the chest. The steel skullcap he wore under his hood connected with Firanu's breastbone. With a groan, the old retainer pitched backward over the porch rail.

The sound of the crowd was getting louder. A woman appeared, a matronly elf with a strong family resemblance to the dead girl. She saw the shadowy agent, his face paint adjusted to the gray night.

She screamed, "Kidnap, kidnap! My brother's child is taken!"

She offered no resistance as he rushed by on his way to the bridge. He pounded up carved steps three and four at a time. On either side he could see the glow of lamps gathering. He ran to a swinging bridge of planks and vines. Behind him, someone shouted for help.

Elves, some armed, gathered at both ends of the bridge. One pointed at him and cried out. The agent spared them a glance and began to run in earnest.

Nothing matters but the completion of your mission. Not your life, nor the life of any who oppose you.

A spear-wielding elf appeared at the near end of the bridge. The agent dropped his prize and sprang at his new foe. Before the elf could raise his weapon, the wraithlike agent was on him, bearing him down to the plank floor of the bridge. They grappled, and the agent used his steelclad head to bludgeon his enemy into submission. Blood streamed down the agent's face, mixing with the mimetic ointment. He rolled the dead elf's body off the bridge and let it splash in the dark waters below. He picked up the fallen warrior's spear.

More torch-bearing elves filled the landings at both ends of the bridge. They were carrying whatever weapons came to hand—snake-fang maces, flails, tree-limb knobkerries—but luckily no bows. He slung the blanket-wrapped body over his shoulder. Elves filed onto the bridge.

"There he is!"

"What is it? A demon?"

"No demon—see, it bleeds!"

That brought forth calls for more of the agent's blood. He calmly positioned himself on the bridge and raised his captured spear. A thrown mace hurtled past him. He faced his nearest pursuers and bared his teeth in a snarl. Torchlight gleamed off his steel fangs. A refinement, his masters called it, pulling his natural teeth and giving him these metal spikes. Now the angry elves hesitated, transfixed by the weird apparition between them.

The spear was useless, so he flung it at his pursuers. He grabbed one of the bridge's supporting vines and clamped down on it with his metal teeth. The cable parted with a crack. The left side of the bridge sagged. Elves began to scramble back to the platforms. The agent turned and just as efficiently bit through another cable.

The broken bridge fell. He'd judged his place perfectly. His portion of the bridge was just long enough to drag the surface of the water and stop before slamming into a tree trunk.

Clasping his burden, the agent plunged into the murky water. His shroud and body paint took on the deep color of night, and he was soon lost in darkness.

He knew it wasn't over. The elves were master hunters and trackers. By daylight they would be after him in force, and his escape portal was far enough away that day would be well underway by the time he reached it.

Failure is not an option. You will complete your mission whatever the cost.

Clasping the dead girl's waist, he swam faster.

* * * * *

Light dispels darkness—a fundamental principle, a law of nature, on every known world. But on the plane of Phyrexia, nature does not exist. On Phyrexia, light serves the dark, it does not rule it.

The Fourth Level of this unnatural plane was the realm of great furnaces. Here were forged many of the components of Phyrexia's living machines. Around the clock (for there is no night or day), gangs of slave gremlins fed the scrap of redundant mechanisms into the mile-high furnaces. Molten metal was drawn off, alloyed and tempered in greater automatic rolling mills, and the resulting mixtures poured, pressed, or stamped into parts for new Phyrexian machines. If the gremlins faltered, they too were recycled, their ranks constantly renewed with more expendable laborers.

Strange, then, was the mission of the gremlin Dabir. A minor gremlin of trifling wits, he was best known for his reliability and his utter subservience to his masters. His immediate overseer, the vat priest Paax, had given him an unusual task. Dabir stood for hours before a shimmering portal to another plane, impatiently awaiting the arrival of . . . what was it again he was waiting for?

"A sample," Paax said.

"What sample?"

The hulking Paax extended an oiled, acid-etched arm until his black fingers were half an inch from Dabir's beaked nose. A blue spark arced from the demon's hand, and the gremlin collapsed on the greasy metal floor of the Fourth Sphere in agony.

"Ask not the will of your betters," said Paax, his voice punctuated by tiny clicks. He was bothered by a sticky breathing regulator. "Only obey."

Dabir picked himself up, fingering his throbbing nose. The smell of scorched flesh made even his feculent stomach churn.

"Dabir always obey great, wise Paax," he whined.

Paax swiveled his slender undercarriage and started away on four delicate, articulated legs. His rear mouth warned, "Be at the portal at the appointed time. Receive the sample, and deliver it to Monitor 8391 at Processing Mill 44. You know the penalty if you fail."

The vat priest maneuvered his bulky upper body around a steaming flue and was soon lost in the maze of heat exchangers and lubricant chases.

And so Dabir waited by the open portal—a glowing pane twelve inches square—for the sample. He could see through the dimensional doorway glimpses of a world far removed from the inferno he'd always known. The surface of that distant place was soil and stone, not oily metal, and living plants waved in the wind. If the gremlin got too close, the portal would shimmer, like the air near the mouths of the great furnaces. Fearful of damaging the ethereal portal, Dabir kept his distance.

He waited through an entire shift of work, rubbing his haunches when they numbed from sitting so long. He turned his back on the portal and laced his taloned fingers through his yellow-nailed toes, bored as only a vapid gremlin can be bored.

Suddenly there was a flash of blue light behind him. He spun and saw the portal had enlarged itself four times. A hooded figure was running across a plain of tall, dry grass toward the portal, pursued by a dozen flesh beings. Their mouths worked, but Dabir could not make out what they were saying. Sound did not traverse the portal.

Several of the tall beings, clad in painted hides and feathers, nocked arrows and loosed them at the fleeing figure. Three arrows struck and bounced off. A fourth found a chink in the agent's armor and buried half its length in his back. He staggered, and for the first time Dabir recognized the hooded figure bore a weighty bundle over his left shoulder.

"Hurry! Come!" Dabir shouted uselessly. He cared nothing about the wounded agent, fearing instead his own punishment if the agent failed to reach the portal. More arrows flashed. A second broadhead found its mark, and the shrouded figure fell, pitching his burden to the ground.

Dabir wet himself in terror. He thrust his long arms into the vibrant portal. A teasing sensation, not unpleasant, played over his oily skin. The precious sample was just beyond his grasping claws. Galvanized by visions of his own lengthy and painful death, Dabir shoved his head through the dimensional window.

He felt cool air, free of oil or soot. Then came the shouts of the hunters. An indefinite light from above dazzled the gremlin's eyes. He reached out for the cloth-wrapped bundle. His movements seemed slow, as if he were swimming through thick oil instead of fresh, open air.

His fingers felt oddly numb, and the sensation was spreading up his arms. Desperately, the gremlin snagged the edge of the wrapping. With a tremendous heave of his long legs, Dabir pulled himself and the bundle back through the portal. Both landed with a thump on the gritty metal plates of the Fourth Sphere.

The portal began to dwindle. The wounded agent raised a hand, either in a final plea or in final salute. Dabir watched six tall beings surround the fallen figure. They had spears. Shafts rose and fell in pitiless repetition as the portal shrank to a few inches, then winked out.

Dabir bobbed up on his knees. He sat in the shadows cast by the eternal glare of the furnaces, biting his own hands to restore feeling to them. His normally glossy black skin had turned ash gray on those parts of his body he'd stuck through the portal. The numbness slowly faded, but his color did not return.

A whiff of something delectable teased his formidable nose. Inserting it in a hole in the tattered blanket, he sniffed. The ugly white thing inside smelled like the air on the other side of the portal. No oil, no soot, no tang of acid aerosols . . . he replaced his nose with his tongue and gave the sample a quick lick. Flesh, newly dead and still sweet. The Phyrexian agent had died to deliver a corpse.

Dabir delivered the body to Monitor 8391 as ordered and departed to other tasks. Monitor 8391 ran a laboratory for the analysis of organic specimens. The Monitor put the slender corpse on his examining table. A chemical spray removed the creature's hair. The Phyrexian precisely measured every critical dimension of the body with calipers, then carefully laid a square of flowsheet over the corpse's head. At the Monitor's command, the tiny machines in the flowsheet crawled over the cold skin, conforming themselves to every contour. When they were done, he had a perfect mold of the dead girl's face.

Monitor 8391 passed on the corpse to the Necrometric Unit 725 for further processing. Body fluids were drained. The blood was contaminated by poison and therefore useless. A substitute would have to be used. The flesh was carefully stripped off and sent to culture vats so the corpse's tissues could be preserved for eventual reuse. The sterilized, polished bones were sent back to the Monitor, who applied his meticulous skills to them once more, measuring them to the finest calibration of his instruments. These figures were forwarded to the engine controlling the mighty apparatus of Processing Mill 44.

The rollers and stamping presses of the factory began to churn. Bars of duralumin and steel were fed into the machinery, which formed a hard, metal skeleton identical to the one measured by the Monitor. Each bone was copied, right down to the individual metacarpals of the hands and phalanges of the feet. The girl had once broken her right arm, and the calcified break was mirrored in the new duralumin humerus.

Jointed and joined, the sparkling new skeleton was sealed in a sterile copper shell to shield it from the ever-present oil rain of the Fourth Sphere. Gremlins loaded the shell into a pneumatic tube and sent it whistling away to the culture vats. Organs and tissues were re-fitted to the gleaming bones, along with certain mechanical improvements added by Phyrexian engineers. The crude and wasteful processes of eating and sleeping were eliminated by filling the body's veins with Phyrexian glistening oil in lieu of ordinary blood. The new body would have six times the speed and strength of the purely organic creature it was based on. It would be resistant to heat and cold, and its senses would surpass those of any elf or human. As a final touch, the mold made by Monitor 8391 was used to restore the old face to the new creation.

The lifeless body was placed in another copper capsule and routed downward to the Sixth Sphere, where it would await the attention of the Inner Circle member, Abcal-dro, servant of the Dark Lord of Phyrexia himself.

* * * * *

She awoke standing in a domed, circular room. It was cold. She looked down at her bare arms and legs, flecked with goose pimples. A moment's concentration dispelled them as heat coursed through her veins.

How strange it was, this shell of flesh. Strange and yet familiar. She stood easily, testing the articulation of her hands, arms, and legs. Breath plumed from her nose in soft wisps. All parts worked. All systems were in order.

The chill walls were blue glass, polished and seamless. Without effort, she calculated the height of the dome at 16.39 feet. She walked slowly toward the only other object in the room, a five-foot-high chrome tripod, above which floated a small black sphere four inches in diameter.

Some things she knew, others she didn't. She knew she was alive and on Phyrexia. She knew the periodic table of the elements, the expansion rate of live steam in a turbine, and the speed at which flowstone multiplied under optimum conditions. She knew where to strike a human body to cause the most damage, but she could also set a broken leg with her bare hands. She did not know her own name.

"That has not been decided yet," said a calm, genderless voice.

She darted away from the hovering sphere and crouched near the wall. It wasn't fear that made her crouch. Fear was not in her design. Her posture was defensive, a position from which to strike at the unseen speaker.

"I am Abcal-dro, your master. Stand up."

She obeyed.

"Speak. You have the means," said the voice.

"Who am I?"

"You are called 'Belbe.'" The name had two syllables, bell-be.

"What does it mean?"

"It derives from the ancient Thran language, *be'el-be*. It means 'a lens.'"

She went to the gleaming tripod in the center of the room. "Lens. A device that focuses to a point or spreads apart rays of light or other forms of energy," she recited.

"Correct."

Belbe looked at her hands. "Do I focus light?"

"In your case, the name is metaphorical. As you are going among flesh beings, you are therefore expected to have a name."

"Where am I going?"

"The plane of Rath."

She closed her eyes and thought. "Rath. An artificial world, created by our supreme master, composed of flowstone nano-machines, inhabiting its own plane at coordinates—"

"Stop." The command was mildly expressed, but absolute. Belbe not only ceased speaking, she ceased moving at all.

"Learn not to speak what you're thinking. By so doing, you give away too much and bore your listeners."

Belbe remained immobile, like a statue of flesh and metal.

"Speak," commanded Abcal-dro.

"I do only your will, Great One."

A strange, liquid, bubbling laughter filled the dome. It subsided to a sigh. "Listen well, Belbe. You are going to Rath soon, as our emissary to that world. Our lens, one might say. The time approaches when Rath will be in congruence with Dominaria, the prime plane of our ancestors. When the conjunction of planes occurs, all that is on Rath will be on Dominaria—"

"And all that is on Dominaria will be on Rath."

A pause. "True." Cold clutched at her fabricated heart. Even the mildest pique of the high priest raked her entrails like a razor blade of ice.

"You were made to resemble the inhabitants of Rath, not your masters on Phyrexia. In fact, the native environment of Phyrexia is inimical to your existence, which is why you must be kept in this environmental chamber until your departure. You are as much like them as we could make you, and that is an important parameter in your mission.

"The governor of Rath has abandoned his post for the sake of personal vengeance. His dereliction is contrary to our purpose, and it will not be tolerated. A new evincar must be found to take his place. You will choose the new evincar for us. Since natural selection is the best scalpel for dividing the weak from the strong, allow the candidates to struggle among themselves until one of the specimens establishes himself as the superior candidate. You will observe this struggle for us. You may choose—" more bubbling laughter rippled through the chamber, "—we give you leave to participate in the competition as you see fit.

"Only one task must remain inviolate. Under no circumstance is the conjunction of Rath and Dominaria to be altered, delayed, or interfered with—*by anyone*. Do you understand?"

"Yes, Great One."

"You may encounter certain beings who, by an accident of breeding, have the power to pass from plane to plane. These planeswalkers may attempt to thwart our plans to overlay Dominaria. You will not let them interfere. Your own life means nothing compared to the success of our plan. Is that clear?"

She bowed with all the grace of her copied body. "It is, master."

"Approach the sphere."

Belbe closed within arm's length of the black orb. It floated a scant inch above the polished tripod. The ball's surface was smooth, yet did not reflect her face as she gazed at it.

"Stand still."

Belbe locked her legs in place. The sphere silently rose and came to her. It touched her at the base of her throat, and for an instant she felt nothing. The sphere melted into her flesh without breaking the skin or causing any bleeding. Pressure built inside her chest, pushing on her newly-placed organs. She gasped with newfound pain.

"This is our 'lens.' It will be the connection from you to us."

"What is this feeling?" she whispered.

"It is called pain. As it is part of mortal existence, you must learn to recognize it. To rule creatures of flesh, you must make pain your ally. Use it whenever you can, Belbe. It is the foundation of power."

Her mock-blood roared in her ears. She feared her heart would rupture, her lungs collapse. Belbe's vision filmed with gray, and her breath caught in her throat. She opened her mouth to scream, but no sound came out. Her knees buckled.

Stand!

The voice of Abcal-dro was no longer in her ears, but inside her head. Despite intense pain, Belbe kept her feet. She staggered against the tripod, blinking through the haze of her suffering. The tripod abruptly vanished, and she stumbled forward, blind and gasping. Something warm ran down her lip.

The eye is now in place. You will soon adjust to its presence. She heard the words, but behind them there was something else. Behind the cool voice and godly demeanor of the high priest, Belbe sensed this:

Sweet, sweet the hall of flesh! The song of blood, what ancient joy! Too long have I slept—why, in this shell I can walk a thousand worlds, renew the sensations of lost millennia! It is mine, it is mine. Who is better than I? I take them all in my hands, caress them or crush them. My little puppet, my lens. Shrink from nothing, please your maker—

Belbe struck herself in the face with her open hand, twice, three times. The thin, shrieking voice submerged in the throb of her raging pulse. She wiped glistening oil from her lip. Slowly the room came back into focus. It seemed so empty without the orb and tripod.

She became aware of being watched. She saw in her mind an image of herself, standing naked under the cold glass dome. The lens was working—she was seeing herself as Abcal-dro saw her.

This frail creature was her? Standing erect on two thin legs, Belbe was the color of fresh parchment, slightly flushed from her exertions. A spray of pale blue freckles dotted her face and shoulders. Her hair, an unruly shock of brown, began at a peak in the center of her forehead and arched back over her high, pointed ears. Along her arms, legs, buttocks, and back were matte black lines in geometric patterns, like tattoos, but in fact were strips of reinforcing carbon fiber. Her face was angular, her chin sharp. Thin white scars remained where her flesh had been reattached to her metallic skeleton.

She raised her eyes to the apex of the vault. The azure glass gradually became transparent, and Belbe saw her hidden master peering down at her from outside the dome.

The room was 29.5 feet in diameter—she knew because her master knew it. Pressing against the clear shell was a mass of translucent tissue. Pulsing black veins, distended with the same glistening oil that filled her blood vessels, lined the shapeless body. Dozens of pseudopods as thick as her waist gripped the base of the dome. Drops of thick blue slime clung to the dome.

Rhythmically twitching green bladders and complex multi-lobed organs were visible through the dirty gray protoplasm. At the very peak of the dome was Abcal-dro's true eye: a swirling green and black iris fifteen inches wide, a trio of red-rimmed pupils in the center.

"Is this how you see me?" asked the high priest. She nodded once, slowly. "How does my appearance strike you?"

"My master is beautiful," she said. "Such power and efficiency must be beautiful."

The Phyrexian's liquid laughter resumed as the dome went opaque again. "One last warning, little one. On Rath you will be on your own. Though backed by the power and authority of the Dark Lord, you will succeed or fail by your own efforts."

"I will not fail, great one."

"See that you don't. It is time to leave."

The seamless floor split apart, revealing dark descending steps. Humid, sulfurous air wafted up from the hole. Unhesitatingly, Belbe went down the steps to a wide, noisome corridor where four priests in full regalia stood waiting for her. Behind them was a full entourage of lesser constructs and functionaries, and lastly a gang of gremlins bearing her new wardrobe—robes of woven chrome and onyx brocades, headdresses of flash-formed obsidian. To the rear were the bearers of her arms and armor. Each piece had been forged in the Fourth Sphere from Monitor 8391's original specifications, resulting in perfectly tailored armor that would fit no one but Belbe.

The suit was made of black diamond, the hardest substance on Phyrexia. It was so hard in fact, it had to be shaped and cut with fluoric acid, since no tools existed that could cut the plates. The acid treatment left the armor matte black, as dead a color as the lens now embedded in Belbe's chest.

She coughed and felt the first drops of sweat form under her arms. The priests bowed as Belbe passed. She thought it odd the exalted clerics of Phyrexia should bow to her, a newly made creature more flesh than metal, but then she heard a whisper deep inside saying *my lens, my eye* . . .

Their obeisance made sense. It was not her they were bowing to, it was their master.

"Monsters."

The room was crowded with elf warriors, stained with sweat, smoke, and the blood of battle. They had not assembled here to fight, but to mourn. Their chieftain's daughter was gone, her fate unknown.

Eladamri knelt by Avila's empty bed. "Monsters," he said again. "I knew the evincar was vicious and unnatural, but I didn't think he would stoop to this!"

"The fiend responsible will be found, we swear it," said Gallan, Eladamri's lieutenant. The warriors around him grunted in agreement.

Eladamri put his hand on the boughs where his daughter had lain. This treachery soured his success at the Stronghold. His warriors had confronted Volrath and his warlord, Greven *il*-Vec, and survived—a victory as signal as any ever recorded on Rath. Now this.

He withdrew his aching hand, bruised by recent combat. The motion stirred the soft boughs, revealing the soft glint of snake bone.

"What's this?"

The agent's knife had fallen to the bottom of the bed. Beside it was a small glass vial, still upright, and a single blue feather.

"I know this weapon." It was plainly of elven make, the garnet pommel bearing the intricate engraving of Skyshroud artisans.

"Gallan, whose knife is this?" Eladamri asked sharply.

His lieutenant held the blade close. In the poor light it wasn't easy to see.

"The emblem is of the clan of Carodonal."

"Yes." Eladamri stood. "Tenesi."

It was too awful to believe, but it was the evincar's style all right. Avila's own fiancé. He was lost in a skirmish twenty nights past.

"I'd hoped he'd found death rather than capture, but ..." Eladamri made a fist around the tiny glass vial.

"What's that?" asked Gallan.

"Something for our healers to study, I think. Now, my brothers, don't dwell on what's happened! Volrath thinks he can frighten me into inaction by taking my child. This will never happen.

"From this moment, I count Avila among the dead. Let her name be added to the roll of warriors who've died to make our land free."

He fixed the narrow blue feather to the brow of his helmet. It would be his talisman during the coming fight for freedom.

The next day, the hunting party returned with the agent's body, tied hand and foot on a pole like a trophy snake. Though he had been altered with many Phyrexian implants, including a control rod in place of his spine, every elf in the village recognized him as Tenesi, once the finest hunter in the Skyshroud Forest, and the betrothed of the lost Avila.

CHAPTER 1
Prisoners

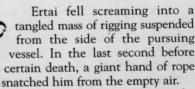

Ertai fell screaming into a tangled mass of rigging suspended from the side of the pursuing vessel. In the last second before certain death, a giant hand of rope snatched him from the empty air.

The airship *Predator*, reeling under accumulated battle damage, scarcely noticed the addition of one to her complement. She had an eight degree list to starboard, her speed had fallen to a scant four knots, and her steering gear was so damaged the ship could not maintain a straight course. Dead sailors and mogg goblins—*Predator*'s boarding troops—sprawled everywhere. Smoke billowed from hull scuttles along the battered starboard side, filling the deck with choking black streamers. Into this chaos strode Greven il-Vec, *Predator*'s master.

The crew—what was left of it—dashed about in ratlike frenzy, each man pursuing his own task. Greven shook his head in disgust. Not a brain to be found in any of them! He spied four sailors by the starboard rail, hacking at tangled rigging with cutlasses.

"Never mind that!" he roared. Leaning against the slant of the deck he shouted, "All free hands to the port side! Can't you feel the list? Do you want to capsize us?"

"But Commander—" said one, blade poised.

Greven seized the man by the throat. The sailor's face purpled; his cutlass clattered to the canted deck.

"Question me, will you?" Greven said, seething. The choking man could not reply. "Worthless meat! Lightening the ship will solve two problems!" So saying, he hurled the sailor over the side. The remaining three scampered for their lives to the port side of the ship.

Predator trembled, and a forward hatch cover blew off. A jet of flame erupted from the hold. The heavy hatch cover passed within a finger's breadth of Greven's head—the wind of its passing cooled his cheek—but he never flinched. The shrieks of men burning in the engine room below had as little effect.

"Engineer, dead stop! Direct all power to lift! Firefighters to the forward hold, now! The rest of you, form a work party and clear the decks!" His voice cut through the terror and confusion, and *Predator*'s crew fell to saving their battered ship. Thanks to Greven and the fearful discipline he instilled, the airship slowly righted itself and maintained its altitude.

Stepping over deck wreckage, Greven reached the forecastle. Here the ship had taken most of its punishment. Bulwarks were shattered, the alloy casing peeled back like gray flower petals. Colliding with the closed portal had caused the worst damage. The ship's prow had been crushed backward to the fourth hull frame. The serrated ram had broken off and was lying at the bottom of Portal Canyon somewhere. The forward harpoon gun had been dismounted, the barrel jammed into the upper boarding mandible overhead. It would be days, maybe weeks, before such extensive structural damage could be repaired.

Greven stood with his feet braced widely apart on the twisted deck and stared at the ancient portal through which *Weatherlight* had vanished. He'd lost a battle, something he seldom did, and he'd failed in his pursuit of the enemy, something that had never happened before. High atop the portal structure, the great Phyrexian control center, styled like a fiercely staring face, mocked Greven's failure.

"Someday, Gerrard," he muttered. "Someday you'll bleed for Greven. I swear it."

Far below, clinging to the rigging draped over the starboard side of *Predator*, young Ertai debated his chances. From this height he would never survive a fall to the ground. He knew a flying spell, but it required calm and the utmost concentration—not very likely conditions at the moment. He briefly considered hiding in the wreckage until *Predator* landed, but the Rathi airship was still hovering and gave no sign of an intention to land. Ertai's arms ached. He couldn't hang on forever. The only sane choice was to climb to the ship above. Talent like his should not be wasted on a meaningless death.

He'd just begun to climb the skein of lines when a body hurtled past. A sailor hit the rigging a few feet from Ertai, and the back of his shirt snagged on some wires. He hung helplessly for a moment, then his clothing slowly began to tear. Ertai and the sailor's eyes met, and for a few seconds, Ertai saw the approach of death in the man's eyes. The sailor clawed at the rigging, but he could not find a handhold. As he tore free, the only sound the man made with his mangled throat was a horribly muted gurgle. Ertai watched him fall.

With renewed purpose, Ertai resumed climbing. The wire rigging tore his hands. What a shame, he thought. Such well-shaped, expressive hands he had. The old masters who had trained him in the nuance and gestures of spellcasting always complimented his fine hands. Now they were being cut to ribbons. A great—and painful—shame.

The shouting from the hull above him abated. *Predator* climbed slowly. Ertai was a few yards below the keel when he heard a voice boom out, "Prepare to clear away the fouled rigging!" His heart contracted into a hard knot when he saw axes and swords glinting above the rail. They were going to chop his lifeline off!

He tried to climb faster, but his feet kept tangling in the rat's nest of metallic rope and wire. When speed failed, he fell back on his greatest asset, his magic. With one arm wrapped around a thick bundle of lines, Ertai used his other hand to begin the gestures of a spell.

The sailors at the rail awaited Greven's command to cut away the downed rigging. With a nod, he set them to work. The first sailor raised a heavy ax, but before he could bring it down on the mass of lines, it flew backward from his hand. Despite the strain of battle and their fear of Greven, the men laughed at their comrade's apparent clumsiness. The next sailor wielded a cutlass. It tore out of his grasp and hurtled over the side. More laughter. The third man had a hatchet. It left his hand and struck him between the eyes. Down he went, bleeding from a serious gash in the forehead. The laughter died.

Greven approached. He turned his head from side to side as if sniffing the wind.

"Magic? Who dares to cast spells on my ship?" he said aloud. Sailors stood by with blank looks. "Haul up the rigging," Greven commanded.

Ertai almost fainted from fatigue. No one ever expected a sorcerer to cast spells one-handed while dangling a mile in the air, he mused—no one but Ertai could have done it! The last one was particularly satisfying, seeing that yokel get his own hatchet back on his thick skull.

The rigging trembled and began to rise. They were drawing him up. It was about time!

Rough hands grasped his arms and collar and hauled Ertai over *Predator*'s rail. He would have liked to have arrived on the deck in a civilized manner, but the angry sailors threw him on his face. Ertai gathered his wits for a suitable response, but before he could do anything, a pair of massive booted feet appeared in front of him.

"What's this?" Greven said. To Ertai, his voice sounded like the scrape of a dull knife blade on a whetstone.

The young sorcerer got to his feet with as much dignity as he could muster. He drew a breath to announce himself, but it caught in his throat when he saw who—and what—he was facing.

Greven *il*-Vec bore little resemblance to the man he once was. Head and shoulders taller than anyone else on *Predator*, he towered over Ertai. It was impossible to tell where his armor ended and his body began. Grafted muscles coiled around his limbs, shoulders, neck, and chest. The unnatural patterns of sinew and armor plate lent Greven a reptilian look, a resemblance heightened by the waxen gray cast of his skin. Add to that the cuts and scars of countless combats, and Greven was a forbidding sight to the newly saved young sorcerer.

"You're from Gerrard's ship," Greven said.

Ertai bowed. "Ertai's the name. You made the right decision, pulling me aboard." So saying, he stood back from Greven and folded his arms across his chest—mostly to conceal his bleeding palms.

Greven's brow arched ever so slightly. He pointed at Ertai and said, "Kill him. And take your time."

Ten crewmen, who moments before had been panic-stricken sheep, formed a ring around Ertai. They were armed with whatever came to hand—cutlasses, hatchets, crowbars, lengths of chain. Inwardly Ertai's heart raced. Outwardly he projected utter calm.

"Guests not welcome, eh?" he said. "You're making a mistake, Captain."

Greven waved aside his warning. "Go on, kill the runt. If any man fails to strike a blow, I'll have his ears cropped."

Ertai closed his eyes and summoned the deepest resources of his magical strength. Images of his far-off homeland flashed through his mind, and power flowed through him. Even with his eyes shut, he could see the auras of his attackers maneuvering to strike. Since they were so hot for his blood, Ertai decided to cool them off. He brought his battered hands up and projected a quick and dirty spell at the closest trio of sailors.

The deck seemed to come out from under them. They rushed forward, weapons raised, and in the next instant, their feet were where their heads once were. It was like trying to run on ice—their boots could find no traction.

Ertai half-turned and hurled three quick bursts at the next group of attackers. Crowbars and cutlasses flew backward out of their hands, some striking their comrades behind them. Then Ertai had to dodge a killing blow from a hatchet. He touched the hatchet man with a single finger, and at such short range the ambient force sent the man sprawling.

The hilt of a cutlass connected with the back of Ertai's head. Stunned, he staggered forward, stray magical energy escaping from his body. It condensed the air, creating an impromptu fog bank of ice and mist on deck. Ertai dropped to his hands and knees and crawled to the foot of *Predator*'s mainmast. If he could put a little distance between himself and his tormentors, he'd show them a thing or two.

Greven leaned one arm on the ship's binnacle and watched his crew fumble through the fog trying to find Ertai. Normally his men were accomplished fighters, but they seemed unable to come to grips with a single, unarmed child. It was the most diverting thing he'd seen in days.

Ertai reached the mast. He started up the iron rungs, then someone caught his heels and dragged him back. Having no time for proper concentration, Ertai flung the first spell he could think of—and the sailor grasping his feet disappeared under a sudden growth of hair. The man's eyebrows, mustache, beard, and the hair on his head exploded into a silky mat that completely covered his astonished face. He reeled away, unable to see or breathe through the hirsute mass. The man staggered blindly to the rail and somersaulted over it. Greven nodded and smiled in grim humor. The runt wasn't bad.

Ertai was running out of strength. He had a small reservoir remaining, but it wasn't much. He made a fist and flung a last magical gasp onto the deck ahead of the charging sailors. The dry planking splintered as thick green shoots emerged from the deck. *Predator*'s crewmen, caught by the sudden garden of tendrils and vines, tripped and fell, piling up in a heap in front of Ertai. Gamely, a few rose from the tangle to advance again. A sergeant in the regular Rathi army, Nasser, reached the exhausted Ertai first. He raised his sword high.

"Hold," said Greven. Nasser froze. He looked to his captain. "He's spent. Chain him up. I'll take him back to the Stronghold."

"Yes, Dread Lord," Nasser said. His comrades fought free of the rapidly withering vines and seized Ertai. They took out their frustrations on the helpless young man by raining blows on his ribs and skull. Heavy hobnailed boots thudded into his side, forcing Ertai to curl into a protective ball.

"Fists only," Greven warned them. "I want a prisoner who can give me information."

Fists it was, and Ertai shrank under the merciless pounding. How could this have happened to him, the most talented student of Barrin's school, the most valuable recruit on *Weatherlight*?

Clearly something was wrong, deeply wrong, on the strange plane called Rath.

"Enough," said Greven. "Take him below."

Nasser dragged Ertai's limp body away by his heels.

* * * * *

Greven set the rest of the crew back to effecting emergency repairs. As he walked the deck observing their progress, Greven noticed that the battle damage in the deck planking was gone. The wood was like new where Ertai's spell had hit it, and the renewal was slowly spreading outward from the initial spot to the rest of the deck.

Repairs by magic—now there was a useful skill. Greven looked back at the hatch where Nasser had disappeared with Ertai. The boy had talent, that was certain.

* * * * *

With a clap of thunder, the canyon portal closed.

The shock wave blasted down the ravine, hurling him to the ground. This fall, on top of the wounds dealt him by the cat warrior, Mirri, were too much. He tumbled and rolled across the abrasive ground, brush and rock tearing at his already ragged flesh. *Weatherlight* was gone. He expected to follow it shortly into oblivion. He no longer cared. Since Selenia's death, he was more afraid of life than death.

He spread his arms wide, feeling the wind tugging at his clothes. The warship chasing *Weatherlight* had been caught in the field of residual energy when the portal closed and did not look like it would be aloft much longer. Serves them right, he thought. Death was the proper reward for failure.

He closed his eyes and drew his arms and legs in close. This made him roll faster. He wanted to believe, after he smashed to bits on the canyon floor, that his soul would depart for some higher, better realm. If he could not be an angel, he could at least dwell among them for eternity.

Death eluded him. As the canyon widened onto the adjacent plain, the sound of the wind in his ears changed pitch. He opened his eyes. For the duration of one heartbeat he saw the jagged walls of the canyon in bold relief—boulders, gravel, the odd wire grass that was the predominant growth on Rath—then it was all blotted out by a pall of blackness that swallowed him whole. All sensation of movement ceased. He was adrift in an endless sea of ink, floating between nowhere and nothing.

Crovax.

"Who calls my name?"

You are needed, Crovax.

He twisted around, trying to see who spoke. There was nothing to see.

Is this death? he wondered. Is this the end of life?

It's the beginning of your life, Crovax.

The mysterious voice could hear his thoughts. Very well, answer me: Where am I?

You are suspended in a bi-planar field. It was necessary in order to save you.

What do you want with me?

Only to offer you a greater destiny than death.

And if I want to die?

You were born to command, Crovax. Generations of leadership have been bred into you. You've had some conflict, some personal loss. Will you abandon your destiny over these setbacks? Wouldn't you rather strike back at those who've hurt you than surrender your life as their victory?

Yes, I would. He repeated it out loud. "Yes, I would!"

Then fly, Crovax. Fly to your ultimate destination.

"Speak clearly, damn you. What am I supposed to do?"

Fly, Crovax. Will yourself to your destiny.

He felt stupid, but he imagined himself flying through the air, encased in a cloud of darkness. In the weird, visionless void, he did feel he was moving again. Was that a breeze on his face? Was it possible?

Good, Crovax. You will be there soon. I am waiting for you there.

Neither mountains nor walls were a barrier to him. Sightless, he hurtled like a shooting star through the darkest of night skies. He flew on, and the despair he'd endured shortly before gave way to anger, hatred, and a deep, gnawing emptiness.

Nemesis

* * * * *

When Ertai regained consciousness, he found he was below deck, his hands and feet chained around one of the ship's masts. A strong, regular pulsation, not unlike a heartbeat, echoed through the airship's hull. The throbbing was equal parts *Predator*'s damaged engine and the pain in his aching head. The crew had not been easy on him. Ertai licked his parched lips and grimaced.

"Not a pleasant experience, tasting your own blood."

His eyes adjusted to the dim light. A few feet away, seated on a keg, was Greven *il*-Vec. He sat so still it was hard to distinguish him from the hull frames behind him. In repose, the massive warrior was no less fearsome than he had been on the open deck. Even in the feeble light, a dark glint of violence shone in his eyes.

"It's not been pleasant on your ship," Ertai said thickly.

"You were not invited aboard."

Even shrugging hurt. "I'm not here by choice."

"Why are you here, boy?"

There was no sense lying about it. "I was manning the portal, keeping it open for *Weatherlight*. I jumped from the control station onto the ship as she maneuvered to enter the portal. You were coming at us like you meant to board us, and they put the helm over to avoid you. The course change was so violent I missed *Weatherlight* completely and got caught by your rigging. If your ship hadn't been so hard on our heels, I'd've drilled my own grave in the soil of Rath."

"A sorcerer as skilled as you killed by a mere fall? I find that hard to believe."

Ertai said nothing but leaned his aching head against the mast.

"Still, I can't imagine anyone trying to plant a spy on my ship in such a careless manner—not even Gerrard Capashen."

Mention of his *Weatherlight* companion sent a spark of anger through Ertai. How could Gerrard have abandoned him, left him in the hands of this grotesque savage? Such ingratitude!

"We are returning to our citadel," Greven continued. "Once there, your fate will be determined by my master, the evincar."

Was that resentment Ertai heard in Greven's voice? Tired as he was, he tried to read the warrior's aura, the invisible halo of power surrounding every living thing. It was one of the first feats apprentice wizards learned, aura reading. Ertai could practically read auras in his sleep.

He closed his eyes and let the visible image of Greven fade from view. In its place came a dark silhouette, a broken outline in black on a background the color of old blood. No other forces existed in Greven's aura but strength and destruction. Not surprising. What did interest Ertai was the distinct break in the brute's aura. Instead of a complete circle of life-energy, the lines broke at Greven's neck. Something was there that absorbed the life force and did not allow it to radiate in the usual manner. Something artificial.

"—what to do with you," Greven was saying. Ertai's eyes popped open. Sweat beaded on his brow.

"What?" Ertai said.

Greven ground his teeth, a noise the crew of *Predator* knew to fear. "I said, you can't expect mercy from the evincar. He has no tolerance for enemies of the state. Your only hope is to cooperate with us. Then Volrath may find a use for you," he said, voice growing.

Ertai hung his head. "I see."

His compliant manner made Greven unclench his jaw. "Your friends have fled, never to return," he said, rising to his feet. He had to stoop to avoid banging his head on the deck above. "If you are as practical as you are talented, you'll make the correct decision."

Alone, Ertai glared in the direction of the departed captain. Stupid hulk. Ertai knew his kind. Bluster and violence, that's all men like Greven knew. They were the easiest types to manipulate. Appeal to their pride, yield to their anger; that was how to do it. Greven hated and feared his master, Volrath, and that was a handy foil too. Ertai began to feel a little better about his chances of survival.

He tried his best to open the manacles that bound him to the mast. Neither his physical strength nor his depleted magical abilities were up to the task, and after long, fruitless effort, he resigned himself to temporary captivity. His earlier fit of confidence faded when he found he couldn't erase the image of Greven's aura from his mind. That black, broken aura spoke of terrible, unnatural things, of a man not alive, yet not dead. He was controlled by the thing in his spine, yet aware of his own lack of free will. Such a man was like a handleless sword—no matter how you tried to grasp it, it was always lethal.

He and Greven had something in common, then. In each their own way, they were both prisoners of war.

CHAPTER 2
Brothers

Darkness was his friend. It came to him intimately, enfolded him in its profound embrace. No aspect of light could ever compare to the sensual companionship of darkness. It caressed him, flowed over and through him, squeezing out the last vestiges of light he'd known. Once his being was suffused by the black void, he felt himself stretching out to infinity.

The gray orb of Rath was like an acorn in the palm of his hand. He closed his fingers around it and laughed. Near his left hand floated another, brighter world, but when he tried to grasp it, it melted between his fingers. Irritated, he tried again. His hand closed on nothing—it was like trying to grab smoke. His blood warmed, then became fever-hot. He released Rath and tried to seize the evasive second world with both hands. Forming a cage with his fingers, he caught the phantom inside. Now it was his! He closed his hands together and awaited the visceral thrill of possession.

It never came. A brilliant stream of white fire forced its way through his clenched hands, pushing back the darkness with its hateful rays. He tried to smother the light, but it just got stronger. It pierced his shut eyes and speared through his brain. His back arched in torment. His jaw locked with such violence his teeth cracked under the pressure.

Let go, let go, massed voices seemed to say. *Let go of it before it kills you.*

"Never!" he cried. "Dominaria will be mine!"

Crovax opened his eyes. He was lying on the floor of a vast hall in twilight. He leaped to his feet, heart racing. What was this place? How did he get here?

Suspended a few inches from his head was a black, spidery contraption studded with short spikes, shaped like a cupped hand. A silver, pearl-like object nestled within the "hand". At first he thought it was hard and glassy, but as he stared at it, the surface throbbed like a living thing. Crovax reached out for the strange object, but the hand whizzed away, retracting upward on a thin black cable with dizzying speed. It vanished into the cyclopean heights of the hall, leaving Crovax alone on the long, polished floor.

His hands were bleeding. He'd forced his fingernails deeply into his own flesh.

"Dream," he muttered, rubbing his stinging palms on his legs. Bright smears of blood contrasted starkly against the cream-colored leggings.

A quick check proved he was standing in his underclothes: a light jersey, matching leggings. His feet were bare. The wound on his neck where Mirri had bitten him had mysteriously healed. A smooth, livid scar covered the spot. Where were his clothes, his weapons, his armor? Without arms or armor, he might as well have been naked.

"What is this?" he shouted. Far above him, indistinct movements and soft clicking sounds responded to the sound of his voice. Crovax had the unpleasant feeling he was under observation.

He walked along, scrutinizing his surroundings. The dimensions of the hall were vast. *Weatherlight* could have easily navigated above the concourse. At equal intervals the vaulted roof was supported by enormous pilasters, decorated in a baroque, mechanistic style. Each pilaster featured a grotesque face of greenish black and chrome, yards across, its stylized mouth open in a silent roar of rage. In the distant recesses of the arched ceiling, unseen mechanisms clicked and whirred. Crovax could not imagine the purpose of such a mammoth hall.

He doubled over, shaking violently. Gerrard. Hanna. Mirri. *Selenia* . . . Crovax toppled forward to the black marble walkway, his bloody hands sliding on the smooth, cold stone. A toothy demon leered at him from the pavement. The demon's face was his own, contorted with hatred, anger, and suffering.

He smote the floor with his fist. "Why am I here?" he bellowed.

Don't you know?

The speaker was quite close, almost on top of him. Crovax lashed out in the direction of the voice. His fists met nothing. He scrambled to his feet, panting.

"Show yourself, coward!" he said. "Stop playing these stupid games!"

The air before him shimmered, and an image formed. Crovax shook his head and rubbed his eyes. The being before him was like nothing he'd ever seen. Fully seven feet tall, the transparent phantom resembled a grisly statue made of meat and metal. Its long arms were covered with pink skin only to the elbows; above them its limbs were made of metal rods and pulleys. The creature wore a beaded leather wrap around its waist. The head was the most arresting feature of all. Atop a skeletal torso perched what looked like a massive head in a mask of fantastic gray and red plumes, bone, and black fur. Crovax saw no visible eyes or mouth, though corrugated tubes emerged from the being's shoulders and chest and entered the mask at various points. It made audible breathing sounds, like a winded dog. A gorget of brass circled the thing's wide neck. Jewels gleamed all over the creature, and some glowed and blinked with their own inner light.

"I am Kirril, servant of the Hidden One," said the creature in a papery voice. Crovax could discern no lips moving on the creature, yet he heard it plainly. "You are here because you wished to be. My master has taken an interest in you."

"Who is your master? Volrath? Do you serve the evincar?"

Kirril's cadaverous arm made a dismissive gesture. "Speak not the traitor's name! The one I serve has many names—The Dark

Lord, the Hidden One, the First Master. He is our great lord, ruler of all Phyrexia."

Crovax was impressed, but he didn't allow himself to show it. "What does your master want with me?"

"The Hidden One has watched you, Crovax, since the day you were born. He has seen the seed of greatness in you and bided his time until you recognized it in yourself. That moment has arrived. Once you chose to follow the path to power, you became his servant. But greater things await you, Crovax, if you have the vision and the strength to accept them."

He scowled at the Phyrexian. "I am no man's servant, do you hear? I am certainly not submitting myself to your Dark Lord! I've ruined my soul already with hatred and murder, but I will not bow to anyone in this world—or yours!"

Kirril glided past Crovax. The hair on his arms prickled as the Phyrexian's projected image passed. In his wake Kirril left a strong odor of ozone, as if his presence singed the very air.

"It's common for birth pangs to be painful," Kirril said, proceeding down the concourse. "What's important is how one deals with the pain. Do you let it defeat you, or do you return it tenfold upon those who caused it?"

"What are you saying?"

"The deaths of the angel Selenia and the feline Mirri were not accidents. Who is responsible for these acts of pain?"

"I am."

"That is the weakling's answer. You were not bred to be weak, Crovax. Who started you on this journey? By whose hand did you arrive on Rath?"

His face burned. "Gerrard Capashen!"

Kirril moved on. Crovax watched him go. It was unsettling to see the wall reliefs and pilasters through Kirril's image—or was it his words that were so disturbing?

"Wait," Crovax said.

Kirril vanished, only to reappear directly in front of him.

Crovax recoiled, then recovered his nerve. "If all these things are Gerrard's fault, why do I feel so—so bereft?"

For a moment the Phyrexian's only answer was his blinking jewels. Then he said, "Every being arrives at a moment of choice between avoiding their destiny or embracing it. The weak turn away from power and decry in others what they cannot accomplish themselves. The strong throw off the constraints of restrictive morality and recognize that ultimate good is that which is efficient and successful. You, Crovax, have not made the choice yet. You've acted according to your true nature as a predator, but you haven't accepted the truth of your superiority yet. Thus you are in torment, like the fools who brought you here."

Kirril pointed to the floor between them. A conical vessel with a flat lid materialized. It was made of dark translucent stone or glass. Inside the vessel a dimly glowing yellow object moved about furtively.

"Your new life can provide rewards you've never imagined. Do you hunger, Crovax? Is there an emptiness deep within you?"

"Yes, damn you."

"Pick up the container."

Crovax hefted the jar. It was a foot high and quite heavy.

"Remove the cap," Kirril commanded.

The jar was sealed with a strip of lead. Crovax peeled away the seal and lifted off the thick cap.

"Take care it doesn't escape."

Crovax peered into the jar. A lobed ball of light the size of a plum floated inside. It moved in slow circles, stopped, and reversed direction like a caged animal. Suddenly, it seemed to sense the lid was off and darted for the open mouth. Crovax clamped his hand over the jar. The globe touched his raw palm and melted into it. He saw the glow through the back of his hand.

A shock passed down his arm, followed by an intense sensation of pleasure. Crovax's dour face broke into a wide smile. The emptiness, the anguish inside him evaporated. He felt invigorated and strong.

"What was that?"

"The life-force of a living creature. Every living thing contains it. Most creatures replenish their supply by eating common food and expend it through physical and emotional activity. Because you deny your natural role as a hunter and master of flesh beings, you expend your life-force needlessly, fueling useless emotions like pity, anguish, and regret. You have progressed beyond mortals, Crovax. You now have the ability to absorb the life-force from other beings. Will you use it, or perish like a miserable, weak human?"

The cuts on his hands were gone. "How has this happened?"

"The power was always within you. By your acts on *Weatherlight* you have awakened the latent instinct."

Crovax dropped the jar. It smashed to flinders on the black pavement. "I want more," he said. "Give me more. I *need* more."

The image of Kirril spread its bony hands wide. "You will have more—as much as you desire—if you meet the Hidden One's final test." With another fluid turn of his hand, Kirril summoned the dream catchers. Spidery claws descended rapidly from the ceiling, surrounding Crovax in a ring of spiny black "hands."

"What are these for?"

"Your education, Crovax. It is important you know the history of Rath so that you will not repeat your predecessor's mistakes. These appliances will allow you to experience the past as it actually happened. Are you prepared for that? You will know terrors and pleasures few mortal men have known."

This time Crovax wasn't alarmed. He kicked aside the fragments of the broken jar and stood in the center of the dream machines.

"My appetite is very large," he declared.

"Good," Kirril answered. "It must be. Now prepare yourself for your lesson."

* * * * *

Crovax lay spread-eagled on an operating table, somewhere on the Fourth Level of Phyrexia. Tubes filled his nose, and a breathing mask covered his open mouth. No less than four Phyrexian birth priests were working on him at the same time, each with his own quadrant of Crovax's body. In the hazy recesses of his mind, Crovax knew this was happening. He had seen the full history of Rath, and he realized he was getting the same treatment Volrath had—he was being modified to fill the role of evincar.

"What conclusion do you draw from Volrath's history?" Kirril asked him.

"Volrath was a fool and a weakling," Crovax replied.

"He was for many years a highly effective governor."

"For suppressing some ragtag elves and whipping moggs, he was fine. The first time a real challenge appeared—*Weatherlight*—he bungled everything. Worse, he became so out of control he abandoned his post to pursue his private quarrel with Gerrard. Not good form for a man with his responsibilities."

"You would not make such mistakes?"

"Never," replied Crovax.

"How would you deal with an incursion by *Weatherlight?*"

"*Weatherlight* is not important. It's a vessel, a means to deliver an end."

Delicate microtomes scraped at Crovax's flesh. Through all the detachment and anesthesia, the sensation—or his thoughts about the sensation—seeped in. Through Kirril's eyes he saw his own naked body laid open on the Phyrexian operating table, his ebon skin pinned back like supple leather, his organs still alive, quivering, his heart pumping. . . .

A high-pitched whine distracted Crovax. He saw again his own transformation. This time a small whirring saw blade was being used to open his skull. The hulking priest wielding the saw had three arms, each tipped with slender metallic digits of excruciating delicacy. The Phyrexian touched the bright blade to Crovax's head, and the former member of the *Weatherlight* crew screamed inwardly.

He felt he was hurtling through an abyss of total darkness. The plunge was all the more terrible because he knew it would last forever. He would never reach the bottom, never feel the absolving impact of death.

Below him a dim light gleamed. It grew steadily larger and brighter, resolving into the form of a glowing angel.

Selenia!

He tore past her, twisting and grasping at her diaphanous, trailing robe. Her sorrowful face seemed blurred, indistinct. Yet when they recognized each other, the angel folded her beating wings and dropped after him. Crovax strained to reach her outstretched hands. Their fingertips brushed many times and failed to meet. Despair gave way to frustration, then to anger. Crovax knotted both hands into fists and hurled himself at Selenia. A dull red halo surrounded him as he shot upward to meet her. She opened her arms wide to embrace him, and he did likewise, flushed with triumph.

They met in midair, and he clasped the bright angel to him. She was not dead, not dead, not dead . . .

Selenia writhed in his grasp. "Let me go! Let me go, Crovax, you're hurting me!"

"I would never hurt you!"

"Let me go, I cannot bear it!"

Crovax drew back far enough to see her agonized face. He knew instinctively the power he exuded was hurting her. The same force that allowed him to stop falling and reach Selenia was now killing her.

"Let me go, Crovax! I'm burning!"

"I won't let you go! You're all I care about!"

Feathers from her wings fell away, scorched brown. She became dead weight in his arms, and they slowly turned in the air until she was hanging limply beneath him. Her robe smoldered, her gossamer hair was singed.

"Crovax, you've killed me."

He kissed her lifeless face. Where he touched her, her lips and cheek blistered. Rather than see her beauty entirely consumed by his raging heat, Crovax released her. She spiraled down into the darkness, wings rigid in death.

He covered his face with his hands. If he could tear out his memory, expunge Selenia from his mind, he might be saved from the torment of her death.

"Kirril? Kirril! Can you hear me? Grant me this boon!"

"No," said the Phyrexian. "You must preserve memories of all your deeds."

"Why? I don't want to remember the awful things I've done!"

"They only seem awful because you cling to inferior concepts of right and wrong. You must learn to savor your experiences. In that way, you will be strong. You'll be superior to those mortals who live in fear and react to pain."

"Can you give me this strength, Kirril?"

"You have it already. All that needs to be done is to delete what remains of your useless moral sense."

"Then do it."

"Are you certain? What is taken away cannot be restored."

"Do it!"

An electrode, tipped with a miniature cauterizing iron, slipped into Crovax's brain. With a hiss, what remained of his painful conscience burned away.

CHAPTER 3
Arrivals

At low speed, and with considerable cursing on the part of Greven *il-*Vec, *Predator* approached the airship tunnel high on the slope of the Stronghold. It had taken two days to return from Portal Canyon instead of the usual five hours. Negotiating the usually roomy tunnel through the slopes of Rath Peak appeared impossible. *Predator*'s steering was a jury-rigged shambles, and none of the bone-headed crew could do anything to correct it. They made three approaches to the tunnel mouth, only to abort each one at the last instant to avoid piling up on the side of the crater.

Furious and desperate, Greven stormed below to where Ertai was still chained to the mast.

"Are we there yet?" Ertai asked cheerfully.

Greven dearly wanted to wrench the boy's smirking head off, but he settled for stomping a cider keg to kindling. It was a full keg, and the sweet smell of cider filled the cramped hold.

Predator lurched heavily to port. Shouts of alarm penetrated from the deck above. Greven's scarred lips curled in disgust.

"Well?" said Ertai. "I can't do much chained up down here."

"Who says I want you to do anything?" Greven snarled.

"You didn't come down here to offer me cider, did you?"

Greven's normally sallow face darkened. He reached out with his massive, sinewy hands, and Ertai feared his time had come. Greven grasped the chain between Ertai's hands, and with little more than a shrug, snapped them in two.

Ertai just stared in amazement. Greven did the same with his leg shackles, and the young wizard stood up for the first time in more than a day.

"Many thanks, Captain. I was beginning to cramp—"

"Shut up," Greven said. "Get on deck!"

* * * * *

Ertai shuffled up the gangway, chains jingling as he went. He emerged on the main bridge. The sailors were trying to steer *Predator* with her tattered mainsails. Even if they had been in top condition, such methods were too coarse for steering the airship into its home base.

Ertai craned his head and gazed at the Stronghold. A vast rounded cone rose steeply from the surrounding plain to a height of over three miles. The barren slopes were yellow stone, streaked with red and brown mineral deposits. The western side was covered by a silver-gray cascade of newly fabricated flowstone. At the peak, the great Hub floated on a continuous stream of sizzling blue energy. This vast cylindrical object received the energy lancing down from indefinite space above. Though not bright in the sense that the Dominarian sun was bright, Ertai's eyes began to water from the light.

"This is no time for tears," Greven said.

"I'm the sensitive type," Ertai said, dabbing his eyes.

Greven dragged Ertai to the forward rail. "We have a steering problem." He really loathed what he was about to say, and it showed clearly on his brutal face. "You will use magic to get us through the tunnel."

"I'm a prisoner of war."

"You're on my ship," Greven replied, his teeth beginning to grind. "If we crash, you go down with us."

Ertai couldn't help but smile. "That's persuasive." He strolled to the port side of the bridge, then to starboard. *Predator* was making a large, slow turn that would eventually bring it back on course for the tunnel opening.

"The rudder is wrecked?" Ertai asked. Greven nodded. "Can you steer with differential thrust from your engines?"

"Normally, yes, but the starboard engine is off its mountings. Only the port engine is supplying thrust."

Ertai shaded his eyes from the blue glow of the peak and studied the sailors trying to manhandle the port mainsail to counteract the off-center push of the engine. Even as he watched, the flapping sail whipped loose and swept three men off the boom. They plunged to their deaths, and no one paused to mark the fact, least of all *Predator's* captain.

"Can you abandon ship?" asked Ertai.

"That's not an option," Greven said, folding his arms across his chest. "What can you do? Remember, if you fail, you'll follow those clumsy fools over the side!"

"As you so eloquently stated, Captain, we're all in this bucket together."

Ertai closed his eyes and extended his hands. Power crackled from his fingertips. There was plenty of energy in the air here, even if it was primarily of a destructive variety. He drew in some of this harsh background energy. It felt bad and made his bruised body ache, but desperate times sanctioned daring actions.

"What are you doing?" Greven demanded.

"Making a road," Ertai murmured. He visualized a great rod of magical energy emanating from his hands to the distant tunnel entrance. That was simple enough, but then he drew the stream of force down his arms and pushed it through his body to his feet. By anchoring the power stream through the hull, he would force *Predator* to follow it. The sensation was akin to hugging a flaming tree, but it had to be done.

Predator shivered and turned smartly toward the Stronghold.

"Prepare for a crash landing," Ertai gasped. "This will be rough."

Greven gave the order, and the surviving sailors and moggs hunkered down behind bulwarks fore and aft. Disdaining danger, Greven remained on the bridge with Ertai.

"Moron," Ertai whispered.

"What?"

"Uh, I'm more on course." His limbs began to tremble. Sweat soaked through the filthy rags he wore.

The bow sank, and the airship gathered speed. Here was the real danger, though Ertai didn't bother explaining it to Greven. His spell could easily keep the airship straight, but he didn't know if he would have enough strength left to stop the ship once inside the crater.

"Cut engines."

Greven sounded far away. Ertai struggled to keep his balance. Heat was building where his body touched the ship. The soles of his feet blistered. Under them the decking began to smolder. Someone—presumably Greven—threw a bucket of water on Ertai's feet.

"Thank you," he gritted.

"We're almost there," Greven replied. "Shouldn't you open your eyes?"

"I can see better this way."

Without the hum of the engines, *Predator* was alive with seldom-heard sounds—the creak of the masts, the pop of the hull under stress, the odd metallic twang of cables automatically adjusting themselves to changes in tension. In his mind's eye, Ertai saw the yellow cone of the Stronghold loom before him. The magical beam pierced the center of the airship tunnel. *Predator* entered it at high speed. The slipstream from the interior of the crater blew warm on Ertai's cheek.

With a whoosh, *Predator* burst into the hollow center of the Stronghold. Crew members cried out, and Ertai opened his eyes.

They were hurtling toward the broad column of energy passing between the Hub above to the Citadel below. Greven laid a hard hand on Ertai's shoulder.

"Steer wide of the beam," he said. "If we hit it, we're dead."

Ertai closed his hands to fists and tried to will the invisible stream away from the energy column. The stream was strong, and it liked flowing into the beam. Veins stood out in Ertai's neck as he wrestled with the channeled power.

Bend, bend, he thought furiously. Go where I will you!

The conjured stream bent to starboard until it was just clear of the energy column. *Predator* roared past in a full 20 degree dive. The port main boom brushed the glaring energy field and sizzled into instant oblivion. Ertai held the turn, and the airship rocketed into a downward spiral toward the landing dock, located at the highest point of the Citadel.

"Better slow down," Greven said.

Here was the point Ertai had contemplated, even in the extreme duress of his conjuration. Rath was his prison, Greven his jailer, and *Predator* was an instrument of oppression to thousands of free people. Why should he save it? Why not let it crash into the Citadel, doing as much damage as possible? At least then he could strike a blow for the oppressed.

"Slow down," Greven repeated, more urgently.

Dying is easy, his old teacher once told him. Dying is passive—living is active. A true mage must live in order to accomplish the goals of his art. What have you accomplished in your short life, Ertai?

"Slow! Slow!" Greven roared.

Predator was just one ship. Greven, just one commander. The coils of Phyrexian domination would scarcely tremble at their loss. He, on the other hand, might accomplish great things—if he lived long enough.

Ertai flung his arms wide. The magical stream, visible only to him, spread out in front of the plunging airship. It piled up against the tower in waves, and each rebounding crest struck *Predator* a hammer blow, slowing her. The already smashed prow struck the mooring ring and demolished it. The great ship slammed into the platform and skidded sideways, shearing off its ventral landing blade. Greven was catapulted from the bridge to the deck below. Only Ertai, rooted in place by the power flowing through him, kept his feet.

Predator came to a hard stop against the flowstone carapace. Greven leaped to his feet amid the tumbled-down wreckage.

"You! You wrecked my ship!" he said, pointing a thick finger at Ertai.

"It was already a wreck," Ertai said weakly. He staggered to the slanting rail. "We're alive. What are you complaining about?"

That said, he slumped to the deck. Where he'd stood, two blackened footprints were scorched into the planking.

* * * * *

Dorlan *il*-Dal, chamberlain of the evincar's palace, awaited the arrival of Greven *il*-Vec with trepidation. Everything was in chaos—the Citadel had been breached for the first time in history, the garrison was in disarray, the mighty airship *Predator* was a steaming wreck, and worst of all, Evincar Volrath could not be found.

Dorlan paced up and down outside the evincar's private chambers, unsure of how to proceed. Greven would no doubt be in the foulest mood, given his failure to catch *Weatherlight*. The shocking debacle at the Citadel would not salve his conscience either. What Dorlan feared most was what might happen when word spread that Volrath was missing. Would the evincar's subjects revolt? Would the rebel elves and their allies attack again? What of the moggs—would they obey their overseers without Volrath's authority to back them up?

The tramp of heavy feet brought Dorlan out of his gloomy reflections. Greven *il*-Vec descended the spiral ramp from the airship dock, followed by the remnants of his crew. Two crewmen carried a limp body between them, a young man clad in foreign clothes.

"Dread Lord!" Dorlan began, bowing hastily. "We are blessed you've come back to us unharmed!"

"Save the oil for someone who needs it," Greven said. He directed his men to lay the unconscious man on the floor. "Where is His Highness? I must report."

"His Highness Volrath is, uh—"

"Yes?"

"He's not here."

Dorlan thought sparks would fly from Greven's tooth grinding. The warrior seized Dorlan by his elaborate sleeves, lifting him until his toes danced on the mosaic inlay.

"Where is he?" Greven demanded.

"I-I don't know, Dread Lord! After the intruders were expelled from the Stronghold, he was nowhere to be found!"

Greven's anger vanished. He set Dorlan on his feet. "Nowhere? Have you searched?"

"Yes, Dread Lord."

* * * * *

Greven stared at Dorlan. From the base of his skull to the small of his back the warrior had a Phyrexian control rod implanted in place of his natural spine. This rod gave him enormous strength, but it also obeyed the mental commands of the evincar of Rath. To disobey brought instant retaliation in the form of unendurable pain. Greven had been so busy saving *Predator*, he'd not noticed the empty sensation left by Volrath's lack of control. Now he swept all points of the compass for his hated master and felt nothing. If Volrath were on the plane of Rath, Greven should have been able to sense him. Yet Volrath could not be dead, for the sudden severance of the evincar's control would have struck his spine like a thunderbolt.

"He's gone," Greven announced. "The evincar is not on this world." Having spoken the words, he made the leap of logic and deduced the truth. "Volrath was on *Weatherlight!*"

"What?" Dorlan said tremulously.

"Gerrard might have captured the evincar. No, that's not right. Why would he flee if he had Volrath as hostage?"

"Then His Highness willingly went on the enemy ship?"

Greven fingered the control rod where it entered the base of his skull. "Yes, that's what he did." The fool! Greven raged to himself. He used his shapeshifting powers to stow away on *Weatherlight!* What did he hope to gain?

"Ah, Dread Lord?" Dorlan was whimpering now.

"What is it?"

"What are we to do?"

"About what?"

"Everything. Who will rule in His Highness's place?" His pudgy face brightened. "You're the evincar's second-in-command. You must take over, Dread Lord! Let the people know a firm hand still holds the reins of Rath!"

The airship sailors cheered and loudly urged Greven to assume the governorship. He glared them into silence.

"This is not a robber band—we don't elect our chiefs here," he said. "There's an order in things that must be observed. Evincars have died before, and new ones were found. Our distant masters must be notified, and their will obeyed. I will consult them."

Dorlan and the sailors blanched as one.

"Do we dare?" asked Nasser, *Predator*'s veteran sergeant.

"You do not dare. I do," Greven said. Inwardly, he was not so eager. For the first time in many years he was free of domination. He could take the Stronghold as his own, but he knew he couldn't keep it. The overlords would not allow it, and his punishment at their hands would make Volrath's casual brutality toward him seem like a child's game.

He strode from the evincar's antechamber to the nearest lift. There were four of these large square platforms, each supported by a flowbot arm, passing through the many floors of the Citadel. Dorlan and the airship crew followed reluctantly.

"Bring the prisoner," Greven reminded them. Ertai was carried along.

The lift lowered them smoothly to the throne room. The oval chamber took up an entire floor. The decor was a mishmash of earlier evincars' tastes, from the brutal efficiency of Davvol to the mechanistic fetishism of Burgess. Volrath had seldom used the throne room. He had preferred the larger convocation hall, deeper in the Citadel, for his state functions.

High above the throne of Rath hung a large, inverted, three-sided pyramid made of some translucent gray Phyrexian alloy. It was cradled by an intricate, multi-armed flowbot carriage. This was the "Window" to Phyrexia. A voice and image portal only, it could not send or receive artifacts or travelers.

Word of Greven's return and Volrath's disappearance brought out the evincar's court. Chosen from the cooperative families of the Dal, the Vec, and the Kor, the courtiers of Rath were servants, sycophants, and spies of the evincar. Their stock in trade was gossip and treachery as they jockeyed among themselves for honors and privileges. During the two-pronged attack by *Weatherlight* and the army of the elven rebel Eladamri, Volrath's collaborators had taken refuge in their Citadel apartments. The danger past, they emerged in their court finery, ready to be seen and counted when the Window to Phyrexia was opened.

Sailors deposited Ertai at the foot of the empty throne. Greven planted his fists on his hips and declaimed, "Overlords of Rath, hear me!"

The pyramid remained dim and inert. Greven repeated his summons. The surface of the pyramid began to sparkle.

Encouraged, Greven said, "I am Greven *il*-Vec, commander of the armies of Rath! Our evincar has left us, and we request that our overlords restore him to us or send another in his place."

A slender red beam lanced out from the mechanism perched atop the pyramid. It raked harmlessly across Greven's face, tracing every contour and comparing it to images of the warrior stored in its memory. When it was satisfied Greven was who he claimed to be, the flowbot flexed its limbs and lowered the Window. The brass-yellow machinery whirred and squeaked until the pyramid reached head height over the throne. The Window came to life with an ominous crackle of power, sending skittish courtiers shrinking back in alarm.

"Be brave," Greven sneered. "It's only a machine."

Dark colors ricocheted through the pyramid, corner to corner to corner. It stabilized in the center and assumed a bluish tinge. Greven squared his broad shoulders and awaited his masters' command.

"Greetings." The Phyrexian voice sounded slurred and mechanical. "Greetings, our loyal warrior, Greven *il*-Vec."

He knelt on one knee. "Humblest greetings, Great Lords. We have a grave problem—"

"The matter is known to us. The Hidden One is not pleased with the evincar's desertion or your soldiers' failure."

"Shall we track down Volrath and punish him, Great Lords?" asked Greven.

"That is not necessary. It is more important for you to strengthen your forces on Rath and crush the rebellion brewing among the elves."

"Yes, Great Lords."

"To this end, we are sending a special emissary who will find a new evincar, reorganize the government, and improve the schedule of flowstone production."

A murmur circled the room.

"Would it not be simpler to appoint a new governor to do all that?" Greven said. Fatigue made him more blunt than usual.

The red beam returned, but this time it was not harmless. It struck Greven in the chest, and the powerful warrior groaned and collapsed. He twitched on the floor several seconds until the beam relented. Courtiers at the rear of the room quietly slipped out lest the overlords' displeasure spread.

"Do not question, only obey," the pyramid intoned. "Expect the emissary in seven intervals. She will appear in the Dream Halls at that time. All will obey the emissary or be punished."

Greven winced as he stood. "We'll obey without question, Great Lords."

The light within the pyramid began to swirl and dart about again, then became inert once more. The flowbot retracted the device back to its former position near the ceiling.

Ertai hobbled on burned feet to stand beside Greven. "Seems we're in the same boat again," he said.

"How so, Runt?" the warrior rumbled.

"There's always someone bigger around who expects you to bow and scrape just to get along, isn't there?"

"Some of us are bigger than others."

"And some of us stand to fall from a greater height," the young man replied. "Now, where can I get some salve for my feet?"

* * * * *

Life is sweet.

This was Crovax's conclusion as he stood at the extreme end of the Dream Halls, gazing down on the royal laboratory and prison tower, the map tower, and the chaotic mogg warrens. Below, the minions of Rath scurried about their tasks like the residents of an anthill. Each life could be his, to take and savor. He smiled, and the dark face in the flowglass smiled back at him. Why not take them all eventually? The value of cattle was as food for the lion.

With a wave of his hand, the flowglass parted. Crovax stepped up to the sill and stood on the edge, hundreds of feet above the laboratory roof. He raised one foot and was amused to see the flowstone sill rapidly extend to support him. He lifted the other foot, and the nano-machines swiftly advanced under that one, too. Crovax repeated the process until he was standing on a spindly flowstone platform six feet out from the ledge. He stood with his arms outstretched and laughed at the absurdly great power that was now his.

With an ominous crack, the thin flowstone structure bowed

under his weight. Crovax's euphoria disappeared. He leaped back to the Dream Halls, just as the feeble platform crumbled away. Crovax hit the sill square in the chest, driving the wind from his lungs. Gasping, he heaved himself over the ledge and rolled back inside the hall. The window flowed shut behind him. Crovax lay on the cold stone floor, heart hammering. Then he laughed.

* * * * *

At the far end of the Dream Halls, the delegation led by Greven had just arrived. Normally only Volrath could have opened the flowstone locks on the doors to his sanctum, but when the group arrived, the massive twin doors were already mysteriously apart. Greven entered boldly, as if he were a frequent visitor. Behind him came Dorlan *il*-Dal and a select group of courtiers, an honor guard drawn from the palace garrison, and Ertai. Dorlan had voiced a concern over bringing the captive wizard along.

"He's an enemy," the chamberlain said. "Surely he belongs in prison?"

"All in good time," Greven answered. "For now, let him see the power he opposes."

Ertai slipped along quietly on bandaged feet. The honor guard was close behind him, so he had no chance to slip away. He only considered escape for a moment. The prospect of meeting an emissary from Phyrexia was far too interesting to miss.

The Dream Halls were their widest where the structure joined the main part of the Citadel. None of them had ever seen the interior before, and the austere monochrome reliefs, starkly stylized images of Volrath, and weird flowbot machinery kept the delegation in a tight group, heads turning in all directions. Only Greven kept his dignity and strode straight on. He drew ahead of the rest until Dorlan called to him.

"Dread Lord, wait for us!"

"Stop dawdling. You've lived in the Stronghold most of your lives, and you act like you've never seen such sights before."

Ertai sat down on the polished black floor. "Might as well wait here," he said.

"On your feet!" said a shocked Dorlan.

"My feet hurt. Ask Lord Greven why they do."

"Leave him," said Greven. "When the emissary arrives, he'll stand like everyone else. How many intervals has it been?"

Dorlan consulted the time meter he wore around his neck. The dial was as big as a dinner plate but as thin as leather. In between ordinary numbers, intricate runes and sigils—Phyrexian numbers—appeared and disappeared irregularly.

"Six intervals and a half," he said when the yellow symbols appeared on the meter's face.

"Stand at ease," Greven said to the honor guard. The guardsmen, led by Sergeant Nasser, slouched in their stiff, conical suits of ceremonial armor.

No one spoke for several minutes. Ertai amused himself by reading the auras of the courtiers. Their strongest components were fear and greed. The honor guard was a different story. They all wore haloes of violence, and their leader, Nasser, had a powerful aura that spoke of great personal ambition. Ertai looked back at Greven and wondered if he knew.

Poking at the floor, Ertai discovered the marble was just another variety of flowstone. He concentrated as he pushed with his finger, and for a fleeting instant, he thought he felt the substance soften. Surprised, he lifted his finger. There was no sign of any indentation—but the sensation must have been genuine. He was far too practiced to mistake a thing like that.

The silence was broken by a far-off whistling. Everyone in the delegation pricked up their ears. Ertai stood. The honor guard snapped to attention.

"The emissary!" said Dorlan breathlessly.

Greven peered down the dim, cavernous hall. "Don't be an idiot. Do overlords whistle like steam kettles?"

Dorlan sidled up to the towering warrior. "Who—or what—is it then?"

The trilling grew steadily louder. It didn't sound like a person whistling, more like a pipe or a tin whistle.

"Could it be Volrath returned?" Ertai asked.

"That sound is not Volrath," Greven replied.

A voice filtered down, distorted and sourceless in the odd acoustics of the hall. As everyone strained to hear, the noise grew more distinct.

Greven ordered the guards forward. They formed a wedge in front of Greven and leveled their spears. The whistling was louder and clearer, but there was still no one in sight.

"Whoever you are," Greven shouted, "show yourself!"

The whistling stopped and was replaced by quiet, eerie laughter. All eyes rose, and they beheld Crovax in his new Phyrexian finery, standing on the vertical wall of the hall, twenty feet above them. His position defied reason and gravity, for he was standing at a ninety degree angle to the floor with no more support than the soles of his boots.

"By the colors," Ertai muttered. "How did he get here?"

"You know him?" Greven said mildly.

"His name is Crovax. He's a sullen, tormented man who came here with us on *Weatherlight*."

Greven parted the line of soldiers. "What are you doing here? This is the sanctum of the Evincar of Rath—trespassing here means death!"

Crovax turned to face the floor and walked effortlessly down the wall. A small bone-white flowstone device perched on his shoulder began to whistle the melancholy nomad song again. Crovax reached the floor and stepped down.

"I *am* the evincar of Rath," said Crovax.

CHAPTER 4
Messenger

Greven drew his black-bladed sword in a swift, fluid motion. "You're either a madman or a liar. In any case, your life is forfeit. Get him!"

The guards lowered their spears and charged. Crovax, utterly composed, made no immediate move to evade them. When the soldiers were ten paces away, the smooth black floor suddenly turned to jelly. The soldiers' feet sank into the black goo and were held fast.

"Dread Lord, he commands the flowstone!" Dorlan cried.

Greven circled wide around the mired troops. Crovax edged away from Greven, drawing his own sword. He seemed wary of engaging the hulking warrior.

Greven leveled his weapon. "You have some influence over the flowstone, but you don't command it as Volrath did, do you?" He cut wide circles in the air with his wickedly curved blade. "Can you direct my control rod, impostor? You have this one chance before I kill you!"

He made a terrific overhand slash at Crovax, who parried shakily. Ertai pushed to the front of the crowd of frightened courtiers. Crovax's aura was astonishingly dense and dark, far

50

stronger than it had been on *Weatherlight*, and it extended to where the soldiers were stuck in the grip of the flowstone. He had little power left to fend off Greven, however.

Greven came on fiercely, cutting at Crovax's head, thrusting at his stomach and legs. One underhand lunge was blocked in the last second by Crovax's lighter blade. Greven's great muscles bulged, and he brought his blade up against Crovax's full resistance. The latter's sword snapped, and the flowstone blade went skittering away, stopping at Ertai's feet. To his astonishment, the broken blade sprouted tiny legs, stood up, and began marching back to rejoin itself to Crovax's hilt.

Taking his sword in both hands, Greven raised it high for a death blow. The flowstone released the soldiers, and the section of floor between Greven and Crovax heaved up to ward off the warrior's blow. Greven's blade stuck fast in the flowstone shield. He grunted and tugged at the imbedded blade. Crovax, breathing hard, searched for a weapon with which to strike the distracted Greven.

Three deep, even tones echoed through the vast space like the tolling of a great bell.

A shock wave blasted down the Dream Halls, silent and powerful. Lightly dressed courtiers went sprawling. Ertai dropped on his face and clawed at the hard pavement. To his amazement, his fingers probed shallow handholds in the flowstone.

The soldiers, buffeted by the noiseless blast, struggled to keep formation. Crovax's flowstone shield receded. Greven recovered his sword but stayed his hand. The tremendous displacement of air could mean only one thing—the emissary was coming.

Tumbling through the air down the center of the hall came a gray cube, turning successive faces toward them as it came. It grew rapidly in size. Only Greven and Crovax held their ground; the courtiers and soldiers, cowed by the enormous power confronting them, backed away. Once the wall of wind ceased, Ertai raised his head to see what was happening.

The cube stabilized, hovering a few inches off the floor. It was at least 30 feet to a side, and its boiling, misty surface revealed no details of its purpose or composition. Behind the veil of gray there was movement. Bumps rippled the facing surface of the cube.

The phantom gong tolled three more times, and a hand appeared through the cube—a lithe, slender hand, gloved in a black gauntlet. A knee and toe appeared, then the leg connecting them. In a simple, natural movement, the emissary stepped through the portal into the Dream Halls.

The emissary was dwarfed by Greven. Clothed head to toe in attenuated sable armor plate, the emissary was only slightly taller than Ertai. The closed helmet turned this way and that, surveying the scene. The emissary raised a hand, but not in greeting. A small device the Phyrexian held made a chirping sound, and the portal began to shrink. As it did, it spat out four large black metal boxes. The cube shrank to the size of a small nut, tumbling in the air as it hovered. The emissary's control device chirped again, and the tiny cube vanished. Back went the device into a pouch on the emissary's belt. Air rushed in to fill the space of the departed portal.

Soldiers and courtiers dragged themselves into some semblance of order. Ertai stood up, absently combing his tousled hair with his fingers.

The emissary stood motionless, and Ertai wondered for a moment if the Phyrexians had sent a mechanical creature like Karn, his former crewmate. Slowly the stranger raised its hands to its helmet. The headpiece slipped off with an audible hiss.

"It's a girl," Ertai said.

"Be silent!" Greven said. He went down on one knee. "All hail the plenipotentiary of the Supreme Master of Phyrexia!"

With much rustling of stiff cloth and squeaking metal, the delegation knelt before the emissary. Ertai was the first to stand. He wanted a better view of this girl from another plane.

Her features were sharp, like the elves of his world. She had high, pointed ears and the spatulate cheekbones of a pureblooded elf. Her eyes, he saw, were identically hued. Incongruous freckles dotted her nose and cheeks. Her armor fit as if a matte-black skin, and where it ended, her own pale complexion revealed strange dark crosshatching lines. In spite of the awesome presence of Phyrexia she bore with her, the emissary looked to be little more than Ertai's age—the human equivalent of nineteen years old.

Crovax bowed smoothly. "Greetings, Excellency. Welcome to Rath."

She looked at him blankly. "Who are you?"

Ertai sniggered. At a nod from Greven, two soldiers seized the young sorcerer in an unfriendly grip.

"I am Crovax, the new Evincar of Rath."

"I've heard of you," the emissary answered coolly. "You exceed yourself. I am here to appoint a new governor, and I have not chosen you yet."

Crovax visibly recoiled. Around him the flowstone floor rose in tiny peaks, like a tempest-tossed lake. It quickly subsided.

Greven stepped forward. "Greven il-Vec, commander of all Citadel forces and captain of the airship *Predator*, at Your Excellency's service."

"Commander."

What a flat, emotionless voice she has, Ertai thought. The members of the court, led by Dorlan il-Dal, greeted the emissary in turn, each swearing undying loyalty to her and to the power she represented. She accepted their boot licking and toadying with the same indifference with which she received Crovax's arrogance.

"What about me?" Ertai called out. The soldier holding his right arm let go and gave the sorcerer a resounding rap on the back of the head.

"Who is that?" asked the emissary.

"No one, Excellency. A prisoner of war," Greven explained.

"You bring prisoners to me? Why?"

"Good question," said Crovax.

"This one has a certain talent for magic," Greven said. "I brought him along to witness your arrival, Excellency, as an object lesson."

"Has he been interrogated?"

Greven steeled himself for punishment. "No, Excellency."

"The first task of a captor is to extract information from prisoners," the girl said. "You will see to his interrogation, Greven il-Vec."

"At once, Excellency." He signaled the guards to drag Ertai away.

Ertai looked between the hulking soldiers and said, "You haven't told us your name!"

Greven was about to order Ertai silenced, but the emissary stopped him. "A logical question. My name is Belbe."

"My name is Ertai. I was first in my class—"

"Take him away," Greven said irritably. "I will question him myself."

* * * * *

Crovax extended his arm to lead Belbe from the hall. She ignored his pretense of gallantry and walked briskly on. Greven asked about the crates sent with her.

"Have them taken to the evincar's quarters. I will occupy them," she said.

This was mogg work, but the smelly brutes were forbidden to enter the Dream Halls. Greven moved as if he was about to order the guards to remove the crates when Crovax made a suggestion.

"Let the courtiers do it," he said. "The palace is their business, isn't it?"

Dorlan blanched at the prospective exertion. "We're not laborers!"

Belbe said, "Do as Crovax says."

"But Your Excellency!" Dorlan protested.

"This man is an intruder, as much an enemy as the wart Ertai," Greven said, poinying at Crovax. "By rights he should be in a cell, too."

"No," Belbe said. "This one has received the attention of the overlords. He's not evincar yet, but he stands in contention for the post. So long as his orders do not contradict mine, he will be obeyed."

Crovax's altered face split wide in an unpleasant grin. "What are you waiting for? See to the emissary's baggage."

Dorlan and the others filed past Crovax. The metal cases were six feet long and half as wide. The pampered, in some cases elderly, courtiers struggled to lift the heavy containers to their shoulders. Crovax could not restrain himself from laughing when one aged Dal collapsed, bringing a crate down on himself. Dorlan directed the rest of the courtiers to hoist the box off the fallen man. Blood stained the old man's gold-trimmed robe, and his face had gone the color of cold ashes.

Dorlan lifted the man's wrist. "He's dead." His voice choked.

Crovax stood over them. "Useless parasite," he said. His brow furrowed, and a segment of the floor detached itself and formed a stretcher. Walking on short flowstone legs, the stretcher bore the body of the elderly courtier from the hall.

Dorlan looked up at him with tears in his eyes. "If you command the stone, why don't you order it to carry the emissary's baggage?"

Crovax grabbed Dorlan's collar and effortlessly lifted the corpulent chamberlain to his feet.

"Prove your devotion to the overlords by carrying Her Excellency's baggage! All of you!" he roared.

Ertai and his escorts had lingered, watching this scene unfold.

"This is bad," Ertai muttered. "He's gone mad, utterly mad."

He was hustled away. Belbe, Greven, Crovax, and the honor guard stood by as the aged and soft-living members of the evincar's court struggled to carry Belbe's crates.

Belbe gestured to Dorlan. "What is that on that man's face?"

"Tears," said Greven.

"A saline solution, excreted for the purpose of removing irritations from the surface of the cornea—"

"The old man who was killed was chamberlain before Dorlan," Greven said. "He was Dorlan's father."

Belbe started for the evincar's quarters without waiting for her baggage. Greven excused himself to see to Ertai's interrogation.

Before he left he said, "If Your Excellency needs assistance—or protection—you need only call. There are guards posted throughout the Citadel." He shot Crovax a warning look and departed. What remained of the honor guard awaited her orders.

"What shall we do, Excellency?" asked Nasser.

"Carry on with your duties," she said.

"And I?" Crovax asked.

"If you're to command the forces of Rath, you should inspect the army and become familiar with it. They have performed poorly of late, have they not?"

"It's true, Excellency," Nasser said grimly. "There was great confusion when we found we had to deal with both rebels and an enemy airship."

"Very well, in five intervals, I expect to hear your military report, Crovax. Inform the chamberlain and Greven *il*-Vec that I want them present as well."

She walked away. Crovax watched her go.

"Man to man, what do you make of her?" mused Crovax.

"Very strange," the sergeant said. "Why would the overlords send a young girl on such a mission?"

"There's a reason, Sergeant. We just don't see it yet. The overlords do nothing without a well-thought-out reason. By the way, what's your name?"

"Nasser, sir."

"How long have you served Greven *il*-Vec?"

"Seven years, sir."

"Seven years, and you only command a troop of palace guards? Greven does not appreciate you."

Nasser met the other man's gaze. "No, sir, he does not."

"We'll have to remedy that." He held out his hand. "Lead on."

Nasser formed the honor guard and marched them away. Crovax strolled behind them, smiling at some private amusement.

* * * * *

The sound of marching feet receded in the distance. Belbe took a deep breath. Alone again, thankfully! Though she'd been on Rath scarcely an hour, she was feeling bruised by the experience. She found the company of the Citadel's inhabitants wearing—the great hulking presence of Greven, the soldiers so wrapped in armor as to seem less alive than the Phyrexian priests she'd encountered, the court officials with their washed out, anxious faces, always ready with a whisper and an open palm. . . .

Her master, Abcal-dro, never told her that people were like this. The only two that interested her were the young one called Ertai and the dark one called Crovax. They were very different types. Ertai radiated brash wit and vast self-confidence, even with shackles on his feet. Crovax was dangerous. She could tell he'd been to Phyrexia and received the special attention of Fourth Level artificers.

She walked unerringly to the flowbot lift that could take her to the evincar's suite of rooms, halfway up the great tower. A detailed schematic of the Stronghold had been implanted in her mind when she was made. Every strut, every brace, every creeping fleshstone appliance was as familiar to her as her own hands. Yet everything was strange, too, because she knew she'd never been here before.

She stepped into the flowbot lift. The conveyance didn't budge, so she prompted it. "To the evincar's quarters."

The Citadel had existed a long time, and successive occupants had altered, decorated, and embellished it as they saw fit. Belbe passed through floors reflecting the tastes of six previous evincars, each new master having overlaid his predecessor's alterations. The basic structure was a shell of brassy Phyrexian alloy and ceramic, over which were layers of flowstone designed to resemble wood, marble, glass, and so forth. Its organic form survived every decorative whim, and centuries of human habitation afflicted it like scars on the body of a great sea beast.

A squeaky voice announced each floor as they passed. "Observation deck . . . courtiers' apartments . . . flowbot repair shop . . . evincar's museum . . ."

"Stop," Belbe said. The lift shuddered into place. They were halfway between floors. "Go down to the evincar's museum."

The lift obediently climbed down several feet. Belbe stepped off the platform. The floor was dark, with only a few reflective glints showing.

"Light," she ordered. Nothing happened. "I want light!"

Some flowstone globes burst into full illumination. Other contrary appliances refused to light at all. As a result, the room was harshly shadowed, a condition made worse by the bizarre contents of the museum.

Volrath had made it his business to catalog all forms of life on Rath. Specimens of every species were here, carefully preserved and mounted on "marble" flowstone pedestals. There were animals, birds, reptiles, and fish, all with staring glass eyes. Some of the specimens were old and suffered from neglect and decay. As Belbe walked slowly past, she touched the plumage of a stuffed bird. Pale blue feathers turned to dust in her hands. Belbe brushed the powder away, and a small two-legged machine scuttled from the shadows, its bell-shaped proboscis noisily sucking up the offending dust.

Volrath hadn't settled for just animals. Each sentient race on Rath was represented by four preserved specimens: adult male, adult female, child male, child female—all in appropriate costume and with typical accouterments. She passed exhibits of the Kor, the Dal, and the Vec. Sleek, powerful merfolk were artfully displayed inside blocks of transparent green flowstone, simulating the sea in which they lived.

The last race displayed were the Skyshroud elves. Only a single example was provided, a fully grown male. Belbe paused, arrested by what she saw. The face, though masculine, was very similar to hers. She climbed on the pedestal with the embalmed elf and stared curiously into his long dead face.

Who were you? Some hunter, some fisher the evincar's soldiers caught one day? Where did you live? Why do you look like me?

Belbe touched the elf's face. It was cold, dry, and hard. The taxidermist had given the·elf blue-gray eyes. She touched the dusty pupil with her fingertip. It was not glass. It yielded to her touch.

Belbe jumped down from the pedestal, trembling. She rubbed her hands repeatedly on the skirt of her armor. The room had suddenly grown small and oppressive. She had to get out, now.

The lift was waiting for her. She leaped aboard and said, "Go."

"Go where?" asked the device.

"To the evincar's quarters. At once!"

By the time the platform stopped at the lowest level of the evincar's suite, the structure had narrowed to a mere two hundred feet in diameter. The antechamber was cool and dim.

"Give me light."

The room gradually brightened with an intense, pulsating blue light. Belbe moved to the center of the room as the walls passed from opaque to translucent. The throbbing blue light was the energy beam outside. She could feel the energy bleeding through the walls on her skin. The bottom floor of the suite was one large room with inward curving walls, and as she stood, fascinated by the energy passing between the Flowstone Factory and the Hub, the floor began to flicker. Languorous waves of color circled the floor in alternating bands of red, orange, yellow, green, and blue. Centered in this silent vortex of color, Belbe stood in silence. The chromatic waves circled the room around her feet. She knew this was caused by feedback in the flowstone as it soaked up the energy seeping through the walls, but it was delightful, whatever the cause.

She drifted a few steps toward the stairs leading to the next floor. As she did, the color wheel shifted to re-center on her new position. Amused, she backed up a few feet. The clockwise swirl followed her.

Belbe trotted around the room. Her re-engineered legs were capable of formidable speed, but in the confines of the tower, she did not test her limits. The spectral bands in the floor chased her, no matter how fast she ran. Static charges built up in the air. Belbe held out her hands, laughing as white sparks discharged from her fingertips.

On her twentieth circuit of the room, she noticed Crovax standing by the lift. She skidded to a stop. The floor went through noiseless paroxysms of clashing color, finally settling into its wheel pattern once more.

"Light," she said. Her heart was beating rapidly, and her hair was damp with sweat.

The walls became opaque as the artificial lighting came up. Crovax, hands clasped behind his back, looked somber in his black robes and acid-etched Phyrexian breastplate.

"What do you want?" Belbe asked.

"I came to see if you were all right, Excellency." He used the language of a subordinate, but he did not speak like one. "From below we could see colored lightning playing about the tower. I didn't realize you were . . . enjoying yourself."

"An amusing effect," she replied. "I discovered it by accident."

"An interesting substance, flowstone. It can be controlled, if one has the will to do so. Half-controlled and half-influenced, it is unpredictable. Please be careful, Excellency."

Without a spoken command, the sides of the lift rose to enclose Crovax.

"Until later," he said as the device sank through the floor.

She was tired. Being on display was wearing, and her sprint around the room used up what vitality she had left. Belbe climbed the ornate stairs to the next floor. An evincar could have willed the stairs to carry him, but she had to make her own progress.

She wandered through chambers filled with paintings and statues, mostly warrior's portraits and battle scenes. Most of the individual images bore the face of Volrath. Belbe found it odd anyone would want to be surrounded by pictures of himself, especially such exaggerated, extravagant images. Volrath slaying an entire army with just his sword. A colossal Volrath, wreathed in cloud, standing astride the Stronghold. Volrath trampling nations and worlds beneath his feet.

Interspersed among the statues, paintings, and tapestries were more useful items—cabinets, cupboards, shelves, chairs, settees. The furniture was uniformly hard when Belbe sat on it. From its dished and bulged shapes, she deduced it was flowstone and that it would soften for the evincar but no one else.

She found a bed at last, a large circular mattress laden with handmade quilts and pillows. These were gifts of the evincar's subjects, and thankfully were not flowstone. The bed was sized for a very tall occupant, so she had to boost herself up. As she sat there, her feet dangling, she noticed another statue, much different from all the others. It was sited so that only a person lying on the bed could see it in the adjoining room. Belbe hopped down for a closer look.

The statue, executed in genuine white marble, depicted two figures facing each other. The taller figure was inescapably Volrath, though this was the only statue in which he wore royal robes instead of armor. His hand was extended, clasping the hand of the facing figure. Belbe circled the twelve-foot-high statue, trying to see who the other figure was.

The figure facing Volrath was shorter and proportioned like a normal man. He had neck-length hair and the suggestion of a beard, and was likewise dressed in peaceful fashion. When Belbe finally reached a spot where she could see, she discovered the figure with Volrath had no face at all.

* * * * *

"Let's talk this over," Ertai said.

Greven nodded to his two mogg warders, who tore Ertai's shirt from his back. He didn't regret the loss of the garment, as it was in tatters anyway, but he did take exception to the assorted irons roasting in a brazier not three feet away.

"This isn't going to accomplish anything," Ertai added. "I have nothing to say."

Greven took an instrument from his belt pouch: a slender red rod, wound in a tight, flat coil. He pinched the end of the coil between his fingers and it slowly unrolled into a rigid rod.

"What is that?" Ertai asked, clearing his suddenly tight throat.

The hulking warrior loomed over him. He gave one end of the rod a twist, and short spikes appeared on the opposite end. Ertai decided he preferred the branding irons. He backed away. The wall stopped him.

Again Greven gestured to the moggs, who seized Ertai's ankles. They jerked his right foot up, and Greven bent over it, rod in hand. . . . Ertai shut his eyes.

Click. The heavy shackle fell from his leg. Ertai opened his eyes in time to see Greven withdraw the spiky rod from the keyhole. He repeated the operation to the other shackle.

"Keyworm," the warrior said, tucking the slowly coiling creature back in his pouch.

"By all the colors," Ertai said, sighing gustily. "I thought—"

The warders slammed him against the wall. Greven picked up an iron. The tip was pale orange, almost white hot.

"Now," said Greven, "tell me about *Weatherlight*."

Ertai, his hands pinned, closed his eyes and conjured a psychokinetic blast from his locus, his solar plexus. Such conjurations were not as controllable as ones channeled through the hands, but considering his situation, he had little choice. He

61

mentally hurled it at Greven and was rewarded by the sound of the iron clattering to the floor.

"I can keep this up longer than you," Greven said. He retrieved the fallen iron, now cooled to cherry red, and returned it to the fire. "This can take all day, or it can be over when you wish it to be. What do you say?"

"A modicum of resistance is mandatory," Ertai said faintly. "After all, I am the most naturally talented sorcerer of the age."

Greven picked up fresh, hot irons in each hand. "Down here, Boy, you're just meat."

CHAPTER 5
Gifts

Belbe relaxed in Volrath's bed for an hour and rose feeling stiff and a bit disoriented. A few seconds of concentration dispelled the cobwebs in her head.

Some discreet servant had left a tray of soft cakes and wine for her refreshment in the outer chamber, but she didn't eat. She knew about food and drink, but the Phyrexians had designed out of her such weaknesses as hunger and thirst. Belbe sniffed the cake and nibbled off the corner of one. To her it had no taste. She sipped the amber wine, then spat it on the floor. To her inexperienced palate, the drink was vile.

Her baggage had been delivered to the floor below. Belbe touched the flowstone seals with her index finger, and the crates opened like black metal lilies. The first two boxes held her clothing. The third held a variety of weapons and spare powerstones for them. The fourth box held three smaller cartons of thin metal, each labeled in Phyrexian. The largest carton was marked: *Nano-machine Conversion Accelerator*. The small one merely said *Power Unit*. These were equipment updates she was to install in the flowstone factory, deep in the bowels of the Citadel. *Remote Transplanar Portal* read the middle-sized box.

Belbe shed her confining suit of armor. Once the lightweight ceramic plates were off, she stretched luxuriously and scratched her sides. What freedom! She never realized mere garments could make such a difference in comfort.

It was dusk, near the time she'd set for the council meeting. To celebrate her newfound freedom, she chose a loose fitting pair of billowing red trousers, topped by a waist-length silver tunic. She went to the lift, stopped, and doubled back to her cast-off armor. The belt kit was still around her cuirass. Never be separated from your kit, Abcal-dro warned her. It contained her single most valuable piece of equipment.

* * * * *

Dorlan *il*-Dal greeted her. He looked wan and worried. With him were two scribe machines, set to take down every word of the meeting. They crouched on either side of Dorlan's chair, looking like severed gray arms. Each of the flowbot's four fingers was stained black with ink. The nail of each finger served as a nib, and all four fingers wrote at once, not only keeping minutes of the meeting, but making triplicate copies at the same time.

Greven was there, as tidy and groomed as he ever could be. Both men bowed when Belbe entered the room.

"Where is Crovax?" she asked.

"I don't know," Dorlan replied, gnawing his lip. "Shall I send someone to find him?"

She considered the idea briefly and dismissed it. "No. He knows we're meeting at this hour. If he chooses to miss us, that's his choice."

They seated themselves around the table, Belbe assuming the tall chair reserved for the evincar. She first asked for an account of the Stronghold's assets. Sweating, the chamberlain wedged a monocle in his right eye and began to read from a lengthy scroll in a sing-song voice: so many retainers, so many courtiers, so many men-at-arms resided in the Citadel. They ate so much meat per day, so many loaves of bread, so many gallons of water, beer, and spirits. Belbe listened attentively for the first half hour, but as Dorlan drew a second scroll from a hamper that contained another five, her mind began to wander.

The doors flew open, revealing Crovax at the head of a band of soldiers.

"You're late," Belbe said.

He saluted rather than bowed. "Your Excellency set me to a considerable task. I did not wish to arrive with it incomplete."

Greven narrowed his eyes. The troops at Crovax's back were led by Nasser and included all the senior sergeants in the garrison—an unusual selection of men.

"You're not allowed to bring armed troops into the Citadel. Only the evincar rates a bodyguard," Greven chided, glaring at the newcomers.

Crovax strode in, a slight swagger in his step. "These fellows? They're not armed. Her Excellency asked me to inspect the state of the garrison, and who better to ask than the men who lead the men, the sergeants?"

Greven leaned on the table and growled, "You men are dismissed."

The doors closed behind the departing soldiers. Crovax took a seat opposite Greven. He sat down without waiting for Belbe's leave. Dorlan gasped at his insolence.

"You sound distressed, chamberlain," he remarked, folding his hands in his lap. "Was it something you ate?"

"No, just something he can't swallow," Greven said.

Dorlan made to resume his monologue, but Belbe stopped him. "I will hear from Commander Greven."

The imposing commander spoke without notes. "The captive, Ertai, was questioned by me for eighty-three minutes," he said.

"Is that all?" asked Crovax.

"No more was needed."

Belbe said, "What did you learn?"

"Until recently, he was a student at a school of magic run by one Barrin. He was recruited from the school by Gerrard Capashen to accompany Capashen to Rath for the purpose of rescuing the woman Sisay, a prisoner of Volrath's."

"The prisoner was freed?" she asked. Greven nodded curtly.

"I could have told you all that," Crovax said, bored.

Greven bristled.

Belbe held up her hand. "The essence of a successful interrogation is not always what you're told but how completely the prisoner gives up what he knows. Go on, Commander."

"It was Ertai's job to hold open the old valley portal, allowing *Weatherlight* to escape from Rath. His magical skills are considerable for one so young, as he will tell you given the slightest chance. During *Weatherlight*'s escape, he was thrown from the deck of Gerrard's ship to *Predator*, where I captured him."

Greven put a tightly wound scroll on the table. "This record contains every detail Ertai told me about *Weatherlight* and her crew—construction, specifications, armament, everything." His enormous hands closed into fists. "Soon I'll know that ship better than I know *Predator*. Next time, I will crush *Weatherlight*."

"Yes, 'next time,'" Crovax said. "The refrain of the defeated."

Without any warning words or grinding of teeth, Greven reached across the table and grabbed Crovax by the throat. Crovax tore at Greven's thick forearm with both hands. Slowly he began to unlock the commander's powerful grip. Surprised, Greven landed a smashing blow to the smaller man's nose. Crovax flew backward, skidding several feet on the polished floor.

"Your Excellency, do something!" Dorlan cried.

Belbe leaned back in the evincar's chair. "I am doing something."

Greven advanced, kicking Crovax's overturned chair out of the way. The would-be evincar was quickly on his feet, ignoring the blood streaming from his busted nose. His hand flashed to his armpit and out came a short dagger.

At this point Belbe said firmly, "No blades, Crovax."

He shrugged and tossed the weapon aside. Greven threw two heavy punches, left hand first, then right. They met only air. Crovax ducked under the bigger man's reach and kicked Greven hard in the gut. It was like kicking a tree trunk. Crovax, concern showing in his face for the first time, sprang away, avoiding his foe's massive fists.

"A little unfair, don't you think?" Crovax panted, circling nearer to Belbe.

"Why do you imagine combat has to be fair?" she replied.

Snarling, Greven snatched up an empty chair and flung it at his evasive enemy. Crovax leaped impressively, dodging the flying furniture. He executed a whirling kick that connected solidly with Greven's jaw, snapping the warrior's head back. Greven shook off the blow and climbed on the table, forcing Crovax to give ground.

Dorlan whimpered and went to huddle behind Belbe. Her boredom had disappeared. She watched, fascinated, as the two men fought around the room—Crovax, wily and agile, Greven, impossibly strong and resilient. When one or the other connected, the impact sent a hot, fleeting pang through her. It wasn't like the pain she felt when Abcal-dro inserted the Lens in her chest. The sensation left a warm feeling in her face and belly. She found herself wanting Greven to hit Crovax again. That surprised her. What difference did it make to her who won?

A rake from the ring on Crovax's left hand opened Greven's scarred scalp, and the commander began howling with unconfined rage. He moved with a speed astonishing in so large a man, hemming his opponent into the doorway. Crovax stepped in, pummeling Greven's throat and face with blows. He paid for his temerity. Greven's backhand sent him crashing against the closed doors.

"Why don't you command the flowstone to save you?" Greven sneered.

Belbe was wondering the same thing. Crovax had been given enough psionic ability to control the nano-machines in a rudimentary way. He could have tripped Greven with the floor, or raised a shield like she'd heard he had done in the Dream Halls. Why didn't he?

Greven took the stunned man by the wrist. He intended to wrench Crovax's arm out of its socket, but even as he steeled himself for the effort, a low, unnatural laugh filled the council chamber.

Crovax raised his head. His eyes blazed with unfathomable mirth. "Do your worst, savage. This is the last time you'll ever lay hands on me!"

In the time it took Greven to draw his next breath, he understood what Crovax meant. The control rod in his spine awakened and began to shriek, pouring torrents of pain through every square inch of his body. Wracked with agony, he released Crovax.

Belbe could see the livid implant between Greven's shoulder blades. To her enhanced eyes, the rod glowed with excess power that the Phyrexian mechanism converted to unendurable pain. She shivered. Her mouth went dry.

Crovax wiped the blood from his lips. "Strike me down, Greven. I'm right here."

Greven's knees buckled. He clawed at the rod, which he couldn't even reach due to the massive width of his own shoulders. Crovax lifted a foot and lightly pushed Greven's chest. The huge warrior toppled backward. Lights, scrolls, and chairs were upset by the force of Greven's fall.

"This is just a taste," Crovax said. "When I am evincar, you'll lick my boots every morning or know my displeasure."

Belbe came up behind him. Crovax's control of the spinal rod was not without effort. Sweat stood out on his face and neck, and dripped from his elbows. He trembled violently—from exertion or excitement? She could not tell. Belbe put a hand on Crovax's shoulder. His skin burned feverishly.

"You've made your point," she said.

"Have I?"

"Commander Greven is a valued member of our forces. I do not want him damaged."

Crovax went back to the council table and set his chair upright again. Once he was seated, he visibly relaxed. Greven let out a long gust of breath and ceased writhing.

"Proclaim me evincar," Crovax said in a low voice. "I have command of the flowstone. I've just demonstrated my ability to affect control rods. What more proof do you need? Discharge your commission and name me governor!"

Belbe went silently to her chair. Dorlan was still peeking out from behind it. When she stood aside waiting, the chamberlain sheepishly resumed his seat.

"Well?" said Crovax.

"You're the leading contender," Belbe said, "but there are others who have not yet had the opportunity to display their talents."

"Others? Who? Him?" Crovax indicated the prostrate Greven with a thrust of his chin. "No one approaches my power!"

"As I see it, your power is limited. You can influence flowstone in your immediate vicinity but only with great concentration. The shapes you create are not permanent. Just now you were too busy evading Commander Greven to think about the flowstone, were you not? And at what range can you affect a control rod? One yard? Ten yards? More is required than psionic ability—can you command the army? Can you execute the orders of our overlords faithfully and without question?"

Crovax sullenly said nothing.

"My decision will be deferred until I have sufficient evidence as to who is best qualified to be evincar," Belbe said. She sorted through the scramble of scrolls on the table. "Do I have your report on the readiness of the garrison?"

He took a flattened scroll from his inner jacket pocket and tossed it in front of her.

"Thank you. Briefly, what is your estimate of the military situation?"

Several long seconds passed before Crovax replied. "The Stronghold garrison is in disarray. They're afraid the rebels are equipped with airships, and they know Volrath has left them in the lurch. The rebels think they won a victory because some of them penetrated the Citadel and escaped with their lives. They'll be full of bluster and confidence and will no doubt be planning new raids."

She opened the squashed scroll Crovax tossed at her. "What do you recommend?"

"Attack without delay."

Belbe and Dorlan exchanged looks. "Are you certain, my lord?" asked the chamberlain.

"It's the course of action the rebels least expect."

Belbe read Crovax's report in seven seconds flat. "How will you do it?"

"I'll form a hard-hitting force, the cream of the garrison," he said, warming to the subject. "Nasser tells me Volrath had agents among the rebels who've provided maps of the Skyshroud Forest. I'll locate and destroy the village of Eladamri, the rebel leader." He tapped a finger against his forehead. "Take out the brains of the rebellion, and the rest are just carrion."

Belbe quickly rolled Crovax's scroll closed. "How many troops will you need?"

"Ten thousand should do it."

"What support? Supplies?"

"I'll take an equal number of moggs along as porters," he said. "No pack animals or clumsy machines—we'll move fast and strike hard." He struck the tabletop with a scratched and bleeding fist.

"You have leave to try, Crovax."

He stood and saluted. "I'll bring you Eladamri's head in a basket."

Belbe blinked several times. "Why would I want his head in any container?"

Crovax limped from the room, smirking. He'd taken some punishment and couldn't quite manage the swagger he'd come in with. On his way out, he deliberately stepped over Greven, still supine with remembered pain.

After the doors closed behind him, Belbe called out, "What do you think of Crovax's plan?"

Greven, white as death, crawled to a chair. "Eladamri will do what I could not," he said hoarsely. The emissary and the chamberlain looked blank. "He will kill Crovax. Unfortunately, he may also kill the best part of my army."

* * * * *

Half a hundred humans and elves gathered in the silent night. Their meeting place was a small hummocky island in the swamp near the edge of the Skyshroud Forest. Here, free-thinking Rathi rebels had come to hear the gospel of resistance. All the world's races were represented save the merfolk, who were blood enemies of the elves and would not seek their company even if it meant avoiding total extinction. Most of those present were Dal and Vec. A single Kor male lingered on the edge of the crowd.

No torches were lit. Darkness was the rule for this gathering.

"I don't like this," said a mature Dal man. He was richly

dressed and wore a jeweled dagger on his belt. "Agents of the evincar could be here—our lives are at hazard, and for what?"

"Why did you come, if you're so afraid?" This from an elderly Vec woman, leaning on a tall staff.

"I'm not afraid," said the Dal. "Just cautious."

"Caution is our enemy now, as much as Greven and his army," proclaimed a ringing voice.

Into the milling circle of men and women came Eladamri and his lieutenants. The elves were well armed with captured weapons. They fanned out to the edge of the little island, watching the night for signs of an ambush.

"Eladamri, hail!" said the old Vec woman.

"Greetings, Tant Jova," said the elf leader. They clasped hands. "How flourishes the tribe of Jov?"

"We are many, and there is metal in our hands, O Eladamri. In the past twenty days we have seen but few of the evincar's men. The skyship does not fly over us, and we have slain many moggs found wandering in our territory."

"This is just the beginning, Tant Jova," said Eladamri. "As we grow stronger, you will see fewer and fewer soldiers on the plain and in the air."

The rich Dal harrumphed. Eladamri turned to him. "Skeptical, Darsett?"

"Yes, I'm skeptical. A raid is not a campaign."

"All winning campaigns should start with a victory," said Gallan, Eladamri's friend and second in command.

"Yes, but you have a long way to go," Darsett replied. The bulk of the Dal behind him murmured in agreement.

"*We* have a long way to go," Eladamri said, raising his voice for all to hear. "The time is past when my people alone could resist the Stronghold with any hope but survival. Now is a chance for victory, for the overthrow of the evincar and his tyranny! We must forge an alliance of all free people on Rath to fight the evincar and his forces. Only then can we be truly free."

"A pretty speech," Darsett said. "But speeches won't beat Volrath's army."

"We'll build our own army," Gallan countered.

"What about the airship? If we openly revolt, Greven *il*-Vec and *Predator* will come and destroy us," said Tant Jova.

Mention of the terrible commander and his flying warship provoked a fresh round of unsettled muttering. Gallan tried to calm the Dal and Vec leaders, but they were plainly afraid of arousing the wrath of Greven.

Darsett raised his voice over the noise. "Already those Dal in the Stronghold who resisted the evincar have vanished—Lady Takara, my cousin Sterba—"

The lone Kor had gradually circled into the crowd until he was close to the elves. He caught Eladamri's eye.

"I don't know you, friend. Who are you?"

"Furah," he said in his odd, lisping way. "Of the Fishers of Life."

All comment ceased. The Fishers of Life were a tribe that lived near the summit of the Stronghold itself. No one knew the peak as well as they. It was rumored the Fishers of Life even had access to the inner crater through secret fissures in the flowstone.

"Speak," said Eladamri. "Tell us your mind, Furah."

The whiskered, catlike Kor shoved his face close to the elf chieftain's. "Volrath is no more," he said.

Four full seconds went by, then the assembly burst into spontaneous cheers. Eladamri alone frowned.

"How do you know this?" he asked.

"We know. The Fishers of Life see into the Stronghold, as you see into the water beneath your village. Volrath left Rath on the other flying ship, the one pursued by Greven *il*-Vec."

Gallan excitedly rattled his sword in its scabbard. "If this is so, our task is half done!"

"There's more," said Furah. "Greven's flying ship lies in ruins atop the Citadel. I myself have seen it there."

Without *Predator*, the evincar's troops have no long range reconnaissance and no ability to strike at great distances from their base in the Stronghold. There were small outposts stationed here and there on the plain, but without the airship, they would be easy targets for Eladamri's raiders.

Everyone began talking at once. Furah's news changed the Dal and Vec leaders from cautious conspirators to fiery revolutionaries. Some actually wanted to storm the Stronghold at once.

"I want Greven *il*-Vec's blood," Tant Jova said darkly. "For all the members of my clan who've perished at his hands!"

"Wait! Be still!" Eladamri barked. "No offense to you, honorable Furah, but we must be sure of news of such importance. Gallan, I want confirmation of what the Kor says. Is Volrath gone? Is the airship out of action?"

The young elf nodded. "It shall be done, Eladamri." He immediately sprinted into the night to carry out his orders.

"This changes things," Eladamri said gravely. "We have an opportunity to strike a blow for freedom. In time, a new evincar will be chosen by the overlords—it may be happening even now. Before the enemy can reorganize, we must strike! If the leaders of the free Dal and Vec pledge their support and send warriors to fight with us, I'll take every royal outpost between the Stronghold and the Skyshroud Forest."

Tant Jova whistled through her gapped teeth. "There must be thirty outposts in the territory you describe," she said. "How many warriors would you need to do such a thing?"

"As many as I can get, my friend."

"Where will you attack first?" asked Darsett.

He pondered only a moment. "The block house at Chireef."

"That's within sight of the Stronghold!"

"Yes. Not a likely place for us to attack—so all the better a place to strike."

Darsett and the young Dal fighting men began proposing various battle plans. Eladamri listened with half an ear, then he noticed Furah was no longer present. Damn him, he thought. He wanted to trust the Kor, but their ways were so strange, and they were so close to the Stronghold. Could Furah's news be a ruse to lure them into open battle? Gallan would find out the truth. Until then, they would plan for an attack.

Tant Jova took Eladamri aside. "Your liege Gallan told me your daughter Avila is dead at the hands of a Stronghold assassin. I grieve for a father's loss."

"Thank you. Volrath thought by such means to break me, but this foul murder only hardens my resolve."

Tant Jova's copper-colored face softened. She was very, very old for a Vec. She'd seen many terrible things in her long life, all coming from the Stronghold.

"I'll make a pact with you, O Eladamri," she said. "We shall never submit to the evincar, never cease to fight his forces, and never put down our swords until Greven *il*-Vec and all his minions have paid the price of justice."

Eladamri grasped her ancient hand. No words were spoken, but even if faced with death, neither would break their solemn bond.

* * * * *

After many hours, the pain had not subsided. His mind flickered in and out, seeking a place to hide from the terror. Solace was brief because his body would not let his mind go.

Tormented by thirst, Ertai crawled across the floor of his cell to the flowstone spigot mounted high on the wall. The warders had teased him, pantomiming that Ertai had to speak to the spigot in order to get water from it. So he crawled from the filthy pallet on which Greven's moggs had thrown him, crawled despite the burns on his legs and chest, and despite the fact that most of his fingers were broken.

"Wa-ah," was as close to the word "water" as he could manage. The spigot could not, or would not, understand him and remained closed. Ertai hated these machines. They were so inelegant and inefficient. Why duplicate the power of magic with crude artifacts? It was an old argument, one he remembered having with Hanna, Barrin's daughter, and *Weatherlight*'s navigator. How he wished he could have an argument with the stubborn, serious Hanna right now.

He yearned for a cool drink. He had to focus past his pain. Ertai called forth memories of water—the clay jar that stood in the corridor, outside the bedroom of his boyhood home, the one with the leaping fish painted on it . . . the waterfall at Jendary, all thunder and cold mist . . . the blue ocean around Tolaria, the rich, ever-changing basin on which the magical isle shimmered . . .

A single cool drop hit his forehead.

Water, water, water! he shouted with his mind. A trickle rewarded his effort but no more. What little liquid fell moistened his parched lips, and he croaked, "Wa-ter."

The spigot opened with a gush. Eagerly, Ertai gulped at the silver stream. It had a hard, mineral taste, but at that moment it was finer than any rare vintage.

"Enough," said a voice. The flow stopped.

He wiped his eyes and discovered he wasn't alone. The green-freckled girl, the emissary, was standing inside the cell door, watching him.

"You'll flood the room," she said, pointing to the spreading puddle on the floor.

Licking his lips, Ertai rasped, "I have nothing to say."

"I didn't ask you anything."

"Oh." He tried to stand, but there was no strength in his limbs. "Forgive me for not standing." He straightened with difficulty. "What do you want?"

"I observed you just now. You opened the valve using magic, didn't you?"

"So?"

"It shows considerable skill for an unaugmented person to have any influence, however small, over flowstone," Belbe said.

"I have considerable skill," Ertai replied with futile dignity.

Belbe came closer and squatted down. Ertai shrank from her until he realized she wasn't there to hurt him. She examined him with keen eyes. He felt a bit like a butterfly in a collector's jar. Her expression was without any feeling but curiosity.

"I want to release you," she said. "Give me your word you won't try to escape, and I'll parole you."

He could hardly believe it. At best he expected a quick execution after telling Greven everything he knew.

"What's to become of me?" he asked.

"I want you to work on developing your ability to influence flowstone."

Ertai let out a short, high-pitched giggle. Then another. A moment later he dissolved in a fit of coughing when he tried laughing with his broken ribs.

"Water," said Belbe. She held her cupped hands under the spigot. They filled, and she said, "Enough." Kneeling beside the wheezing Ertai, she offered him water from her own hands. With trembling fingers, he guided her hands to his lips.

"Thank you," he whispered.

"If you can control the flowstone," she went on, unaffected, "great things await you."

"Are you offering me a job?" asked Ertai wryly.

Belbe separated her hands. The last drops of water fell to the damp floor. "I'm offering you a chance to become Evincar of Rath."

CHAPTER 6
Enemies

With Volrath gone, the empty throne lent an air of uncertainty to every activity in the Stronghold. Crovax stepped into this maelstrom of confusion and doubt. Armed with Belbe's commission to strike at the rebels, he threw himself into the task. Troops of the Royal Army were marched out of the Stronghold and mustered on the plain by companies. Battalions of moggs, less disciplined and less intelligent, massed behind the soldiers and awaited their new commander. Crovax disdained the elaborate military ceremonies favored by Volrath and went on foot among his troops, followed by his newly formed personal guard, the Corps of Sergeants.

The one thing missing from this gathering of martial might was Greven *il*-Vec. Since Crovax did not ask him to join the expedition against Eladamri, the erstwhile commander of all Rathi forces chose not to appear on the plain with the army. He remained in the Citadel, overseeing the extensive repairs being made to *Predator*.

Crovax, hand on his sword hilt, approached the Corps of

Sergeants. Nasser stepped out of line and saluted.

"The army is mustered as ordered, sir."

"Very good. Do you have the list?" asked Crovax.

Nasser slipped a hand under his breastplate and pulled out a folded slip of parchment. Crovax studied it briefly, then walked to a spot in full view of the massed troops. He closed his eyes and extended his hands, fingers spread. The flowstone substrate humped up. A murmur went through the soldiery.

The hump became a rectangular stage six feet wide and ten feet long. Crovax raised his hands, and the platform bulked higher. When the stage was a full six feet off the ground, he lowered his hands. Just before his boots touched the side of the platform, steps indented themselves, allowing Crovax to easily climb to the top.

Only the front ranks had seen Crovax command the flowstone, but word filtered back through the assembled troops. They stirred restlessly, arms and armor clanking as they fidgeted and stretched to get a glimpse of their new leader. Far in the back, the moggs grunted and hooted and climbed on each other's backs to see Crovax.

"Soldiers of Rath!" he exclaimed.

One hundred companies of 200 soldiers each snapped to attention in unison. The moggs quieted.

"I am Crovax of Urborg. The emissary of the overlords has appointed me to command an expedition against the enemy, the rebel Skyshroud elves. We will shortly undertake this expedition, but first I have some things to tell you.

"An aerial vehicle came to Rath from a far-off place and lent support to an attack by the rebel leader Eladamri." He did not mention he came to Rath aboard that same vehicle. "The enemy airship has been dealt with and will not be a factor in our fight."

More muttering rippled through the ranks. Crovax let them talk for a few moments, then held up his hands for silence.

"Our own ship, *Predator*, is under repair and will soon be flying again. The rebels believe we don't dare move against them without our airship. They're wrong. Starting today, I will lead this force against the home village of Eladamri, whose location our spies have made known to us."

He paused, expecting cheers. When none came, Crovax glowered. Nasser and the sergeants raised a shout, and the soldiers half-heartedly joined in. Crovax waved for quiet.

"We will exact revenge for the defeat the elves dealt Greven *il*-Vec. But first I have another task, a solemn and sacred warrior's duty." He unfolded the parchment Nasser had given him. "When I read the following names, I want the officers named to come to me."

He cleared his throat. "From the First Company, Captain Thayer *il*-Vec; from the Third Company, Captain Ulan *il*-Dal; from the Seventh Company, Lieutenant Shirzod *il*-Vec . . ." The list grew until eighteen officers, all company commanders, stood nervously at Crovax's feet.

"You commanded companies during the recent fight with the elf rebels," Crovax said. "All of you were either outfought or outthought by your foes. Because of your dereliction of duty, cowardice, and incompetence in the face of the enemy, for your abject failure as commanders and as soldiers, you are hereby condemned to death."

The officers milled around in shock. They had no place to run; on the right they were hemmed in by the Corps of Sergeants, and on the left by a band of moggs who'd been summoned by Crovax for just such an eventuality. Several of the officers fell to their knees and raised open hands to Crovax, who stood above them glowering.

"Mercy, mercy, Great Lord! The fault was not ours!" they cried.

With a nod, Crovax set the moggs on the pleading men. The shambling creatures dragged six screaming officers from the crowd and dispatched them with their heavy clubs. It was considered a great disgrace to be killed by a mogg, and the surviving twelve officers closed ranks and drew their swords, ready to slay any mogg that approached them.

"Hold," said Crovax. The moggs lowered their bloody clubs. Crovax turned to the surviving officers. "For your last soldierly action, I've decided to suspend your sentences. You are reduced in rank to common soldiers and assigned to the scout battalion. You will lead our column into the Skyshroud Forest. If you distinguish yourselves in combat, you may yet be restored in rank."

Paul B. Thompson

Again Crovax wanted hurrahs, but the troops were uniformly silent. The spectacle of six Rathi officers bludgeoned to death by moggs did not encourage anyone to cheer.

Irritated, Crovax dismissed the men. "The designated companies will muster on the plain for the expedition in six intervals!" he shouted.

The stage sank back into the ground. Nasser and the sergeants assembled in front of him.

"Worthless rabble," Crovax said. "Did you see their faces? They were sickened by those cowards' deaths! No wonder they lost their last fight. What can be done with such weaklings?"

"They will recover once they taste victory," Nasser said.

"They'll win if I have to whip them all the way to the Skyshroud!"

"About the route, sir. Have you given any thought to what part—?"

The smell of freshly spilt blood teased Crovax's nostrils. His attention kept wandering to the slain officers. Finally the lure proved too strong, and he walked away, losing Nasser's question in mid-sentence.

The six men lay in a heap, their skulls crushed. Not one man drew so much as a dagger to defend himself. Crovax could not understand it. He announced their deaths, and still they didn't fight. Spineless worms.

There was one among the slain officers who hadn't quite surrendered his life. Crovax could sense it. His hands and face tingled, and the strange hunger awoke inside him. He kicked aside two corpses to uncover the one who was still alive. The soldier's face was white, and his chest barely moved to draw breath. Crovax knelt in the gore and gently turned the man's face to him. A faint current of life-force played over Crovax's fingers. Just a feather touch, but it was there.

The jar Kirril had given him in the Dream Halls had contained a primitive life taken from some animal. The remembered thrill of absorbing the glowing orb made Crovax shudder. By the time he'd mastered himself again, the officer was about to expire. Crovax pressed his hand to the dying man's face, ignoring the crushed bone and purplish blood clotted there.

Yes, he had it. Invisible by daylight, the escaping life-force of the soldier was snared by the tidal pull of Crovax's appetite. Though it was but the last gasp of a dying man, it was far sweeter than the crude sample he'd taken from Kirril's jar. What delight, what ecstasy he endured. He felt uplifted, ennobled, enriched. Here indeed must be the food of the gods . . .

He heard his name being called, distantly, over and over. Gradually he became aware of a hand on his shoulder. In a sudden burst of action, Crovax leaped up, scattering Nasser and two other sergeants who'd been standing over him.

"My lord, you were in a trance," Nasser said.

"So? If it was my trance, why do you presume to interrupt it?"

"Uh, my lord, it's been a full hour since you dismissed the army. There are preparations to be made."

Crovax looked wildly at the sky. Time had passed. The pile of gray clouds, which earlier had been stationary in the sky, were now billowing on a brisk northern wind.

"It was only a moment," Crovax whispered.

"My lord?"

"Never mind. Carry on with the preparations. Send a squad of moggs to clear the bodies away—"

"—and burn them?" Nasser finished. Cremation was the custom on Rath.

"No," Crovax said. "Have the moggs set up a gibbet by the causeway and hang the bodies from it. I want the whole expedition to march past them. It will motivate them, don't you agree?"

"As you say, my lord."

* * * * *

Supported by two somber guards and accompanied by Belbe, Ertai was ushered into a small chamber within a large tower outside the main Citadel. It was an unsettling place, filled to the ceiling with vats, vessels, and urns of unknown purpose. Some tanks held rank solutions that bubbled and seethed, even though no fire burned beneath them. Here and there flowbots continued in tasks Volrath had set for them. One rotated an hourglass-shaped flask at precise two-minute intervals. A muddy brown solution drained endlessly from one half of the flask to the other. Another long, insectlike arm switched bowls of red and yellow gelatin from under a device emitting colored rays.

Ertai could feel the air was alive with power. Most of it was destructive energy, the forces of corruption and decay. It was so strong, he reasoned there must be a powerstone somewhere in the laboratory—a very large powerstone.

"What is this place?" he asked, thinking he'd been better off in his cell.

"Volrath's laboratory," Belbe said. "He did considerable work with animals here. I understand his collection of artificial creatures is quite fascinating. Would you like to see them?"

"No, thank you!"

She shrugged. "Perhaps later. Here's what we came for."

In the center of the room, almost obscured by other apparatus, was a large circular slab of crystal. The flat top was grooved with five concentric rings, the sides were lined with narrow vertical flutes. Made of some smoky, transparent mineral, the slab was sited under an elaborate metal tripod fifteen feet high. Rendered in the skeletal, organic style of the fortress itself, the tripod supported a second faceted crystal, about half the diameter of the slab below it. Wires were attached to the smaller crystal, running off to all parts of the laboratory.

Here was the source of the power Ertai had sensed since entering the room. Both crystals were saturated with it.

"Help him onto the device," Belbe told the guards.

"Wait a minute," Ertai protested. "You're not putting me on that thing! Do you know what it is?"

Belbe crossed her arms. "You want to be well, don't you? This machine can alleviate all your injuries in a few minutes. Otherwise, you'll have to be confined to bed for days, maybe weeks. Even then, your hands may not heal properly."

Ertai tried not to look at his ruined hands. Greven had allowed his moggs to crush his fingers with thumbscrews after he'd outlasted the branding irons.

"Crovax is leaving this day with a force to destroy the rebels," Belbe went on. "If he succeeds, I must name him evincar. Once that happens, I can do nothing else for you."

"He'll have me killed," Ertai said. He looked up at the tall soldier holding his left arm. "Wouldn't you think so?" The guard nodded.

Why was he hesitating? So he got an infusion of negative energy—so what? He'd handled amounts of such power before, on an experimental basis. It was distasteful, but he'd suffered no ill effects from it. Power was power. Only stumpwater witches and country bumpkins still believed types of power were "good" or "bad."

He had no illusions about becoming Evincar of Rath. So absurd was the whole idea, his first response after Belbe proposed it was to laugh in her face. The laughter quickly died, smothered by the fire in his tormented flesh and the look of disappointment on Belbe's face. When she offered the option of rapid healing and a far more comfortable existence than either a barren cell or a headsman's ax, he chose to play along for a while. Once he regained his strength, he might be able to escape to Portal Canyon, open a gateway to Dominaria, and get back home. At least there was a chance . . . the loss of such a talented wizard would be an infamous crime, a terrible loss to civilization.

"What do you say?" Belbe asked, breaking in on his reverie. "The choice is yours."

"I suppose I can handle a little," he said.

"Good." Belbe smiled. Ertai found himself feeling glad he'd pleased her.

The soldiers hoisted the young wizard onto the crystal slab. Belbe ordered them back. She fiddled with the alignment of the upper focusing crystal, centering the stream of power on Ertai's chest.

"Don't overdo it," Ertai said, trying to sound nonchalant.

She didn't answer but went to the shielded control station to make a few adjustments. "Volrath used this infuser to heal experimental animals after he'd surgically altered them. On higher settings, it can mutate living creatures into drastically different forms."

Belbe clicked over several switches. "I'm using a lower setting in this case," she announced. "Beginning now—"

With a loud crack, sparks flew from the array of wires above the focal crystal. Ertai, helpless because of his injuries, could do nothing but watch the fireworks overhead.

"Stand by," Belbe shouted over the throb of the machinery. "I'm diverting power from the laboratory flowbots."

One by one, the automatic mechanisms in the lab shut down. Jars fell to the floor and smashed, spilling their unnatural contents. Horrible odors wafted through the room.

Ertai noticed the focal crystal had begun to glow darkly. It was an odd concept, a dark glow, but there was no better way to describe the presence of negative energy. He expected to see a beam emerge from the stone and touch him, but it never did. Instead, the glow got wider and darker, gradually blotting out everything else in sight.

Unlike the power he'd tapped to bring *Predator* in for a crash landing, Ertai discovered this dark energy, in its pure form, felt cold. His body felt flooded by ice, and the cold spread rapidly through his chest and down his legs. It did blot out the pain of his injuries, and for that he was grateful.

With a snap, the surge of power ceased. Ertai pushed up on one elbow and saw the laboratory was hip deep in mist. Each breath he exhaled made sparkling ice crystals in the air.

Belbe appeared, swimming out of the fog. She looked disheveled, her hair awry.

"How do you feel?" she asked.

"Wonderful." Ertai flexed his hands, formerly crumpled like a bundle of broken reeds. "I feel like new—no, better than new."

He hopped off the slab and patted himself all over. His burns were gone. His ribs were healed. Even the bruises from the beating *Predator*'s sailors had given him were gone.

What about his mind?

He held up a finger on his right hand, and a tiny flame appeared at the tip. Ertai extended the next finger and made the little flame leap to it, and then the next finger, and so on. It was an elementary magical exercise, one he could do since he was a small child.

By the time the flame had jumped to his fourth finger, it flickered and turned orange, then red. It dropped down to his pinkie and became purple. When Ertai transferred the violet flicker to the thumb of his left hand, the tiny flame went jet black.

He stared at the black flame.

Belbe watched him. "Are you all right?"

Ertai snuffed the flame with his other hand. "It's nothing," he said. He'd never seen the finger flame change color before. He was suffused with dark energy, true, but he'd created a yellow flame and not willed it to change. That it did so by itself was disturbing.

Belbe gently pulled his hands apart. "Come, it's time you had a proper bath, clean clothes, and food."

She led him by the hand through the misty lab. On his way out, he saw two empty suits of armor standing near the door. The men inside, the two guards who'd brought him there, were gone.

"Where are the soldiers?" he said.

In answer to his own question, Ertai's foot snagged something soft. Behind the shelves was a five-foot-long gray slug, oozing a trail of iridescent slime across the floor. Another monster slug nudged at the base of one of the suits of armor.

"Perhaps I used too high a setting after all," Belbe said mildly.

* * * * *

The Skyshroud Expeditionary Force tramped down the long causeway from the Stronghold, their faces wrapped in scarves to keep out the swirling dust. The wind had picked up in the past few hours. A Hub reversal was nigh, and that always unsettled Rath's weather. The massive device atop the Stronghold periodically rotated itself to equalize the wear on its energy-focusing apparatus. When the Hub turned, rapidly changing winds scoured the surface of Rath.

Crovax raised another flowstone reviewing stand from which to watch his troops march out. He had a total of fifty companies, ten thousand men, and ten thousand moggs acting as porters, carrying supplies for a sixteen-day campaign. Two-thirds of his force was infantry, while the other thirty-five hundred men were Rathi cavalry. They rode mutant two-legged beasts called kerls, created by Volrath as cavalry mounts. It was a powerful force, far larger than any sent out by any previous evincar.

Soldiers marched down the causeway to the plain, passing the six corpses twirling in the Hub wind. Moggs had stripped the bodies of anything of value, leaving the dishonored officers clad only in rags. Confronted by this sobering display, the Skyshroud Expeditionary Force marched out in total silence.

Crovax fumed as the long column of men and moggs slogged by. The troops had no spirit. On Dominaria, an army left home singing, with pipes and drums playing martial tunes. The army of Rath was a dull, sullen force compared to the warriors Crovax remembered.

When half the column was past his reviewing stand, Crovax dissolved the platform and mounted his kerl. He took the reins from a mogg who'd held them patiently. Crovax spurred his mount, bowling over the mogg and sending him rolling in the dust.

In the vanguard of the army were the twelve condemned officers acting as scouts. Behind them rode Crovax's orderlies from the Corps of Sergeants. Each orderly had a percher on his shoulder. These were another of Volrath's creations—pigeon-sized flying creatures with leathery blue wings and flaring, trumpet-shaped mouths. Perchers understood simple commands and could repeat short messages verbatim. They flew back and forth over the army, relaying orders.

Before nightfall the scouts had reached the outpost of Chireef. This was a two-story blockhouse situated on the edge of a flowstone "sea", a basin consisting of miles and miles of flowstone frozen in motionless waves like the surface of an ocean. The garrison of Chireef stood ready to receive Crovax and his force.

Crovax and his aides galloped up to the blockhouse in a flurry of jingling arms and flapping banners. The commander of Chireef, Gunder il-Dal, was plainly stunned by the size of the army Crovax brought with him.

"My lord," he said. "Where are you going with so vast a force?"

"Where I will," Crovax replied curtly. "How are conditions between here and the Skyshroud Forest?"

"Quiet as the grave, my lord." Gunder il-Dal mopped his brow, pushing his helmet back to get to his generous forehead. "No rebel would dare get so close to the Stronghold."

"Yes, yes. The cavalry needs water for their mounts. After they've had their fill, let the moggs drink what they can." He reined his black-spotted beast around.

"Will you be staying the night, gracious lord? I can offer what accommodation our humble outpost affords."

"The column marches all night," Crovax replied. "If in two days' time any rebels come your way, I want you to stop them. They'll be fleeing their defeat, and I don't want any to escape."

Gunder looked puzzled. "Defeat, my lord?"

"Yes, the defeat I shall inflict on them."

The first company of cavalry lined up by a row of spouts set high on the walls of the blockhouse. Crovax rode by and mentally commanded the valves to open. Out gushed fresh water from the blockhouse cisterns. Kerls pushed their fleshy faces into stone troughs and lapped the cascading water with their flat black tongues. Only yards away, thirsty moggs, weighed down by almost two hundred pounds of supplies each, licked dry lips and anxiously awaited their turn at the troughs.

* * * * *

Gunder slowly walked down the line of his troops, eyeing them carefully. Chireef had only a normal garrison of forty-eight soldiers. Fifty-five were mustered on the plain, and that made Gunder nervous. Suppose someone noticed?

Crovax and his leading elements swept on, and Gunder ordered his men back inside. Once the metal door was closed and barred, he pulled off his helmet and poured a pitcher of cold water over his profusely sweating head.

"Wine!" he shouted. "Can someone find me wine?"

"What's the matter?" asked Eladamri, emerging from the shadows. "You should be pleased, Darsett. You've met this new warlord Crovax face to face, and he didn't see through you or your men."

Darsett and his Dal followers shed their helmets and heaved a collective sigh of relief. Eladamri's raiders had taken Chireef by stealth only hours before. They were about to set fire to the place when they spotted the huge dust cloud raised by Crovax's oncoming army. Rather than be caught in the open by a vastly superior force, Eladamri kept his warriors inside and sent Darsett out disguised as the late commander of the outpost.

"What do we do now?" Darsett said, peeking through an arrow slit to spy on the troops passing by outside.

Paul B. Thompson

"Wait until they're gone," said Eladamri. "Then we'll proceed as planned."

Gallan, who had wrapped his elven hair and ears with a scarf to pose as a Dal soldier, said anxiously, "We know where they're going, Eladamri!"

The elf leader nodded. His snakehide armor was freckled with blood. He dipped a rag in an open barrel of water and dabbed at the stains.

"Crovax is heading for the forest. He thinks he can destroy us by destroying our homes," he said calmly.

"Are we going to let him?" Gallan demanded.

"He's welcome to try. Evincars as far back as my grandfather's day have tried to impose their rule on us. This Crovax seems no wiser than they. In fact, so far he shows less wit than the departed Volrath. Our late evincar used infiltrators and the airship to hunt us down. His tactics were very dangerous, as our losses in the past year show." He paused in his scrubbing. "Even my daughter wasn't safe in my own house, but we have little to fear from a big, blundering mass like that. Where they go, we'll fade away, and when they're tired and low on food and water, we'll strike."

He stooped to pick up Gunder *il*-Dal's helmet, tossed on the floor by the nervous Darsett. Upon seeing the grim visage of Volrath on the brow of the helmet, Eladamri's face darkened with implacable hatred.

CHAPTER 7
Baptism

The army marched all night around the edge of the flowstone sea. By daybreak, the men were dragging spears and shields in the dust behind them. Moggs, normally hardier than humans, were staggering under the burdens Crovax had imposed on them. Disciplined formations broke down. Gaps appeared in the long column, and still Crovax led them on.

Crovax's hand-picked aides galloped the length of the column, cajoling and threatening the men to close ranks and move forward. Soon they were faltering too, reeling in their saddles like the exhausted cavalry screening the army's flanks. Perchers took over their job, relaying Crovax's increasingly shrill orders to the rearmost elements of the force.

Crovax's outriders spotted a band of elves on the open plain some miles from the forest. They weren't rebels, just a hunting party, but the Rathi cavalry rounded them up and herded them back to Crovax.

Tired, his sable armor coated with gray dust, Crovax was in a foul mood when the elf prisoners were brought before him. They did not cower or beg for mercy from him. That annoyed Crovax. Without even asking any questions, he ordered five of the eight elves beheaded on the spot.

The remaining three hunters, ashen-faced, huddled together in a circle of Rathi lancers. Crovax willed the flowstone up around their ankles, both to restrain them and to demonstrate his mastery of the nano-machines.

He dismounted and walked over to the eldest elf. "Where is Eladamri?"

The elf, whose white hair was turning amber with age, shook his head. "I do not know Eladamri."

Crovax clasped the elf around his waist and thrust a long dagger through his ribs. He held his blade there, staring into the eyes of his victim as the elf's blood coursed over his feet.

Crovax withdrew his dagger with a swift jerk, releasing at the same time the elder elf's feet from the flowstone. The hunter folded like a candle held too near a flame.

Crovax wiped the blood from his blade with two fingers. He stood close to the next prisoner and flung the dead elf's blood in his face.

"Where is Eladamri?" he asked again.

The second elf held his chin up and shook his head, unwilling to answer. Crovax, dagger in hand, crossed in front of him. The elf shut his eyes, dreading the thrust he thought was coming. Crovax circled behind him while his eyes were closed. He put the dagger in his teeth and leaped into the air, kicking the elf in the small of his back. Because his ankles were held by the flowstone, he couldn't fall naturally, and when Crovax bore down on his back with all his weight, the elf's legs snapped at the knee. He screamed as Crovax stood on his back, unmoved by his agony.

"My lord—" began one of the troopers.

"The next man who speaks will be given to the moggs," Crovax said quietly.

He squatted on top of the moaning prisoner and asked his question again. The elf could only choke in the dust. Crovax took the prisoner's head in his hands and, in one powerful wrench, broke the elf's neck.

The third prisoner was the youngest, and he openly trembled when Crovax approached.

"Eladamri lives in the village of Sweetwater!" he said, unconsciously tugging at his captive feet. "He left there five days ago to meet Dal, Kor, and Vec chiefs, to convince them to join the rebellion!"

Crovax's face shone with pleasure. Everyone around him assumed he was pleased to finally be getting information, but in fact he was in the throes of ecstasy after imbibing the life-forces of the two elves he'd killed. He smiled at the third elf in a dreamy, languorous way.

"Where did this meeting take place?"

"I don't know. I don't know, great lord! Spare me, please spare me!"

Crovax, still smiling, laid a hand on the young elf's cheek. "What's your name, boy?"

"Valin, merciful lord."

Crovax nodded. He drew back his hand and struck the prisoner hard on the jaw. With a crunch of bone, the youth fell to the ground unconscious.

Crovax released the elf from the flowstone. "Chain him, and put him in with my personal baggage. He may have more information to tell us."

* * * * *

Hidden among the "waves" in the flowstone sea, the rebels watched the gradual disintegration of Crovax's army with satisfaction. Years of soft living inside the Stronghold had taken the iron out of the soldiers' legs. Eladamri's ardent young followers urged him to make a spoiling attack on the column before it reached the Skyshroud Forest.

"Not yet," the elf leader said. "It's a long march to the forest, and a lot of useful obstacles lie in between."

"But our homes—our families!" Gallan and the others protested.

"Send word for them to retreat to the tree tops, deeper in the forest."

Word was sent, but the hotheads around Eladamri continued

to seethe with pent-up frustration. Their anger was fanned when they heard about the capture of the hunting party. Eladamri's scouts saw the whole episode and reported it to their chief. Eladamri received the news impassively.

"We must save the survivor," Gallan urged.

"He's lost," said Eladamri. "He was lost the instant the riders took him."

"But he lives!" said Cardamel, another of his youthful followers.

"What would you have me do, lose ten to save one? That's what our enemy wants us to do."

"Our people are dying, and we're doing nothing!" Gallan said.

Eladamri swept the remains of their meager lunch from the stone around which they sat. "I shall destroy their army. Isn't that enough?"

"But when?"

"In less than a day the enemy will reach Skyshroud. By then the column will be stretched out halfway back to Chireef. We'll hit them before dawn, when most of them will be asleep." He threw down a snakeskin scroll and added, "Two thousand warriors from Skyshroud, the Dal and the Vec, will combine for the attack. If the gods favor us, Crovax and his men will be snake food by this time tomorrow!"

The elves cheered fiercely and clasped each other's arms, pledging their lives to victory. Eladamri did not join in, but silently left the rock crevice where they'd been eating. When he was gone, Cardamel took Gallan aside.

"Some of the lads want to do something about the hunter held by Crovax," he said, his voice low. "His name's Valin. He's Firanu's grandson, did you know that?" Gallan shook his head. "There's four of us ready to take Valin away if you give us leave."

"I won't go against Eladamri's orders," Gallan replied. Cardamel's face fell. "But if you four should happen to slip away tonight, I may not be able to remember where you've gone."

The elves clasped hands. "May the gods bless your faulty memory," Cardamel said, grinning.

* * * * *

On the underside of the Citadel, near the lava inlet to the great flowstone works, Greven *il*-Vec was supervising the repair of his airship. Workmen, mogg labor gangs, and flowbot machinery swarmed over the broken hull, slaving around the clock to rebuild the ship.

Greven applied himself to the task at hand. He tried to forget his humiliation at the hands of Crovax, tried not to think about the fact that the insolent usurper was leading the army—*his* army—against the rebels even now. Greven had hunted Eladamri for years, and he respected the elf's cunning. He sensed, deep in his much-altered chest, that Crovax was courting disaster. Ruthlessness was no substitute for experience, and in his own brooding way, Greven welcomed the day when Crovax would meet defeat.

Overhead, a hull frame slipped from the grasp of a flowbot crane and crashed to the floor, crushing a pair of moggs loitering there. Greven threw down the blueprints he was holding and stormed out onto the dock.

"Dung for brains!" he bellowed. "Don't you know you can't hoist a hull frame with just one crane? Use two, you worthless worms!" A second flowbot arm lowered and grasped the fallen frame. "Now you see, you've bent it!" Greven raged. He ordered the damaged frame to be returned to the foundry and pounded straight again.

Greven retrieved the fallen plans. When he straightened, he found a slender, ethereal Kor standing not two feet in front of him.

"How did you get in here? What do you want?"

The Kor pressed a hand to his chest, a gesture of respect Kor performed instead of bowing. "Greetings, Dread Lord. My name is Furah, of the Fishers of Life."

Greven knew the tribe; they lived outside the Stronghold crater. They were harmless, almost invisible people who never troubled the authorities.

"What is it?" Greven asked impatiently. "I'm quite busy, as you can see."

"Certain information has come to me, information of value to you, I believe."

"About what?"

"The activities of a certain resident of the outer lands—the Skyshroud Forest, perhaps."

Greven's teeth began to grind. Talking to a Kor was like trying to swat flies with a broadsword—things never seemed to connect.

"Speak plainly before I have your legs broken!"

"I speak of the elf Eladamri, Dread Lord."

"You have news of Eladamri?" Greven tried to take the Kor by the arm, but he missed somehow—his hand swept through empty air. Furah stepped back just beyond his reach.

"Forgive me, Dread Lord, but I dislike being touched—a quirk common to my people."

"Get to the point!"

Furah pressed a hand to his chest again. "Eladamri has been trying to enlist the cooperation of the Dal, the Vec, and the Kor in his war against you," Furah said. "I myself went to a conclave in the forest on behalf of my people."

"And how was Eladamri's message received?"

"With great enthusiasm, Dread Lord."

"But not by you? Why are you informing on them, Furah?"

Behind Greven, a trio of moggs overturned a crucible of molten flowstone on their way up a ramp into the airship. The liquid stone, immune to commands or programming, formed into legions of tiny silver spheres and skittered in all directions. Workers who stepped on the flowstone slipped and fell, all over the dock. With a snarl, Greven left the Kor man and roared for all work to cease. The tumultuous airship dock fell silent, save for the hiss of the waiting flowbots.

"Everyone stand still!" Greven shouted, and he was heard throughout the dock. "When the stone solidifies, it will be safe to move again."

A tiny silver bead whirled in place at Greven's feet. As it cooled, the flowstone slowly flattened into an egg, then a disk, and finally spread itself as thin as paper. It lost its silver color and took on the patina of whatever substance it was lying on.

"Resume work!" Greven called. The dock exploded with activity all over again.

He turned around, expecting to find the Kor waiting for him, but there was no sign of Furah. What should he make of this information? If Eladamri had forged an alliance with restive elements among the outland Dal and Vec, then the simple, annoying elf rebellion could turn into a full-blown civil war.

Crovax . . . Crovax had taken half the army on a mogg's errand into the worst swamp on Rath. He was expecting to trample over a few hundred elves, when in fact he was facing an unknown force of much greater size.

He shouted for his Vec foreman and ordered him to keep the repairs going no matter what.

"Where are you going, Dread Lord?" asked the foreman.

"To see the emissary."

He found Belbe in the evincar's suite. She was sitting in one of Volrath's grand chairs, watching Ertai wash himself in the evincar's ornate bath.

"Hello, Greven," Ertai said breezily. He sat in steaming water up to his hips while a jointed fleshstone appliance scrubbed his back with a sodden rag.

"What in the overlords' name—?" Greven spotted Belbe in Volrath's chair, observing Ertai's ablutions.

"It's called a 'bath,'" Belbe said. "Evidently a custom among humans. The ritual serves both as relaxation and hygiene."

"I know what a bath is, Excellency." Greven's molars were ready to pulverize iron at that moment. "Why is this enemy of Rath, this prisoner, in the royal bath?"

"Because I was dirty," Ertai replied. "It's hardly fitting for a sorcerer of my skills and a candidate for evincar to go around smelling like one of your moggs."

Words failed Greven completely. He spread his powerful hands and looked to Belbe for enlightenment.

"It's true," she said. "Crovax, while presenting excellent qualifications, cannot be the sole candidate. It wouldn't be efficient to award the position to him without competition. Since Ertai has demonstrated outstanding magical ability, including some untutored influence over flowstone, it's efficient to offer him a chance to try for the job as well."

Belbe descended from the high chair. She was clad in a large, belted scarlet tabard that flowed from her shoulders like a cape and swept to the floor. Against the monochrome décor, she blazed like a flame.

"Which reminds me, Lord Greven. Would you like to be considered for evincar as well? You have many years of effective service on your side and manifest talents for the job."

There it was, plainly stated at last. Greven had pondered this possibility since Volrath's departure, and he knew what his answer must be.

"Thank you, Excellency, but I must decline," he said.

"As you choose, but why?"

"I'm content to remain a loyal servant of the throne."

"It would mean the end of the control rod."

"I've considered that. I served Volrath for many years, and I've seen firsthand the effect unfettered power had on him. I would rather be the blade than the hand that wields it."

Ertai plucked the washcloth from the fleshstone scrubber's soft claw. He wiped his face with it and said, "Why is that?"

He could not explain his past to these—children. Greven had once been *en*-Vec, a leader of a great warrior nation. Treachery and jealousy cost him his position, his clan, and his life. With no other recourse but ignominious death, he fell into the hands of Volrath and became *il*-Vec, the hated outcast.

He said simply, "Because the victim curses his killer, not the blade that cuts him."

"Blades have no choice who they cut. Men do," Ertai replied.

"I have given my answer!" Greven thundered. He struggled for calm in the presence of the emissary. "Excellency, I have news of grave import." Greven recounted his odd conversation with Furah. Belbe listened while walking around the edge of the tiled bathing pool.

"You believe Crovax has led his army into a trap?" she asked after some contemplation.

"I do, Excellency."

"How would you remedy this situation?"

"I doubt I could reach Crovax with a relief force before the rebels strike," Greven said. "Worse, Crovax would probably commandeer any companies I brought, enlarging Eladamri's bag of killed or captured."

"That sounds like him," Ertai said, digging at his ear with the washcloth.

Greven ignored him. "I can, if Your Excellency desires, put

together a force and go to Crovax's aid," he said. "I can have a scratch force prepared in two hours."

"No," said Belbe.

"No?" Greven and Ertai asked together.

"This expedition is Crovax's audition, his way of proving he is strong enough to be evincar. Very well, let him prove it. If your informant is correct, Crovax faces a more skillful enemy than he imagines. This is his chance to prove his mettle."

"Cold," muttered Ertai. When Belbe asked him to repeat himself, he said, "The water's gone cold."

"Then get out," snapped Greven.

Ertai looked from the hulking warrior to the gamine emissary and shook his head. "I can wait."

Greven gritted his teeth, then he continued. "We may lose many soldiers, Excellency."

"Yes."

"And valuable arms, and a host of moggs."

"Quite possibly."

"Does any of this concern Your Excellency?"

"What matters in a test of strength is who wins," Belbe said. She paused, looking into the pool where Ertai sat. Her crimson-draped reflection wavered with every ripple of the water. "Victory belongs to the strong."

"Don't forget luck and brains," Ertai added. "The strongest wrestler may fall if he slips up—and a smart fighter provides his own bar of soap." So saying, he squeezed the cake of soap in his fist. It squirted free, landing at Greven's feet. He kicked the perfumed bar back into the tub.

"So, I am to do nothing?" Greven asked once the metaphors had settled down.

"Put the garrison on alert," Belbe said. "And try to trace this Furah—if he spies on his friends, he may be spying on us as well."

"I fear insurrection should Crovax be defeated," Greven said gravely. "There are thousands of Dal in the crater city, and thousands more Vec and Kor below the Citadel. I don't think the shorthanded garrison could defend the Citadel in the face of a general uprising."

"Hostages," said Ertai.

"What?" Belbe and Greven questioned in unison.

"Take hostages from the leading families of the Vec, Dal, and Kor," Ertai said. "That way they'll not be inclined to act up, should the worst happen."

Greven was inwardly surprised. This cocky boy, not long ago his helpless victim, had hit upon a real stratagem. Was he a serious contender for evincar after all?

"A useful idea. Dorlan il-Dal knows the people in the Stronghold. Have him work out who will be taken and how many from each race," Belbe looked up from the tub. "Lord Greven, you will round up hostages as Ertai has suggested. Be firm, but don't rough them up. Hold them in a secure place until Crovax's fate is known."

"It shall be done, Your Excellency." With that, the stalwart warrior departed.

* * * * *

Once Greven was gone, Belbe sat down on the edge of the bath and dipped her bare feet in the water. She smiled with delight at the sensation, swishing her feet back and forth in the suds.

Suddenly she stopped. "This water's still warm."

Ertai slipped carefully through the shallow pool until he could lean on the edge beside her.

"Belbe," he said confidentially. "Whatever happens, don't let anyone hurt the hostages."

"Why? If no threat is perceived, taking hostages has no strategic value."

He laid a damp hand on her knee. She froze, shocked by the sudden, intimate contact. "If you hurt the hostages, you really will have a civil war on your hands."

"Then why did you suggest it?"

He looked around furtively. "May I speak freely?" She nodded. "It's part of my plan to become evincar."

"I don't understand."

Ertai lowered his voice further. "Past evincars ruled by fear, yes? Fear of death, fear of soldiers, fear of the overlords and their machines? I won't rule that way, Belbe. Should I become evincar, it will be with the support and acclaim of the people, not through terror. If Crovax wins his battle, I want to present the hostages their freedom. If he loses, I want to save them from Greven's revenge."

There was no sound but the drip, drip of water from the flow-stone spigot. The humidity was such that Belbe's hair relaxed, and dew formed on her cool skin.

"Rulership is imposed, not granted," she recited, as if reading a text.

"Tyranny is imposed," Ertai countered. "Freedom is the will of the people."

"Freedom—a lack of political or social control. Also known as anarchy, democracy, or mob rule."

Ertai pushed away. He waded to the opposite end of the pool where a heap of towels and a dressing gown lay. He glanced back once out of self-consciousness, then climbed out of the bath. Belbe did not look at him. She stared blankly at the lapping water.

"I forget who you are, where you come from," he said, even though she wasn't listening. "You don't understand anything but brute force, do you?"

On a hunch, he read her aura. To his surprise, she was not so dark as Crovax or Greven. Belbe had a streak of violence in her makeup, but radiating outward from her physical self were the bright coronas of other attributes—passion, intelligence, reason. The strongest force at work in Belbe was curiosity—an interesting discovery.

Ertai tied the sash of the gown tightly around his waist. His fingers twinged from the effort, as if from rheumatism. Not fully healed, he mused. Perhaps he should visit Volrath's laboratory later for another infusion. That would make his studies in magical flowstone manipulation go much easier.

"Good night, Belbe," he said.

Still pondering, she didn't answer.

* * * * *

Night fell, and Crovax allowed the army to halt its headlong advance. The Hub had completed a half-revolution that night, and wind from its motion whipped through the camp in heavy, humid gusts. On the horizon, the dark profile of the Skyshroud forest beckoned. Tomorrow the army would penetrate the forest.

In his tent, Crovax received the reports of his scouts. Of the twelve condemned officers, only eight had returned from the forest to relate what they found. The other four entered and were never seen again.

"Large sections of the forest are impassable, my lord," said one scout. He was coated head to toe in sticky gray mud. "The ground below the forest canopy is very swampy and entirely unpredictable in depth. I walked for a mile in knee-deep water, then without warning, stepped in a hole deeper than my head."

"So the swamp is a swamp," Crovax said dryly. "Thank you for that valuable information! How do the elves traverse the Skyshroud? The hunting party we captured hadn't a speck of mud on them."

Another scout saluted. "They use the trees, my lord. I saw bridges made of vines connecting tree to tree."

"They may use trees for small groups, but I can't believe they use them exclusively," Crovax said. "There must be dry paths built up above the level of the swamp. I want them found." A jingling sound from the next compartment distracted him. He glanced that way and added, "Find me a way into the forest. I don't care if it takes all night, you hear? Find it!"

The filthy, fatigued soldiers saluted and filed out. When they were gone, Crovax dismissed the guards from the door and sent his aides to inspect the camp. Once alone, he went to the large brass-bound hamper in the corner of the tent and threw back the lid. A thin scrap of tapestry inside squirmed. Crovax slowly lifted the cloth.

"Hello," he said.

He reached in and dragged out the elf prisoner, Valin. The youth's hands and feet were chained, and a strip of rag gagged his mouth. Crovax sat down on a pile of carpets and regarded his prisoner.

"Do you believe in curses, boy?" he said. Valin could only grunt in reply. "You should believe—they're real. Somewhere in the distant past, my family was cursed by the gift of an amulet. My ancestors thought it was just an heirloom, but it held a captive angel inside, who served our family for generations."

His tone was so measured, so reasonable, Valin regained his composure. He sat up with his back against the hamper, cradling his shackles in his lap.

"Her name was—well, it doesn't matter. Suffice to say, I destroyed the amulet out of anger, and the angel was freed because of me. She fell under Volrath's spell and fought for his cause until I was able to find her again. We fought. I killed her.... As my family's heir, my soul was bound to hers, though I didn't know it. When she died, part of me died with her. That was the curse, you see—that my life should continue only by the death of others."

Crovax poured wine into a heavy silver goblet. "At first I was devastated by her loss, but I know now that Selenia's death was a necessary part of my evolution. The overlords instructed me. They changed what seemed like a foolish tragedy into the source of my strength. I know now the path of greatness is strewn with corpses. I'll pave my way with as many dead bodies as it takes."

He downed the wine in a gulp and let the cup fall to the carpet. The flowstone lanterns in the room dimmed. Crovax stood, his eyes glowing pale red.

"They blotted out my feelings to cure me of my weakness," Crovax said flatly. "Funny, the changes carry over to so many small things . . . wine has no taste anymore. Eating is just exercise for my jaws. The only food I crave now is the life inside other living things. So far, I've only tasted life from the dying. Tonight I'll dine on the living."

Valin's eyed widened in terror. He struggled to stand and run, even though he was hobbled by thick chains. Crovax watched him thrash toward the door. In two steps he caught the elf and seized him by the back of the neck.

"It's an honor, really," Crovax whispered in his ear. "At least I know your name, Valin. The thousands who follow you will be as anonymous as cattle."

CHAPTER 8
Failure

Four shadows slipped through the wire grass. Wrapped head to toe in dark gray cloth, they were armed with short-shafted spears, cut down to allow for fast handling in tight places. The four elves were going to a tight place indeed: the camp of the Skyshroud Expeditionary Force.

Cardamel and his comrades Kameko, Darian, and Sanyu, dropped to the ground side-by-side a dozen yards from the picket line. Every few minutes a pair of kerl-mounted men rode by. In between the mounted patrols, two foot soldiers marched past in the opposite direction. Barely thirty seconds passed between the concentric rings of sentries. Not much time to run twenty yards and stop somewhere out of sight.

"Let's take out the men on foot," Kameko suggested. Even close together, it was hard to hear each other. The wind was up and would stay up until the Hub ceased rotating.

"The first riders to miss them will sound the alarm," Cardamel said.

"So what do we do?" asked Sanyu.

Cardamel eyed the long rows of tents. If they could reach them, there were plenty of dark places to skulk there.

"We'll have to do it one at a time," he said. "Run straight for the tent line and hide until the last one crosses over."

No one had any better idea, so Cardamel's approach was adopted. After the next pair of kerls clopped by, he sprinted for the tents. Massed campfires inside the camp robbed the night of its cloak of black, and Cardamel knew he was highlighted against the sky. He ran for all he was worth and slid to a stop between two tents, just as the paired foot soldiers appeared around the curve.

"He made it," said Kameko. "I'm next!"

Kameko sprinted into Cardamel's arms, and they hugged the dirt as the next patrol came by.

Darian rubbed dust on his hands and crouched in the tall grass, ready to run. The cavalrymen passed, and Sanyu slapped him on the back.

"Go!"

Darian wasn't much of a runner, but he was a leaper. He was six feet from the tents when the foot guards appeared, so he gathered himself and jumped headlong into the shadows with his friends.

One of the Rathi soldiers unslung his crossbow. "What was that?"

"What? I didn't see anything," said his partner.

"You didn't see something hurtle across, right there?"

"No. What was it?"

"I don't know. Kind of big—a bird, maybe." The soldier licked his lips. "Fresh meat would be great! We could roast it when we got off duty."

He left the path and probed cautiously into the shadows, bow leveled. His partner waited at the perimeter.

"Hurry up," he said. "We'll be punished for leaving the path!"

"Here, birdie," chirped the Dal soldier.

Kameko rose up and snatched the crossbow from the astonished man's hands. Cardamel clamped a hand over his mouth and dragged him into the darkness. Darian shoved a knife under the hungry soldier's breastplate, and he stopped struggling.

"Come on," called the waiting sentry. "We'll get in trouble."

Kameko raised the crossbow and put an iron-tipped quarrel through the second sentry's throat. Sanyu burst out of hiding, grabbed the dead soldier's feet, and dragged his body to the tents just as the next mounted patrol appeared.

Cardamel thought fast. He donned the bird hunter's helmet and cloak, took the crossbow from Kameko, and stepped out into the open.

One of the oncoming riders called, "Sentry! What are you doing?"

"I had to answer nature," Cardamel replied.

The riders snorted derisively. "Where's your partner?"

Sanyu was ready for this question. He donned the other guard's helmet and cloak and stepped out beside Cardamel, shaking a leg as he went.

"Ah!" he said broadly. "I needed that!"

The riders spurred on. The two elves kept their faces averted under the helmet brims.

"Peasants," said one rider as they trotted by. "Stick to your assigned route! You've seen what Lord Crovax does to those who fail in their duty!"

"We know," Sanyu muttered.

Before the next patrol came, the elves conferred. They had no choice. Cardamel and Sanyu would have to walk post for the dead sentries, or the game was up.

"It'll work," Cardamel said. "Once you find Valin, come back here and wait until you see us march by—then you'll know it's safe."

"How will we know which sentries are you?" asked Darian.

"Wait at this exact spot," Cardamel explained. "Each time I march by here, I'll tap the bow against my helmet like this." He tapped out a *ping-ping, ping-ping* sound against his helm. "Then you'll know it's us."

They ran to catch up to where the sentries were supposed to be, leaving Darian and Kameko to rescue Valin.

The camp was very large, and the elves had to make certain assumptions if they hoped to find their brother elf. A prisoner held for interrogation would likely be near the commander of the army—Crovax, in other words. Crovax's quarters would be the largest in camp, probably in the center of the sea of tents.

The elves made for the heart of the enemy camp, skirting bright campfires and small groups of moggs. The soldiers were dead tired from marching all night and all day, so most of the tents were full of snoring men.

Kameko crouched between two tents and pointed ahead. The center of the camp was an open square, dotted with posts newly sunk in the ground. Several Rathi soldiers were tied to posts. Their bare, bloody backs were mute evidence of the floggings they'd received, no doubt for some petty violation of army rules. A tall Vec soldier with sergeant's insignia on his helmet was directing the distribution of water to the punished soldiers.

"A provost! If we grab him, he'll know where Valin is," Kameko said. Darian nodded.

They watched the sergeant tick off that each flogged soldier had received a dipper of water, then he rolled up his scroll and made to leave. The elves flitted between tents ahead of him, and when he turned off the main path to reach his bedroll for the night, they tackled him high and low.

The sergeant fought, but Darian pressed a snakebone dirk against his windpipe.

Kameko hissed, "Be still or die!" The Vec soldier stopped fighting but remained tense, ready to spring.

"Where's the elf prisoner? Where is Valin?"

"Elf prisoner?" repeated the sergeant loudly. Kameko nicked him with the dirk for being noisy.

"Do that again and you'll have a second mouth in your neck! Where's the elf prisoner?"

The sergeant smiled. "In Lord Crovax's quarters."

His smirk infuriated Darian, who punched the sergeant hard in the gut. "Take us there! If you give us away, you'll be the first to die!"

The two elves followed the sergeant to a complex of conjoined tents in the northeast corner of the square. There were no guards at the entrance. The sergeant ducked inside. Kameko and Darian followed, and Kameko pulled the sergeant back.

"If this is your commander's tent, why are there no guards?" he said.

"Lord Crovax doesn't require them." The elves exchanged looks. "Do you want to find him or not?"

Darian shoved the sergeant forward. "Go on."

The tent was a maze of flaps and canvas rooms. It seemed deserted until Kameko heard a sigh emanating from an adjoining room. Using the Vec soldier as a shield, he pushed into the room. The sergeant promptly stumbled over a body on the floor.

"Kameko, look!"

Stretched out on the carpet was the young hunter Valin, empty eyes staring at the ceiling. The sergeant had fallen to his knees, but in the center of the room, sitting slumped on a heap of carpets, was Crovax himself. He looked passed-out drunk.

Kameko knelt by the dead elf. There were no signs of violence on him, no blood, no bruises.

Crovax did not react at all to the intruders. Darian rushed forward, ready to kill the enemy commander where he sat. His blade went up but froze there.

"Kameko . . ."

The elves looked into Crovax's face. A strange, rosy light shone in his open eyes, even though they were rolled back in his head. Thin vapor, like breath on a cold morning, trickled from his open mouth. His teeth appeared sharp, like those of a wolf or a shark, and his body was larger and stronger than it had looked when the elves had seen him for the first time back at Chireef. Worst of all, something was moving under Crovax's skin—small bumps in the flesh of his face moved about of their own volition.

The forgotten sergeant threw himself on Darian. Down they went in a heap, grappling for the elf's bare knife. Kameko was about to help his friend when the seemingly inert Crovax grabbed him by the wrist.

"Darian! Help!"

Darian had his own problems. The Vec sergeant was strong and outweighed him by thirty pounds. Darian raked the Vec's cheek with his knife tip, drawing blood. The sergeant responded with several pounding blows to the face, and Darian saw the room swimming away in a black haze.

Crovax lifted his head. He pursed his lips and whistled—a slow, eerie tune. Kameko drew his knife with his left hand, but before he could thrust it through a joint in Crovax's armor, the enemy commander effortlessly crushed his wrist. Bones snapped and ground together, a sickening sound. Kameko screamed and fell to his knees, dropping his knife.

* * * * *

Marching side by side in their stolen helmets and cloaks, Cardamel and Sanyu heard shouting inside the camp. All the cavalry on the perimeter turned and galloped down paths between the tents, toward the center of the camp.

"What do we do?" Sanyu asked.

"Keep walking. We're sentries—we can't leave our post," Cardamel replied.

After much shouting and dashing about, a percher appeared, flapping its narrow wings and blaring the message given to it.

"Assassins! Assassins have tried to kill the commander! Two elves are caught! More may be around! Stand your ground! Assassins! Assassins . . ."

"We've got to get out of here," Cardamel said, throwing down the crossbow.

"But our comrades—"

"Our comrades are dead, and we will be too if we don't leave now!"

They bolted for the wire grass. Twenty-five yards away, four kerl riders spotted them and gave chase. The elves split up, Cardamel running to the right and Sanyu to the left. Two riders followed each fugitive. Cardamel knew he couldn't outrun the tireless kerls, so after topping a slight rise, he whirled and drew the short spear off his back. He knelt on one knee and braced the spear with his foot.

The first rider came tearing over the hill and plowed right into Cardamel's spear. The kerl made a flat, bleating sound and heeled over, greasy green blood gushing from its chest. The rider hit the ground heavily and lay stunned. Cardamel planted a foot on the thrashing kerl's chest and yanked out his spear. The second rider hauled on his reins, twisting his beast away from the fallen kerl. Cardamel leaned back and cast his spear. It caught the cavalryman in the chest. His armor saved him, but the impact knocked him backward off the kerl's abbreviated rump. Before he could rise and call for help, Cardamel cut his throat.

Running for all he was worth, Cardamel despaired. Kameko and Darian lost—Valin was as good as lost. He prayed Sanyu would evade pursuit and make it back to Eladamri.

He ran more than a mile before he felt safe enough to check

behind him. Wire grass whipped in the Hub wind, but there were no signs of further pursuit. Weary, Cardamel slumped to his knees. His bold plan was in ruins, and his brave comrades sacrificed. What a terrible farce!

"Get up."

He looked up into the grim face of Eladamri. Cardamel opened his mouth to speak, but the rebel leader cut him off with a curt wave of his hand.

"Save your entreaties! You disobeyed me, Cardamel! How many warriors did you lose on your mogg's errand?"

Mutely Cardamel held up three fingers.

"So. That's the price we've paid for your night of foolishness."

Just then a courier ran up. "Eladamri! Eladamri, a message from Tant Jova!" He handed the elf leader a square of cloth on which the Vec matriarch had penned a note. Eladamri read it and hurled the scrap into Cardamel's face.

"Worse news! Your bungling has raised a general alarm in the enemy camp, and their cavalry have found the Vec warriors hiding at the edge of the swamp! All our preparations are in jeopardy!"

Miserable, Cardamel drew his knife. He sat there, despondently fingering the blade. Eladamri took it away from him.

"There's no point in dying now," he said evenly. "There's fighting to be done."

Cardamel looked at his leader. "May I go in the vanguard?" Eladamri nodded, and gave him back his knife.

The clamor of distant combat grew until it overcame the constant wind. It was not yet midnight, hours before the planned attack, but all of a sudden the elves had a major battle on their hands.

* * * * *

Ertai slid off the crystal base of the power infuser. His formerly aching body felt supple and fit after a few minutes of exposure to the power stream. Cracking his knuckles, he tried the passing fire exercise again. This time the tiny flame was black from the start, even though he willed a yellow flame. He snuffed the ebon flicker and for a moment had the frightening thought that the treatments would alter him permanently, like the unfortunate guards who first brought him there.

Scrounging around the laboratory, he found a metal tray among Volrath's equipment and anxiously studied his reflection in it. It was still Ertai who gazed back at him—wasn't it? Same shock of blond hair, same flat nose, same weak chin. He thrust his jaw forward as he often had when he was a boy, trying to correct the receding line of his chin. It sank back into place when he relaxed. Same old Ertai.

He was glad to be healed. His talent was too valuable to waste on a meaningless death, but he wondered what sort of bargain he'd made. Could he really become ruler of an entire world? Ruling Rath could not be a comfortable position. Mysterious overlords above and seething revolution below—no, being evincar was no job for a sane man. Let Crovax have it. Sanity was not a handicap Crovax enjoyed.

His stomach growled. Meals were a problem in the Citadel. Belbe never ate, and neither did Greven. Of course, he was sure he didn't want to see what—or who—Greven *il*-Vec ate. But hungry he was, so he returned to Volrath's study deep in the laboratory. Amidst the bizarre apparatus and dripping, vile-smelling beakers was an island of cabinets, chairs, and a monumental desk. A dark, polished wood cabinet looked promising, and the lock broke easily when he applied a psychokinetic spell. It contained a number of obvious wine bottles and some paper-wrapped bundles that Ertai assumed were food. The bundles contained hard yellow biscuits. He sat down in one of Volrath's many oversized chairs and nibbled a biscuit experimentally. It was dry and slightly salty but better than nothing.

Ertai propped his feet up on a misshapen mogg skull lying on the floor. Marks on the bony cranium revealed the former master of Rath once had the same habit.

What was his best course of action? Crovax would likely murder him given the slightest provocation, likewise Greven. Belbe was friendly enough but cold as ice. If it served her mission for him to die, he wasn't sure she would object.

The cracker gone, he began on another. There was still the Phyrexian transplanar device in Portal Canyon. If he could get there, Ertai knew he could operate it. Trouble was, Portal

Canyon was a long way from the Stronghold. Getting there was a problem, and getting there without being stopped was an even bigger conundrum.

The only course, as he saw it, was to continue to play along with Belbe. That way he had the freedom of the Citadel and could improve his magical knowledge and his control of flowstone. Then, when the time was right, he'd get to Portal Canyon.

"There you are."

Ertai saw Belbe standing nearby. Lost in thought, he hadn't noticed her arrival.

"What are you doing?" she said.

"Contemplating my options."

She pointed. "What's that?"

"Food. Do you want some?" He handed her the package, now half empty.

"I don't eat," Belbe said, sniffing a biscuit. "Where did you find these?"

"In there. Volrath must have kept them on hand for snacks."

"Volrath was energy sufficient, like me. He didn't need to eat." She read the Phyrexian script on the biscuit wrapper. "I'm sure he never ate this."

"Why?" asked Ertai. "What is it?"

" 'Mogg wafers,' it says."

Ertai grimaced. "This is mogg food?"

"No, it's made of moggs. I imagine Volrath fed these wafers to his experimental animals."

* * * * *

Crovax emerged from his stupor to find three dead elves in his tent, Sergeant Tharvello wounded, and his entire staff ranting about a night attack by the rebels. He shouted for silence.

"Send the First Cavalry Company to fend off the rebels," Crovax said. "Hold the Third and Fourth Cavalry in reserve, north of camp. Get the infantry and moggs moving. I want a standard echelon formation with no more than ten yards between each company. String the moggs out in front as skirmishers. What is the strength of the enemy?"

"Unknown," said Nasser. "The scouts estimate more than a hundred, all on foot."

"It may be a diversion," Crovax said. "Maintain a sharp watch on other fronts. To your posts!"

He stepped over the corpses without a second look. Tharvello, his face bleeding, went to his company without any questions or thanks from his commander.

Crovax emerged from camp and stalked quickly through the wire grass. The night was tinged cobalt by the distant glow of the Stronghold's energy column. Overhead the clouds swirled in a wide spiral pattern, flashes of green lightning arcing from one band of clouds to another.

A cavalry officer galloped in, his lance bloody. "My lord! The enemy is retreating to the swamp!"

"Who are they? What were they doing?" Crovax demanded.

"They're Vec, my lord. Our riders first spotted them crawling through the grass toward the camp."

"Vec? So Eladamri has allies. No matter. Harry them to the forest edge, Captain, but don't enter the swamp. There may be more of them lying in wait for just such a move."

The captain saluted and galloped away.

Crovax called for his kerl. Behind him, the Expeditionary Force was drawing up on the plain in a checkerboard formation. Each block represented a troop of fifty men, and four blocks made a company. Moggs formed a ragged line ahead of the regular troops. The Rathi battle formation was a mile long from west to east, with the camp nestled behind the center of the line. The balance of Crovax's cavalry was positioned north of the tents, in reserve.

Crovax rode out to see the actual fighting. In the eerie half-darkness, the Rathi cavalry was circling small groups of Vec warriors, who popped up now and then to throw hatchets or stone-tipped spears at the kerls and riders. Crovax saw a stone spearhead shatter on a cavalryman's shield and laughed.

"Move in on them!" Crovax cried. "They're just savages! They're using stone spears! What are you, a gang of moggs?" Stung by his taunts, the cavalry overran the Vec, lancing nomad warriors right and left. Groups of Vec not yet engaged began to run for the swamp, half a mile away.

Crovax slumped in his saddle. This was no contest. "Recall the troopers," he said. Perchers took to the air, screeching his orders.

Nasser approached and Crovax called to him. "Any movement on other fronts?"

"No, my lord. I've sent scouts out in all directions. They report no rebels in sight."

They rode together back to the battle line. To Crovax's surprise, the soldiers in the front ranks raised a ragged cheer.

"They've changed their tune," he said.

"All soldiers want is victory," Nasser replied.

The wind died for the first time in many hours. A fragile stillness ensued. The night grew darker as the clouds spread apart, filling the whole sky. A series of wavering orange lights appeared on the plain north of the Rathi camp. Far away, the Hub reversed its rotation, sending a fresh wind rushing from the north. It arrived on the battlefield heavy with the odor of smoke.

"Campfires?" Nasser wondered. Crovax stood in his stirrups. A smear of white smoke rolled down the plain. With his enhanced eyes he could plainly see his reserve cavalry silhouetted against the wind-driven cloud.

"Something's wrong."

Flames leaped skyward from the dry prairie. The plain north of the camp was on fire, and the wind's change of direction was propelling the flames toward Crovax's army.

"Face about!" Crovax shouted. "The enemy's behind us!"

Elves, whirling torches around their heads, ran through the high grass, applying brands to the thickly growing weeds. Now a wall of flame a mile long came sweeping toward Crovax. Behind it were more than a thousand elf warriors.

The cavalry kerls were dumb beasts, bred for endurance and passivity, but they would not stand in the way of fire. Two cavalry companies milled about in confusion as their mounts bleated in growing terror. Reluctantly, Crovax ordered them out of the way and sent the infantry marching back through the camp to meet the enemy. Tents and stacks of equipment disrupted the tight battle formation. The formal checkerboard broke down into streams of soldiers, leaning forward into the wind and smoke.

The gap between the Rathi soldiers and the elves closed to a few yards. Tents were burning all along the north side of the camp. Behind the smoke and flames, the elves hurled salvoes of spears. Their snakefang tips were keen, and though they didn't always pierce Rathi armor, they did find enough chinks to inflict casualties on the advancing infantry. When the soldiers slowed under the hail of spears, the fire caught up to them. The lead ranks wavered and began to fall back. Moggs were already scampering through the camp, hooting in alarm.

"Why are they retreating? I ordered no withdrawal!" Crovax shouted.

"Men can't fight in a fire," Nasser said. "We must abandon the camp!"

"Give up the camp to rebels? Never!"

He spurred forward, trampling men and moggs who got in his way. A wave of fire was inundating the tents and had almost reached the center of camp. Soldiers staked in the square for punishment screamed for help as the flames advanced. Some of their comrades tried to reach them, but the conflagration rapidly engulfed the area, turning the square into an enormous funeral pyre.

Crovax held his shield over his head to ward off the rain of elven spears. His kerl blubbered and pranced, anxious to escape the flames. Crovax ignored the protesting beast, standing in his stirrups and staring through the fire for a glimpse of Eladamri and his rebels.

Commander or not, the kerl had had enough. It lay down, rubbed Crovax off, bounded to its feet and galloped away, bleating. He didn't have time to curse the stupid beast before flames washed over him. He threw an arm over his face and waited for the searing pain.

It never came. Crovax felt the heat, but it never crossed his threshold of pain. Pleased, he jumped to his feet. The fire had passed him, still propelled by the Hub wind.

In the flickering light, hundreds of lightly armed elves darted in and out, lofting their spears over the advancing fire. Roaring, Crovax charged into the nearest group, slashing at them with his sword. Every elf evaded his blade, melting back into the darkness beyond the firelight.

"I am Crovax! Crovax of Urborg!" he bellowed. "Come out, Eladamri, and fight me face to face!"

Less than thirty yards away, Eladamri saw Crovax striding about, shouting and waving his sword. The rebel leader simply watched Crovax rave.

"Will you fight him?" Gallan asked.

"Look at him," Eladamri said. "He's utterly mad."

"He's the enemy commander. Why don't you kill him?"

Eladamri leaned on his spear shaft. "Did you see what he did? He fell from his animal, wallowed in the fire and got up, unhurt. He's not flesh and blood—he's been altered, like Volrath. He's not going to fall to a snakefang spear." He laid his spear on his shoulder. "It's time we put an end to this battle. Lord Crovax will have to wait another day to die."

Eladamri put a hand to his mouth and uttered a loud, trilling cry. It was echoed by the throats of a thousand elves along the battle line. The sound halted Crovax's futile ranting, and he turned his back on the elves, walking swiftly back to his singed and shaken troops.

Elves circled wide around the western flank of the burning camp. There Darsett waited with over four hundred Dal in full battle gear. Beside him was Tant Jova and the main Vec force, three hundred strong, most armed with Rathi weapons scrounged from Crovax's fallen soldiers. Eladamri whacked Darsett on the back and clasped hands with Tant Jova.

"Time to wash our spears in enemy blood," he said.

The three rebel elements swept forward, shouting, screaming, banging their weapons on their shields. To the Rathi infantry, it seemed as if an entirely new enemy force sprang out of the darkness and hurled itself on them. The flustered Stronghold troops formed a hollow square and fended off waves of rebel attacks, the dead and wounded piling up deeper each time a fresh attack broke over them. Moggs outside the infantry squares were slaughtered in great numbers. Gradually, the exhausted Rathi line was pushed backward, changing from a square to a narrow triangle. Eladamri kept the pressure on all through the night while segments of his force were sent away to safety in the forest.

The Hub wind died before daybreak, and the fire went out. The camp was a heap of cinders. Of the ten thousand soldiers who arrived on the edge of the Skyshroud the night before, two thousand were dead or dying, and another three thousand were wounded. Only a few hundred moggs could be found. Crovax had lost over half his army in a single battle.

Eladamri was not in a celebratory mood. With far slenderer resources, his loses numbered just over one hundred elves, three dozen Dal, and nearly two hundred of Tant Jova's Vec nomads killed. No rich haul of captured weapons could be expected following the all-consuming fire.

He blamed himself, and he blamed Cardamel for ruining his trap. "Another six hours and we could've had them all," he stormed at the post-battle council deep in the forest. "Not just their lives but all their weapons and supplies too! That's what your little adventure cost us, Cardamel."

The young elf, who lost a hand in the fight, said nothing.

Tant Jova tried to calm Eladamri. "We have beaten them in open battle for the first time, my brother," she said. "Their new commander, Crovax, is disgraced. There's no one to lead them now. We've gained time as well as a victory—time we can parley into a bigger and better army."

The aged Vec matriarch shuffled to the center of the tree house. "Another thing, perhaps most important of all—I have this morning received a summons from the Oracle *en*-Vec. She has tidings, she says, of the *Korvecdal*."

The *Korvecdal* was the fabled deliverer of Vec prophecy, a hero who would overthrow the Stronghold and lead the peoples of Rath to freedom. When *Weatherlight* came to Rath there was talk that her captain, Gerrard Capashen, was the *Korvecdal*. No one thought so now, as he'd left in his flying ship, and the Stronghold was unbowed.

Every eye in the room turned to Eladamri. Eladamri sighed deeply. He'd won an expensive victory, and his first thought was the preservation of his army. Holy prophets were not his concern.

"We'll withdraw to Korai," he said, rubbing the smoke from his eyes. "There we can take stock of our losses and maybe gain a glimpse of the future."

CHAPTER 9
Victims

The operation began at sunrise. It was not going well. It should have taken a few hours to cull hostages from the leading families of the Dal, the Vec, and the Kor, but as Dorlan *il-*Dal stood on a broken wall in the ruined city quarter, studying his timepiece, he saw the roundup was entering its eighth hour. It would take longer still to get things recorded properly.

Greven descended on the crater with two thousand soldiers and as many moggs. He had a list of names drawn up by Dorlan and his fellow courtiers, and he had to go house to house to find the people he wanted. Quotas called for no less than two thousand hostages from each group.

Word quickly spread about the roundup, and finding the listed hostages got harder and harder. There were scuffles but no real fighting. Most of the hostages were quietly anxious or stubbornly sullen, but few offered open resistance.

Lines of captives, sorted by family and race, marched four abreast out of the City of Traitors under the Stronghold to the ruins beyond. Soldiers lined the way with arms ported.

"If I put whips in the hands of my moggs, the lines would move faster," Greven mused.

Dorlan was horrified. "You can't do that! Moggs whipping the evincar's subjects! They'll riot—they'll rebel."

"Easy, old man," Greven said. "This job's about stopping a rebellion, not starting one. I was just thinking like a soldier."

Thinking like a savage, Dorlan thought.

So the chamberlain stood on a tumbled-down wall with a trio of scribes below him, totting up the people as they trudged by. Each list was checked against Greven's master list to make certain the exact number from each group was represented. In an operation like this, Dorlan stressed, no one race should be seen as being favored by the authorities. The resentment thus caused would undo the salutary lesson of taking hostages in the first place.

Greven turned away from surveying the operation. "What's the count?"

Dorlan slapped his secretaries on the shoulder in turn.

"One thousand, three hundred and forty-four of the Dal," said the first.

"One thousand, two hundred and eighty-nine of the Vec," said the second.

"Eight hundred and seventy-five of the Kor," added the third.

"Why so few Kor?"

"They're more elusive," Dorlan said. "I've had reports that Kor from outside the Stronghold have not been taken at all."

"The Fishers of Life?"

The chamberlain consulted a scroll. "Yes, that's the clan. How did you know?"

Greven didn't answer. Instead he asked, "Have the holding areas been prepared?"

"Such as they are. If we have to hold these people more than a few days, they'll not stand for the conditions here."

"They'll stand for what they're told to stand for," Greven snapped. He signaled his escort to form up. He wanted to see the holding area himself.

At the far edge of the ruins, near the city moat, three large squares had been cleared by mogg laborers. Rough walls made from the debris of fallen houses were piled up to create crude stockades. Each stockade had a single entrance. Hostages were marched into the stockades according to their race.

Some hours passed, and the lines began to thin. Eventually

Dorlan and his secretaries appeared with the soldiers who'd been driving the lines forward. The chamberlain looked happy.

Greven turned his eyes to Dorlan. "What's the final count?"

"We made up the Kor tally. A whole band of them arrived at the last minute," Dorlan said under his breath. "The quota is within 20 persons of being prefect."

"Where are the Kor?"

"There, at the end of the line. They turned themselves in."

"What!"

Dorlan shrugged. "They appeared on their own behind the escort detachment. One of them spoke to me and asked to be added to the tally."

Greven grasped Dorlan's soft arm in a painful grip. "The Kor you spoke to—was his name Furah?"

The chamberlain grunted in pain. "Dread Lord, you're hurting me."

"What was the Kor leader's name?"

"Furah sounds right, or Furdah—some such uncouth name."

Greven released Dorlan with a shove and waded through the ranks of guards. In front of them were the last hostages, in this case over a hundred Kor in identical gray leather outfits. Though Greven had lived his entire life on Rath with both Dal and Kor as neighbors, he'd never seen an entire clan look so identical.

Startled, Greven called out, "Furah! Furah, I want to speak to you!"

In one motion, a hundred-plus Kor turned and looked back at Greven. *They were all Furah.* The warrior shook his head.

"Did you see that?" Greven asked a nearby soldier.

"See what, Dread Lord?"

"Nothing. Never mind."

* * * * *

The night of the Hub wind, Belbe made her first inspection of the flowstone factory. She did this alone, or rather, with six moggs to carry the new machinery sent with her from Phyrexia. The court advisors she quickly dismissed as useless sycophants. Greven and Dorlan were busy rounding up thousands of hostages, and Ertai was nowhere to be found. This last fact annoyed her in some ill-defined way. Belbe found herself wanting Ertai's company, and not having what she wanted made her feel thwarted.

She soon forgot about Ertai, Greven, hostages, and everything else once she was deep in the flowstone works. Unlike those parts of the Citadel adapted for habitation, the factory was the most Phyrexian part of the Stronghold, and in Belbe's short life, Phyrexia meant home.

The structure of the factory was purely organismic—the adamantine frames of the building were like bones, and the cladding was applied like muscle and skin over the factory's skeleton. The entire fortress cantilevered out from the side of the Stronghold cone and was studded with flues, exhaust ports, and enormous conduits channeling liquid flowstone outside the crater. Over the years, residue from the great works accreted outside like scar tissue, blunting the lines of the severe architecture. By the time Belbe arrived, the Citadel was like a vast wasp's nest, growing organically and infested with thousands of poisonous inhabitants.

In the domed control center atop the factory, Belbe stood in rapt fascination of the great cauldron at the heart of the Citadel. Here lava, the raw material of flowstone, met the energy beam sizzling down from the Hub. Atoms disintegrated in the energy stream were whirled about at extreme velocities and reformed into programmable nano-machines—flowstone. It was all so wonderful, magnificent, and efficient.

Moggs lolled on the floor behind her, taking a breather while Belbe was lost in admiration of the factory. She recovered her sense of purpose and ordered them to bring up the Nano-Machine Conversion Accelerator. This was a globe eighteen inches in diameter, whose outer skin was encrusted with extruded tubing, wires, and output jacks. It was a self-aware device, capable of accepting verbal orders and implementing them throughout the factory. Phyrexian technicians had designed the Conversion Accelerator to optimize production of flowstone. As things stood, the factory ran at one speed all the time. Actual output varied, however, according to the amount of energy from the Hub, the quality and amount of lava, and the purity of the raw materials used. The Conversion Accelerator would harmonize these elements so as to produce more flowstone when conditions warranted, and expend less energy when conditions were unfavorable. Overall production efficiency was expected to increase by almost twenty-seven percent.

The moggs maneuvered the heavy module into place. Belbe made the master power connections, and the Accelerator came to life.

"Implement final installation," she commanded.

"Understood." The device extended sharp-edged feelers to the control console. The tubes punched through the flowstone skin. Thin yellow oil wept from the incisions, but they quickly healed.

"Connection complete," said the Accelerator. "Input flow nominal. Output flow at 117 percent."

"Reduce output to 100 percent."

"That is not maximum," countered the machine.

"This is a test of your verbal command structure. Reduce to 100 percent."

The Accelerator vibrated slightly on its new mountings. Lights all over the factory dimmed, brightened, then settled down. The constant drone of the molecular whirlpool in the factory core declined half an octave.

"Output flow 100 percent," the Accelerator announced.

Belbe adjusted some of the external controls on the module. One of them was the voice command recognition circuit.

"Who am I?"

"Emissary from Central Control, unit number 338551732—"

"Stop, you are correct. Do you acknowledge my authority?"

"Command authority is authentic."

"Are there any default authorities?" she asked, curious.

"The Evincar of Rath."

"Any others?"

"No others."

"Very good. Seal command authority to my voice and the evincar's."

The unit clicked loudly and said, "Sealed."

One task done, another major task remained. The moggs had a second carton to deliver. In her belt pouch she had the control unit for a transplanar portal, the only portable device of its kind on Rath. The second carton in her baggage was a Portal Generator, a special device that could open a portal to any plane in the multiverse.

The portal, if opened, would need space. It also needed to be out of the way. Where to install it? Belbe ran through the complex floor plan of the Citadel in her head. There was a place ... she called the moggs. Installation of the Accelerator had taken so long, the moggs had fallen asleep leaning on the second carton. She shouted at them, and they twitched awake.

She took the catwalk that circled the mighty central crucible. This close to the factory, static from the tremendous energy input could be felt through the walls of the furnace. The moggs didn't like it one bit and slunk along, scratching their tingling skin on every available protrusion. Belbe found the prickling sensation stimulating, not unlike her experience with Volrath's bath.

When she reached the place she'd chosen, she checked carefully to be sure she was not observed. Location of her portal equipment had to be secret. There were people in the palace who would kill for a chance to leave Rath, and Belbe had explicit orders from her masters not to allow anyone access to the portal.

An hour later, the portal device was deposited in a seldom-visited part of the Citadel. Belbe made a mental note to ask Greven to execute the moggs who helped her install the machinery as a standard security precaution.

Belbe had minimal need for sleep. The glistening oil in her veins kept her active long after ordinary beings craved rest. At daybreak, she descended to the lower airship dock to see what progress was being made on *Predator*. She found the hull had been reassembled and new deck fittings were being installed. All that remained after that was the tricky job of installing the engines and rigging.

She spotted Greven's Vec foreman and asked him where his master was.

"I haven't seen him since yesterday, Excellency," said the Vec. "He left with Lord Dorlan, and I haven't seen either of them since."

"Thank you—"

"Excellency, when you find Lord Greven, ask him please to come back as soon as he can. We don't dare set the engines in place without him."

Belbe promised to pass the word to Greven. On her way out of the ship dock, a guard stopped her.

"If you're looking for Lord Greven, Excellency, you'll find him in the ruins beyond the City of Traitors."

She searched her implanted memory and found she didn't know this place. "Where is that?" Belbe asked.

The guard stepped to the edge of the docking platform and pointed to the floor of the crater.

"See the lights down there, Excellency? That's the City of Traitors. If you head that way," he pointed to the far side of the crater, in the direction of the mogg warrens, "there's a lot of fallen-down buildings. That's where you'll find Commander Greven."

Belbe leaned on the railing. A warm updraft, smelling of molten rock and ozone, ruffled her hair and the tight sleeves of her teal gown.

"What's Greven doing down there?"

"Haven't you heard, Excellency? That's where he's taken the hostages—the hostages from the City of Traitors."

Belbe had a sudden urge to descend to the ruins and observe the operation for herself. Without the airship, it was a long journey to the crater floor. Belbe dismissed the guard and stood by the rail, gazing down at the haze-shrouded area, pondering how best to get there.

"Your Excellency?"

The second word was enunciated with ironic precision. There was Ertai, leaning casually on one of the inverted buttresses supporting the airship dock. Something was different. It wasn't just his appearance, though he had finally given up his tattered robes and donned Rathi garb—high collared doublet, knee breeches, and ankle-high fleshstone boots, all in different shades of gray. It was something else about him, less tangible than a change of wardrobe. Ertai's presence was different.

"Someone needs to speak to the tailors in this place," he said. "They have no sense of color at all. But I did want to be presentable, since you called me."

"I didn't call you."

"You were thinking about me. I came to find you."

"I had work to do," she said, pretending not to care. "In the factory."

"Then I'm glad I missed it. There's nothing as boring as machinery." He came to the rail and looked down on the city. "Awful place," he remarked. He glanced upward at the vast overhanging bulk of the Citadel. "It's like living in a well with a boulder balanced over your head."

"I want to go down there," she said, pointing to the distant ruins. Ertai asked why. She reminded him of his hostage idea. "Greven and Dorlan are down there now, gathering them."

Ertai's face darkened. "I'm sorry I suggested it. I don't know how such an idea came into my head." He shrugged. "Of course, it's a very good idea, from a certain point of view—like all my ideas. But no good will come of it."

"I want to go there," Belbe repeated.

Ertai took hold of her hand. She made a mild attempt to free herself, but he held on.

"Let me take you there, Excellency."

She stopped struggling. "You don't have to call me that."

"Don't I?"

"No."

"Very well, Belbe. I can get you down there faster than an airship or any silly flowbot crane."

"How?"

He let go of her hand, turned, and walked about six feet away. He sat down on the gritty floor, folding his legs in front of him. Ertai pressed his palms together and closed his eyes.

"Visualization," he said softly, "is the most important part of spellcasting."

Belbe watched him closely. Ertai trembled. His fingers went white from the pressure, and most of the color drained from his face. The collar of his new doublet wilted from perspiration.

Something disturbed the air behind her. Belbe turned and saw a large, vague shape with flapping wings hovering a few yards from the platform. Ertai's expression grew more strained, and the outline of the flapping object grew more distinct. Air itself seemed to be congealing to form the creature, which gradually assumed the form of a great predatory bird.

"What is it?" she asked, impressed.

Ertai did not answer. He opened his eyes and stiffly unbent his legs. His brow was etched with deep furrows as he fiercely maintained his concentration even with the distractions of open eyes and movement.

He extended a hand toward the phantom bird, drew it back, and closed his outstretched fingers into a fist. The giant bird flew into the dock, its wings and head passing through the solid structure of the platform without resistance. Yet when it reached Ertai, it extended a taloned claw and grasped him around the waist. He repeated the clasping gesture and the spectral falcon took hold of Belbe's waist as well.

"What's this?" she protested, trying to open the bird's talons. Though solidly in the creature's grip, her efforts to repel the bird met no solid flesh at all. It was most disturbing, being lifted by visible, yet untouchable claws.

"Stop it," she said. "I'll use the Citadel egress. It'll only take a few hours to go down there—"

Before she could finish the sentence, the spirit falcon rocketed away from the airship dock. Belbe, to her consternation, saw she was dangling beneath the translucent creation, hundreds of feet in the air. Some primitive part of her was thrilled with terror—an emotion she was learning on Rath—but her good sense told her interrupting Ertai's mental focus would be disastrous for them both.

The falcon descended in a rapid spiral through the hot, lava-scented air. They circled quite close to the upward flowing column of lava. Between the giant falcon claw clamped around Belbe's waist and the stifling heat of the lava, it was hard to breathe. Fortunately, the falcon's next loop took them away from the lava flow, well out over the City of Traitors.

As they coursed through the thin clouds, Belbe started to enjoy the experience. The sweep, the feeling of speed and power flying conferred was intoxicating. She looked down on the city below, marveling at the gridwork of streets and houses. It was some minutes before she realized the streets and squares were devoid of activity. Not a single Vec or Kor could be seen.

Ertai started to choke loudly. His face had gone ghastly white, and blood was dripping from both nostrils. He let out a wracking cough, and to her horror, Belbe felt the falcon's claws thin and slip. They were two hundred feet above the city. If she fell from this height, not even her metal skeleton would save her, and Ertai would surely die.

They descended too rapidly as the falcon's wings faded in and out of existence. At fifty feet, rooftops rushed by, and chimneys became serious hazards. Ertai was hanging limply in the falcon's evanescent grip, blood staining the front of his new clothes.

Thirty feet. Belbe looked up. The body and wings of the falcon were almost gone, just the faintest outline was left. Abruptly, the magical creature vanished. Belbe lunged for Ertai. She caught him, twisted in mid-air until her feet were down, and braced for impact.

They hit the roof of an empty house, broke through, hit the floor of the second story, and went through that as well. When Belbe hit the ground, her legs jackknifed hard, but the Phyrexian alloys took the stress. Her augmented nerves signaled massive pain, then shut down. Over and over they rolled in the dust and debris of the abandoned dwelling, coming to a stop against an outside wall.

Belbe rose from the rubbish. Her ill-used legs quivered from the strain. Already her implanted healing systems were kicking in, repairing torn muscles and ligaments, and liberally dosing her nervous system with pain suppressants. She turned Ertai over. His color was already coming back, and his nose had stopped bleeding. Belbe had taken the full force of the fall for him.

"Ow," he said, clasping his head. "What a headache. What happened?"

"Your magical bird failed."

"My spell, fail? Impossible!" His conviction, strongly spoken, made his head throb unmercifully.

"It dropped us. If I hadn't caught you, you'd be dead now."

The dim interior of the ruined house, the drying blood on his face and neck, and Belbe's unflinching manner must have convinced Ertai that she was telling the truth.

"The Spirit Falcon is a taxing spell to perform, but I've never heard of it failing like this," he said, genuinely puzzled.

"It began to fade after just a few minutes."

He scratched his rusty blond head. "There must be something interfering with the flow of magical energy."

"Perhaps it's your healing treatment. The native energies of Rath must be very different from those of your home world."

Belbe helped him stand.

"Good thing we fell on an empty house," he said quietly.

For reasons she did not entirely understand, Belbe leaned forward and pressed her lips to Ertai's. He was so startled by this unexpected action he failed to respond in kind. Belbe drew back, expressionless.

"Did I do it incorrectly?"

"I don't know," he said. "I wasn't prepared—"

"Prepare yourself then," she said. "It may happen again." In awkward silence they made their way out of the ruined house.

The unpaved street was covered with sickly yellow moss and gray lichen, and clogged with blocks, fallen pediments, bricks, and shards of pottery. Belbe and Ertai picked their way through the ruins to the next street. This wide path was clear of debris, and the thick dust had been stirred recently by a large crowd of people.

"The hostages came this way," Belbe said.

"Must be hundreds of them."

"Thousands. Lord Greven is not one for half measures."

They walked down the broad, empty road. Ruddy light from the rising column of lava painted the ruins in shades of pink.

Ertai looked at Belbe. "May I ask you a question?"

She put her arms behind her head and stretched her healing limbs. "Of course."

"Do you ever ask yourself if you're on the right side or not?"

She looked at her feet. "Of the road?"

"No, in this struggle."

"No."

"Why not?"

"The right side is the side that succeeds," she said simply. "This is the basic truth my masters taught me."

"They could be wrong."

"It is possible but not likely. Time will tell."

"I used to think I knew right from wrong," Ertai said. "That was before I began my advanced studies in magic. Then I learned that power is power, regardless of its origin. Any species can be used to kill or cure, and if that's so, how can any of it be good or evil? It simply *is*. I think people are like that, too. We simply are."

"I will ask you a question," she said. He agreed. "Do you regret coming here? Do you miss your comrades on *Weatherlight?*"

He stopped, feet stirring little gouts of fine dust. "They left me here," Ertai said. "I was angry at them for that. Now, in an odd way, I think they did me a favor."

Amid the ruins, the sanguinary light of the lava column, the still, humid air at the bottom of the crater, Belbe had a strange, new experience. A more worldly woman could have told her she was feeling affection for the first time. As it was, she had to figure it out herself.

* * * * *

The hostages filled the stockades with resignation. Each family staked out a place in the dusty enclosures and waited for word they could go home again. Soldiers stood atop the low rubble walls, eyeing their quiescent charges.

Belbe and Ertai arrived to find Greven seated on a broken monolith. Dorlan il-Dal was with him, a picnic lunch spread out on a cloth between them. When they saw Belbe approaching, both men rose and bowed.

"Greetings, Excellency! You are looking well today. Why didn't you let us know you were coming? I would have prepared a repast for you as well." Dorlan said effusively.

"It's of no matter," she replied. "I do not eat."

"Are the hostages here?" Ertai asked impatiently.

"Six thousand of them," confirmed Greven.

"Five thousand, nine hundred eighty-eight, to be exact," said Dorlan. He held up several loose scrolls. "I have the tallies here if Your Excellency would care to see."

She ignored the proffered scrolls and walked to the mouth of the Dal stockade. Moggs grunted and sidled away from Belbe. Guards on the wall snapped to attention.

Dorlan, Ertai, and Greven came up behind her.

"What does Your Excellency require?" asked the chamberlain.

"A better view, first." She looked left and right, judged the far wall to be straighter, and sprang from a flat-footed stance to the top of the seven-foot-high structure.

Belbe looked out over the dusty arena, jammed with almost two thousand Dal. With designed thoroughness she catalogued the crowd: one thousand, five hundred and thirty-three adults, four hundred and sixty-one children. Most of the adults were elderly or female. She started counting crutches in the crowd and stopped when she passed one hundred and fifty. Distaste rose in her throat. She turned to the trio of men waiting below her.

"Who chose these people?" she shouted.

"Why, I did, Excellency, with Lord Greven's help," Dorlan replied.

"Why take these particular people—women, children, the aged?"

"Come down, Excellency. I'd rather not have this conversation yelled from the stockade wall," Greven said, his face hardening.

She did come down, landing inches in front of the towering warrior. "Explain your choices, Chamberlain."

Dorlan's lip trembled. "The—the Dread Lord and I discussed it. We agreed these would make the most effective hostages."

"Go on."

Greven stepped up. "Our goal is to keep peace inside the Stronghold. We chose people who have strong bonds with those not chosen. Dal men will think twice about rising against us if they know we have their mothers, fathers, wives, and children in our power."

"I think you've erred, Commander," Belbe said. "Now we're as much hostages as those people beyond the wall!"

Ertai spoke up. "What do you mean?"

"If any harm comes to these people, it will foment rebellion rather than quell it." She was angry, and she didn't know how to handle the emotions stirred up by the plight of the hostages. "Why didn't you round up young males instead? They're the potential allies of Eladamri, not these helpless folk."

"In matters of civil unrest, there are no innocent bystanders," Greven said.

"Be at ease, Excellency!" Dorlan pleaded. "No one wishes harm to these people. When Lord Crovax returns triumphant, all will be well."

"And if Crovax loses?" asked Ertai.

The silence that followed was suffocating.

CHAPTER 10
Rivals

The Skyshroud Expeditionary Force remained on the field for two days, burning its dead and building temporary defenses out of turf, rocks, and the wreckage of the army's equipment. Everyone expected the rebels to attack and wipe them out, but they didn't. Cavalry patrols were sent out to locate Eladamri's band, but they returned in a few hours and reported finding no sign of the enemy.

The rebels didn't leave behind a single scrap; every thrown spear, every bent sword, every broken helmet was scavenged from the field of battle. Nor were any rebel dead left behind. The plain around the burned Rathi camp had been trampled flat by men, elves, moggs, and kerls, but no other evidence of Eladamri's force remained.

Crovax withdrew to his makeshift quarters—a pile of scorched sod with a square of canvas for a roof—and brooded over his defeat. Organization and defense of the Rathi position fell to Nasser. Aside from grunting approvals to Nasser's suggestions, Crovax did not speak for two whole days. Late in the afternoon on the second day after the battle, he emerged from his hut. Nasser had been lingering outside, waiting for his commander to appear.

"My lord," said Nasser when Crovax stood unblinking in the late day sun. "What are your orders?"

"Any sign of the enemy?" asked Crovax quietly.

"None, my lord."

"Break camp. We will march." Crovax turned to go back inside.

"Very good, my lord. Where to?"

"The Stronghold."

The army had been waiting for just such an order, and in less than an hour they were ready to march. The cavalry fanned out to watch for rebels, and the infantry column, much reduced in length, shouldered their weapons and started off.

The Corps of Sergeants waited patiently for Crovax to join them. The commander's kerl was tethered to the stump of a lance outside his quarters. More than half the army was on the path back to the Stronghold, and there was no sign of Crovax.

"Someone should rouse him," Tharvello said. The other sergeants shook their heads. No one wanted to incur his wrath.

"Nasser, you're his favorite. You do it," said Tharvello.

"I can wait."

"Ha! You're afraid of him too!"

Eyes narrowed to slits, Nasser dismounted his soot-smudged kerl and tossed the reins to the nearest mogg. He squared his shoulders and walked to the door of the little sod hut—just a flap of tattered canvas, waving slowly in the light breeze.

Five feet from the hut, Nasser halted and called out, "My lord! The army is underway. Will you take your place with us?"

A muffled thud, and a cloud of dirt whirled away from Crovax's hut. Shafts of blinding white light burst from every crack and crevice in the sod walls. Nasser threw an arm over his face, and the hut collapsed with a spurt of gray dust and ash.

"Sergeants, to me!" Nasser cried. A dozen seasoned warriors ran to the destroyed shack and tore through the poles and clods of earth looking for their commander. When they found themselves scraping at virgin soil beneath the hut, the sergeants realized Crovax was gone. Everyone spoke at once.

"What happened?"

"Eladamri—"

"—elven magic!"

"Some new weapon—?"

"—Eladamri—"

Nasser squatted in the remains of the hut, toying in the debris with his fingers. His careful contemplation of the situation gradually calmed his fellow sergeants.

At last someone said, "Where did he go?"

"Maybe back to where he came from," Tharvello said. "What do we do now?"

The senior sergeant dusted the drab soil of Rath from his hands. "I will take command."

They were more than happy to let him shoulder the burden. Tharvello said, "What are your orders, Nasser?"

"Without a body, I can't assume Lord Crovax is dead. The commander's last order stands," he decided. "We go home."

* * * * *

Predator was airborne again, thanks to Greven's tireless efforts. After the hostages were secured, Greven returned to the airship dock, where he oversaw the replacement of *Predator*'s powerful engines. The hull was floated out the lower dock and carefully steered to the upper landing pylon. There the final refit would take place, and Greven would take on new crew to replace those lost in the costly battle with *Weatherlight*.

Ertai disappeared into the libraries of the Citadel, beset by the conundrums of his place in the scheme of things. Days passed, and Belbe saw little of him. When she finally did, she was amazed by the changes slowly transforming him. Early one morning she found him perched on a table in one of the old scroll depositories, surrounded by heaps of discarded documents. It was stifling in the narrow room, and Ertai had stripped to the waist to better bear the heat.

Never a muscular fellow formerly, Ertai now displayed a formidable breadth of shoulder as he sat hunched over a scroll. That, and the fact his hair had become copper-brown made Belbe doubt she was seeing him at all.

"Hello," she said uncertainly. "I see you're making use of the libraries."

"These scrolls are all wrong," Ertai said, pushing the heavy scroll aside. "Their description of energy crossover—"

"What's happening to you, Ertai?"

He looked at her from under heavy-lidded eyes. "What are you talking about?"

"You're changing. Your hair, your physique—"

"It's to be expected," he said, stretching his bare arms, now covered with thin, ropy muscles. "The energy infusions you started me on are doing it. Every time I go back to Volrath's laboratory, I change a little more."

She drew back. "You're still using the infuser? Why?"

"Imagine my chagrin when I discovered the effects of the device were only temporary. When my injuries return, I have to go back to the infuser for another treatment. I should've known it wouldn't actually heal me. If I hadn't been so hurt, I'm sure I would have thought of it."

"Thought of what?"

Ertai leaned his cheek against his knee. "Only natural life-energy can heal human flesh. Other varieties can mask damage by transforming it into something else. In my case, Volrath's device seems to be making me into a lesser version of our friend Greven."

"No!"

"It doesn't matter. I can't stop now, anyway. If I miss a day at the infuser, the misery of the torture session comes back. I can't bear it. . . . a little muscle won't hurt me, and my mind is still my own. Maybe even better, if that's possible. I'm reading eight books a day, did you know that? I'll be through this library soon, then I'll move on to the next."

"Be careful, Ertai."

He smiled in his own wry way. Ertai held up his hand, palm out, to the closest scroll-laden shelf. The flowstone rippled like a reefing sail. He sustained the motion for several seconds before it faded.

"Your influence is improving," she said, pleased.

"Yes. I may give Crovax a surprise before long."

She wanted to speak to him about his growing power, but Ertai lowered his head to his reading again and quickly forgot Belbe was present. She backed out of the close little room. Her heart was beating fast, and she didn't know why. It took several minutes to slow it to a normal rhythm.

Belbe continued her rounds of the Citadel, stopping by the factory control room to check on the Accelerator unit she'd installed. The stubborn device kept trying to raise production to inefficient levels above 100 percent, which forced Belbe to improvise a method to hamper the machine's excessive enthusiasm for production. She settled for tampering with the output meter, resetting it by hand to fool the Accelerator into thinking the factory was producing more flowstone than it actually was. However, there was a problem with her makeshift solution. Like every other mechanism in the factory, the output meter was self-correcting. In the course of several days' production, it would discover its readings were inaccurate and correct itself. Thus Belbe would have to return to the control dome every other day to reset the output meter to maintain maximum efficiency.

While she was adjusting the output meter for the first time, she spotted a ball of white light, about two feet wide, circling and descending the energy column. The ball darted first in one direction, then another. Belbe lost it for a second against the glare of the beam, then adjusted her vision to see past the column's corona. High above, the white ball of light hovered over the upper airship dock. It dipped behind the pylon and was lost from sight.

Curious, she left the control station and made her way back to the residential wing of the Citadel. Everything seemed normal. Servants and courtiers bowed as she passed. Guards stood at their stations, unalarmed.

She reached the main intersection in the heart of the palace. From here, stairs and flowbot lifts branched out all over the structure—up to the evincar's quarters, down to the laboratories, libraries, map room, armories, and prison. Belbe strained every nerve in her being, searching for the fiery intruder. The strongest trace (which was very weak indeed) came from a window in the outside wall. From there she looked down on the mogg warrens, map tower, Volrath's laboratory, and the roof of the Dream Halls. The arched roof of the hall bore ghostly heat trails, crisscrossing back and forth. The phantom visitor was there.

For the first time in her short life, Belbe ran. Her legs were quite healed after her fall in the ruins a few days ago, and she ran to the physical limits of her alloy frame. Flashing down the dark corridors of the palace, she passed unsuspecting courtiers and soldiers in a blur. Within seconds, Belbe was at the doors of the Dream Halls. Her hands were just about on the handles when the tall double doors swung silently inward. Belbe rushed into the vast, silent hall.

"Ah, my young mistress."

"Crovax!"

He was still in his dusty armor. She could smell blood and smoke, and saw bits of wire grass snagged in his boots.

"Was that you?" she said, incredulous.

"You saw me? Oh yes, you're the emissary, you see everything." He seemed dizzy and shuffled his feet to keep his balance. "A bonus from our masters," he said. "I can will myself from point to point."

"Teleportation."

"Is that what it's called? Hard on the head, if you ask me." He called up a flowstone stool out of the floor and sat down.

"What about the army? Why did you leave them?"

"My army?" he exploded. "Worthless, cowardly cattle! I would have killed them all if I were Eladamri!"

"You lost your entire army?"

Crovax's face contorted. "I lost little of value."

"How many survived? Where are they now?"

He leaped to his feet. "Who are you to question me?"

"I am the emissary of the overlords," Belbe said calmly. "I ask you again, where is your army?"

"Out there." He flung a hand. "We fought a night battle. The rebels started a fire upwind of our position, and many of the soldiers were trapped by the flames."

"And Eladamri?"

Crovax's voice was almost inaudible. "He escaped."

The distant dream machinery near the ceiling clicked and whirred. For some seconds, it was the only thing moving or making noise in the Dream Halls.

Then Belbe spoke. "You failed."

The cold, hard edge returned to his voice. "This is only the first round. There are many acts yet to play."

"A new evincar must be named soon."

"Then name me! Who else can you choose? Greven? He's been a slave too long to know how to rule."

"There is another candidate." The flowstone around Belbe heaved like a sea swell. She ignored it, and when it was calm again she said, "I refer to Ertai."

"That boy? Do the overlords know you're considering that arrogant little cur?"

"The overlords know everything I do," she said stiffly. "Ertai has magical gifts far in excess of anyone else on Rath. His influence over flowstone grows daily."

"Can he command an army? Can he govern? Can he rule?"

"Those are questions still unanswered about you, Crovax. As for Ertai, he's intelligent, clever, and has many insights. It was Ertai, for example, who devised the stratagem of taking hostages from the local population to insure they wouldn't lend support to Eladamri's rebels."

Crovax broke into an awful, face splitting grin. "Hostages? What a delightful idea. I give the pup credit." He walked a slow circle around Belbe, close enough for her to feel his cold breath on her face. "How many hostages?"

"A thousand." Why she gave him the wrong figure, she didn't know.

"Where are they?"

"The ruins outside of the City of Traitors."

He stopped his perambulation directly behind her. "I see. Thank you, Excellency."

"For what?"

"For restoring my faith in the wisdom of our masters," he said. Cool fingertips brushed the back of her neck. "But hear me, girl. I *will* be Evincar of Rath."

"Are you threatening me, Crovax?"

The fingers were withdrawn. "Certainly not, Excellency. I merely pledge to do my utmost for the cause. You do your best for the overlords, don't you?"

"I do the task I was made for."

He suddenly enfolded her from behind in his powerful arms, one around her waist, the other around her neck. In a split-second decision, Belbe decided not to struggle but remained as relaxed as possible.

"We're allies after all," he said softly in her ear. "Cooperation can be as satisfying as competition—with the right company."

"I'm here to choose the best person for the job, whoever that is." Belbe still didn't move.

"No emotion involved?" Crovax asked.

"Emotion is not efficient."

Crovax tightened his grip.

"You can't overpower me, Crovax."

"I wouldn't dream of trying, Excellency." He dropped his arms, and Belbe stepped away. Adrenaline coursed through her. She felt like a coiled spring, all wound up. Crovax appeared quite calm.

"I want a full report on the battle in writing, detailing your losses, Eladamri's tactics, and the state of the army," Belbe said, inwardly shaking with excitement. She kept thinking about what it would be like to break Crovax's arms and legs. She knew just how to do it, even through his armor.

"As you wish. When shall I present my report?"

"You will wait upon my pleasure." Belbe imagined his face exploding in a shower of blood and bone fragments, his teeth falling like hailstones to the polished floor. "Where are the survivors of your force?"

"A few days' march from here."

"Will they make it back on their own?" With one kick she could crush his windpipe, and he would slowly strangle to death. . . .

He shrugged. "That has more to do with Eladamri than my soldiers."

"*Predator* is flying again. I'll send Greven to find your men and escort them home. The ship has no weapons on board yet, but the rebels won't know that." With one blow she could drive the cartilage in his nose back into his brain.

He saluted. "Your Excellency is wise and frugal."

Crovax departed, and the Dream Halls doors closed silently behind him. Belbe leaped into the air, kicking her feet and pounding the air furiously with her fists. When this failed to satisfy her, she ran to the wall and punched an elaborate bas-relief depicting one of Volrath's dreams of glory. The flowstone walls, made to imitate marble, splintered under Belbe's blows. No sooner had the fragments fallen to the floor than they began climbing back up to rejoin the broken structure. She pounded on the wall until her knuckles were scored and weeping glistening oil. Panting with excitement, she stood back to catch her breath.

Her violence triggered the dream device overhead. With a hiss of servos and uncoiling wire, three dream catchers dropped to Belbe's eye level. In each was a dirty white "pearl", representing some dream experience the device thought appropriate to Belbe's current state of mind. She stared at the trio of machines and with a howl of pure fury, seized one in each hand and ripped them loose. The third dream catcher hastily retracted.

Belbe enjoyed crushing Volrath's dreams under her heel.

* * * * *

The army reached Chireef, the last outpost before the Stronghold, three days after the battle. A march that had taken Crovax a day and a half Nasser was content to do in twice the time. His men were tired, many were wounded, and no one was in a hurry to return home from a defeat.

Riders came back with the news that the blockhouse at Chireef seemed abandoned. The doors were closed and barred, and none of the garrison responded to the scouts' hails. Alarmed, Nasser and the Corps of Sergeants rode ahead of the main body with all the remaining cavalry to investigate what happened at Chireef.

The blockhouse looked deserted. Arrow slits were vacant. No sentries walked the roof. Some unknown banner hung limply from the flagpole—the air was too still to stir it. Despite repeated calls, no one inside the blockhouse responded.

The door was a massive bronze affair, and the Rathi soldiers were not equipped to batter it down. A team of four men was ordered to scale the blockhouse walls with ropes and grappling hooks. The outside of the blockhouse was as smooth as glass (to prevent just such attempts at climbing by the enemy), so it took some time before the soldiers were able to reach the roof. Three men were detailed to enter the blockhouse and open the outer door while the fourth hauled down the mysterious flag and tossed it to Nasser.

It was a triangle of rough green cloth with a simplified image of a red snake's head, fangs bared, in the center.

With a loud clank, the doors of Chireef rolled back. The cavalrymen who'd entered the blockhouse emerged looking puzzled. No one was inside, alive or dead. The place had been stripped clean—not even garbage was left.

"What about the cisterns?" Nasser asked. The army was thirsty.

"Empty," the scouts reported. Someone had broken off the flowstone valves, allowing all the water to drain from the storage tanks.

This was plainly the work of Eladamri and his rebels, but the mysterious state of the blockhouse was unsettling. Why were there no signs of a fight? Where were the dead or the wounded? They couldn't even find any bloodstains. How could a band of rebels, armed only with hand weapons, capture a well-defended blockhouse the army had visited only a few days earlier?

A smudge of dust on the horizon warned Nasser the foot column was on its way. Tharvello and some of the sergeants wanted to keep the troops away from Chireef, hide the strange fate of the garrison from the rank and file. Nasser would not allow it.

"Let everyone know," he said grimly. "This is what they can expect at rebel hands! Let them contemplate Chireef and fight harder to avoid their comrades' fate."

Each company marched past the empty blockhouse. Smashed valves and puddles at the foot of the wall made it clear there was no water for them. Word filtered through the ranks about the disappearance of the entire garrison, and a chill enveloped the already dispirited army.

Nasser ordered the march to continue until dusk. Though they were within a night's march of the Stronghold, the senior sergeant didn't want his dejected troops to arrive home in the middle of the night. He decided to camp one more night and march into the city by the full light of day. Nasser sent a percher ahead with this news. Not knowing where Crovax was, he addressed his message to Greven *il*-Vec.

He halted the army astride the main road from the Stronghold to Chireef. The tired men filed out of formation and dropped their packs in the dirt. Details were sent to gather tinder for campfires, and the communal pots were unpacked for dinner.

These mundane tasks occupied the army in the last hour of daylight. Nasser and his comrades were about to sit down when sentries reported an unknown light in the sky.

Nasser overturned his bowl in his haste to stand. He didn't have to go far before he spied what the sentries had seen: a bright golden light, low in the air and moving with considerable speed. It was approaching from the southwest, directly away from the Stronghold.

"Airship?" suggested Tharvello. "An enemy airship?"

"I don't know. Alert the troops. If we're going to be attacked, the men must disperse."

Trumpets and perchers blared, and the soldiers gave up their meager meals to stand to arms. The aerial beacon was easily visible to all now as it maneuvered below the sluggish clouds. Anxious murmurs passed through the ranks.

The hum of aerial engines reached the soldiers. The first dim outline of the ship behind the light could just be made out.

"It's a big one," Tharvello said.

"Shut up," Nasser replied.

The gilded searchlight raked the grassy plain, right, left, ahead, and back. Some cavalry were caught in the beam, and the kerls pranced nervously when the light hit their weak eyes. Nasser raised his hand to alert the troops. At his signal they would scatter to avoid the airborne attack.

No missiles or bombs erupted from the airship. Instead, it slowed and began to descend. The searchlight swung down, highlighting the patch of ground where the ship would alight. In the reverse glow, Nasser recognized the long prow, the jutting boarding mandible.

"It's *Predator*!"

The Rathi troops let out a concerted shout of relief, and hundreds rushed forward to greet the landing vessel. *Predator* dropped to within a few feet of the ground and hovered. Lamps blazed fore and aft, and against the light Nasser could see crew members scurrying about on deck.

A rope ladder unrolled to the ground, but the first man off the ship didn't use it. Greven *il*-Vec jumped from the deck, landing lightly. He stooped to clear the overhanging bulk of the airship, standing erect once he saw the Corps of Sergeants drawn up to greet him.

"Dread Lord!" Nasser said, over the throb of the hovering ship's engines. "It's good to see you!"

"Is this all that remains of the force?" Greven said sternly, surveying the men clustered around *Predator*.

Taken aback, Nasser recovered his professional demeanor and replied, "It is, Dread Lord."

"Where's Crovax?"

Nasser looked Greven in the eye. "He's not here, sir. We haven't seen him since this morning."

"What?" Greven thundered. Every man present, veteran or recruit, flinched. "Where is your commanding officer?"

Nasser explained how Crovax vanished when the strange explosion demolished his hut. He expected a further display of temper, but instead the giant warrior seemed pleased to hear of Crovax's unexpected departure.

"Gone, is he? His chance to be evincar is gone, too." Greven noticed the press of soldiers around him and snarled. "Do you men have nothing better to do than stand here, gawking like a bunch of hungry moggs?"

The relieved soldiers returned to their campfires. Greven ordered *Predator* aloft to watch for trouble while he remained on the ground. He wanted to hear a full account of the battle with the rebels. Then he announced he would personally lead the remnants of the Skyshroud Expedition into the Stronghold.

Greven got the whole story from Nasser and the sergeants. They blamed the wind and fire for their debacle and confirmed that Eladamri had Vec and Dal allies in the fight.

Greven listened to every word. His inhumanly hard features were a mask to the assembled sergeants. As Greven sat there, thinking yet saying nothing, one by one the sergeants slipped away to catch a bit of sleep. Nasser was the last to go.

"If there's nothing else, Dread Lord, I'll say good night." Greven gazed at the dying campfire. Nasser saluted curtly and disappeared into the outer darkness.

He hadn't gone ten yards before Tharvello grabbed him from behind.

"What is it?" said Nasser.

"You heard Greven back there. This means the end of Crovax, doesn't it?"

"Such decisions occur far above my head."

"Come now, you and I took up Crovax's mantle gladly, thinking it would advance us in the army and get us out from under that bastard Greven's thumb. Well, Crovax botched it! We should make amends to Greven."

"You talk like a soft-handed courtier," Nasser said. "I'll not sell my loyalty at the first sign of adversity."

Tharvello grinned. "So you're staying with Crovax?"

"I serve Rath, not any one man. If you think Crovax is finished, you're badly mistaken. Defeat or no defeat, he'll be back stronger than ever. Mark what I say."

Nasser left him.

* * * * *

Tharvello opened his hauberk and pulled out the percher he'd hidden underneath. Perchers remembered the last words spoken in their presence.

Your words are marked, Tharvello thought, stroking the winged creature.

CHAPTER 11
Banquet

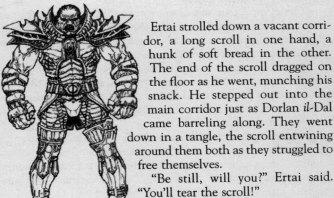

Ertai strolled down a vacant corridor, a long scroll in one hand, a hunk of soft bread in the other. The end of the scroll dragged on the floor as he went, munching his snack. He stepped out into the main corridor just as Dorlan *il*-Dal came barreling along. They went down in a tangle, the scroll entwining around them both as they struggled to free themselves.

"Be still, will you?" Ertai said. "You'll tear the scroll!"

"Help! I've no time for this foolishness! Ugh! Where is the emissary, young man?"

Ertai slid out of the tangle. "I haven't seen her."

"I must find her! She must be told about this terrible thing!"

"What terrible thing?"

Dorlan tried to shuck the coils of parchment and untangle his legs from Ertai's. "The hostages! The hostages have disappeared!"

Ertai shoved Dorlan backward. The chamberlain's head thumped on the floor, and when it did, the flowstone gripped his balding head and held it there.

Eyes wide with shock, Dorlan babbled, "You control the stone!"

143

"In small ways," Ertai replied, rising and dusting himself off. "Now, what's got you in such a panic? Six thousand people don't just disappear. Greven must have moved them."

"Greven flew out in *Predator* this morning—and not a single hostage remains in the holding area!"

His words speared Ertai through the heart. With his concentration rattled, his control of the flowstone evaporated. Freed, Dorlan sat up and clutched Ertai's leg.

"I received a report from the commissary officer not two hours ago. He went to the stockades to distribute food and water and discovered everyone was gone."

"What about the guards?"

"Gone, too." Dorlan began to weep. "There were large numbers of footprints leading out of the city into the caverns, but there's no way out of the crater there."

"Did you send anyone out to search?"

Dorlan nodded, wiping his nose on his sleeve. "Of course I did! Some came back saying the tracks lead right up the crater wall—but there's no tunnel or cave at the spot, just a blind wall! Four men were lost during the search. I fear the Death Pits—"

"What's that?"

Dorlan squirmed with reluctance. "A fable, mostly. The residue of the flowstone creation process is pumped into remote caverns and crevices. It looks like tar, but it's very poisonous. The credulous believe the Death Pits are sentient. It's just a myth."

"You said you feared it," Ertai objected.

"It is poisonous!" Dorlan began to tear up again. "If a single hostage dies, it will be very bad for us!"

"Come," said Ertai, hoisting the rotund chamberlain to his feet. "We'll find Belbe."

"I've looked and looked. No one knows where she is."

Ertai closed his eyes and held his hands six inches apart, right in front of his chest. Magical energy crackled between his palms, quickly solidifying into a spinning star-shaped object.

"What's that?" asked Dorlan, drying his eyes.

"A ferret." Ertai imparted a single mental command to his magical creation: *Find Belbe*. The star spun away. He grabbed the front of Dorlan's robe and said, "This way! Don't lose sight of it!"

They followed the flying ferret through dark halls and light, and before long it became obvious where it was going.

"She's in the great hall," Ertai said. "Where she arrived."

One of the huge doors was ajar. The spinning star hovered outside, unable to pass the powerful wards placed around the Dream Halls. Ertai dispelled the ferret with a wave of his hand. With Dorlan in tow, they entered the vast hall.

Ertai's foot crunched something. The floor was littered with shiny gray shards. It wasn't flowstone but some kind of crystal. As far as the eye could see, the concourse was peppered with the stuff.

Several yards away there was a crash, followed by the tinkle of broken bits. Ertai raced ahead and found fragments of a newly smashed globe still spinning on the mirror-black floor.

"Belbe?"

He heard a low voice muttering, and another gray globe came crashing down a few feet away. Ertai looked up and saw a figure moving in the dim heights overhead.

"Belbe?" he called more loudly.

"Go away, I'm busy."

He frowned. What had gotten into her? "It's about the hostages! They're missing!"

She was silent for a moment, then said, "Come up."

He cast about for a ladder, stairs, any way up. "How?"

"You're the magician."

Angrily, he went to one of the monumental pilasters that supported the glass roof. He placed his hands against the hard flowstone surface, and scooped handholds formed for him. He climbed steadily, noting the handholds smoothed out after he passed them. The ceiling was very high, and it took him several minutes of climbing before he reached a sort of mezzanine made of a black metal lattice, invisible from below. Here were stored all the strange devices Volrath used to explore and preserve his dreams. Belbe had been going along the platform prying out all the dream storage globes and hurling them to the floor.

She sat astride the mesh ledge, her feet dangling in the open air. Ertai cautiously slipped onto the platform and tried not to look down.

"What are you doing?" he demanded.

"It's called 'cleaning house,'" she said. "I've been getting rid of Volrath's collection of terrors and pleasures." She held up a broken shell. "In his case, there wasn't much difference."

"Belbe, the Dal, Vec, and Kor hostages are missing!"

She tossed the shell into the void. "Did they escape?"

"I don't know! Dorlan says even the guards have vanished."

"Ah. I wonder . . ."

"You know something?" He leaned over and grabbed her hand. "Belbe, what's going on? The safety of thousands is at stake!"

She looked away. "It's probably Crovax's doing."

"Crovax? Is he here?"

"Crovax has returned, and his powers have greatly increased. He could open a tunnel through the crater wall with a wave of his hand."

"By all the colors—if he hurts those people, every member of their families will join Eladamri's rebellion!"

"Crovax . . ." She gripped the mesh platform on either side, each finger in a different perforation. When she said Crovax's name, she closed her hand, tearing the enormously strong metal lattice like rotten cloth.

"Let's get down from here," she announced.

"I can make handholds, if you want to go down with me."

"Too slow." She grabbed an empty dream catcher and hugged it close. "Come here, Ertai." He crept to her. She scooped him in with her free arm. "Hold on."

"What are you—?"

Before he could finish his question, Belbe slid off the platform. They plunged down, Ertai yelling all the way. Halfway to the floor the dream catcher's wire spool tightened, slowing them. It adjusted for their extra weight and lowered them gently to the concourse.

His feet on solid ground again, Ertai said, "You could have warned me!"

"Candidates for evincar should be bold," she said. She opened her arms, releasing Ertai and the dream catcher. The empty mechanism whirred, and with a snap, flew back to the rafters.

With Dorlan in tow, Belbe and Ertai rushed out of the hall. She detoured through the garrison to turn out the palace guard.

Seal the Citadel, she ordered the guards; no one was to get in or out without her approval. Then she, Ertai, and Dorlan piled into one of Volrath's fleshstone walking machines. Even with extreme haste, it would still take a couple of hours to circumnavigate the crater to the point outside the Stronghold where the hostages' tracks had led.

* * * * *

Deep within the Skyshroud Forest lay the Eye of Korai, a flat-topped mound created over the course of several centuries by the elves of the forest. Baskets of dirt and stone were brought from outside the Skyshroud and deposited in a spot located within the densest part of the swamp. Over the years, an artificial island was created, rising some twenty-two feet above the stagnant black waters. The flat top covered an acre and a half and was paved with thousands of carefully fitted stones, brought in by hand by generations of elves. The mound was called the Eye of Korai after the great elf chieftain who began it.

Early in the rebellion, Greven *il-Vec* found the Eye from the air, and the site was badly damaged by bombs. The Eye was repaired, and a giant camouflage net was fabricated to cover the mound. Woven of living vines, the net blended in with the natural tree canopy, hiding the elves' sacred assembly site.

It was at the Eye of Korai that the elf tribes gathered to celebrate their most solemn ceremonies, to honor their dead (who were buried in tomb chambers deep in the mound), and to consult each other on important issues. It was only natural the Eye was chosen as the place Eladamri and his allies were to meet the most revered holy figure on Rath, the Oracle *en-Vec*.

No one knew her real name. She was incredibly old, far older than matriarch Tant Jova or any of her sisters. It was rumored the Oracle dwelt on other planes and could see not only the future of this world but the future of other worlds as well.

No one saw her arrive. Eladamri and his people went to bed one night after their arrival and awoke the next day to find a strange pavilion had appeared in the exact center of the Eye. The pavilion resembled a Vec nomad's tent—conical roof, sloping walls—but was larger and changed color constantly as light and shadow played over it. There was no obvious entrance. Eladamri was amused when Darsett walked around and around the pavilion, looking for a door and finding none.

"It's a blasted trick," Darsett growled.

"Of course," Eladamri said. "What better way to preserve your privacy than to live in a house without a door?"

Tant Jova and her young female bodyguards joined the Dal and elf. She leaned on the arm of one of her proud granddaughters, the warrior Liin Sivi.

"Lady, how do we speak to this oracle of yours?" Darsett finally asked.

Tant Jova answered, "You can't, O Darsett. When the Oracle has something to say, she will call you."

They lingered by the mysterious pavilion for some time, half-hoping to be summoned into the presence of the famed oracle. When minutes turned into hours, Darsett grew irritated and left. Eladamri likewise had pressing matters to attend to and took his leave. Only Tant Jova remained. Sivi found a folding stool for her grandmother to sit on and stayed with her.

After his defeat of Crovax, Eladamri sent runners to every district bearing the news. As he hoped, new recruits trickled in, wanting to fight the disarrayed government forces. He established a number of recruiting camps on the fringes of the forest. There, trusted lieutenants weeded out the treacherous and the lazy from the stream of volunteers. Those who showed commitment and staying power would be taken deeper into the Skyshroud and begin training for war.

Daylight was failing when Eladamri and Darsett were alerted by Tant Jova that a door to the oracle's tent had appeared. The three allied leaders stood side by side outside the pavilion, gazing at the fluttering canvas opening. The oracle's tent was haloed by a faint greenish glow. This troubled the Vec matriarch.

"It's a bad sign," said Tant Jova.

"How so?" asked Darsett.

"To my people, green is a color of ill-omen."

"Among mine, it's a good sign," Eladamri said cheerfully. "Green is the color of our ancient trees. Perhaps she wears this aura to honor me." Tant Jova did not look convinced.

"I suppose we should go in," Darsett murmured. Eladamri

nodded and took the lead. Darsett followed, and a worried look-ing Tant Jova brought up the rear.

Entering the tent was like walking into a fogbank. Every vis-ible feature, including the entrance, disappeared once they were inside. The faintly greenish mist smelled strongly of incense and rare spices. The odors were strong enough to make Eladamri's head swim. He kept going straight ahead—at least he assumed he was—for several yards, which didn't make sense. The pavil-ion was no more than fifteen feet across as seen from the out-side. Was he walking in some kind of dazed circle?

"Seeker, come. You are welcome," said a sourceless voice.

"Where are you?" said Eladamri.

"Here, all around you."

He fumed a little. Why were these mystical types always so obscure? "I want to speak to you face to face," he called out.

No sooner had he said so than a dark outline appeared in the mist. Eladamri approached cautiously. The silhouette resolved into a seated Vec woman, dressed in nomadic robes densely pat-terned with green and brown embroidered swirls. She sat at a tall, bowl-shaped table filled with a silver liquid. Her face was averted, her arms gripped the bowl on either side.

"Are you the Oracle *en*-Vec?" asked Eladamri.

"I'd hoped your first question would be more intelligent."

Startled by her impudence, the elf leader replied, "What is this? Did you admit me to snipe at my wits?"

"Peace, O Eladamri. Take no offense at my free tongue. When past, present and future exist in your mind at the same time, it's difficult to spare enough thought for manners."

She raised her head. Eladamri had heard the oracle was an aged crone, but the face he saw was as fresh as an open lily. He took her to be no more than fifteen years old.

"I'm much older than that," said the oracle. "What you see is an illusion I will you to see."

"You read minds?"

"When they're simple enough, I peer behind the thinker's eyes and read his words before they form on his lips."

"More insults! Why am I here, O Oracle?"

She blew on the surface of the bowl, and the silver liquid rippled to the edge and back. "Your cause is just, O Eladamri, and your triumphs genuine, but final victory is beyond your grasp."

"All things are possible with the gods' help," he said. "Are you telling me the rebellion is doomed?"

"It will never succeed on Rath."

He didn't want to believe it. For all his invocation of the gods, Eladamri was a realist, believing first and foremost in Eladamri. It rankled him for this ancient oracle, this freak, to tell him flatly his cause was hopeless.

"Not hopeless," she said. "You will defeat your enemies one day, elf lord, and be hailed as the savior of a world not your own."

"Enough vagaries," he said. "Tell me something useful. What is Crovax doing at this moment?"

She pursed her brown lips and blew again over the silver pool. Though Eladamri could see nothing in it, the oracle peered closely at the bowl. She shuddered violently and struck the fluid mirror with the palm of her hand.

"Oh! Oh!" was all the Oracle could say.

"What is it?"

"Horrible! I cannot—"

"What?"

"Blood and more blood . . . he feasts on their lives! Abomination!"

Eladamri leaned forward, resting his hand on the edge of the bowl. He thrust his face close to the oracle's and for a instant caught a glimpse of her true visage—deeply wrinkled skin the color of mud, sunken eyes, a nose little more than two holes in her face. He blinked and the impression was gone. The dewy eyed girl was back.

"Speak plainly," he urged. "I must know Crovax's doings."

"I cannot speak it. . . ." she whispered.

He turned away in disgust. "This is useless! Can you tell me nothing of value?"

"Two things, O Eladamri. Your destiny lies in the Stronghold, not in the forest or on the plain. A door will be offered to you, and you must enter. To do otherwise is to doom all you cherish!"

"The Stronghold! Should I attack there before a new evincar is chosen? Is that what you're telling me?"

The oracle sagged in her chair, covering her face with her hands. "No . . . no attack on the Stronghold will succeed. It will fall to the quietest of all, no man, no elf. You must go there in chains, O Eladamri. Go in chains, go in chains. The Dead One will open a door for you, and you must go."

"I don't understand! Will I be captured? Is that what you mean?"

The mist thickened between them. He tried to reach through it and take hold of the oracle, but it was like seizing a shadow.

"Where will this door take me?" he cried.

Her reply was a fast fading whisper. "To a land of light and color. Go there. Go there and be the Korvecdal . . ."

The mist disappeared, and Eladamri found himself standing in the open atop the Eye of Korai. The oracle's tent was gone. Darsett and Tant Jova were a few feet away, their eyes closed. Eladamri shook off the aftereffects of the oracle's intense illusions and called to his friends.

Both awoke at the same time.

"She's gone!" said Darsett.

"Was she ever here?" Eladamri asked, even though he knew the answer.

"I heard everything," Tant Jova said. "Her prophecies and her proclaiming you the Korvecdal!"

"I heard it too, but I couldn't see or speak," Darsett said, puzzled.

"Yes, yes," Tant Jova said. "The word must be shouted in every village and every tent—Eladamri is the Promised One. Eladamri is the Korvecdal!"

Rebels on the mound gathered quickly when they heard the Vec matriarch shout. They took up the refrain, "The Promised One! The Korvecdal!" and shouted it as loudly as they could, over and over. Liin Sivi and Gallan raised Eladamri on their shoulders. Despite his misgivings about the oracle's murky predictions, Eladamri was vastly relieved. All his life he had dreamt of this moment. So much had been sacrificed, not least by him—his wife, his only child, a safe and normal life—all lost to the dark forces of the Stronghold. Now the final fight could begin. He would be the Korvecdal, no matter what gloomy and ambiguous prophecies the Oracle *en*-Vec made.

They carried Eladamri around the perimeter of the Eye, shouting and singing war songs. They were about to start a second circuit when four weary, bleeding elves appeared at the edge of the mound. The triumphant parade abruptly ceased, and Eladamri was set back on his feet.

He greeted the harried new arrivals. "I know you, Brother," he said to the eldest elf in the group. "You're Raydon, of Moss-bridge village?"

"I am. Health to you, Brother." Raydon had a number of siz-able sword cuts on his arms and visible blade marks on his breastplate. "My nephews and I are all that's left of a band forty strong. We were on our way here to join you, Eladamri, when we were attacked by the evincar's flying ship."

Alarm ricocheted through the crowd.

"What?" said Darsett. "*Predator* flies again?"

"It does, or its twin," said the weary Raydon. "We took a shortcut across the plain from Mossbridge, and the devils fell upon us without warning."

"You have hand weapon injuries," Eladamri said. "How did that happen?"

"It was their method, Brother," said the elf. "They did not rain fire and arrows on us, as in the past. The flying ship alighted, and a hundred soldiers came out. Greven *il*-Vec led them."

Mention of the Rathi warlord provoked fresh outcries for vengeance. Eladamri quieted his friends and allies.

"This changes much," he said. "I had hoped to forge an army to meet the Stronghold's soldiers in open combat, but we dare not expose ourselves to destruction from the air."

"What can we do?" asked Gallan.

Eladamri pondered for a moment. "We must go on," he said. "We'll go back to the old ways—ambush, hit the enemy, and run. We'll steal their weapons and bide our time as our strength grows."

"We can't win by ambushing outposts," said Darsett.

"It's that flying ship," Tant Jova said, striking the ground with her staff. "Without it, the Stronghold would collapse like a rotten cask!"

The allies fell to arguing strategy. Voices rose as they dis-agreed on how to fight under the threat of aerial attack.

Gallan turned to Eladamri. "What is our best course of action, Brother?"

"Destroy the flying ship."

"You make it sound easy," Darsett said sourly.

"It won't be easy," Eladamri answered, "but it must be done."

"But how? *Predator* roosts inside the Stronghold," Gallan objected.

"Yes."

Darsett snorted, "Are you proposing we storm the Stronghold just to destroy the flying ship?"

"Not 'storm,' Darsett. Just pay a little visit, a few friends and I."

Tant Jova looked stunned. "You're not going to raid the Stronghold, O Eladamri!"

"No," he said. "I'm going to give myself up."

* * * * *

It would have been faster to seek Crovax by air, but Greven had taken *Predator* to find the Skyshroud Expeditionary Force, so they were forced to rely on one of Volrath's old two-legged walkers. The Headless Turkey, as Ertai called it, lumbered across the undulating landscape below the crater. The walker made slow progress over this uneven terrain.

Opposite the Stronghold's main causeway, the plain was level and covered with knee-high yellow grass. As the Turkey climbed out of a shallow gully, Belbe's acute eyes spotted a smudge on the horizon—a crowd of people.

"Faster," she said.

Volrath's old machine covered the flat ground at an admirable clip, each sweep of the metal-toed feet tearing up a dusty divot. Ertai was at the controls, which consisted of two levers, one each for the right and left leg. He had them shoved forward as far as they would go, maximum speed. Belbe stood at the front of the car, hand to her brow, scanning ahead for obstacles. Bouncing in the back was Dorlan, gripping the sides of the walker with white-knuckled hands.

When they were still a mile away from the evident crowd, Belbe stiffened and signaled for Ertai to slow down. He hauled back on the levers, bringing the Turkey from a gallop to a lazy lope.

"What do you see?" asked Dorlan.

"People," she replied, puzzled. "They seem to be floating above the ground."

A far-off shriek reached out to them, a thin wail of pure terror and utmost anguish. Ertai dropped his hands, and the walker stopped.

"He's not—!"

"He is." Belbe vaulted over the side. It was eight feet to the ground, but she landed lightly on her toes and took off running. Ertai shoved the controls forward, sending the walker pounding after the fleet emissary.

Belbe covered the last eight hundred yards in seconds. What she thought were people "floating" was not that at all. Ahead the plain was thickly studded with sharp poles, formed from the flowstone substrate under the thin layer of topsoil. Impaled on the poles were the hostages—thousands of them.

Belbe stopped, frozen in her tracks by the scene before her. Crovax had commanded the spikes to thrust out of the ground, impaling the victims where they stood. Some died immediately. Others took time to find death, and a few still clung to life. Their moans were like a swirling wind, coming from every direction at once.

She didn't hear the walker thump to a halt behind her. It squatted, and Ertai got out. Dorlan couldn't. He buried his face in his hands and sobbed.

Next thing Belbe knew, Ertai's hand was on her shoulder. She shrugged it off.

"How could he do this?" Ertai whispered.

"His power over flowstone is developing exponentially," Belbe said. "He's learned to fix the forms into permanent shapes. Impressive."

"Impressive? How can you say this savage is impressive?" Ertai took a step back, a horrified look on his face.

Slowly, Belbe walked into the forest of death. Most of the poles were eight to ten feet high, tall enough that the victim's feet couldn't reach the ground. The gray metal spikes were black with gore, and the air was heavy with the smell of blood. Ertai tried to follow Belbe, but within a few yards he broke down, nauseated.

Dazed, Belbe wound her way through the maze of spikes.

Since they'd sprung up wherever a person had been standing, there was no order, no pattern to their placement. Where a family huddled together for safety, a spike for each of them had erupted. Standing alone was no safer. Many victims looked as though they were caught in mid-stride. Age and gender made no difference—all had fallen to Crovax's insatiable vengeance.

A scream came from close by. Numbly, Belbe turned toward the sound. She saw a band of moggs manhandling a Dal man. Without thinking, she hurled herself at them, lashing out at the loathsome gremlins with her fists and feet. Bewildered, the moggs let their prey go and fled, whooping.

Belbe tried to help the man stand, but he was crazed with fear and kept trying to crawl away on all fours.

"It's all right, it's all right," Belbe said over and over. The man, mired in gore, looked up at her and started to speak.

His words were cut short by a spike bursting from the ground beneath him. It thrust up so powerfully that the man was carried four feet in the air before Belbe could even react. She grasped the still growing post and tried to break it, but even her considerable strength could not affect a metal pole eight feet tall and now almost seven inches thick. Blood cascaded down the pole over Belbe's hands. Trembling, she backed away and screamed.

Ertai heard her cry. Sick and shaken, he ran to her, calling her name. He dodged around a cluster of thick spikes, and they fell into each other's arms. Belbe was bathed in gore up to her elbows, and a thick spray of blood had at some point struck her in the face.

"Belbe! Belbe!" he shouted, shaking her by the shoulders. He raised a hand to strike her, but with her lightning reflexes she caught his hand long before it could connect.

"Hit me and I'll kill you!" she cried. To emphasize her point she squeezed his hand. Ertai bent his legs to relieve the pressure on his hand, and Belbe forced him to his knees.

"Don't hurt me," he said. "Haven't enough people been hurt today?"

Suddenly shamed, she released him. "Crovax. I must find Crovax."

Blood and dust made a dense brown mud that clung to Ertai's knees. "I'll go with you."

They wandered through what seemed like an endless field of carnage. Ertai kept his eyes on the ground, but Belbe gazed wide-eyed at every horror. The sights and smells of death assaulted her at every turn, and the relentlessly analytical mind given to her by her Phyrexian masters made her catalog each victim as she passed:

Male, Dal, estimated age, 60. Impaled through the chest.

Male, Vec, estimated age, 72. Impaled through thigh, abdomen, armpit.

Female, Vec, estimated age, 11. Impaled through foot, thigh, and head.

Female, Dal, estimated age, 44. Impaled through abdomen.

Female, Dal, 28. Impaled.

Male, Vec, 6.

Female, Kor.

Female.

Female.

Male . . .

Ertai was clutching her hand. She ceased her macabre catalog and said, "Do you still want the job?"

"How can I defeat a man who does things like this?" he said. "How can you allow a monster like him to rule this entire world?"

"I must choose the best candidate for evincar," Belbe said faintly. "I exist to make this choice."

Belbe heard voices ahead. Ertai dropped her hand and went on. Belbe followed, methodically counting the dead.

At the epicenter of the death field was a clear space twenty yards wide. In the midst of the clearing sat Crovax at a long rectangular table covered in a spotless white tablecloth. His back was to them. Assorted moggs armed with axes and clubs stood idle around the edge of the clearing. Others in weirdly comic livery—fancy velvet uniforms and wigs—bore silver trenchers laden with food to the table.

"Welcome, Excellency," Crovax said, keeping his back turned. "Is my rival, young Ertai, with you?"

"Bastard," Ertai spat, starting forward. Belbe restrained him.

"Are we having lunch?" she said. Some coolness had returned to her voice. The sight of Crovax gave needed focus to her outraged senses.

"A light repast. It's been a busy morning. Please join me."

Ertai's face purpled, but Belbe cautioned him with a glance. "I do not eat, but thank you," she said. She motioned Ertai to follow her.

They circled the end of the table Crovax had raised from the ground. Two high-backed chairs bubbled up and solidified across from Crovax. Belbe slid gracefully into one chair. Ertai fell heavily into the other.

It was an extraordinary scene. Crovax had discarded his customary black garb and was clad instead all in white—bloodless, sterile white, without a speck of gore or dirt on him. A white mantle, edged in gold, draped across his shoulders, and on his head he wore a plain circlet wrought in gold and white enamel. He'd cut off his long pigtail at neck length and let his hair hang loosely. Had he not been backed by a panorama of violent death, Crovax would have been the epitome of a peaceful, civilized monarch.

"Wine?" he said. A mogg, in an ill-fitting white cravat, hopped to Belbe's elbow and held out a silver urn. "It's one of Volrath's vintages. He drank it for pleasure, I'm told." Belbe said nothing, so the mogg filled the heavy crystal goblet by her plate. The wine was brilliantly scarlet and smelled faintly of flowers.

"Give some to the boy, too. I assume he can drink," Crovax said. The mogg waddled to Ertai.

"Why have you done this?" Belbe said. "Why slaughter these innocent people?"

"You surprise me, Excellency. Didn't the overlords teach you that the most valuable tool of rulership is fear? This small exercise will insure the loyalty—or at least, the compliance—of the civil population during the coming campaign against Eladamri."

"Small exercise?" Ertai shouted. His goblet overturned, spilling bright red wine over the snowy tablecloth. Before it lapped the undersides of the heavy silver dishes, the scarlet liquid vanished, as did Ertai's cup.

"No more wine for you," Crovax said.

"Five thousand, eight hundred sixty-eight killed hardly qualifies as a 'small exercise,'" Belbe said.

"It's more than a thousand," he said, tweaking her for her lie. "But they were expendable. Dorlan chose only the old and the weak."

"You're a monster," Ertai said flatly.

Crovax sawed off a bit of rare cutlet and forked it into his mouth. "This from the boy who would be evincar! I'm told the hostage idea was yours."

"No one was supposed to get hurt."

"You're sentimental, Ertai," Crovax said. "There's no room for sentiment on Rath."

"What you call sentiment, I call prudence," Belbe said. She could see her reflection in the empty silver plate before her. The wild, blood-smeared face could hardly be hers. "Your actions are precipitate, Crovax. There's no evidence the people of the Stronghold intended to rise in rebellion against us. It is you who've given them common cause with Eladamri by murdering their families."

"With all respect, Excellency, you don't know what you're talking about. I was with the army when we were ambushed by the rebels. There were Dal and Vec warriors with the Skyshroud elves."

"So you avenge your defeat on helpless old people and children?" said Ertai.

"Yes." He sipped wine. "As evincar, I will brook no resistance to my rule. The only law of the realm shall be—obey, or die."

"You're not evincar yet," Belbe said.

Crovax slammed down his goblet, snapping the stem. "Then declare me so! Now!"

"There are other factors to consider."

"What? Him?" Crovax whipped a knife off the table and thrust it at Ertai. "I can kill him without leaving my chair!"

"We've seen what you've learned to do," Belbe replied. "Your mastery of the flowstone increases daily, but you lost a battle and a sizable part of your army with it. You show little understanding of how people should be governed, relying on naked force instead of statesmanship. In short, Crovax, your methods are inefficient, and as far as I'm concerned, the issue of who will succeed Volrath is still unresolved!"

He sat back. "You constantly amaze me, Excellency. Of course, you're right. We'll see in the coming days who the best man is, won't we?"

CHAPTER 12
Ghost

Beneath the main causeway leading into the Stronghold, the remnants of the Skyshroud Expeditionary Force marshaled, awaiting the orders of Greven il-Vec. *Predator* droned overhead, searching the wide plains for the enemy. The airship had attacked several bands of rebels the previous day, landing troops beside (and sometimes among) the startled foe. These small actions had done much to restore the army's morale, and Crovax or no Crovax, they were marching into the Stronghold as an army, not a defeated rabble.

A percher landed on Greven's shoulder. "Urgent from *Predator!* Urgent from *Predator!*" it squawked.

He hated the raucous, leathery creatures. "What now?"

"Unknown intruder! Unknown intruder—" Greven grasped the irritating creature by the neck. The percher's heart fluttered wildly.

"Land in the hollow below Three-Toe Hill," he said to the messenger. "I will meet you there."

He flung the percher into the air. It circled once, then flapped away to find the airship.

Greven hollered orders at Nasser. "Take the men to their barracks. Send the wounded to the healers, then confine everyone to quarters until I return."

"Trouble?" asked Nasser.

He had no idea but answered, "No."

Three-Toe Hill was a forty-foot high promontory half a mile east of the causeway. There was a wide but shallow hollow below the hill where the airship could land and not be seen while on the ground. By the time Greven walked there as no kerl existed big enough to carry him, *Predator* was waiting.

The airship's boatswain, Narmer by name, was on the ground waiting for Greven. He ran up the slope when the commander's huge silhouette appeared on the hilltop.

"Dread Lord!"

"What's this about an intruder? Can't you handle a lone man on foot?" said Greven.

"There's more to it than that, Dread Lord." Narmer looked quite disturbed. He wrung his hands and scuffed his feet continuously in the dry turf. "I thought this should be brought to your attention immediately."

"All right." Greven unlocked his jaw. "Let's find this intruder of yours."

Narmer put a hand to the warrior's massive chest. Greven was frankly surprised the boatswain dared touch him.

"There's no need, Dread Lord."

"What? Why not?"

"We picked him up," Narmer said. He pointed to *Predator*, hovering a few feet off the ground. A figure appeared at the rail, deeply clothed in the shadow of the hill behind them. "He wishes to speak to you."

Greven went slowly to the dangling rope ladder. For one of the few times in his life, he actually experienced a feeling of dread. The shadowed figure leaned on the rail. As Greven's eyes accustomed to the shade, he saw the intruder's face.

* * * * *

"Eladamri, you're insane."

Darsett *en*-Dal and the inner circle of the rebellion were

Nemesis

eated in the great room of Eladamri's home. Their host sat on
he floor by the door, casually whittling a block of wood. The
garnet on the pommel of his carving knife gleamed in the cool
light of four foxfire lamps.

"I mean that with all due respect," Darsett added when no
one seconded his opinion. "What I mean is, this scheme of yours
seems far more desperate than circumstances require."

"I've been hunted by the airship for years," Eladamri replied.
He scored a hole in the end of the stick and blew away loose
wood chips. "My wife died in an airship attack. There's no way
he rebellion can proceed with that machine flying over us,
spying on everything we do and raining death on us from
above."

"Granted, O Eladamri, but why must you go on this raid?
How do you know Greven il-Vec won't have you killed on the
spot?" said Tant Jova.

"I know him," said the elf. "If he thinks he can lay hands on
me, killing me is the last thing he'll want to do. Greven will
want to know all the details of the rebellion, including the
names of my allies." He smiled at his Dal and Vec friends. "In
either case he'll want me alive, for a time. That's all I need."

In the past few weeks, Eladamri had aged noticeably. The
hard, determined elf he'd always been had given way to a con-
templative, almost wistful one. He'd not worn a helmet since
meeting the Oracle en-Vec, going bare headed with his long hair
tied back in a rough ponytail. Deep lines etched his face, and his
eyes betrayed a weariness never present before.

"I wish you'd let some of us go with you," Gallan said.

"That would only increase the danger," Eladamri replied.
There are no elves in the evincar's army, and my escort must
pass close inspection as Rathi soldiers."

"There are no women in Volrath's army, either," Gallan
protested. "Yet Liin Sivi is going with you!"

"Sivi is the best fighter in my clan," Tant Jova protested.
She's an adept of the *toten-vec*." This was the unique whip-knife
combination weapon used only by female warrior societies of the
Vec. "I'm not happy Eladamri has chosen this course, but I feel
better in my heart if Sivi is with him in the Stronghold."

"It's settled," Eladamri said. He slipped together the two

halves of the fetish he'd carved. A little glue and the joint would be invisible. "We'll leave tomorrow at sunset. Do we have enough captured uniforms and equipment?"

"Enough for a regiment," Darsett said, grinning. "There's a surfeit of officer's outfits. We can all be Rathi officers if we want. They died especially often."

"If I show up at the Stronghold the prisoner of ten officers, I think they'll be a little suspicious," Eladamri said. "It would be best if you went as the lowliest of privates."

Eladamri's plan called for a hand-picked force of ten warriors drawn from his Dal and Vec allies to don Rathi uniforms. They would walk to the Stronghold with Eladamri as their "prisoner" and present him to the authorities there. Once inside the Stronghold, they would find where *Predator* was moored and destroy the airship. Gallan and Tant Jova would assemble the rebel army, now almost eleven thousand strong, and when Eladamri and his team returned, a full scale war on the Stronghold would commence.

"What if you don't find the *Predator* conveniently docked, waiting for destruction?" asked Gallan.

"Then we'll wait until it returns," replied the elf leader.

"And if Greven murders you before the airship comes back?"

Eladamri was momentarily silent while he bored a hole in the top half of the image he was making. He licked the end of a length of string and threaded it through the hole.

"This war is not about me, Gallan. Understand that now. Whether I live or die, this is not Eladamri's rebellion. It belongs to every free person on Rath, not to me. If I die on this operation or any other, you must fight on, do you hear? Otherwise everything we've fought for becomes just vanity, an empty struggle for glory. Will you swear to carry on the fight no matter what happens to me?"

"It is sworn, O Eladamri," said Tant Jova.

"I swear," Liin Sivi added.

"You're a fool," Darsett said, scratching his bearded cheek. "A gallant, dedicated fool I'm proud to know. I swear, too."

Gallan was alone. Everyone in the room watched him struggle for the words.

"I will fight on," he said at last. "But if you die, I further swear to show no mercy to Crovax, Greven *il*-Vec, or any other Stronghold leader. They will all die—by my hand, if necessary."

Eladamri continued to carve. The pile of white shavings at his feet grew larger.

"Thank you, Gallan," he said.

* * * * *

"Crovax's army has returned," Ertai said.

He was standing by one of the odd, protruding egg-shaped windows in the evincar's quarters. Far below, he could see the soldiers fanning out from the causeway to the Dal city located on the lip of the crater wall. Overnight word had spread about the massacre, and there'd been trouble in all the settlements. Nothing major—no attacks were made on the Citadel—but small bands of outraged city dwellers had roamed the streets all night. Some moggs had been killed and small groups of soldiers set upon, but when the Citadel garrison turned out, the troublemakers went home. The knowledge that both Crovax and Greven were present in the crater deterred the common folk from taking matters too far.

Inside the Citadel, however, a siege mentality took over. Patrols constantly circled inside the fortress, making sure all entrances were secure. Dorlan *il*-Dal was prostrate after witnessing the aftermath of Crovax's revenge, and he had abandoned his regular duties. Fearing assassination, courtiers locked themselves in their rooms. Belbe withdrew to the evincar's suite. Before long, Ertai joined her, his clothes stuffed with scrolls borrowed from the Citadel's libraries. They spoke little. Ertai dragged a chaise to the window and read there, occasionally glancing outside to see what was happening. Belbe huddled in one of Volrath's oversized chairs, her knees drawn up to her chin. She stayed there for a complete night and half of the following day.

"I'm afraid," she finally said.

Ertai looked up from his scroll. "Why are you afraid? You're the emissary of Phyrexia. Of the people here, you're probably the safest one of all. No one dares harm you."

"Perhaps I misuse the word. I've never felt this way before. I think it's fear."

"What are you afraid of?"

"Hurting someone."

Ertai left the chaise and leaned on the arm of Belbe's chair. "You're afraid of hurting someone else, not being hurt yourself?"

"Yes."

"Who're you afraid of hurting?"

"Crovax."

The young sorcerer did a double take. "By all the colors," he said. "Why should you be afraid of that?"

"Because I *want* to hurt him. I think about it all the time. I want to break his limbs, put out his eyes, dismember him, castrate him—"

"I get the idea," Ertai said hastily. "No one would weep if you did kill Crovax."

She seized his hand in a powerful grip. "Listen to what I say! I want to *hurt* him, and when I'm done, I want to hurt him all over again. Killing him would be mercy. I don't want him to find any mercy!"

"Belbe, my hand—"

"At first the images were just fleeting. I could distract myself with other things. In the Dream Halls I broke Volrath's dream records because I really wanted to break Crovax's skull."

Her fingers were digging into his flesh. Ertai tried to pry her fingers loose, but even his newly grown muscles were no match for Belbe's enhanced strength.

"I'm not supposed to care what Crovax does so long as it serves the purposes of my masters. His methods are coarse, but he is the strongest candidate for evincar. Why don't I name him to the post and depart? I have the means. I'm not responsible for the people here. Is it because I know in time Crovax will kill every living thing on this world to feed his appetite for destruction?"

Ertai made a fist and hit Belbe as hard as he could on the jaw. Her head snapped back, and for a brief instant he saw the light of rage in her eyes. His heart shrank to a hard ball, and a hollow place opened in the pit of his stomach. Belbe must have seen the expression of fear on Ertai's face, and she abruptly released him. He backed away quickly, rubbing his sorely bruised hand.

"I'm sorry. I didn't mean to hurt you, Ertai."

"I hope I'm not around when you do mean to hurt someone," he said ruefully. His mood quickly changed. "Do you really have a way to leave Rath?"

"Of course. I cannot allow you to go," she said, lowering her feet to the floor.

"Even if it means Crovax kills me?"

"Yes."

Ertai paced up and down. "You know I can't compete with him for the evincar post. Although my knowledge and talent far exceed his, I can't match him in sheer power."

"No one can. Crovax feeds on death. Every time something near him dies, he absorbs the life-force from it, increasing his own power. Combined with his innate lust for destruction, no one will be able to stop him."

"How long have you known this?"

She lowered her head to her knees. "It became clear to me yesterday. I kept trying to determine why his power keeps increasing, despite the mistakes he makes. Then I realized his modifications on Phyrexia were largely neurological, not mechanical. Though he was obviously given muscular and size enhancements, the important changes must have been made on the inside. He still eats food like a normal being of flesh, but it's just a habit he hasn't given up yet. His command of the flow-stone is growing exponentially. It doesn't come from rare cutlets and sour wine. Obviously, he has another source of power.

"Then I realized what was happening—the deaths of so many soldiers in battle fed Crovax enough energy for him to teleport for the first time from the battlefield to the Citadel. Slaughter of the hostages has boosted his power a thousandfold more. Soon he'll be unstoppable. That's why I want to hurt him. I want him to know what it feels like to suffer at another's hands."

For a moment, Ertai forgot about escape. "Why don't you kill him? He'll kill us both if we get in his way."

"I must put the best possible candidate on the throne of Rath."

"Why?" he shouted. The flowstone around him rose in a hundred tiny peaks.

"It's my purpose," she replied hotly. "It's the reason I exist."

"I have a notion for you, Belbe. Exist to be yourself! Loyalty is an admirable trait, but you can't cling to it in the face of certain destruction!"

She stalked across the floor, flattening the flowstone waves with her feet. An inch from his face she stopped.

"This is why you and your kind will fail—you think only of yourselves, your own petty individual concerns above the welfare of your race! My masters will destroy you and anyone else who stands in their way. It's the law of nature that the efficient shall displace the inefficient . . ."

Ertai carefully lifted her hand and clasped it with his own. "You're the same race as I," he said. "You've no common cause with beings whose sole purpose is to force people like us into slavery."

His touch was firm and warm. Belbe stared at him, at their hands. She dropped Ertai's hand and turned away.

He put his arms around her. Unlike Crovax, his touch was gentle. "Why do you always turn away at the last moment?" he said.

"I cannot do what I imagine."

"Why not? What stops you?"

Belbe shuddered. "I am not alone and never have been. There is a . . . device in my body which transmits everything I see and do to my masters on Phyrexia."

He turned Belbe to face him. "Where is this device?" She took his hand and pressed the tips of his fingers to her breastbone. He felt the curved surface of the Lens imbedded there.

"Can it be removed?"

"Perhaps on Phyrexia. Not here."

He closed his eyes and probed the Lens with his mind. Touching it, even psychically, was like entering a vast empty well, black and bottomless. There seemed no end to it, as it stretched all the way from Rath to the secret plane of her overlords.

Belbe lowered her head to his shoulder.

Ertai sighed in awe. "That thing could swallow me whole."

"Could you break it, or block it?" she murmured. "At least for a little while?"

"Hmm, maybe. Your masters can't bear the natural life-force, right? Perhaps if I send a charge of such energy into this device it will blind them."

He cupped his palms together over the imbedded orb and summoned all the natural magic he could reach on this unnatural world. Belbe felt a buildup of heat in her chest. It didn't burn, but slowly diffused outward through her neck, arms, and abdomen. Ertai removed his hands.

"Did it work?" she asked.

"There's no way to know for certain."

She draped her arms around his neck. "I don't care anymore. I'm tired of being a lens. I want to be alone with you, if only for a while."

* * * * *

After some hours in each other's arms, Ertai was spent and Belbe drained of her stormy emotions. He fell asleep on the chaise. She watched him a while, breathing deeply, his lips just apart. His hair was russet brown now, and next to her pale skin the increasing grayness of his flesh was quite noticeable. He was indeed beginning to resemble a lesser version of Greven *il-Vec*.

Belbe got up, careful not to disturb her sleeping lover. She was cold, and though she tried to dispel the goose pimples on her arms and legs, she found she couldn't. This puzzled her until she decided it must be due to Ertai's spell. Her Phyrexian systems weren't meant to handle natural magic, and her loss of metabolic control was probably due to the presence of his magical charge in her system. She glanced back at the naked, sleeping Ertai. It was worth it.

She wandered through the empty suite, letting her fingers drift across Volrath's strange artwork. She hadn't touched them before, and she discovered some of the statues had latent flowstone responses to being touched. Though they looked like stone, when caressed the statues became soft as velvet, supple as leather, and warm to the touch. What a strange person the evincar must have been, wasting his intimacy on inanimate, though responsive, objects.

In Volrath's bedroom, she paused by the mirror. Her hair was disheveled, her face flushed, and her lips bruised. These were superficial things. Belbe stood closer to the mirror. She traced the line of her face and throat as she had on Volrath's statues. Her skin was cool to the touch, and it didn't change texture as her fingertip passed over it. Why was that? Was she less responsive than flowstone? No one would have said so two hours ago. Now that her passion was spent, was she the same as she was before?

* * * * *

Ertai rolled over, empty arms seeking Belbe. Not finding her, he opened his eyes. Across the chamber, in the shadowed recesses of the ceiling, he saw what looked like a suit of black armor hanging by its feet from the ceiling. The armor moved.

Ertai bolted from the chaise.

"Who is it?" he demanded. He raised his hand. "Come down, or I'll knock you down!"

Lilting laughter was his answer. The intruder dropped from the ceiling, somersaulted, and landed on his feet.

"Crovax!"

"Congratulations, Boy," Crovax said. "Met the emissary on equal terms, have you?"

"How long have you been there?"

"Long enough. Who would've thought the overlords would send us such a spirited representative?" He sauntered over and picked up a piece of Belbe's discarded clothing. Ertai snatched it from his hand.

Crovax laughed. "Now you're going to defend her, as any rustic swain would."

"You're a filthy animal," Ertai said. He was terrified to be found like this by Crovax, his fear compounded by not knowing what Crovax would do to him or Belbe.

"And you're a stupid boy, today's performance not withstanding." Crovax sat down on the same chaise where Ertai and Belbe had made love. "It's a good trick, though, I'll give you that. Seducing the emissary is bound to be good for your candidacy."

"That's not what happened!"

Crovax's dark eyes shone. "Are you going to tell me it's love?"

"I-I don't know."

There was a sharp intake of breath. Both men saw Belbe

standing in the doorway. Ertai snatched up the first available garment—his doublet—and hurriedly draped it around her.

"The proper answer was 'yes,'" Crovax said, stretching.

"Shut up!" Ertai said.

Crovax stood, hands falling slowly to his sides. "You're welcome to try and make me, Boy."

"What passed between us was not about human love," Belbe said archly. "I had some curiosity about the practice of copulation, and Ertai was obliging me."

"So I saw. If all you wanted was experience, you could have done better," Crovax said. "I'm always available for Your Excellency's enlightenment."

Ertai started forward, but Belbe stopped him.

"Don't," she said. "He's trying to provoke you. I've seen it before."

Crovax shrugged and sat down again. "Better listen to her, Boy. I can kill you any time I want." He flung out his hand suddenly. Ertai flinched, affording Crovax a hearty laugh. "You're not a total fool. You're smart enough to be afraid of me."

"What do you want, Crovax?" said Belbe.

"I came to tell Your Excellency that order has been restored in the Stronghold cities," he said. "When the army returned, I posted soldiers in every square, tavern, inn, and gathering place in the crater. There'll be no more trouble."

"Good. You may go."

"One thing, Excellency. Since Master Ertai has 'obliged' you, don't you think it prejudices you in the matter of his candidacy?"

"I will choose the new evincar based on total ability, not by military or magical skill—or biological prowess."

Crovax chuckled and made to leave. He'd gone a few steps when Belbe, moving with blinding speed, rushed up behind him. She uttered a short, sharp cry. Crovax whirled, but his fists met only air. Belbe lashed out with her bare foot. It caught him under the right breast and he flew backwards, his cuirass deeply dented from the blow.

"Belbe, don't!" Ertai shouted.

Crovax sprang to his feet, and the flowstone furniture between them coalesced into a solid wall seven feet high and four inches thick. Belbe could not stop her rush in time to avoid slamming into the barrier. Crovax grinned, and the wall slammed Belbe twice more. He was about to smash her against the wall of the Citadel when she leaped over the ponderous bludgeon and landed a kick squarely on Crovax's forehead. Down he went, but the floor boosted him back to his feet. Crovax had a sword, but he didn't draw it. Instead he willed the floor to hold Belbe by the ankles—but he was too slow. She leaped to a nearby pillar made of natural iron—outside Crovax's influence—and clung there by her fingertips and toes, panting.

Crovax shucked off his breastplate, wincing from the blows he'd taken.

"You've made your point, Excellency," he said. "I shouldn't try to bully you. But in the interests of—shall we say, efficiency?—will you set a date at which time you will name the new Evincar of Rath?"

Belbe remained on the pillar, her hair awry, looking like one of Volrath's exotic statues. She drew a deep breath, swallowed, and said, "I will set a date."

"When?"

She glanced at a timepiece on the wall. The Phyrexian numerals dissolved into simplified Rathi ones.

"Two days from now. At midday exactly."

Crovax slung his dented armor over one shoulder and bowed slightly. "I await Your Excellency's wise decision."

When he was gone, Belbe dropped to the floor. Ertai hurried to her, thinking to comfort her. He found her shaking from head to foot.

"It's all right," he said. "He won't hurt you. He dares not, at least until you choose the next evincar."

Belbe wasn't shaking from fear. "That was wonderful!" she declared. "I want to demolish him with my bare hands!"

Ertai dropped his comforting arms. Without another word, he retrieved his discarded clothes and hurriedly dressed. Belbe was so overcome with excitement she didn't even notice him until, half-dressed, he started to leave.

"Where are you going?" she asked.

"To the library," he replied coldly. "I've a lot of reading to do. My final examination is in two days, is it not?"

He slammed the ornate flowstone door behind him.

Nemesis

* * * * *

Sergeant Nasser, bathed and attired in a fresh uniform, waited on Crovax's pleasure in the evincar's council room.

"I have my account of the army's march back to the Stronghold, my lord," Nasser said, holding up a slim scroll. When Crovax did not reply, he laid it on the star-shaped table before him.

"Where is Greven *il-Vec*?" asked Crovax.

"Called away to the airship. Something about an intruder on the east plain."

"I see. Let him chase as many wanderers as he likes. In two days, the overlords' emissary will convene a special assembly. Her purpose is to name the new Evincar of Rath."

"The choice is clear, my lord."

"So you say, but our esteemed emissary is under all sorts of pressures and influences. In such circumstances, she may not make the correct decision. We can't let that happen."

"No, my lord."

"Tomorrow, I want the Corps of Sergeants to return to the Citadel—all of them. Every man is to bring his sword, shield, helmet, and dagger."

"The palace guards won't allow armed troops inside," Nasser protested.

"Then smuggle the arms in! Use your imagination." Crovax glowered. "The ceremony will be at midday two days from now. At midday less two hours I want the Corps of Sergeants to gather in the evincar's antechamber. Arrive in twos and threes—don't come in a body. Be fully armed."

Nasser nodded. He knew what Crovax intended, but part of the price of his complicity was making his new lord and master admit it out loud.

"What do you intend, lord?"

"The succession cannot be left to the whims of a hot-blooded girl," Crovax said. He drew his dagger, held it point up for a second, then drove it into the table to the hilt. "Before you and all the sergeants, the emissary will name me evincar or die on the spot. Her paramour, the boy Ertai, will die regardless."

Nasser folded his arms. "It shall be done, my lord."

CHAPTER 13
Traitor

Beset and bewildered, Belbe escaped the intrigues of the palace by retreating to the factory. No one else could stand the noise and crackling atmosphere of the flowstone works for long, so it was an ideal place to hide—no, sequester herself. Amid the intake jets, centrifugal distributors, and flow regulators she found a measure of serenity.

Or so she thought. Even under the faceted dome of the control center Belbe was haunted by memories and choices she didn't want. Her life, her total existence she owed to Abcal-dro and Phyrexia. There was no disputing that. But did she have the right, as Ertai suggested, to exist for her own sake? She had never considered what would happen to her once her task on Rath was done. Would she be recalled to Phyrexia? Life there would be severely circumscribed by her need for an unpolluted environment. Could she live under Abcal-dro's dome like one of Volrath's experimental animals, always under the eye of her polymorphous master?

Clearly no, if it was up to her.

Could she remain on Rath? This option had positive and negative aspects. Once an evincar was chosen, she'd no longer have any role to play. Belbe might stay on as advisor to the new

172

governor, but tolerance for her position seemed doubtful. Perhaps she could find some minor role in the Citadel—maintaining the flowstone production facility, for example.

No, even that job was destined to be short-lived. The conjunction of Rath and Dominaria was not far off. The final invasion would begin then, and she'd be lost in the tidal wave of the Phyrexian onslaught.

Belbe gazed through the many-paned dome at the energy beam pouring through the heart of the artificial crater. Beyond it, like an azure-tinged ghost, was the pinnacle of the palace, topped by *Predator*'s high landing dock.

The Accelerator broke into her daydreaming. "Output flow is sub-maximum," it bleated. "Increasing output to 114 percent."

Absently, Belbe dialed the output meter down to 86 percent and recalibrated it to read 100. The entire factory shifted with the fluctuation in production.

The Accelerator accepted the doctored information with a flat, "Increasing output to 114 percent."

Her hand was on the dial. What did that suggest?

She had only a moderate knowledge of planar mechanics, but she knew enough to know Rath and Dominaria were slowly coming into the same planar coordinates. When they matched, the worlds would interlock and become one. Rath would overlay on top of Dominaria and be the bridgehead for invading Phyrexian forces.

She looked over the mosaic of dials and switches, and the image of the massacred hostages filled her sight. All those people, those innocent, loyal subjects, killed to gratify the vengeful hunger of one man. How is it different, her remorselessly logical mind went on, to allow the Hidden One to slake his hunger for power with the lives of innocent Dominarians?

How is it different? How?

"There is no difference," she declared out loud.

The critical factor in the congruence of Rath and Dominaria was mass. The two worlds actually occupied the same interspatial niche, but Rath had insufficient mass to affect a hold on the older, naturally created world. The greater Rath's mass, the slower its vibrational rate became, until at last it resonated at the same rate as Dominaria. That's why the flowstone factory had the highest priority for resources on Rath—each layer of nano-machines, no matter how thin they appeared to be, increased the mass of Rath and hastened the day when the two worlds would be joined.

What if it didn't happen? What if Rath lacked sufficient mass to permanently overlay Dominaria?

Belbe's hand still rested on the output meter. She could make a choice—*the* choice—for Rath. If the final conjunction failed to take place, Rath could be changed. The absolute rule of the evincar could be dispelled. Negotiations with the rebels could put an end to the guerrilla war. Law and reason could take the place of rule by fiat. The overlords would surely strike back, but before that could happen, the energy imbalance on Rath could be reversed, resulting in a toxic environment for any potential Phyrexian invaders. Ertai knew enough about magic to help make this possible.

Unfortunately, for all his talents, Ertai was no match for Crovax. She could not depend on him alone to alter the course of Rath's destiny. Greven was more capable, but his control rod prevented him from openly opposing Crovax. Dorlan and the court were useless. The real subversive power to change things lay in her hands alone.

Belbe touched the Lens lightly. Ertai claimed he had blinded the implant. Did she dare believe it?

She had to. Belbe could not face the balance of her life, no matter how short it might be, knowing she was responsible for the destruction of two worlds and the deaths of millions.

She adjusted the output meter to 50 percent. Warning lights flashed throughout the factory until she curtly ordered them stopped. Belbe quickly recalibrated the meter to read 100. If she could maintain the sub-normal flow until the predicted time of conjunction, the mass of Rath would be too low to overlay on Dominaria.

She was confident no one in the Citadel would notice her tampering. The meter would have to be adjusted daily if the reduced output was to be maintained, otherwise the self-regulating factory would compare flowstone production to past rates and correct its output. Belbe regularly visited the factory anyway, so no one would suspect her if she made daily trips to the control center.

As she was permanently disabling the alarm system, *Predator* entered the crater, passing several thousand yards over the control center. The dome vibrated as the powerful airship circled around the energy beam. Belbe watched the vessel glide smoothly to the upper dock and moor there, wings folding back against the hull. She finished her alterations and left the dome.

She'd just reached the central corridor of the palace when Greven il-Vec and the airship crew arrived on their way down from the dock. Belbe noticed among the usual crew a tall figure, wrapped in a floor-length brown cape and hood. No one else in the crew was so attired. She used her infrared vision to peer through the disguise, but discovered she couldn't penetrate the apparently simple cloth wrap. What was going on here? Curious, she changed her path to intersect Greven's. They met at the foot of the staircase that led to the grand convocation room.

"Excellency," said Greven, bowing.

"Greetings. How do you find your repaired vessel?"

"Sound enough, though I'll be glad when the armament is back aboard. Scouting is weak tea for a fighting ship like *Predator*."

The crew waited patiently in Greven's shadow—all except the hooded one. He sidled to one side, as if to slip away unnoticed. Belbe stepped directly in front of him.

"I don't know you, do I?"

The hood snapped sharply in Greven's direction.

"Excellency," explained the warrior. "This is a delicate matter. I'd be glad to explain it to you in a less public place."

She gestured up the steps. "The room is empty, I believe."

Belbe mounted the steps, followed by Greven and the hooded figure. The doors to the convocation room—once the throne room of evincar Burgess—consisted of a series of giant disks rolled together to form an irislike barrier. At Belbe's command, the enormous door dilated to admit them. With a scrape like glass on glass, the disks rolled back together.

"Well?" said Belbe. Her voice echoed in the vast empty hall.

"Your Excellency knows we have a network of spies and assassins operating outside the Citadel?" Greven said. "This is one of our agents."

The hooded figure kept his distance, standing aloof with his hands crossed. Belbe tried once again to see through the heavy cloak but with no more success. She had a fleeting impression the person beneath the cloth was evading her, changing even as she tried to identify him. It was an unsettling experience.

"Is there anything else you require?" asked Greven impatiently.

"Let me see your face," she said directly to the hooded one.

"Excellency—"

"Let me see your face."

Gloved hands rose and folded back the deep rim of the hood. A lean, feline head emerged with a wispy goatee and bifurcated upper lip. Greven's mysterious companion was a Kor.

He pressed his hand to his chest in formal fashion and said, "I am Furah, chief of the Fishers of Life."

"Furah must not be recognized inside the Citadel," Greven said. "It would compromise his safety as our agent."

"Of course," Belbe said. "Thank you for indulging my curiosity."

* * * * *

Belbe departed and Furah raised his hood again.

"Simple enough," said the Kor. "She won't be a problem."

"Don't underestimate her," Greven replied. "She may look like a child, but she was made by the overlords and has many talents."

"You've grown cautious, Greven. You didn't used to be."

"We're playing a very dangerous game. I value my life, wretched though it is."

Furah folded his hands into his voluminous sleeves. "Don't betray me, Greven."

The bitter warrior held his chin up and replied, "I betray no one! Just understand, this is your gamble, your fight. I will not hinder you—but I can't help you much, either."

Greven stalked away. The doors opened for him. Furah remained in the convocation room for a time, contemplating the tapestries and bas-reliefs commemorating the deeds of the previous evincar.

Nemesis

* * * * *

Ten rebels, clad in captured Rathi uniforms, walked single file across the dry plateau. The six Dal were lead by Teynel *en*-Dal, Darsett's nephew, wearing the helmet of a Rathi corporal. The four Vec followed Liin Sivi, now disguised as a Vec male. She'd cut off her long black hair close to her scalp and disguised the break between her hips and waist with a bloodstained bandage. The blood was real—Sivi had taken the wrapping from a dead Rathi soldier. Her ancestral weapon, the toten-vec, she coiled around her waist under the bandage. The toten-vec consisted of a bone handle, six feet of braided snakeskin leather fashioned like links of chain, and a double-ended, double-edged knife blade eight inches long. The snakeskin whip was threaded through a hole at the base of the knife. Because Vec nomads had so little access to good metal, they developed weapons like the toten-vec in lieu of traditional swords. A skilled user could cut an enemy's throat from six feet away or take out an eye with a flick of the wrist. Sivi was an acknowledged master of the whip-knife, hence her title "Liin," which literally meant "striking viper."

Eladamri, suitably clothed in rags, sat on the back of a plodding kerl, his hands shackled together. The kerl's reins were carried by Medd, one of the Dal impostors. The elf had a copy of the shackle key hidden in his sash, so he could free himself if necessary. He was unarmed and bareheaded. He squinted against the steady stream of dust blown in his eyes. The tall cone of the Stronghold broke the silver horizon ahead. They were still a day's walk away.

The rebels were bored. They sang for a while, the Dal teaching the Vec their songs, and the Vec returning the favor with their own ululating repertory. After a few hours the songs ran out, and their throats grew dry. Eladamri refused to let them bring adequate water rations. They were supposed to be stragglers, survivors, not well-equipped commandos. If they arrived footsore and dried out, so much the better for verisimilitude.

Teynel shaded his eyes. "No sign of the airship," he said. "I kind of hoped they'd spot us and pick us up."

"Are you mad?" Sivi responded. "You couldn't get me into that flying machine!"

177

"It's better than walking," offered Khalil, one of the Vec warriors.

Sivi shook her head vigorously. "That machine is an unnatural creation. Some day the gods will strike it from the skies!"

"Strike away, but until then, I'd rather ride than walk," said Teynel.

"Want the beast?" said Eladamri, holding up the reins in his manacled hands.

Shamed, the young Dal declined. "I wouldn't ask Your Lordship to walk."

"I'm not a lord," the elf said sharply. "I don't carry any rank, either. Call me Eladamri, or brother, and nothing else."

"I thought only elves called each other 'Brother,'" said Sivi.

"Anyone who fights at my side can call me brother."

This put new spring in the rebels' step. They had covered a lot of ground by midday when they paused for a scant meal of Rathi army rations.

What little breeze there was died. Shamus, the Dal on lookout, spotted a rising column of dust in the distance.

"Someone comes," he announced.

"Keep your places," Eladamri advised. "You're not supposed to be alarmed by the sight of your fellow Rathi soldiers."

The origin of the dust proved to be a band of Kor a hundred strong, males, females, and children, marching in loose formation and bearing everything they owned on their backs. The sight was so unusual even Eladamri got to his feet. He whispered a few words to Teynel, who hailed the Kor band.

"Hold!" Teynel shouted. "Who are you people?"

Four male Kor bearing a stretcher on their shoulders promptly lowered their burden to the ground. The women squatted in the grass with the children, fanning themselves in the heat. A Kor elder approached Teynel with arms folded.

"Greetings, soldier of Rath!" he said. "I am Theeno, and these are my people, the Fishers of Life."

"Where are you going?"

"To the mountains far to the south, brave soldier. Our chief is dead, and we must leave our homes on Bluefire Mountain."

Now Teynel understood. Many people living outside the Stronghold referred to it as Bluefire Mountain.

"Why must you leave?"

"It was the dying wish of our chief. He was well known to your commander, Lord Greven."

Teynel stepped past Theeno. The body of a middle-aged Kor lay on the stretcher, draped in a diaphanous shroud. Midway between the collar and the hips, a dark brown stain was soaking through the shroud.

"This man died violently!" Teynel said.

"It is too true, soldier of Rath," Theeno said. "Our chief went to meet the lords of the crater, as was his wont, only this time he returned with his death wound."

Eladamri stood over the body. Ruse or no ruse, he had to know who lay dead on the carrier.

"Forgive me. I mean no disrespect . . ." The elf lord knelt and turned down the drape.

The dead Kor was Furah.

Eladamri covered the body again and stood up. He frowned at Teynel.

"Be on your way," Teynel commanded. "We have to deliver this prisoner to Lord Greven."

The Kor stared at Eladamri with slitted eyes. "This is Eladamri? He is an enemy," said Theeno. "Give him to Lord Crovax. He will dispatch him as he did the others."

Sivi stepped forward. "What others?"

Theeno smiled, showing prominent eye teeth. "Lord Greven gathered six thousand from the peoples of the crater to hold as hostage against those who would aid the vile rebels of the forest. When Lord Crovax returned from battle, he spared us, the Fishers of Life. He knew we were his loyal servants. The rest—" Theeno held two clawed fingers in front of his eyes and made a stabbing motion. "They burn even now."

"Crovax killed them all?" asked Sivi, voice rising.

"All but the Fishers of Life. Our chief was friend to Lord Greven, and so we were spared the great lord's wrath."

Teynel again ordered the Kor to move along. The women and children stood, and the bearers hoisted the body of Furah to their shoulders. With much churning of dust and no speaking, the Fishers of Life moved on.

When they were far enough away not to hear, Sivi exploded.

"The butcher! Six thousand people—his people, from his own cities—killed at once! What kind of devil are we fighting, Eladamri?"

"Apparently one with great bloodlust," the elf replied. He divided his gaze between the retreating Kor and the distant cone of the Stronghold. "I thought Volrath ruthless and cruel, but this Crovax can only be pure evil. My overtures to the people of the crater have been roundly ignored, you know. I thought them too afraid or too comfortable to fight their oppressors. Now Crovax and Greven have slain six thousand. The Oracle en-Vec saw it happen, but she couldn't describe it to me, it was so horrible. It's a monstrous crime, but it may yet rebound in our favor. If I send agents to the crater again, this time the response should be favorable to our cause." He folded his chained arms. "Do I sound callous?"

"A little," Teynel said. "Finding advantage in a catastrophe seems cold."

Eladamri remounted his sleepy kerl. "A revolution is not a country dance. We can't save those already dead, but we can pay back their murderers for their crimes.

"See clearly what we're doing, all of you. This isn't a game or a contest of honor. It's bloody, vicious business. The difference between us and Crovax or Greven is that we do what we do to put an end to oppression and bloodshed. For them, violence is a way of life and always will be."

He directed the team to follow the Fishers' track back to the Stronghold. It gave them a clearly trodden path and helped obscure their own footprints should *Predator* or a Rathi patrol discover them. News of the massacre put new strength in their step. When Teynel proposed they walk all night to reach the Stronghold by the next morning, no one objected.

* * * * *

Dorlan *il*-Dal left his chambers for the first time three days after the hostage massacre. He'd not slept in all that time. Hunger finally drove him out, and he roamed the halls of the Citadel in his dressing gown, trying to remember where the kitchens were.

Nemesis

He found no one but guards in the corridors. The first dozen he asked gave him directions to the dining hall, but each time he moved on a few yards, he forgot what he was told. One soldier took pity on him and gave him two salty biscuits from his ration bag. Mumbling profuse thanks, Dorlan wandered on, nibbling the hard bread and leaving a trail of white crumbs on the polished black floor.

Once he'd eaten his biscuits, Dorlan was thirsty. He drifted aimlessly into one of the less used areas of the palace, the storerooms clustered outside the bridge to Volrath's laboratory and the map tower. Dorlan knocked on faceless doors, saying, "Water? Has anyone a cup of water for Dorlan?" The storerooms were sealed, and he encountered no helpful soldiers in the hall.

He started to cry. Tears wore tracks through the flour on his lips and chin. Sniffing, he shuffled along, shaking door handles and muttering hoarsely for water. After trying more than thirty sealed rooms, his hand fell on a door handle that turned. Dorlan brushed the tears from his eyes. Someone in here would give him a drink.

The room beyond was short and wide, with a low, ribbed ceiling. Dorlan went in, and he was roughly grabbed by the front of his robe and jerked into the room. He stumbled and fell to his knees. The door slammed shut behind him, and a light flared on.

He was surrounded by burly men in rough clothes. Arms were piled on the floor—swords, scabbards, breastplates, helmets. As he lifted his head, he saw who held the lamp.

Crovax.

"Ah! Help! Help!" Dorlan shrieked. Lips curled in disgust, Crovax indicated he wanted Dorlan silenced. A callused hand clamped over the chamberlain's mouth, and fists pounded his back and belly. Gasping, Dorlan sank to the floor and whimpered.

"Be quiet, and no one will hit you," Crovax said. "What are you doing here?"

"I want a drink of water."

The sergeants exchanged puzzled looks. Nasser and Tharvello lifted the rotund Dorlan to a kneeling position and shoved a stool under his rump. The chamberlain's face was streaked with fresh tears.

"What's the matter with him?" Tharvello wondered aloud. "The old fool's never been a hale warrior, but I've never seen him wander about the place weeping."

"He seems distressed," Crovax said, rising. Dorlan shrank from Crovax's slight movement. The latter smiled, sharp highlights growing on his face from the lamp in his hand.

"It's me, isn't it?" he said. "Do I frighten you, Dorlan?"

He shut his eyes and shook his head furiously. "May I have a cup of water?"

Nasser looked to Crovax, who shrugged. A sergeant handed Dorlan a bottle. The chamberlain drank greedily, water flowing down his chin.

"Enough," said Crovax. "He's revolting." The bottle was taken away. Dorlan grasped at it and cried when it was taken beyond his reach.

"Be quiet!" Crovax snapped.

"I'm sorry," sniffed Dorlan. "Why are you hiding in here?"

"Who says we're hiding?" asked Nasser.

Dorlan pointed to the heap of arms. "You're not supposed to have those in the palace."

"Your mind hasn't completely left you, I see," Crovax said, setting the lamp on the table. "Too bad. As an idiot, you were harmless. As a witness with his wits, you're a danger."

Whatever else was wrong with Dorlan, he knew when he was in peril. He struggled to rise, but six strong sergeants forced him back on his stool. He tried to scream, but someone shoved a rag in his mouth. Gagging, Dorlan lost his recent meal of biscuits and water.

"Hold him," said Crovax. He drew a double-edged dirk from his belt.

Dorlan's eyes widened in terror. He fought feebly to stand.

Crovax pressed the needle-sharp point of the dirk into the fleshy underside of Dorlan's chin. The chamberlain lost all his color and ceased struggling. Crovax looked down at the helpless man and stayed his hand.

He turned to Tharvello and then tossed the dirk to the young sergeant. "You do it."

"Why me?"

"Because I told you to."

Tharvello put the edge of the dirk to Dorlan's flabby throat. Just as the blade was about to cut the chamberlain's skin, Crovax shouted.

"Stop!"

All eyes were on him. Crovax held out his hand for the weapon. Tharvello laid the dirk pommel first in Crovax's hand.

In one swift motion, Crovax closed his hands around the handle and slashed horizontally with the dirk. He cut a throat in one clean stroke, but it wasn't Dorlan's. Tharvello reeled back against his fellow sergeants, blood pouring down his chest.

"Traitor!" Crovax snarled. "You meant to sell me out to Greven and that worm Ertai!"

"What?" said Nasser. His question was echoed by every man in the room.

Crovax shoved his hand into the crumpling Tharvello's tunic. Out came a percher, its legs and wings tied with strips of ribbon. Crovax held it up and bade it speak.

"'I serve Rath, not any one man,'" the creature repeated.

"Your words?" Crovax asked Nasser.

"Mine, but I said more than that," the senior sergeant said calmly.

"You're right." Crovax gave the percher a little shake, and it spoke again.

"'If you think Crovax is finished, you're badly mistaken. Defeat or no defeat, he'll be back stronger than ever. Mark what I say.'"

Crovax crushed the percher to a bloody pulp in his hand and threw the remains on the dying Tharvello.

"Very prescient of you, Nasser. Our friend Tharvello recorded what you said and went to see Greven *il*-Vec with it. When Greven wouldn't act on what he heard and appoint Tharvello chief of the Corps of Sergeants—over your "retired" corpse, Nasser—Tharvello swore he would take his percher to Ertai and the emissary. As it turns out, I have a certain amount of influence with Greven, and he revealed the whole sordid story to me."

Tharvello's eyes rolled back. His flesh had taken on the color of new parchment. From his stool, Dorlan lifted his slippered feet and tried not to let the blood touch him.

"You'll find me tolerant of many things," Crovax said, wiping the dirk on the terrified chamberlain's gown. "Drunkenness, dueling, gambling—these are normal recreations of fighting men. As long as they don't compromise your duties, I don't care what you do on your own. I can even tolerate failure. We all fail, now and then." He laughed, though no one else in the narrow room joined him.

"What I won't tolerate is treachery. This is the fate of traitors." He kicked Tharvello's still-warm corpse. "Do you know why I gave him the knife first?" The sergeants nodded or grunted ignorance. "To give him a chance to kill me. If he'd tried to strike me down with a quick thrust, I would've spared him. Assassins I can use. Traitors are just carrion.

"You know your places for tomorrow's operation. You're the best men on Rath, the best fighters and true leaders. When I am evincar, you will all share in the bounty of my victory."

Nasser raised a fist in salute. "Crovax! Victory!" The sergeants took up the cry. "Crovax! Victory!"

Dorlan swallowed the bile in his throat and croaked, "Crovax, victory."

"Oh, yes, the chamberlain. I almost forgot you."

He grabbed Dorlan by his thick throat and hoisted him into the air. The portly chamberlain weighed easily as much as two normal-sized men, but Crovax lifted him with one hand. Dorlan's eyes bulged, and froth formed on his red lips.

"I can't trust you any longer," Crovax gritted. "You've always been a fool, but at one time you had enough sense to keep your mouth shut. Losing your wits has cost you your life."

He threw Dorlan against the flowstone door and it held him fast. The door panels flowed outward, gripping Dorlan's head, arms, waist, and legs.

Crovax twirled the dirk between his fingers. "Observe," he said. "I'll show you the stroke I used on Tharvello was no fluke."

CHAPTER 14
Prize

The pile of discarded scrolls spilled off the table and covered the floor. A good third of the bookshelves were empty. Ertai slumped over the latest treatise, head propped on one hand. He couldn't read anymore. For sixteen hours straight he'd labored in this obscure annex where some past chamberlain had stored all the books he found too old or too esoteric for the palace's main collection.

The technical information he gleaned from the scrolls was straightforward enough. The tiny machines were highly resistant to normal magical influence because it was artificial. Flowstone existed on the molecular level. In order to survive programming and recombination, flowstone molecules were extremely well balanced harmonically and therefore resistant to any sort of energy input. In a natural substance—wood, for example—matter was balanced statically. At rest, under normal conditions, wood was wood. Add heat to it, and its balance broke down—burning resulted. No fire in the world could burn flowstone because adding heat to the harmonically stable substance had no effect. Trying to ignite flowstone was like trying to boil an ocean by adding a teakettle full of hot water.

The secret of flowstone manipulation lay in focusing magic or mental energy on individual molecules of the stuff. Ertai imagined it this way: start with a tall brick tower, solid and level. A man could not topple the tower simply by shoving against it or even by battering it with a sledge hammer. But with a chisel and mallet, he could loosen bricks around the base of the tower. When the foundation became unstable, the tower could be toppled with a single finger. The real skill was in trying to make the resulting rubble into something useful.

Evincars were given this psionic ability by the Phyrexians during their physical metamorphosis. Unaltered minds could influence flowstone only through absolute concentration or conversely by a massive outpouring of directed magic. Ertai's effects came from the latter method. His magical skills got him started, and the infusion therapy he'd been taking boosted the available power for him to tap. Now, however, his method was at a dead end. All the natural magical power present on Rath wasn't enough to enable him to raise up a table or turn the floor to putty as Crovax did.

Ertai's candidacy was, in a word, doomed. The trick was to make certain he himself wasn't doomed along with it.

He considered going to Crovax and abdicating his chance to become evincar. Surely the relieved Crovax would spare him, maybe even allow him to depart Rath via the old Phyrexian portal in Portal Canyon?

Of course. Crovax was such a kindly, forgiving fellow.

Ertai shoved the remaining scrolls off the table. The small flowstone lamp overturned, and for a moment he feared it would start a fire among all the loose manuscripts. The yellowish wick kept glowing inside the glass shield. There was no fuel as such in the lamp. Commanded to glow, it glowed. In time the nanomachines in the lamp would break down, disintegrate, and the light would go out. It would take several hundred years at least.

Ertai put his head on the table and stared at the light. It reminded him of Belbe. Bright, purposeful, untiring, and single-minded. What did she think of their solitary encounter? He tried to understand what it meant to him. Since he was a small boy, Ertai's life had been centered on the practice of magic. For nineteen years it was the first thing he thought of in the morning, and the thing he dreamt of at night. At Barrin's Academy he'd been too busy for romance—if something didn't advance his knowledge of magic, what use was it? He could laugh now at his own arrogance, except he didn't feel like laughing.

With thumb and forefinger, he tried to pluck the glowing wick from the lamp. It winked out, throwing the cluttered room into darkness. He took his fingers away, and the element resumed glowing. No flame, no heat. More than ever it reminded him of Belbe.

She had her own portal, she said. If so, she must go and take him with her. As Ertai saw it, they had common cause to leave Rath together. Once Crovax was in power, no one on Rath was safe. Everyone would be fodder for his appetite, his own private herd of two-legged cattle. As a defeated rival, Ertai's life was obviously in danger, and he could see Belbe's would be, too.

Yes, Belbe would be number two on Crovax's "to do" list.

Where to go? Dominaria? It was home, but very soon it would be the scene of a horrible war. Gerrard and the others had told him this, and Belbe confirmed it. In their private moments, Belbe explained how Rath and Dominaria would intermingle, the landscape of one becoming part of the landscape of the other. Once the Rathi overlay was in place, the legions of Phyrexia would pour forth in all their awful, technological efficiency, and life on Dominaria would be either enslaved or extinguished.

Ertai considered himself a realist. Gerrard, Hanna, and company couldn't prevail against the hosts of the Hidden One. He'd thought it possible once but no longer. They would be faced with an army of a hundred thousand Crovaxes, utterly ruthless and totally without mercy. His homeworld was doomed.

Belbe's portal could take them anywhere. There must be a million worlds or more out there populating the void. Even the Phyrexians couldn't reach them all. Perhaps he could find some peaceful world of magic to inhabit, where machines were made of wood and didn't think, where floors existed only to be walked on, and a man and woman of talent could live a good life together until time mingled their souls into the great firmament forever.

Go out, he willed, and the lamp obeyed.

* * * * *

Clouds were piling up in high black drifts over the Stronghold as Eladamri and his team approached the foot of the main causeway. Teynel had gotten on their lone kerl, as befitted his senior rank among the "Rathi" troops. Eladamri walked behind, his manacles tied to a long rope. Teynel looped the other end around his saddle ring.

The causeway rose from the plain, a massive raised bridge of solid masonry. Usually busy, traffic up and down the road was today only a trickle. It soon became clear why: a heavy cordon of soldiers patrolled the end of the road, and guard posts along the bridge were fully manned.

Teynel waved Sivi and the others forward. They lined up and stood at attention. Eladamri came alongside the Dal corporal and got down on both knees, trying to look downtrodden.

"Why all the soldiers?" Teynel asked. "Do they know what's up?"

"No," said Eladamri, his head hanging low. "If they suspected us, they would have swooped down on us long ago. There's something else amiss."

"It can't hurt to ask," said Sivi. "We're all one army, aren't we? We've been lost more than a week, so it won't be strange if we don't know what's going on."

"True enough," said Eladamri. He raised his head. "Look out—we've been seen."

The buff stone barbican at the end of the causeway was a small fortress in itself. A sentry, standing in the open arched doorway, spotted the rebels and hurriedly called his superior. A Rathi captain appeared, eating a bright blue pear. He shouted an order, inaudible from where Eladamri sat, and 40 soldiers poured out of the barbican, fully armed. In ragged order they ran at the waiting rebels.

"Now is the time for cool heads," Eladamri said. "Remember, you're all Rathi soldiers. Those men coming are your comrades."

The soldiers fanned out and encircled the little band. Teynel leaned nonchalantly across the neck of his kerl. Liin Sivi stuck the stem of a long blade of grass in her teeth.

The captain arrived, still clutching his half-eaten snack. "Who are you?" he said sharply.

Teynel saluted. "Corporal Elcaxi of the Fourth Company. It's good to be home!"

The captain squinted at him. "Fourth Company, eh?"

Teynel smiled. "That's right, the Fearsome Fourth."

"Not many of you fellows made it back." The captain extended a hand. "Welcome home."

Teynel shook the man's hand with genuine relief. "We have a prisoner to turn in."

The captain stood over Eladamri, hands on his hips. "Why'd you bother? I'd've cut his throat and left him on the plain."

Sivi stepped forward. "Oh, no," she said. "We caught us an important rebel. This is Eladamri!"

The fruit fell from the captain's hand. "Stuff me with stone! The rebel leader himself? Are you sure?"

"That's who he says he is. Can't think why anyone would claim to be Eladamri unless he was. I mean, knowing what's gonna happen to him, yes?" Teynel said.

"On your feet!" The captain signaled his men to come forward and take the prisoner. Sivi and the rebels closed around the elf, blocking the soldiers.

"He's our prize," she said. "We caught him, we'll take him in."

The captain burst out laughing. "You're the Fourth Company all right! Nobody else has such brass!" He waved his men back. "Come to the guardhouse. I'll give you a token that'll get you through the other stations, and I'll send a percher to Lord Greven with the news."

"Lord Greven hates perchers," Teynel said boldly. "Send a runner instead. We're not in a hurry, and this elf ain't going anywhere without us!"

Flushed with excitement, the captain readily agreed. A runner was dispatched with the startling news of Eladamri's capture. The rebels strolled to the guardhouse amid the admiring looks of the Rathi soldiers. Eladamri dragged his feet and did his best to look dejected.

The captain gave Teynel a pass, an engraved metal disk four inches wide with the Citadel seal on it. Teynel hung the cord around his neck and let the token fall across his chest.

"This is wonderful," said the captain. "Tell me, how did you capture him?"

"It was tough," Sivi said. "Our battalion charged through the burning camp when we saw this band of elves cross in front of us. We chased 'em into the swamp, losing half our number on the way. We killed twenty or thirty rebels and caught this one about to skewer himself. We tried to find our way out of the Skyshroud, but we got turned around in all the trees. The rest of the battalion was lost to potholes, snakes, and fever. We got out eventually, but the army had moved on. We made our way back as best we could."

The soldiers hung on Sivi's every word. When she finished, they cheered lustily. Sivi couldn't help but grin.

"This is the best news we've had since *Predator* was repaired!" said the captain. "With their leader gone, the rebels won't have the stomach to face us again!"

Surrounded by waving, cheering troops, the team herded Eladamri forward. When the barbican had fallen behind them, the elf spoke.

"Nice work, Teynel."

Teynel grinned and nodded. "I was doing my best to sound like an insolent soldier."

"What about my performance?" Sivi asked.

"Splendid," said Eladamri. "You have the gifts of a bard." He trudged on, his arms weighed down by the heavy shackles. "It's one thing to fool common soldiers at the gate, but Greven *il*-Vec will turn up soon and so will Crovax, for all we know. So keep your heads."

"I'm not worried," Teynel said. "Once word gets around we're bringing in Eladamri, no one will look twice at us."

And so it proved. At each guardhouse they passed, soldiers turned out to hail them and to stare at the captured rebel chief. Not all their looks were baleful, however. Many were simply curious to see the famed Eladamri, the elusive guerrilla leader who'd evaded them for so long. Popular rumor made Eladamri a wizard of elven magic, which accounted for his many miraculous scapes. It was disappointing for the legend lovers to see the fabled elf turn out to be a slight, middle-aged fellow wearing rags.

The runner must have had a busy tongue, because everyone they encountered along the causeway knew Eladamri was coming. Soldiers and civilians alike lined the bridge, and more arrived every minute. Civilians from the crater settlements came out to see the procession. The disguised rebels were almost overwhelmed by the hordes of curious Dal and Vec who wanted to see Eladamri.

Suddenly, the crowd in front of them melted away. Kerl-mounted cavalry were cantering down the bridge with lances leveled. People scrambled to avoid the troopers. Behind them came a battalion of heavy infantry in tall, conical suits of armor. In their midst was Greven *il*-Vec, decked out in fearsome battle gear. Eladamri checked the faces of his young comrades. More than one rebel's face lost color at the sight of the towering warlord. Of all the rebels, Liin Sivi was the calmest. Hip outthrust, she casually rested her hand on the handle of her toten-vec.

"Dread Lord," Teynel said, his voice cracking. "Corporal Elcaxi and men, reporting for duty. We have a prisoner."

The heavy infantry parted ranks, and Greven stepped out front of them. "So you do." He was a good two feet taller than the manacled elf, yet as they sized each other up, a kind of equality existed between them. Not respect, but recognition that each was a formidable warrior.

"If you're not Eladamri, you should be," Greven said.

"Do you doubt it, Dread Lord?" said Sivi.

He eyed her as if she were an insect crawling across his dinner plate. "Doubt keeps a soldier alive," he said. "You should cherish it as closely as your sword."

He said, "I am Eladamri, son of Kelimenar. Are you going to leave me standing here?" For a moment, a fleeting fragment of a second, he saw indecision on the other warrior's face.

Then it was gone, and Greven gave his orders. "Deliver him to the Citadel guards on the factory concourse."

"But Dread Lord," Teynel said. "What will happen to him?"

"Is it any concern of yours, Soldier?"

"Yes, Dread Lord," Sivi interjected. "As his captors, we want reward for taking him."

Some of the civilians in the crowd gasped at her impertinence. The genuine Rathi soldiers listened for the telltale grinding of teeth, but none came.

"Everything you've earned will be yours. This is the word of Greven *il*-Vec."

He stood aside and let Teynel lead his team through. The dark, brooding bulk of the Stronghold lay ahead. Eladamri lifted his face to the sky and took what he hoped was not his last look at the turbulent gray clouds of Rath.

* * * * *

The tense atmosphere in the Citadel had reached an unbearable level. Every minute was like the hour before a storm, when all is still, but the threat of an upheaval is clearly in the air.

Belbe sensed things were about to break. She donned her close-fitting armor for the first time since the day of her arrival. To her logical mind, the danger came from the thousands of Dal and Vec people living in the crater. These were the people Crovax had wronged by murdering their loved ones, and despite the relative calm of the past two days, Belbe felt certain a revolution was bubbling just beneath the veneer of normality.

Armored, with her helmet tucked under one arm and a slim Phyrexian sword on her hip, Belbe went forth to find the other residents of the Citadel. She had little luck. Ertai was missing, probably buried in some forgotten library. Dorlan *il*-Dal was nowhere to be found. She went to his private chambers and found the door open. Dorlan's rooms were a shambles. Bedclothes were torn off the bed. Broken pottery littered the floor. His chamberpots were full and reeking.

When she emerged from Dorlan's rooms, the hall was full of people—courtiers, some of whom she hadn't seen in a week, and members of the palace guard. Even off-duty guards in their padded jerkins were milling around in the corridor. Belbe stopped an elderly Dal.

"What's happened?" she said.

"Tremendous news, Excellency!" said the courtier. "They say the elf lord Eladamri has been taken! He'll be here in minutes!"

"Eladamri? Taken?" If the man had told her Greven had changed sex, she could not have been more surprised. "How did it happen?"

"I know not how the rascal was caught, only that he is coming here in chains."

He hurried away after bowing numerous times. Belbe, a bit dazed, stood motionless in a river of moving, chattering people. Eladamri captured?

The ordered tread of guards in formation awakened her. Turning, she ordered them to stop. The twelve guards halted, and their leader saluted.

"We have orders to convey the rebel Eladamri to the palace prison," the senior guard said. "We're to meet Lord Greven on the factory concourse and take custody of the prisoner."

"I'm changing your orders," she said. "You will bring the prisoner to the convocation chamber. I want to see him." The captain of the guard saluted again and continued on his way.

Belbe ascended the stairs to the convocation antechamber. At midday she was scheduled to announce her choice for the next evincar. In preparation for the ceremony, the antechamber had been polished and decorated with banners and martial flags. Guards in black-enameled dress armor already stood by the iris doors. They presented arms when they saw her.

"At ease," she said. "A state prisoner will be brought here shortly. You will admit him, his escort, and anyone that follows, is that clear?"

"It shall be done, Excellency."

She stepped between them. The circular panels hissed apart. "Until then, admit no one," Belbe added.

"Yes, Excellency."

The hall was decked out with a wide semi-circle of crimson and gold banners, each one bearing the heraldic arms of a past evincar. Each company of the Rathi army was represented by a battle flag. The governor's throne, stripped of Volrath's insignia, had been brought down from the upper throne room just for this occasion. Flanking the tall chair were two flaming braziers.

She walked slowly down the aisle, surrounded by symbols of Rath's past and present might. From the odor, she realized the flames she saw were real, not flowstone simulations. The braziers were the size of warrior's shields, mounted on black metal tripods.

Her footsteps were loud in the stillness. She felt strangely numb.

Belbe mounted the shallow steps to the dais and sat down on the throne. Her back had just touched the rear of the seat when she heard a voice say, "How does it feel?"

Crovax walked out of the shadows directly above her.

"Don't you get tired of walking around upside down?"

"An amusing trick of the flowstone, sometimes useful," he replied, walking down the wall. "But you didn't answer the question."

"It's a chair, like any other."

Crovax stepped down to the floor. "Not so. That's the seat of the Evincar of Rath, the sole arbiter of the lives of millions."

"I thought the power resided in the ruler, not the furniture."

"You have so little appreciation of the trappings of power. Anyone who sits there, no matter how base, gets a taste of rulership. That doesn't happen with ordinary bar stools or kitchen chairs."

"On Phyrexia, such trappings are unnecessary. Power comes from knowledge and control, not flags and furniture. My own master . . ." her voice trailed off as she remembered the formless mass of Abcal-dro. "He has no need for chairs."

Crovax descended the dais. "You're here early. Have you come to a decision?"

"Yes."

"Care to share it with me?"

"Not yet."

"Then why are you here, Excellency?"

"Haven't you heard? Eladamri's been captured. Greven's bringing him here even as we speak."

Crovax was electrified. "You jest! No, you never do—Eladamri captured!" He clapped his hands and smiled broadly. "A fitting prize to begin my new era on Rath!"

Noise swelled in the antechamber, and the iris doors scissored apart. Leading an enormous crowd was Greven il-Vec, still clad in his battle armor. At his heels came ten nondescript soldiers with muddy feet in battered, rusty armor. Next were the palace guards in a box formation, four abreast. In the center of the box walked a lone figure in gray rags, his hands bound by heavy chains. Courtiers in their baroque finery filled the hall behind the guards, and a motley collection of off-duty soldiers, servants, and the odd mogg or two filled out the crowd.

Belbe craned to see the famous rebel leader, but with Greven and a wall of guards in the way, she couldn't get a clear view of him.

Greven halted the procession. A few onlookers coughed nervously.

"Your Excellency!" Greven boomed. "The soldiers of the army of Rath bring you tribute!" He stepped to one side.

Crovax stood at the foot of the throne, arms folded. He opened his mouth to speak, but his words were stillborn when Belbe rose from the evincar's throne and descended the steps.

The hall grew deathly quiet. Her boots clicked on the mock-marble floor. She felt as though she was confronting a great mystery, a lost wonder of nature.

* * * * *

Teynel, Sivi, and the rebel raiders held their breath. They never imagined they would get so close to the seat of the enemy's power. The vast Stronghold impressed them. The flow-stone factory puzzled and frightened them. Rank upon rank of tough, professional soldiers worried them. Now, in the very heart of the Citadel, they were face to face not only with Greven *il*-Vec and Crovax, but the personal emissary of the dreaded Phyrexian overlords.

She was a girl. A young *elf* girl.

"These are the soldiers who brought in Eladamri," Greven explained.

Teynel saluted with such force he almost knocked his own helmet off. "C-Corporal Elcaxi of the Fourth Company, Your Excellency."

"Corporal."

"This is my second, Private Vertino." Sivi returned Belbe's vacant look with an icy appraisal of her own.

* * * * *

The rebels parted ranks to let Belbe pass. When they were clear, she got a better glimpse of Eladamri. He was of moderate height, and the color of his hair meant he was past the prime of life for his race. The lofty palace guards, chosen from the ranks of the regular army for their size and strength, still prevented her from seeing him clearly.

Greven nodded, and a door of armored warriors drew back.

Eladamri looked upon her face, and she on his.

His eyes widened, and a rush of blood flamed in his cheeks. Eladamri let out a roar of perfect rage, and though weighed down with thirty pounds of shackles and chains, he threw himself on Belbe and bore her to the floor.

She thought time had stopped. Everyone was fixed, like the statues in Volrath's suite—the guards, hampered by their ceremonial garb; the ragged soldiers who'd captured Eladamri gaped; Crovax, hovering on the periphery of the scene, watched and smiled. Greven, who always seemed on the knife's edge of violence, just looked on with curious passivity.

They're going to let me die, she thought. They're going to let this madman kill me.

Eladamri had both hands around her neck. Because of her gorget he couldn't throttle her, so he raised her head and slammed it against the floor. It hurt, but only superficially. Her alloy skull could turn an ax blow. As it was, each time her head struck the floor there was a dull metallic thud.

"Assassin! Murderer!" the elf cried. "Avila! Avila—!"

The footsore soldiers of the Fourth Company moved first. They grabbed Eladamri by the arms and shoulders and tore him off Belbe. Once they acted, the spell was broken, and the palace guards quickly pinned the rebel leader to the floor with their polearms. Elcaxi and his comrades pushed away the guards' bills and axheads, relying on their bodies to hold the raging Eladamri.

Someone lifted Belbe to her feet. Her vision cleared, and she saw her benefactor was Crovax.

"I knew he was crafty, but I never thought Eladamri was insane," Crovax said mildly. "Are you all right, Excellency?"

Belbe rubbed the back of her head. "No permanent damage."

"Damned murderers! They did it on purpose! Devils! Monsters! Dear Avila, sweet child, how could they do this—?"

Belbe was still holding the back of her head. "What is he raving about?" Crovax and Greven were clueless. "You men, let him go," Belbe commanded.

Sivi and Teynel hesitated but followed orders.

"Up," said Teynel, and the rebels scrambled to their feet. Eladamri arched his back and sprang to a crouching position with one flex. Tears streamed down his cheeks. With a second heave, he regained his feet. The palace guards interposed a wall of polearms between him and Belbe.

"Hold," she said to the troops. "Don't harm him." She turned to Eladamri. "Why do you risk death to lay hands on me? Who is Avila?"

He advanced a step, breathing heavily. "Does my face mean nothing to you?"

"I've never seen you before."

He gripped the polearm shafts barring his path. "Where do you come from, Girl?"

Greven backhanded Eladamri, sending him sprawling. The crowd let out a collective "Oh!"

"You do not question the emissary!" Greven barked.

Belbe held up a hand to the hulking warrior. "Be still," she said. She pushed through the hedge of polearms and knelt beside the elf. Eladamri pushed himself up on one arm and dabbed the blood from his freshly split lip.

"Do you attack me because I'm the emissary of your enemy?" said Belbe.

"I attacked because you're an abomination, a horrible lie," Eladamri said in a low voice. "You should be exterminated, as all unnatural creatures should be."

"I wouldn't speak too lightly of extermination," Crovax said, shouldering through the press. "From where I stand, the best candidate for extermination is you."

Eladamri stood. He was weighed down by his chains, but when Belbe tried to assist him, he pulled away from her, glaring hatefully.

"Remove his shackles," Belbe said. When no one complied with her order she shouted, "Do as I say!"

Teynel shoved the key in his leader's bonds. He tried to urge Eladamri to be calm with a meaningful glance. The elf did not

Paul B. Thompson

meet his eyes. He burned holes in Belbe and kept doing so even after his chains fell loudly to the floor.

"What are your orders, Excellency?" Greven asked.

"What is the first task of a captor?"

He bowed. "As you command, Excellency." At Greven's order, the box of guards was reformed. Teynel and the rebels kept discreetly to the rear.

"Don't kill him," Belbe added as the prisoner faced about. "Find out what he knows, but preserve his life. Do you understand?"

Greven avowed he did.

Crovax sighed. "So much trouble. I doubt he'll tell us anything. Better to strike off his head now and be done with it. I can have the airship drop it on the rebels in Skyshroud Forest—"

"Shut up," Belbe commanded.

Crovax shrugged.

The massive crowd tried to get out of the way of Eladamri's escort, but there were so many packed in the rear of the hall that it took a few minutes to clear the doorway. Just as everyone's attention was focused on the departing rebel leader, the floor of the hall turned to soft clay, and the dilating doors melded into a solid mass. Everyone was lifting their feet, losing shoes and slippers in the sticky stuff.

Belbe's frustration was written on her face. "What are you doing, Crovax? Restore the door and floor."

Crovax was seated on the throne. He looked very natural and comfortable in the tall black chair. Leaning back, he propped his chin on his hands and waited until everyone was looking at him to respond.

"The noon hour is not far off, Excellency. Why not take advantage of these splendid witnesses and announce your choice for the next Evincar of Rath?"

She looked around. "Ertai is not here."

"Should he be?"

"He is under consideration for the post."

Crovax flexed his fingers. Four flowstone rods, like the ones he had used to slaughter the hostages, erupted from the floor around Belbe. Secondary spikes jutted from the foot-thick shafts, isolating her in a ring of artificial thorns.

Belbe glared. "I tire of your displays."

His right eyelid twitched. A fifth rod formed between her feet. It rose slowly to knee level and held there, the tip bending backward to caress her leg like some inquisitive tentacle.

"Name your choice," Crovax said quietly.

"Not yet."

The fifth rod leaped up to her chin. Limp pseudopodia emerged from it and delicately probed the joints of her armor. She knew that with a single thought he could convert them to steel-hard spikes.

"If you kill me, you'll never be named evincar," Belbe said. "Knowing that, do you think you can frighten me into a decision?"

Crovax burst out laughing. It was hard, unfriendly mirth, but the cage of spikes sank into the floor. The rest of the crowd found their footing had firmed up. Their exodus accelerated now that many of them had seen Crovax's talents for the first time.

"I defer my decision until tomorrow morning. By then I will know more about the rebels' plans and can act accordingly."

With that, Belbe strode from the hall. Eladamri's eyes hatefully followed her out of the room.

CHAPTER 15
Pawn

Ertai awoke slowly. The room was pitch black and so hot that sweat from his brow had pooled on the tabletop, matting together several old manuscripts. There was a vile taste in his mouth. Coughing, he sat up and realized he'd chewed on a scroll in his sleep. That explained the awful flavor of ink.

He thought the lamp into working. It flashed to life, first red, then orange, gradually brightening to a soft yellow glow. He had no idea what time it was or how long he'd been in the dusty, arid annex.

Trampling through piles of open scrolls, he reached the door and threw back the bolt. Air poured in like a cool waterfall. He held out his arms and drank it in gratefully. These Citadel rooms were all but airtight with their doors closed. It was a wonder he hadn't suffocated in this book-lined tomb.

Sweaty and with sleep-swollen features, Ertai sauntered down the corridor. From the amount of light coming from outside, it seemed like late morning or early afternoon. Rath had no proper day or night, but diurnal variations in the great energy beam approximated two halves of a day. He wanted a cool drink, some decent food, and a bath. Thoughts of bathing made him smile. He'd use the fancy tub in the evincar's quarters again. Maybe this time Belbe would join him. It would be a good place to spring his plan about the two of them leaving Rath forever.

The side hall connected to a major corridor that was surprisingly full of people. The Citadel hadn't been this lively since he'd arrived. Now the place bustled with servants and elaborately dressed courtiers, some hastening from point to point, others lingering in handy alcoves, conversing in loud, theatrical whispers.

"Pardon me, but what's the stir?" he asked a trio of gaudy loafers.

"Have you not heard? We've captured Eladamri!" The fat courtier, who bowed under a headdress loaded with gems, didn't look like he'd ever captured anything but a free meal.

"Are you certain? When did this happen?"

"I saw him myself in the convocation hall, not half an hour ago," said the fellow haughtily. "He's a savage, no doubt about it. He tried to kill the emissary in front of the whole court!"

He tugged on the courtier's copious sleeve. "Is Belbe all right?"

Lord Widewaist removed his gold embroidered sleeve from Ertai's ink-stained fingers. "No harm came to Her Excellency," he sniffed.

Ertai made a slight alteration to the flowstone around the courtier's feet, uttered a brief thanks, and hurried on. A few moments later he was rewarded by the sound of the bloated courtier falling flat on his face. Ertai had locked his slippers to the floor.

The hall leading to the convocation antechamber widened. Ertai broke into a trot. He dodged around slow moving loiterers then bumped into the broad back of a man who wasn't moving at all.

"Out of the way," he said. "This is a public hall, not a public house."

The big man turned around.

"I know you," Ertai said. "You're a soldier—Sergeant Somebody-or-other."

"Nasser's my name." Another sinewy fellow moved in behind Ertai. "This is Sergeant Valmoral."

The sweat turned cold on Ertai's neck. "How d'you do?" They were both in cloth jerkins and trews, so he said, "Is this your day off, Boys?"

"A sergeant's work is never done," Nasser replied. The one called Valmoral poked the tip of a short but very sharp knife in the small of Ertai's back. "We know you're a tricky fellow, so chose your next act carefully."

"You have my full attention."

"You'll come with us," Valmoral said.

"You really think you can abduct me, here, in front of all these people?"

"You'll come," said Nasser. "The life of the emissary is at stake."

"Belbe?" Ertai's eyes narrowed. He could, with a little effort, send simultaneous psychokinetic bursts from each hand and repel these two roughnecks. But then what? For all he knew, Belbe was already in their hands. He relaxed, letting his shoulders sag.

"Good thinking," Nasser said. "This way."

They moved slowly against the general flow of the crowd. The soldiers stood on either side, steering him with nudges from their broad shoulders. He thought fast and hard.

"At least tell me where we're going," he said out of the side of his mouth.

"To a place of calm reflection," Nasser replied.

"I could use some calm reflection . . . ah!" Valmoral pricked him with the point of his knife.

"You chatter like a percher. Be silent."

They turned off the main corridor to a small side hall, losing most of the foot traffic as they did. They went on quite a ways and turned off again, this time into a passage just wide enough for two men to walk abreast.

"Fourth door on the right," Nasser said.

He slowed his pace until Valmoral reached out to shove him forward. As soon as Ertai shuffled forward out of arm's reach, he commanded the flowstone walls to narrow. Two bulges formed in front of the sergeants, blocking their way. Ertai ran.

"Hold, You!"

He skidded to a stop at the fourth door and glanced back at

the trapped men. One was shouting dire threats, the other was trying to worm past the obstruction. Ertai put a hand on the door handle. It swung inward.

He looked into the smiling face of Crovax.

"Having fun, Boy?" he said. "Good. I'm in the mood for some fun, too."

* * * * *

Teynel, Sivi, and the rebels cautiously trailed behind Eladamri and his escort of palace guards. It was easy to follow them, even through the crowds because Greven *il-*Vec overtopped everyone in sight. As long as they kept the warrior's towering frame in view, they knew where their leader was.

Except for Sivi's toten-vec, they were unarmed. Even as Rathi soldiers, they had to surrender their weapons when they entered the palace. Eladamri had been preternaturally calm through all the danger until he laid eyes on the emissary. His subsequent murderous, implacable rage was something none of them had ever seen in him before.

"The emissary looks like an elf," Sivi noted as they shadowed their captive leader. "Is that what angered him?"

"I don't know," said Teynel, "but I have a bad feeling about it. I wasn't expecting her, and I don't think Eladamri was either. I didn't think they would act so quickly to interrogate him."

"We can't let them torture him!" Sivi said.

Teynel turned back abruptly, coming nose to nose with Liin Sivi. "We have a mission to perform. If you aren't happy with the way I'm leading it, you're free to leave!" Her hostile glare softened, so he added, "I don't intend to lose Eladamri, but he may have to endure some hardship before we can retrieve him. He understood that before we left Skyshroud—didn't you?"

Eladamri and his captors halted near the mouth of a gilded bridge that led out into the open crater. A short way down, a large conical building extended well below the line of the bridge.

They heard Greven speak. "Take a last look," he said, his inflection oddly respectful. "You may not see daylight again."

Eladamri inhaled deeply. "I will know the light far longer than you, Butcher."

Any trace of compassion left Greven's voice. "Forward!" he barked. The guards locked their shields together. Eladamri was now closed inside a living cage. Head held high, he strode in perfect step with the escort.

The rebels were pressed into individual niches in the wall just behind the bridge landing. They saw and heard the exchange between Greven and Eladamri.

"What is that place?" asked Sivi.

"A prison, I assume," Teynel said. "It's isolated from the rest of the fortress."

"How do we get in?"

"We don't. We're following Eladamri's original plan. Sivi, you take half the men and look for *Predator*. I'll lead the rest and search where you don't. Take no action when you do find it— we need to make sure of the one attack we'll get. We'll rendezvous in four intervals at the entrance to the big hall we saw. Then we all go back to the airship and finish it once and for all."

Sivi stepped out of her niche and tapped the shoulders of four of the rebels. Wordlessly they peeled off and followed her. Teynel watched her take her squad up a spiral staircase. Teynel signaled the remaining rebels to follow him. Since Sivi chose to go higher in the Citadel, they would search low.

* * * * *

She could still feel the pressure of his hand around her throat.

What was it that drove this total stranger to attack her in full view of the assembled court? Belbe sat sideways in the throne of Rath and tried to answer the question logically. He called her an abomination, a lie. Both implied representations of truth that were actually false. How was she false? She was who she was, made on the Fourth Sphere of Phyrexia for this exact mission. Did she resemble someone known to Eladamri? She rejected the idea as too absurd.

If that was true, who was Avila?

Belbe shook her head. It throbbed a little where Eladamri had dashed it against the floor. She didn't have enough information to answer her questions. The only place she could get more was from Eladamri.

The convocation room was empty. All that remained were the flags, Eladamri's manacles, and Belbe. She picked up the heavy chains. By now the rebel leader was beginning his interrogation. She remembered what Ertai looked like after Greven was done with him. A sour taste spread up her throat. No doubt Eladamri was tougher than Ertai, but the thought of him being burned and beaten by Greven's moggs made her ill. It was easy enough to send him there when he'd just tried to throttle her. She regretted it now. There'd been enough violence in this place—too much. She was sick of it. If she had authority to stop it, it was high time she exercised it.

Belbe hurried from the hall, still gripping the manacles. She'd had enough of Crovax's bullying, too. He'd humiliated her in the past, but this last time was in public, and she wouldn't stand for any more. If Greven would back her up, she was willing to name Ertai as the next Evincar of Rath.

Crovax wouldn't take it lying down, but she had a few surprises for him. Among the equipment sent with her from Phyrexia was a case of special weapons. She was supposed to supply these weapons to the new evincar, but she had a better use for them. Her masters might not approve, but she had already gone too far down the road of resistance to feel fainthearted. With Ertai at her side, she'd free Greven from his control rod, and together the three of them would destroy Crovax and establish Rath as a sovereign world, no longer the puppet of Phyrexia or a threat to Dominaria. And possibly, if Eladamri were amenable, he could have a post in her new order, too.

The flowbot lift carried her swiftly to the evincar's quarters. When she arrived in the outer chamber, the room was dark. Belbe asked for light, but nothing happened. Annoyed, she climbed the stairs and entered the statuary room. There, lamps blazed brightly.

She stopped short. Something was amiss. Nothing in the room was disturbed, but she avoided the usual path through the statues, preferring to hug the wall instead. The Phyrexian crates were where she'd left them, seals intact. She pressed her thumb into the shallow depression on the back of the seal, and it opened with a click.

Nestled in the crate were two identical weapons—plasma energy dischargers. They were shoulder arms, like crossbows, but instead of a steel bow at a right angle to the stock, there was a long metal casing ending with two sharp metal points pointing forward. Dischargers used a single powerstone. Six were stored in the crate. These stones were so strongly charged they couldn't be loaded bare-handed. She picked up an L-shaped loading tool, pressed it against one of the powerstones, and inserted it into the slot on the underside of the weapon. A row of green and red jewels on top of the discharger began to glow. The weapon was armed.

Cradling the Phyrexian weapon under her arm, Belbe hurried to the lift. She was halfway across the statuary room when she heard a tinny whistling.

Belbe swung the discharger around, aiming the double points in the direction of the sound. The little tune repeated.

"Come out, or I'll use this!" she said. The whistler's reply was mockingly the same.

Her thumb pressed against a smooth pad on the rear of the metal housing. There was a flash like lightning, an ear-splitting crack, and one of Volrath's statues was blasted in two. The tune ceased.

"Our masters make impressive weapons, don't they?"

Crovax was close behind her—too close. She tried to bring the heavy discharger to bear, but he tore it from her hands before she could get it leveled. Belbe leaped at him, trying to snatch the weapon back. Crovax casually punched her on the jaw. She flew backward against a statue of a crouching youth. By the time Belbe shook off the blow, the tips of the discharger were an inch from her face.

"You have an extraordinarily hard head, but I suspect this device can deal with that," said Crovax.

"At this range you'll vaporize my skull," Belbe said.

"Really?" Crovax caressed the weapon admiringly.

Belbe waited for the flash and the oblivion to follow. Crovax raised the tips to the ceiling. "Get up."

He went to the door. Men filed in from the darkened staircase. She recognized them as the Corps of Sergeants. Two of them bore a third man between them, hands tied and mouth gagged: Ertai.

Their eyes met. Belbe made a half step in his direction but froze when Sergeant Valmoral pressed the edge of his knife to Ertai's jugular.

She forced herself to be calm. "Now what?"

"This is a coup," Crovax replied matter-of-factly. "As of this moment, I am taking over the rule of Rath. You will name me evincar in front of these witnesses. Now."

"And if I don't?"

"Sergeant Valmoral will bleed the boy dry."

Belbe folded her arms. "So do it. I'll not be coerced."

Crovax shrugged and nodded. Valmoral drew his knife back to add force to the cut. Ertai's eyes widened, then he squeezed them shut. Down came the stroke of the blade.

Under her arm, Belbe had secreted a broken piece of the statue she'd fallen against. It was a young man's hand—a slender, elegant hand, fingers gathered in, touching the finely carved thumb. Made of flowstone, it weight about a pound. She whipped this at Valmoral with all the speed and power she possessed. It hit him on the forehead just before the stroke of his knife laid open Ertai's throat.

The room erupted. Ertai swung his bound hands at the nearest man, catching him in the gut. Belbe whirled and sprang at Crovax. He pointed the Phyrexian weapon at her, but nothing happened. Alarmed, he dropped it, and the flowstone statue of an androgynous nude between him and Belbe came to life at his command. Belbe tried to dodge it, but the statue caught her around the waist and flung her back. Two sergeants moved in. They wore helmets and breastplates but were armed only with knives. Belbe got a foot against the moving statue and heaved it away. The first man slashed at her. She caught his arm and broke it like a twig. He howled and dropped his blade. She twisted his arm behind him, spinning him around, and shoved him against his oncoming comrades.

The floor crept up around her ankles and hardened. Belbe dodged one soldier, knelt, and hammered the flowstone with her fist. The material around her right foot splintered, freeing it. She promptly used it to kick one of her attackers in the chest. His cuirass indented three inches from the blow. She felt the ribs behind the armor crack, and the man went down.

A knife point raked across the bridge of her nose. This one was going for her eyes! Enraged, Belbe brought her hand across to ward off another attack. The sergeant drove his knife right through the palm of her hand. She blocked the pain and closed her fingers around his knife, crushing every bone in his hand. He groaned and fell to his knees. Belbe slid her impaled hand off the knife blade and delivered a reverse kick to the back of the man's skull. There was a crunch of bone, and he pitched forward. The man was dead before his head hit the floor.

All of a sudden the fight was over. Belbe had disposed of four attackers. Her left foot was trapped in a thick block of flowstone, and glistening oil was leaking from the hole in her hand. Crovax and the rest of the sergeants withdrew beyond her reach.

Ertai, arms and legs stretched wide, was being held by two of Volrath's statues, animated for the task by Crovax. His shirt was torn open, and a bright red slash crossed his chest. Valmoral, an ugly gash on his head, had cut Ertai once and was poised to do so again.

"Finish him," Crovax ordered.

"No!" said Belbe. "Don't hurt him."

"You see," Crovax said to his surviving men. "Love conquers after all."

Two statues seized Belbe by the hands and feet, spread-eagling her off the floor like Ertai. Crovax found the discharger and picked his way over the fallen men and toppled statues to Belbe.

"You're quite formidable. The overlords built you well," he said.

"I'll be sure to relay your compliments," she replied, panting.

He held up the discharger. "Why wouldn't this work for me?"

"The mechanism is protected. It will function only if I use it," she lied.

Crovax tossed the exotic weapon aside. "Too bad. A splendidly destructive device."

He closely examined her wounded hand. "Not blood?"

Belbe shook her head.

"Interesting." Crovax sniffed the glistening oil and without warning licked the thin black liquid oozing from the wound. Belbe strained against the statues' grip. The one holding her wounded hand softened its hold, just for a second. It was enough. Belbe's open palm connected with Crovax's cheek and sent him sprawling.

Nasser and some of his men started toward him. Crovax got to his knees and stopped them with a blood-chilling glare.

"No one moves!" he hissed.

"Why not release me and make it a fair fight?" Belbe taunted, waving her free hand.

Crovax caught her hand in his, and they wrestled for a few seconds.

"Why do you imagine combat has to be fair?" he gasped.

He backhanded her across the face twice. Belbe's eyes filmed with gray until she shut out that pain as well. Crovax was plainly surprised when she took his blows and grimly smiled at him.

"You are the strongest," Belbe said. "There's no point resisting the inevitable. I will name you evincar."

All fell silent.

Ertai chewed through his gag and spat out the wad of cloth, croaking, "Belbe, no!"

"You heard her!" Crovax cried, pointing a finger at the assembled sergeants. "She said it!"

"I said it, and I mean it," Belbe said. "But it's not official until I proclaim you governor before the overlords on Phyrexia."

"How can you do that? Do I have to travel to Phyrexia?"

"No, I must declare you evincar before the open Window." She meant the voice-only message portal in the convocation hall.

Crovax stood back. The statues released Belbe and Ertai. "I give you this much grace, as you are the emissary and a redoubtable fighter," he said. "Summon the court to the Window and proclaim me evincar to everyone."

Belbe rubbed her battered hand. "I will. Tomorrow."

"Why not now?"

"It's late," she said. "We can do this in haste, or we can install you with all grave and proper ceremony. It's up to you. There's also the matter of Eladamri."

"What's he got to do with it?"

"Wouldn't you like to have him at your feet, in chains, when I name you to the throne? Everything in the hall will be seen on

Phyrexia, you know. Wouldn't you like to impress the overlords by presenting them with the defeated leader of the rebels?" She saw the glimmer of vanity in his eyes.

Crovax nodded with satisfaction. "I still don't see why we can't do it sooner," he said.

"Give Greven the night to break him," Belbe said coolly. "You wouldn't have him shout rebel slogans while the overlords are watching, would you?"

"Hardly." Crovax smiled. "You're much too clever for someone whose life is measured in weeks. Why don't you remain on Rath? When I am evincar, I will need clever servants to carry out my will."

She didn't say anything. She cradled her injured hand in her good one and regarded it thoughtfully.

"The idea intrigues you?" said Crovax.

"It's an interesting proposal. I shall consider it."

The sergeants picked up their dead comrade, and the injured men hobbled away to the dispensary. Four of them, including Nasser, remained behind, surrounding Ertai.

"I'll keep the light of your life until tomorrow," Crovax said. "His life is my guarantee you'll not renege on your promise."

"You will be evincar," Belbe said. "You have my word as emissary of the overlords. Let Ertai go."

Crovax laughed. "Shall we say tomorrow, an hour past midday? I'd hate to become governor until after the courtiers have been fed."

"Choose the hour you want. I will be there."

Crovax herded Ertai and the sergeants out. He paused by the door. "I'll have to do something about this clutter," he said. "My predecessor had appalling taste—such a weakness for the human form. Good night, Excellency. I enjoyed the fight."

She picked up the cast-off Phyrexian discharger. The jewels on the top were dark. Belbe turned the weapon over and discovered the powerstone was gone. Someone—presumably Crovax—had removed it during the melee. An impressive feat, considering he'd never handled such a device before. He'd also removed the powerstone without the special tool, bare-handed. An ordinary man would have been struck dead by the potent energy stored in the stone.

CHAPTER 16
Decision

At the very pinnacle of the Citadel, Sivi and her comrades crouched behind a crane on the airship dock. A few yards away, *Predator* floated gently, tethered to the platform by a half-dozen thick cables. The airship's massive deck gun, which fired a huge barbed harpoon against enemy airships, had just been lowered to the deck by another crane. Gangs of moggs tugged on lines, rocking the gun carriage back and forth until it slipped onto the prepared barbette. Sivi counted at least thirty moggs and their Dal and Vec overseers around *Predator*. Maybe a hundred more were close by in various workshops.

"What do we do, Sivi?" asked Khalil, one of the Vec volunteers.

"If we could get on board, we could do some damage," she muttered.

"Teynel told us not to act alone," said Langwin, a Dal kinsmen of Darsett's. "We should meet up with him as planned and tell him we found the airship."

"Yes, and by the time we get back the damned thing may have flown away," Sivi said. "All the while Eladamri is in the hands of Greven! I tell you, we have to do what we can, now." She loosened the fake bandages and uncoiled the toten-vec from around her waist. "Are you with me?"

Her Vec clansmen quickly agreed. The Dal were less enthused.

"Listen," she said. "If we can destroy *Predator*, it will create confusion throughout the Stronghold. It'll be easier for us to rescue Eladamri and get out of here."

The two Dal rebels mopped sweat from their faces.

"All right," said Medd, the elder of the two. "How do we get on board?"

Sivi looked all around. There was too much open floor between them and the floating airship. Though still dressed in Rathi uniforms, they were in a restricted area and were bound to be stopped long before they reached their target.

Sivi raised her eyes. The flowbot crane they were hiding behind was the largest on the dock. The gantry rose forty feet, and the gooseneck section reached out well over the moored airship.

"Feel like climbing?" she said.

She looped the toten-vec around her shoulder and started up the skeletal framework of the crane. One by one the others followed. The gantry was big enough to allow them to climb three abreast, but Liin Sivi took the lead.

She soon reached the end of the vertical section. Sivi paused and looked down. Her hands tightened on the framework. Not only was she forty feet above the platform, she could see over the edge of the dock to the Citadel far below. The ever-present energy beam was on the other side of *Predator*, and the sizzling blue stream almost drowned out construction noises from the dock.

The workers slacked off the lines on the deck gun once it was in place. Moggs with heavy iron mauls circled the gun and pounded red-hot rivets into the weapon's pedestal. Sparks flew, and when other moggs threw cold water on the rivets to harden them in place, gouts of steam clouded the deck.

It was opportunity sent by the gods. Sivi frantically waved her men forward, and one by one they dropped from the crane to the vacant quarterdeck.

They crouched along the port bulwark and worked their way aft to some open hatches. They heard voices and sounds of work below.

Medd looked to their leader. "What now?"

"There must be flammables on a ship like this," she said. "Oil, niter, liquor, something. We'll search below decks until we find some, then *phutt!*" She tossed a hand in the air. The rebels nodded solemnly.

They were about to ease down the first open hatch when a dock worker popped out unexpectedly. He stared at the five Rathi soldiers huddled there.

"What?" was all he managed to say before the rebels dragged him out and pounded him unconscious. They shoved him in a scupper, out of sight.

Sivi unslung the toten-vec. With gestures she indicated she'd go first.

Step by step, she descended the wide ladder into the ship. The air was heavy with the smell of hot metal and freshly cut wood. Sivi let the knife head of her weapon dangle by a few inches of cord. A mogg came out of a side cabin, a bundle of reinforcing rods on his shoulder. He didn't see Sivi frozen like a statue a few feet behind him, so he kept going. She flattened against the bulkhead and peered around the open door. Two more moggs were working inside, bolting rods to the outer hull plating. Sivi waved for her companions to slip past. When they were clear, she boldly walked by the open door, whip hanging loosely from her hand.

They descended two decks and reached an open ventilator shaft above the engine compartment. The ventilator was four feet square, and the metal grating normally covering it was dismounted and leaning against the aft bulkhead. Hot, humid air rose from the quiescent motor. Sivi risked discovery to gaze down into the engine room. She counted five Dal workmen wiping down the powerstone accumulators with rags, polishing the brass fittings until they gleamed like gold. Sivi sniffed. Mineral spirits . . . that would burn nicely.

Where were they getting it from? She leaned out farther. The workmen were passing a tin bucket around, dipping their rags in and wringing out the excess. When the bucket was empty, they refilled it from a cask standing nearby.

"This is it," she whispered. "Get ready."

They poised themselves around the hole. When four workmen were in sight, Sivi nodded, and they dropped one after the other on the unsuspecting men.

The unarmed rebels surprised the workmen and quickly pummeled them into submission. Sivi was hurling one man headfirst against the bulkhead when the fifth Dal returned with a bucketful of mineral spirits. He dropped the container and shouted for help. Engine noise drowned him out. He turned, but before he ran two steps Sivi unleashed the toten-vec. She made a single underhand cast. With a snap, the knife blade spun through the air at the end of its chain and took the fleeing man in the back. He froze, arms outstretched, as if turned to stone. Sivi yanked the toten-vec, and the return impetus spun the man back to fall dead at her feet.

The other rebels looked on in awe. "Did you think it was a toy? Get that barrel over here," she said.

The group wrestled the heavy cask to the starboard side of the engine. Sivi leaned in, and the three of them toppled the barrel over. Brownish mineral spirits washed down the deck, filling the air with a pungent aroma.

Medd turned his head to avoid the fumes. "Someone will notice the smell."

Someone did. The second after his sentence, a heavy wrench hurtled from above, catching one of the Dal in the forehead. He fell like a poleaxed kerl. The rebels looked up and saw the ventilator opening was lined with moggs, growling, gibbering, and waving hand tools.

A barrage of wrenches and mauls banged off the bulkhead and engine housing. Sivi and Medd leaped one way, Khalil and Langwin the other. A couple of moggs got carried away and jumped into the compartment. The floor was slick with spirits, and they slipped and fell heavily. This didn't prevent other moggs from leaping down on top of their friends. Two of them fell on the helpless Dal who had been hit by the wrench and clubbed him to death. The remaining rebels were divided by the massive engine and a growing swarm of moggs.

A mogg, covered in spirits, got up waving his maul. Sivi flicked the toten-vec blade into his warty chest. It hardly seemed to mind. She and Medd exchanged worried looks.

"They're tougher than they look," Medd observed.

Sivi frowned. "I just have to find a soft spot."

She did, burying the eight-inch iron blade in the mogg's left eye. It shrieked and fell, kicking the deck with its stumpy legs.

"Let's get out of here!" Medd shouted. "Khalil! Langwin! Try to make it to the main deck!"

Langwin dodged a blow and waved that he understood.

"We need a torch!" Sivi cried.

A wrench caromed off the bulkhead beside his head. The tool scraped against his borrowed helmet.

"Flint? Steel?"

"I thought this was a raid, not a camping trip!"

They backed out the forward hatch. Medd slammed shut the door. A thrown maul proved useful in jamming the latch.

Footsteps pounded on the deck above. Sivi and Medd ran forward, eyeing the ceiling.

"Sounds like a hundred," the Dal rebel said.

Sivi looked thoughtfully at the ceiling. "No more than sixty, I'd say." The passage ahead was still clear. "Watch that way!" she said. Medd hovered by the next door, dividing his attention between the corridor and what Liin Sivi was doing.

She spotted a lamp on the wall. It was on a pivot, to freely adjust to whatever attitude the airship assumed. Putting aside the toten-vec, she grabbed the lamp in both hands and succeeded in breaking it off. She adjusted the wick control and the lamp began to glow.

Volatile spirit was leaking under the engine room hatch. *Predator* was trimmed heavy at the bow because the deck gun had just been mounted, so the spill was slowly flowing forward. Sivi stood back and hurled the glowing lamp at the darkening pool seeping under the door. The lamp shattered. The light went out.

"Damn! Their lamps don't use flame."

Two workmen appeared in the passage. They ducked when the toten-vec came whistling their way and quickly fled.

"What now?" asked Medd.

"We've got to do some damage," said Sivi.

"Could we use the big crane outside? Batter the ship with it?"

"That works for me. Let's go!"

They ran down the long passage, crossing the hold on a

narrow catwalk. The interior of the airship had the same zoological quality as the Citadel, and running through it was like traversing the belly of a great beast. The deck was planked with wood, but the bulkheads and ribs of the vessel were some sort of reddish alloy, between metal and bone.

At last the passage ended, and they found a metal ladder leading up. Sivi climbed. When she poked her head out, a crossbow bolt plunked into the deck. The fletching creased her cheek. She ducked so fast she knocked Medd off the ladder below her.

"Are we trapped?" asked Medd, rubbing his hip.

"Not yet."

She let the toten-vec dangle down the steps. With a quick flick, she tossed the knife head out the hatch and whipped it in the direction the arrow came from. It stuck in something. Sivi tugged; it resisted. She raised her head enough to see she'd killed the bowman, but the toten-vec's cord was entangled in the dead man's crossbow.

The deck was clear. They scrambled out and slammed the hatch. Khalil and Langwin were ahead on the main bridge, besieged by swarms of angry moggs.

"We've got to help them!" Medd cried.

Sivi frantically untangled her weapon from the dead man's bow. "We'll need more than one toten-vec to stop that mob."

More than a toten-vec? Medd looked over his shoulder at the biggest weapon he'd ever seen. He took Sivi by the hand and dragged her along.

"Do you know how to operate that thing?" she asked, sizing up the weapon on the run.

"How hard can it be?"

The deck gun was loaded with a barbed harpoon, with a shaft as thick as Medd's thigh. The breech end of the gun was a hedge of levers, none of which were labeled.

Men and moggs were gathering on the dock.

Sivi saw the glint of sword blades among them. "Hurry!"

Medd pulled a lever. The deck gun swung left. Making a note of that, he tried the lever on the opposite side. The gun obligingly swung right. A lever between those two made the gun elevate or depress.

He hauled back on the left side control. The gun mount

rotated rapidly until it was pointed dead astern. Medd let off the lever. He depressed the muzzle until the raked tip of the harpoon was pointing not at the mob of moggs menacing their friends, but at the deck below them. A bolt whizzed by his head.

"Hurry!"

Medd yanked a short lever below the three main controls and was rewarded with a spurt of vapor from the gun mount. Sivi twitched her toten-vec back and forth nervously.

"Try again!" she yelled.

On the elevation control knob was a black button. Medd pressed it.

There was a deafening blast, and the deck gun fired point blank into the rear of the ship. Sivi was thrown to the deck. The enormous harpoon barely cleared the barrel before imbedding itself below the bridge. Planking on the bridge peeled back as far as the harpoon penetrated. The impact hurled moggs through the air end over end.

Sivi sat up, holding her head. A loud clanging filled her ears, and it took her a few seconds to realize the noise was real and not coming from inside her battered brain. Medd dragged her to her feet.

He shouted something. She couldn't hear him. He put his lips close to her ear and shouted.

"They've raised an alarm! This place'll be swarming with soldiers soon!"

The breech of the gun opened automatically after firing. A brown, drum-shaped object popped out of a shute alongside the gun, and a pile of harpoons were stacked conveniently on deck. Medd staggered to the scattered pile of harpoons and man-handled one back to the gun. It wouldn't feed through the breech, so he loaded it down the muzzle. The brown drum was exactly the size of the cavity at the rear of the gun, so he inserted it and closed the breech.

Smoke from the first firing drifted across the deck to the air-ship dock. Dock workers had taken cover after the gun was fired, and in their place came heavily armed palace guards. Sivi used the smoke to reach the quarterdeck. Stunned, bleeding moggs lay everywhere. She had to dig under them to find her missing comrades. Khalil was dead, killed by the moggs before the gun fired. Langwin was senseless. She dragged him out and boosted him to his feet.

"You on *Predator!* Stand away from that gun!" shouted a voice from the dock. Medd pulled the right lever, and the harpoon thrower swung smoothly toward the voice.

"Stand away, or we'll storm the deck!"

Medd leveled the gun in the speaker's direction. He waited until Sivi appeared through the smoke with Langwin leaning on her shoulder.

"Loose!"

A wave of arrows swept the deck. Shielded by the massive gun, Medd was safe enough, but the volley caught Sivi and Langwin in the open. Langwin was hit twice. Sivi let the dead man fall and threw herself on the deck.

"What are you waiting for?" she yelled. "Let fly!"

Twenty-odd soldiers came running through the smoke, swords bared. They were in skirmishing order, so Medd depressed the gun at them and pressed the firing button.

There was a double explosion. The harpoon shaft snapped, and the barbed head plowed sideways through the attacking guards. The butt end of the harpoon shot crazily into the air, ricocheting off the dock and flying into the energy stream. It vaporized in a burst of white light and smoke.

Medd had failed to close the gun fully, firing it with the breech plug unlocked. The resulting explosion completely wrecked the gun.

Bleeding from minor shrapnel cuts to his face and hands, Medd staggered to his feet. Sivi was lying face down on the deck a few yards away. Heedless of the danger, he moved across the smoky deck to reach her. There were no obvious holes in her, but she wasn't moving. He knelt and prodded her with a bleeding finger.

"Sivi? Sivi, are you alive?"

She raised her head. "Of course I am." She stood up and dusted herself off. She coiled the toten-vec in her hand. "You're pretty dangerous with that thing."

"I ruined it."

"Good. That's why we're here."

The dock was still, though the alarm bell still pealed. The surviving rebels ran to the edge of the foredeck and rattled down he gangplank. No one on the dock was alive. The sideways-spinning harpoon head had slain the entire squad.

Sivi paused long enough to salvage a pair of daggers. Medd ound a sword that hadn't been bent too much by the blast and shoved it in his empty scabbard.

"Come," he said. "We must find Teynel and the others!"

They reached the side stairs just as another detachment of palace guards arrived on the main lift. The rebels slipped away in the smoke, leaving a damaged but intact *Predator* floating easily on its moorings.

* * * * *

He never cried out. Greven admired him for that.

The questioning went on for hours without result. Greven and the mogg warders went through their standard repertory of branding irons, thumbscrews, and pincers. Eladamri never screamed, never begged for mercy. He cursed for a while, then fell silent. His resistance spooked the moggs, and they began to slip away from the session. By midnight no one was left in the cell but Greven and the stubborn rebel leader.

The Vec warrior poured himself a cup of tepid water. He sat down on a low stool and studied the enemy who had so long eluded him. Unlike the common soldiers of Rath, Greven never believed Eladamri had magical powers. He understood—or thought he understood—the mind of a dedicated fighter. But when Eladamri exhausted his interrogators and revealed nothing of his plans, his organization, or himself, Greven felt bereft of understanding. He was just a middle-aged elf, of no great size or physical strength. He didn't preach about freedom and liberty the way some rebel prisoners did. He said nothing. He endured.

"What's your secret?" Greven asked.

Hanging by his wrists, Eladamri twisted slowly with the torsion of the rope. He'd escaped into unconsciousness, but he was still visibly breathing.

The cell door swung open. Greven jumped up, snatching his bare sword from the table beside him. A shadowy figure stood in the entrance.

"Who's there?"

The intruder stepped forward, and Greven saw the hooded figure clearly.

"It's you," he said. "There's nothing to tell. He won't talk."

The hooded one glided into the room. Pale hands emerged from the wide sleeves and gently folded back the cowl. Greven saw the face of Furah.

"Why are you here?" he asked the Kor.

"I've been interested in this one a long time," said the visitor. "Your usual methods failed, didn't they?" Greven admitted they had. "You can't break a warrior like Eladamri by abusing his body. Someone like you, Greven, whose entire being is wrapped up in his physical form, you would have broken by now."

Greven bristled. "I am no stranger to pain."

"Pain isn't the author of submission—fear is. They're quite different. Ordinary men come to this room filled with terror because they know they will suffer great pain. Eladamri was not afraid. His spirit preserves him from mere physical suffering. To reach him, we will have to find out what he fears."

"Do you have time for this? The emissary has been holding out against Crovax, but she can't withstand him much longer. Will you act soon?"

"There's time. I have certain elixirs with me that will open windows into Eladamri's mind. I'll use them."

Greven set his face like stone. He hated drugs. Under normal circumstances, there was a kind of bond between prisoner and interrogator—strength vs. strength, it was. Though he would never admit it to the visitor, he felt Eladamri had qualified for an honorable death. He was tortured, he held out, and the next step ought to be a dignified execution. Elixirs were a cheat. No one could resist them. Eladamri would tell everything now, and his honor would be lost.

He ordered Greven to bring the elf down. Greven untied the rope and lowered Eladamri to the floor. A heavy chair was dragged over, and the unconscious rebel leader was strapped to it. All the while, the visitor busied himself at the table, mixing powders from various vials into a cup. His stirring rod tinkled in the gloomy cell.

He held out the cup. "Hold his nose," he said. "I don't want to be bitten."

Greven tilted back Eladamri's slack head. He held the elf's nose and pulled his chin down. In came the cup, delivered by a slender Kor hand. Greven got a whiff of the potion. It had a sharp odor, like vinegar.

Suddenly a metallic bell began to clang loudly in the corridor.

Greven released Eladamri's nose. "Intruders!"

"The guards can handle it," said Furah, putting the cup to Eladamri's lips.

"I must see to any disturbance," Greven insisted, pushing the cup away. "You should come too."

"Why me?"

"Things are very unsettled. It's a dangerous time for all of us. If you want to keep up with what's going on, you'd better come along."

"You don't want me to administer my elixir. Are you afraid I'll succeed where you failed?"

"The prisoner's not going anywhere. If the alarm is false, or the situation easily resolved, we can return—nothing will be lost," said Greven.

The visitor raised his hood. "Time will be lost, but I take your meaning. Order must be restored to Rath if my plan is to succeed."

Greven quickly buckled on his sword belt. "What do you intend?"

"To take what's mine. Nothing less."

* * * * *

Teynel and his team descended into the bowels of the Citadel in search of an airship docking station. None of them knew their way around, and the deeper they penetrated the labyrinthine recesses of the flowstone works, the more lost they became.

"Don't these people believe in signs?" Teynel asked in exasperation. He'd thought as long as they kept going down, they would eventually find evidence of the airship dock. No such luck occurred. Before long the rebels found themselves negotiating tunnels too low for them to stand in. The air was oppressively hot and humid, and the lower they went, the hotter it got.

They'd not encountered any people for quite some time. This did not mean the tunnels were unoccupied. As Teynel and his men crept along, stepping over ridges in the ribbed floor, they saw strange creatures moving about in the semi-darkness.

One numerous creature had an egg-shaped body, about the size of a water pail. It walked on two long legs bent backward at the knee. Covered in bare, spotty skin, it had no discernible head. The creature smelled like rotten meat. It paid no attention to the rebels, who pressed themselves against the wall and let the headless thing hop by.

Moving on, they reached a narrow vertical shaft. The top was lost in profound darkness; the bottom glowed brightly with a pulsating red light. A rushing sound, like deep waters pouring over a precipice, boomed up the shaft.

"There's light down there," Teynel said. "It may be a way to the dock."

His clansman Garnan offered to scout the situation. The walls of the shaft were deeply ribbed, so he had no problem climbing down. The other rebels lay on the tunnel floor and watched their comrade descend toward the throbbing red light.

After a few long minutes, Garnan called up, "Teynel! You must see this!"

"What is it?"

"Teynel, come see! It's fantastic!"

They all wanted to go, but Teynel ordered the remaining rebels to stay put. He spit on his hands and began his climb down. The ribbing was coated with some kind of resilient skin, yielding to his grip. It looked oily, but in fact was dry to the touch, and Teynel was able to descend with confidence. Ten feet or so below the tunnel, the glare all but shut out the dark shaft above. Air in the shaft was broiling, yet the walls remained surprisingly cool. Teynel could not see any bottom to the shaft, but he kept going. Garnan was a sound fellow, and wouldn't call him if there wasn't something worth seeing.

He lowered his right foot, but instead of another rib found only air. Teynel held on, waving his foot around, trying to find a place for his toe. Something grabbed his heel.

"Over here. It's me."

With Garnan's aid, Teynel climbed out. There was a platform

made of polished tubing at the bottom of the shaft. Teynel's feet began sliding as soon as they touched the slippery ledge.

"Careful," Garnan said. "This stuff's like glass!"

Teynel gripped the rail circling the platform. They were suspended hundreds of feet in the air at the very lowest point of the whole Citadel. The entire structure was above them, and below, clearly visible through the slatted tubing, was the crater floor and lava well.

"By all the gods," Teynel gasped.

A column of molten rock thirty yards wide rose from the funnel-shaped aperture below the Citadel. It was drawn up to a large cluster of nozzles in the center of the Citadel's belly. The stream of red-hot liquid rock thundered into the tubes with a sound like a hundred waterfalls. The heat was intense, and Teynel had to cover his face with his arm just to glance at the flow.

"Look there!" Garnan said, tugging at his arm. Teynel tore his eyes from the awesome spectacle and followed Garnan's pointing hand. Perhaps forty yards away was a massive pylon, jutting down from the main body of the Citadel. A wide platform served by cranes was built on the end of the pylon.

"The airship dock!" Teynel shouted over the roar.

"Yes, and it's not there!"

"Either Sivi's found it, or *Predator* has left the crater," Teynel said, pushing his comrade to the shaft opening. "Let's go back! We must keep our rendezvous with the others!"

Garnan leaped and caught hold of the ribbed inner lining of the shaft. He pulled himself by his arms alone until he could get his feet on the bottom lip. Teynel watched him climb, then poised himself to repeat Garnan's leap.

The platform quivered beneath him. As the polished surface was almost frictionless, Teynel skidded in a small circle. He grabbed at the rail and realized to his horror that the platform was circling toward the thundering lava stream.

"Garnan! Garnan, hurry!"

The round opening his comrade had entered had become crescent-shaped. This was no mere observation platform—it was part of the huge flowstone works! The shaft was used to convey molten lava to the factory far above!

Teynel leaped. He caught the ribbing with one hand. It wasn't enough. One by one his fingers tore free, and he fell heavily on the bright floor of tubing.

"Teynel!'

Garnan, hanging by his feet and one hand, waved for his kinsman to try again. The inexorable progress of the rotating platform would soon immerse Teynel in molten rock. The Dal rebel threw himself at Garnan's outstretched hand. Their fingers met, but their sweaty palms slipped over each other. Garnan shoved his shoulder down and wrapped his fingers around Teynel's sleeve. For an agonizing second Teynel dangled at the end of his friend's arm. The shaft opening was still waning. Teynel took hold of Garnan's arm with both hands. Face purpling, the young Dal hauled his friend up. Teynel just got his feet through and the opening closed to just a few inches.

"Cousin or no, as of today, you are my brother," Teynel vowed.

"Does this mean I can't marry your sister?" quipped Garnan.

Teynel and Garnan struggled for breath in the relatively cool shaft. When they were able, they climbed to the intersecting tunnel. Kireno, Vellian, and Shamus were not at the end of the tunnel where they'd left them.

They retraced their steps through the tunnel. After calling quietly to their comrades and receiving no answer, Teynel paused to listen.

"Hear that?"

A soft tearing sound was coming from down the corridor.

Garnan nodded. "I hear."

They crept on, senses straining to detect any danger. The tunnel curved to the left and rose. Rounding the curve, Teynel spotted something lying on the floor some yards ahead.

Part of the object was moving. As they slowly closed, Teynel made out a pair of booted feet lying motionless on the floor. The remnant of a dirty Rathi army mantle was draped over the rest.

It was a corpse—one of their men. He couldn't tell which one. Standing on the corpse's back was one of those spotty two-legged creatures. It didn't have a head, but it had a mouth full of crooked, needlelike teeth. It pivoted its jaws down and took another bite of the body.

Garnan saw it too and drew in breath with a sharp hiss. Teynel ran forward and kicked the hideous scavenger with all his might. It squealed and went flying. Ominously, there were answering squeals from the darkness. Lots of them.

"Filthy little monsters," Teynel said. "I wonder how many more of them are out there?"

"I don't care to find out," Garnan replied.

The mysterious death of their comrade and the disappearance of the other two men put haste in their stride. When Garnan and Teynel emerged in a normal-sized, well-lit corridor in the lower palace, they paused again to catch their breath.

"Do you reckon they were captured or eaten?" asked Garnan.

"Neither, I pray. I hope Kireno got impatient and went to meet Liin Sivi at the rendezvous."

The pair moved on.

They were within sight of the convocation chamber steps when the alarm erupted. Teynel knew instantly it meant some part of their team had been found out. He resisted an urge to run. He and Garnan stood to one side as palace guards massed in the hall. Crovax appeared, sword in hand, and demanded a report.

"There's been a disturbance," said one of the guards.

"What a revelation! Speak plainly!" Crovax snapped.

"Some soldiers attacked the workers on *Predator*—"

Teynel gripped his partner's arm. Sivi! Damn her! He told her not to act on her own!

"Soldiers? What soldiers?" Crovax was pacing and swinging his sword. "Sounds like rebel infiltrators to me, probably trying to liberate their leader."

He swiftly ordered army troops into the Citadel. When the captain of the guard protested the use of regular troops in the palace environs, Crovax raised a flowstone tentacle and strangled the man where he stood.

"Any other objections?" he asked. "Good. You men follow me."

Fifty guards formed ranks and marched away to the stairs and lifts. Teynel and Garnan were about to slip away.

"You there! Where do you think you're going?" Crovax was looking right at them.

Teynel saluted. "Returning to our company, my lord."

"Never mind that. I need you now."

Teynel spread his hands. "I've no sword, my lord, nor has my friend."

Crovax raised an eyebrow slightly. Two spires of flowstone rose from the floor. The formed into identical short swords, complete with cross hilt and moon pommel. Teynel and Garnan stared in amazement.

"Take them, you idiots," Crovax said. When the rebels did, the supporting rod of flowstone detached and retracted into the floor. The swords took on the color and weight of standard steel weapons.

"Come." Crovax swept away, mantle billowing. Teynel and Garnan sheathed their new swords and ran to catch up. One way or another, they would find their comrades, even if it meant joining the troops sent to catch them.

CHAPTER 17
Forsaken

He was no stranger to pain. He knew it in many forms, from the bite of a Skyshroud snake to the ragged kiss of a merfolk blade. His had been an active life, and he had endured many injuries. There were worse forms of suffering than the physical kind: The vision of a wife in the burned and shattered remains of the home they'd built together. An empty bed where a gentle daughter had slept and died.

He learned to kill his enemies as revenge for these hurts. It didn't help, but he was never troubled by their blood on his hands. What did weigh on his conscience were all the dead friends and allies, people he led to war who died for his cause. Each of their lost lives was one more scar to bear, a burden he knew would grow larger before life was done with him.

Since he was alone, Eladamri let the tears flow down his lined face. He'd always been awake, even through the worst of Greven's torment. At times his mind departed on its own, leaving him unsure of what he was seeing or feeling. He remembered—thought he remembered—Greven *il*-Vec sitting across the table from him, watching him with something like puzzlement on his evil face. He'd been joined by another, someone

227

Eladamri hadn't known. His erratic eyes showed him the face of Furah, the Kor tribal chief, but Furah was dead. His daughter was dead too, yet someone was walking around with her face. Was this unholy fortress full of ghosts?

Tears softened the crust of dried blood that glued his right eye shut. He opened both eyes and stretched them wide. Coals glowed feebly in the iron brazier by his feet. Thumbscrews, branding irons, and other horrible instruments lay scattered about. He could smell water in the pot on the table. Licking his parched lips, Eladamri yearned for a sip.

Thinking him unconscious, Greven had tied Eladamri to the chair by the wrists and ankles—a mistake. Eladamri relaxed his hands, folding his fingers inward to make his wrists as small as possible. He worked his left hand backward against the cords. The black rope was made of the same mimetic cable used on *Predator* and was thus a form of nano-machine like flowstone. When he pulled against it, it shrank tighter around his wrist. He stopped, and the cord ceased shrinking. Eladamri realized Greven's mistake was not so grievous. If he continued to fight the mimetic cord, it would eventually cut his hands off.

He leaned forward and managed to lift the rear legs of the chair off the floor. The chair weighed a good forty-five pounds, but once he got it rocking, it was easy enough to tip it over. It crashed to the floor hard on his left side. The brazier overturned, scattering embers.

How did magic rope like heat? Eladamri scraped a glowing coal closer with his ruined fingers. What did a blister or two matter when your fingers were already broken?

He pressed the cord against the coal. A stab of heat passed through the binding to his wrist. Nothing else happened. So much for burning off the cords. He heaved the heavy chair forward to a pile of now-cold branding irons. He couldn't quite wrestle the heavy irons into his grasp with just his fingertips. Now what?

He could see the pottery pitcher on the table above him. What he wanted most, perhaps even more than his freedom, was a cool drink of water. Since he couldn't get to the pitcher so long as he was tied to the chair, it was a moot point. Eladamri butted his head against the table leg. He did this again and again until his vision dissolved in a haze of red. This couldn't go on.

With the lightest touch, he let his battered head rest against the table leg and sighed. The jug, shaken to the edge of the table, promptly toppled to the floor. It smashed to pieces in a spray of water. None splashed his face.

Not my best day, he decided.

The pitcher was boneware, a hard, glassy pottery suitable for his purpose. He picked a nicely jagged shard and sawed against the cords. For a moment the mimetic strands tightened, then began to fray. His heart leaped when the cord sprang free of his wrists and wriggled on the floor like a headless lizard. A few cuts more, and his right hand was loose, then his feet.

Eladamri tried to stand, but found his abused knees wouldn't let him. He sat on the floor, free but too hurt to walk.

He tied pieces of cord together and used it to bind an iron to his left leg as a splint. Using the table for support, he managed to stand. He grabbed the cup on the table and prepared to down the contents, but when it neared his lips his nose detected an acrid odor. Poison. Meant for him, no doubt, and here he almost did Greven's job for him!

His meager possessions lay strewn on the table. The only thing he took back was the small wooden fetish he'd carved his last night in the forest. He examined it carefully. It was intact, so he hung it around his neck.

Eladamri found another branding iron with a blunt hook on the end to serve as a weapon. He went to the cell door and found it unlocked. That worried him. Why wasn't he locked in? Was this some kind of elaborate trap so Greven could claim Eladamri was killed "trying to escape?"

A muffled mechanical clangor filtered through the stout walls. Some sort of alarm. That's why Greven had gone. He swiftly made the connection to his young warriors and their mission to destroy the airship. Eladamri did not pray, but he fervently wished his comrades success. The odds were long against them.

He hobbled into the corridor. No one in sight. The conical tower's shape meant the passage ran outboard of the cells, which were arranged around the axis of the tower like slices of pie. As he looked both ways down the vacant corridor, his guerrilla instinct gave him an idea. Never overlook a chance to cause maximum trouble for the enemy!

He went to the next door. It was locked, and the mechanism was protected by a nasty looking flowbot whose jagged jaws encircled the lock. Use the wrong key, or try to fiddle with the device, and your hand could be bitten off.

Eladamri rapped softly on the door. He pressed his ear to the panel and heard shuffling of feet inside. There was a low wicket through which the prisoner was given meals.

He opened the sliding gate and whispered, "Hello? Who's in there? I'm a friend!"

Instead of a voice or a face, a fleshy red tentacle appeared and wrapped itself around Eladamri's leg. A burning sensation started where the thing touched him, and its grip tightened and tightened. He was sorry for whatever beast or freak Volrath had imprisoned, but he wasn't about to lose his leg in a show of sympathy. A few well aimed blows of his iron discouraged the creature, and the tentacle was withdrawn.

The next three doors either were closed on empty cells, or else the occupants didn't feel like responding to Eladamri's summons. At the fifth door he distinctly heard a thin voice talking or singing.

Bending low to the wicket he hissed, "Are you human in there?"

"Are you human out there?" was the sarcastic response.

"I'm a Skyshroud elf, a prisoner as you are. I'll let you out."

No answer. He gingerly inserted the iron into the lock mechanism. Sure enough, the flowbot's jaws snapped shut, deeply indenting the hard iron bar. Eladamri leaned all his weight on the trapped tool, and with a crack, broke the lock without dislodging the flowbot protecting it.

The door opened into the corridor. The smell of filth from inside was overwhelming. Something gray stirred within, and for a second Eladamri thought he'd been tricked by another one of Volrath's monsters. The gray shape became a human form—a gaunt, red-haired young woman of modest height, clad in filthy rags.

She blinked at the light. "You are an elf," she said. "I thought my time had come, and Volrath was playing a little game with me."

"Who are you?"

"My name is Takara, daughter of Starke."

He knew the name from Darsett *en*-Dal. Takara had been part of the early Dal resistance movement. Why was she still alive?

Takara slumped against the door. "Has there been a revolution? Or are you the new chief warder?"

"Neither. I'm escaping, if I can. If you would be free, come along."

Though limping himself, he gave his arm to the stranger. Takara didn't look like she'd been Greven's guest in the interrogation cell. Her skin was unmarked, but she was terribly thin and weak, probably starved for weeks.

She looked down at his makeshift splint and battered hands. "You're not in any shape for this, are you?"

"I'm not alone," he advised. "Some of my people are in the Citadel, but we have to find them."

Takara lowered her head to his shoulder. "Oh well, this has broken the tedium . . ."

The alarm bell ceased. It had been part of the background so long, its sudden cessation seemed louder than the noise had been. In its place they heard footfalls echoing along the curving corridor.

Takara lifted her head. "The world's shortest escape," she said, sighing.

Eladamri held a finger to his lips. He pulled the iron splint from his tortured leg. Without the brace, he almost collapsed. Takara held him up, though her frail arms trembled from the effort.

He nodded thanks.

They huddled in the shallow recess of a shut cell door, waiting for the runners to appear. Eladamri caught a glimpse of Rathi boot and breastplate and swung his iron. It whistled by Kireno's nose, missing him by a hair.

"Brother!" the Vec rebel cried. "It's us!"

The momentum of the swing carried Eladamri to the floor. Takara couldn't disentangle herself and fell on top of him. The two were gently separated by Kireno and one of Teynel's many cousins, Shamus.

They propped the elf against the wall.

"Be easy, brother," Kireno said. He took the water bottle from his hip and gave it to Eladamri. He drank greedily until he saw Takara watching him with parted lips. He wiped the mouth of the bottle and offered it to her.

Takara seized the bottle with both hands and raised it high. Water spurted from the corners of her mouth and ran down her chin, cutting white tracks in the gray grime on her face.

Eladamri smiled. "What news of Teynel, Liin Sivi, and the rest?"

"We fear Teynel and cousin Garnan are dead," Shamus put in. "We were trying to find the lower airship dock we'd heard about and got lost in some tunnels deep in the fortress. Teynel and Garnan went ahead to scout, but we were attacked!"

"Greven? Crovax?"

"Creatures, monsters!" Kireno said. "Poor Vellian put his hand in a nest of them. These two-legged ratballs devoured him . . . we had to run, we had no weapons to fight them with. We were supposed to meet Liin Sivi and her men at the hall where we saw Greven and Crovax, but the bell started ringing and there were guards all over the place—"

"—so we came to find you instead." Shamus finished Kireno's sentence for him.

"What's it like in the Citadel?" asked Eladamri.

"Chaos," Kireno replied. "They're bringing troops in from the city garrison, I heard them say. The whole place will be overrun with soldiers."

"Sivi must have drawn their attention. Very well, we need to get out of sight for a while and wait for things to calm a bit before we try to get out," the elf said.

"Where can we go?" said Shamus.

"Greven's bound to return here to finish with me," said Eladamri. "I can't decide whether to ambush him here or clear out to fight another day."

"Begging your pardon, O Eladamri, but you're in no shape to fight," Kireno said. "Let's find a quiet corner to hide in, as you said."

Takara interjected. "The map room," she said. "It's the next building over, before you get to the mogg warrens. It's for the evincar's use only, so no one goes there much."

"You know your way around this maze?"

She looped dirty copper hair behind her ears. "My father was Volrath's mentor and later his servant. I know something about the Stronghold." She handed the empty water bottle to Eladamri.

"The map room it is," he said.

He and Takara had to be helped to stand. They braced each other.

Takara smiled wryly. "You never know what you'll find behind a closed door, do you?"

* * * * *

When the alarm went off, Belbe was in the control room of the flowstone factory making the third of her subversive adjustments to the output meter. As she suspected, the monitoring units built into the factory machinery had detected the reduced output by comparing current production figures to those of the past. All through the day the production of flowstone steadily increased. By the time she arrived late that night, the works were churning out flowstone at 90 percent of capacity. The speed at which the factory corrected itself troubled her. It meant she would have to be more vigilant in her sabotage if her goal of preventing the conjunction with Dominaria was to be met.

When the alarm sounded, she covered all traces of her tampering and started back to the palace to find out what was going on. She found the corridors clogged with guards. Though the palace garrison numbered over two thousand men, she found hundreds of troops of the regular army mustering on the factory concourse. She accosted a captain of the Tenth Company and asked him what he knew about the situation.

"Forgive me, Excellency, I don't know much more than you do," the officer said. "I heard something about *Predator*—a riot between the moggs and the workers, maybe. I don't know."

"Why would they need so many troops to quell a brawl?"

"There's thousands of moggs in the warrens, Excellency. If they get out of hand, it would take the entire army to put them down."

"Who's commanding this operation?"

The captain frowned and pointed. Belbe followed his gesture

and saw a sergeant standing on a flowbot armature, shouting orders. If the Corps of Sergeants was involved, it meant Crovax was in charge.

Belbe was seized by a sense of foreboding. She smelled a plot. If Crovax had engineered an emergency in order to flood the Citadel with army troops, it gave him an unbeatable advantage in the struggle for power. True, she had offered him the evincar's crown, but that was just a ploy to save Ertai's life. She'd still held out hope that with Greven's help she could suppress Crovax and lead Rath in an entirely new direction. Now things looked very bad, if not hopeless.

Once in the palace, she learned there had been a disturbance at the upper airship dock. She went there immediately and found the pinnacle heavily occupied. The docking platform was littered with slain guards, and the air was spiced with the smell of burnt gunpowder. *Predator* floated evenly on its tether, but there was obvious damage to the deckhouse and main bridge.

She easily picked out Greven and Crovax among the mass of troops. Greven bowed when he saw her. Crovax did not.

She approached Greven. "What's the matter?"

"Things are unclear at the moment, Excellency," he replied. "We're questioning the workers and moggs who were on board when this happened, but we're not getting a coherent story from any of them. The guards who responded to the first call for help are all dead, killed by that." He indicated the twelve-foot-long harpoon head, now imbedded in the far wall of the platform. "Someone fired the deck gun without closing the breech. The gun's mangled, and the harpoon cut down more than twenty men at once."

"What do the workers say?" asked Belbe.

"They say the moggs went berserk and attacked them."

"And what do the moggs say?"

"Moggs are moggs," Greven said. "I've learned not to put much stock in what they say."

"Tell her," Crovax said. He seemed half-angry, half-excited. "Tell her what they said."

"It's not proven," Greven said evenly.

Even this mild contradiction brought swift retaliation from

Crovax. Greven's face contorted as his spinal rod sizzled into action.

"Enough," Belbe said. "You tell me, Crovax."

Crovax made his hulking victim suffer for a few seconds, then released him. "The moggs claim they were attacked by soldiers—men of the army."

"Why would our own soldiers attack *Predator?*"

Crovax leaned closer, and in a mocking whisper said, "When is a rabbit not a rabbit?"

"What?"

"When it's a fox."

Sergeant Nasser, on the foredeck of the airship, hailed his master. Crovax excused himself politely and went to see what Nasser had to tell him.

Belbe turned to Greven. The warlord still had his eyes tightly shut.

"Greven," she said. "Are you all right?"

"He's learned to inflict lingering pain," Greven said through clenched teeth. "He's done this to me several times in the past few days. He punishes me, or amuses himself with my suffering. I think it's over, but he leaves me a surprise. Lately it's been acute pain when light hits my eyes."

Belbe lowered her voice. "I'm sorry to hear that. Would you walk with me a moment? I have a proposal I want you to hear."

"As you command, Excellency. First—" Greven's eyes sprang open. They were shot with blood, and when the normal light of the Stronghold hit them, he grimaced and uttered a short cry of agony.

"Does it hurt so much?"

"I'm getting used to it," Greven grunted. "However, if I don't gratify Lord Crovax's sense of humor by screaming, he will redouble the effect next time."

Belbe shuddered. "Come. I have something important and secret to tell you."

She led him into the shadow of the flowstone carapace, dismissing the guards who were already there. When they were alone, Belbe began.

"The time has come for plain speaking. Crovax has been

pressuring me to name him evincar. After many threats and some violence, I've agreed to do so tomorrow afternoon in the convocation hall."

"I've wondered why you've delayed this long," said Greven.

She was taken aback. "At first, I wanted him to prove himself worthy. Later I became afraid of what he would do when total power was his. I saw what he did to the hostages. I was there. It troubled him no more than you or I swatting a fly. I discovered he gains power when life is extinguished—he absorbs the life-force of dying beings into himself. Don't you see? This guarantees people will continue to die!"

"We will all die sometime, Excellency."

Belbe's hands closed into fists. "What's the matter with you? Of all people, I expected you to understand. He torments you. He mocks you. It will only get worse, can't you see that? Have you no ambition for yourself, Greven? If we could forge an alliance against Crovax, we could change things on Rath."

"Crovax is too powerful. He controls the flowstone."

"Ertai has influence over the stone, too. Not as great as Crovax's but sufficient to even the odds if you and I attack him together!"

Greven made a pretense of looking around. "Where is Ertai?"

"I don't know. Crovax's men are holding him prisoner."

"Then he's a dead man."

"No!" she said forcefully. "Give me your word—promise you'll join with us against Crovax, and I'll find Ertai this night and free him!"

"I cannot." Belbe was visibly deflated by Greven's flat rejection. "There is more at stake here than you know, Excellency. I cannot act as you ask. My loyalties are . . . committed."

"I don't believe it," she said. "I know you hate him. Can it be you're afraid of him as well?"

She thought this taunt, which always enraged Greven in the past, would arouse him again, but the hulking warlord turned away without a word.

"I'm not free to act, Excellency," Greven said. "I never have been. Though I command armies and the flag on *Predator*'s bridge is mine, I do not have command of myself. I'm sorry."

Speechless, Belbe watched him return to the hubbub surrounding the damaged airship. On the way, he was intercepted by an officer of the palace guard in a crimson mantle. Though Greven outranked anyone else in the guards or regular army, she distinctly saw him salute this minor officer.

Crovax really has him rattled, she decided. Her options were shrinking hour by hour. Ertai captive, Greven immobilized, even the rebel leader Eladamri was no longer a threat. Crovax stood alone on the field, waiting for Belbe to place a crown upon his head.

She must find Ertai. Once she knew he was safe, she would go to her last resource. If he didn't help her, then every living being on Rath was doomed.

* * * * *

Kireno and Shamus, still attired like soldiers of the Fourth Company, boldly walked out on the open causeway connecting the prison to the map tower. Two sentries were posted on the bridge between the buildings, one on each side, facing each other. Kireno and Shamus approached in measured step.

"Halt!" the Vec rebel shouted, hoping to sound military.

"What's this?" asked the sentry on the right, nearest Kireno.

"We're your relief."

The rebels waited tensely. The guards relaxed their stance.

"About bloody time," one guard groused. "We should've been relieved two hours ago!"

"There's trouble in the Citadel," Shamus said. "That's why they sent for the Fourth Company."

"Oh yeah? You guys talk a lot, but what makes you so great?"

"We captured Eladamri," Kireno said.

The sentries couldn't top that, and they didn't try. They shouldered their polearms and prepared to march back to the Citadel.

Then one of the guards stopped. "Hey, how do you plan to stand guard without any weapons?"

Shamus and Kireno exchanged quick glances. "Uh, they wouldn't let us through the palace armed," said the Dal rebel.

"What? In a general alarm?"

Kireno dodged the sweep of a poleax and charged in before

the guard could recover. He hit the man high, carrying him along until the reached the edge of the bridge. The Vec gave an extra shove, and the guard toppled backward over the rail. His scream faded as he fell, and it was soon drowned out by the constant background rumble of the factory energy beam.

Shamus had more trouble with his man. He avoided the guard's spearhead, but the back swipe of the shaft caught him behind the knees, and down he went. That would have been the end of him if Kireno hadn't jumped on the guard's back, knocking the Rathi soldier's helmet off in the process. They fell in a tangle on top of Shamus and rolled over and over in a flurry of fists and kicking feet.

Eladamri and Takara came out of hiding at the prison tower gate. By the time they reached the scuffle, the unfortunate guard was hanging by his hands over the side of the bridge. Shamus was out cold, and Kireno was bleeding from a busted lip.

"Help! Help me!" yelled the guard.

Eladamri and Takara stood over him. The Rathi soldier stopped shouting.

"Please help me," he said.

The elf held out his hands. "Thanks to Greven il-Vec, there's not much I can do," he said.

"Lady, please help!"

Takara looked around. She spotted the guard's poleax. In her weakened condition, she couldn't fully pick it up, so she dragged it by the butt end to the edge of the causeway.

"That's it," said the guard. "Hand me the shaft, and I'll climb up."

Takara said nothing, but held the poleax shaft over the guard's head. He regarded her quizzically until she let go. The stout shaft connected solidly with the soldier's bare head, and he disappeared with a screech. The poleax tipped up and followed him into oblivion.

"A waste of a good arm," Kireno said. He knelt by Shamus and patted his face roughly to revive him.

Eladamri leaned on the rail, looking intently at Takara. "That was cold."

"I learned from an early age, if someone gets in your way, put them aside," said Takara.

They cleaned up the bridge of all traces of trouble and hurried to the map tower. The door was locked, but Takara claimed she knew how to circumvent the mechanism. She fearlessly thrust her hand into the flowbot jaws and manipulated the lock inside. Eladamri and the rebels waited to see if the jaws would bite off her slender arm.

"My father taught me this," she said. "Good for sneaking in where you're not allowed . . . I hope Volrath hasn't changed the locks since he threw me in prison."

With a loud clank, the doors spread apart. Takara carefully withdrew her arm from the lock.

"After you," said Eladamri.

The interior of the map tower was suffused with wavering green light, which fostered the odd sensation of being underwater. It came from the tower cone, glazed entirely with heavy, irregular panes of jade-green glass. The upper half of the map tower was taken up by some kind of complex machinery, all gears and cams and glowing powerstones. Takara led Eladamri and the rebels into an amphitheater, which filled the bottom quarter of the structure. This single room was over three hundred feet wide and featured two concentric seating platforms, focused on a central column of intricate design. A set of wide steps descended to this column, and overhead, a segmented gantry curled above the central pillar like the tail of a huge metallic scorpion. As they entered the vast, empty chamber, their footsteps rang hollowly off the green glass walls.

"Welcome to the Map Room," Takara said. Her voice was still weak from privation, yet the acoustics of the map room enabled her voice to be heard easily.

"I don't see any maps," said Shamus, still groggy from his fight on the bridge.

"I'll show you."

She descended a staircase to the inner ring of seats. At the foot of the steps was a panel, covered with strange glyphs and symbols. Takara stood before this arcane altar, hands poised. Then, as if playing a musical instrument, her fingers flew over the controls, touching the symbols in a complex sequence.

With a deep hum, the enormous machine awoke. The broad descending column, covered with brazen cog wheels and bundles of tubing, retracted ponderously into the ceiling. It left behind a thick stump, serrated with large angular flaps. These flaps folded outward and stopped. When the column was about thirty feet up, it locked in place.

"Now what?" Eladamri asked in a hushed voice.

"Here." She stroked a single glyph.

The air between the column and the serrated base shimmered. A swirl of gray and green fog formed, whirling on both axes. It darkened, became opaque, and assumed the shape of an oval spinning globe. More definition developed, and the rapid rotation slowed. In seconds, the globe settled into a mottled gray egg, turning slowly on its vertical axis.

"Rath," Takara said.

Eladamri looked on, fascinated. "This is Rath?" Takara nodded. "For years I've heard philosophers debate priests about the shape of the world. Most of the holy ones taught the world is flat, surrounded by a void, like a stone lying in a stream. Some philosophers claimed it was round, like an egg."

"Which did you believe?"

"I always considered it unimportant. Since no one can see the whole world at once, what difference does it make what shape it is?"

"It's with knowledge like this that the evincar can locate and strike his enemies."

"Show me the Skyshroud Forest," he said.

Takara toyed with the controls, and the gray globe was instantly replaced by a flattened half-sphere. Centered in the portion facing Eladamri was a broad, irregular patch of dark green.

"This is Skyshroud as seen from a height of 100,000 feet," she said. Punching a button made the green patch treble in size. "From 20,000 feet." Takara touched the panel once more, and the image swelled to cover the entire hemisphere.

"From 10,000 feet," she said. "This is how it looks from *Predator*."

Eladamri looked for the Eye of Korai, his village, and other features he knew. None were discernible. There was texture to the image, made up of taller and shorter trees, but the canopy was as featureless as the sea.

"Now I know why Volrath and Greven have had such trouble catching us," the elf said. "Even with this great artifact, the Skyshroud is still our shield and sanctuary."

Intrigued by the maps, Kireno and Shamus came down and joined them. For several minutes, the rebels were lost in the bird's eye view of Rath.

"Here's something none of you have ever seen." Takara played the panel expertly, and the hemispherical view of Rath was replaced by a brilliantly colored globe.

Compared to Rath, which was made up of shades of gray, green, and brown, this world was a blinding array of colors—bright blue oceans, yellow and red deserts, smoky purple mountains. Feathery clouds filled the atmosphere, softening the contrasts between the sharper colors. The whole thing was like a jewel, a bauble fit for an empress's brow.

Something about the colorful world moved Eladamri deeply. "What is that, Takara?"

"Dominaria."

He knew the name. *Weatherlight* had come from there, with its motley crew of heroes—and so had Crovax. Dominaria. The name tripped from his tongue as pleasingly as the rainbow sphere delighted his eye.

"Tell me about Dominaria," he said.

"It's the original home of our kind, yours and mine," Takara replied. "The ancestors of every soul on Rath came from there. Some ancient sages say even the overlords came from there, long ago. There's a prophecy that says the demon world will one day tear apart the clouds and rain destruction on the Bright World. I think the seers knew what we're only beginning to realize—the purpose of Rath is to destroy Dominaria."

"How can that be? They're separate worlds. I know people and machines fly between them, but how can Rath destroy another world?"

Weary, Takara braced herself against the control panel. "I was never educated about such high things. What I can tell you is, Rath is a shadow, created by the overlords of Phyrexia as a gateway to Dominaria. Just as sleeping mortals serve as bridges to the terrors of the night, so is Rath the nightmare bridge to Dominaria. For hundreds of years, Rath has been growing, coming closer to the old home world. The Stronghold is the key point, the focus of the overlords' grand design. This dark fortress is where nightmares are made flesh, the sword-point against Dominaria's throat."

"Gods preserve us!" Shamus muttered.

"You said your father served Volrath—where is he now?" the elf asked.

"Gone. Away." She shuffled backward from the panel. "I don't know where."

"Why didn't Volrath kill you? Does he know of your work with the rebellion?"

She laughed dryly. "Volrath cared nothing about my work with the Dal resistance. He locked me up to make certain my father wouldn't betray him—"

Takara's eyes rolled back in her head. Kireno sprang to her side and caught her in his arms. Without her hands on the controls, the map apparatus shut down. The double sphere of Rath-Dominaria rapidly lost color and definition, finally winking out like a vanishing soap bubble.

CHAPTER 18
Coronation

Ertai had to give Crovax credit. The man was a remorseless killer, but he did have a certain amount of cold-blooded style. Ertai was feeling generous as he waited to die.

He was imbedded up to his neck in a cube of flowstone eight feet wide. At the rear of the cube a thin pipe stretched back to one of the main flowstone conduits. Little by little, the cube was growing larger, and therein lay Crovax's wicked genius: the cube was balanced atop the flowstone furnace. An endless blue torrent of energy plunged into the crucible, meeting the raw lava rock brought up from below the Citadel. When Crovax and his minions placed him here, Ertai had been at least twelve inches from the edge of the furnace cone. In the past four hours the cube had grown at least eight inches per side. In another six or seven hours the cube would be so large the narrow ledge could not support it. He would topple forward into the works and be disintegrated by the furious energy beam.

It took Crovax only minutes to create the cube. He mentally programmed the nano-machines to retain their shape as the cube grew, and thoughtfully provided Ertai with a cavity in the cube sized exactly to his body. Once the sergeants shifted the cube in place atop the crucible, Crovax stood back and watched for several minutes.

243

The flowstone also absorbed radiant heat from the energy beam and got hotter all the time.

"Isn't this all a bit too elaborate?" Ertai said.

"Would you tell an artist his painting was too elaborate?" replied Crovax.

"If need be."

"You have no sensitivity, Boy. The beauty of this arrangement is its slowness. You have half a day to contemplate your end. I hope you use it wisely."

"Why kill me at all? I'm no threat to you. I can't even get out of this cube, much less challenge your command of Rath."

"You really do miss the point. You've been an annoyance to me and therefore deserve to die. Also, because of your close ties to the emissary, killing you should be very painful for her."

Ertai called Crovax all the dirty names he had in his considerable vocabulary. Crovax responded by tightening the flowstone around Ertai's throat until his tongue protruded and his face turned blue. Then, just as suddenly, he relented.

"I'd love to stay and play, but I'm being crowned today," he said. "Duty before pleasure, as they say."

He descended the steps to where his private guard was waiting and never looked back.

Ertai tried to influence the flowstone enough to allow him to escape. He expanded the space around his body slightly, at the expense of enlarging the cube prematurely. It was like wrestling inside a block of cheese. When he concentrated, the stone closest to him softened, but he couldn't influence the outer bulk of the cube. The effort left him gasping, and the growing heat wrung sweat from his every pore.

What a fool he was to agree to this sham. He was a wizard, not a politician or a warlord. All his grandiose plans to escape or become evincar of Rath were the consequences of overweening pride. Now he was paying the price of his folly.

His eyes started to swell shut. He guessed this was from being so close to the blazing energy beam. Such promise, such talent he had. All wasted on this ugly, colorless world, ruled by ugly, colorless people. Was this the ultimate fate of Dominaria, should the Phyrexian invasion succeed? If so, he was glad he would not be alive to see it.

There was Belbe. Why did he care about her? He tried to tell himself he'd seduced her, that his motives were only self-serving. Looking back on it, those hours he spent with her were not just the best ones he'd had on Rath but maybe the best he'd known in his entire short life. He didn't seduce her—he was the one seduced. For the first time Ertai found a woman who didn't ignore him or reject him for his thundering arrogance.

The hole at his neck was just large enough for Ertai to poke a few fingers out. Despite his best efforts, he found he couldn't enlarge the hole. Conjuration was always more sure when the sorcerer could use his hands to gesture, but in this situation he'd have to do without.

Once before he'd searched for Belbe with a magical ferret. Now he summoned up a similar creation, this time a retriever. It was hard evoking anything to appear in the glare of the energy beam, but he managed to create his retriever in the air above his head. It resembled a ghostly ball studded with spikes, like a translucent sea urchin.

"Bring Belbe here," was all he told it. The retriever spun away. Ertai couldn't tell if it survived passing so close to the beam, but it was his last and only chance.

* * * * *

It took a long time for Sivi and Medd to work their way down from the airship dock. They were helped by the flood of soldiers entering the palace. They were able to mix with the new men and gradually put some distance between themselves and *Predator*. By the time the alarm was quelled, the two rebels were within sight of the convocation hall doors.

The antechamber was curiously devoid of troops. As Sivi and Medd entered from the central corridor, they paused to survey the room—nothing. No courtiers, no soldiers, no palace guards.

"When we get out of here, you know what I'm going to do?" Medd said as they proceeded.

"What?"

"I'm going to drink myself into a stupor the likes of which has not been seen before."

Sivi smiled. "Sounds like a good idea. What's your drink?"

"Black Eye." This was a Dal drink made from fermented lichen.

"Never had any," she said. "Why do they call it 'Black Eye?'"

"Oh, it has something to do with the effect. You drink enough, you fall down and wake up the next morning with a black eye."

"That's an old man's tale."

Sivi and Medd whirled. Out of a shadowed alcove in the rear wall came Teynel and Garnan.

"Cousin!" Medd burst out, but Teynel's somber face stilled any further display of joy by the young Dal rebel.

"What have you been doing, Liin Sivi?" said Teynel coldly.

"My duty," she replied.

"You attacked the airship, didn't you?"

She folded her arms. "Isn't that why we came?"

"Did you destroy *Predator*?"

Sivi chewed her lip. "No."

"Where's the rest of your group?"

"Dead. Where are yours?"

Teynel flipped the mantle back from his shoulders. "Lost or slain, I don't know. By now there must be four companies guarding the airship. We'll never get through to it. All we can do now is find Eladamri and get out of here."

She said nothing. Garnan and Medd walked ahead a few paces while Teynel fell into step beside the Vec woman.

"You disobeyed my orders," he said in a voice for her ears only.

"I had an opportunity and chose to take it."

"And failed." Their boots clacked loudly on the faux marble. "If Eladamri is dead, I'll see you die as well."

She raised a single eyebrow. "I'll make my case to any council or court you can raise."

"I'm not talking about a trial," Teynel explained. "I mean just this—if Eladamri is dead, I'll kill you."

Sivi nodded. "You can try."

Thirty yards outside the prison tower they ran into their first checkpoint. A mix of palace guards and regular soldiers had blocked off the passage with a wall of spears and shields. Teynel stepped in front of Garnan and Medd. Piled against the wall were three dead moggs. Their sword wounds were still oozing blood.

"Halt," said the guardsman at the shield line. "Stand and be recognized!"

Teynel saluted. "Corporal Elcaxi of the Fourth Company. This is my squad. We're supposed to patrol out to the prison and back." He rolled his eyes. "Trouble is, nobody's told us what we're patrolling for."

"Don't I know it," said another guard. "The alarm sounds, we turn out, and what happens? Nothing."

Sivi pointed to the dead moggs. "What's that?"

"Bunch of moggs. Tried to force their way through here." The first guardsman grinned. "They didn't make it." The guards pulled two sets of propped-up shields aside and let the rebels pass.

"These fellows aren't very smart," Garnan observed.

"Don't underestimate them," said Teynel. "There's thousands of troops in the Stronghold, so no one can know them all. This little charade of ours can't succeed much longer. As soon as somebody recognizes you two from *Predator*, or figures out there is no Corporal Elcaxi, we'll be in the soup."

They passed through another roadblock before reaching the bridge to the prison tower. The bridge itself was empty. Teynel had the others follow him single file to hide their numbers from any oncoming foe. They entered the lower doors of the prison without encountering anyone.

"This is too easy," Sivi said. "Someone should be on guard here."

"It smells bad, I agree." Teynel looked both ways down the curving passage. "I wonder where they're keeping Eladamri?"

"Should we split up and search?" asked Medd.

"Not this time. Stick with me. We may be in for a fight."

Teynel chose to go right. They moved slowly down the hall, checking the doors they passed for noises. Except for some soft shuffling and scraping sounds, they heard nothing.

"I guess prisoners don't last long here," said Sivi.

The farther they went, the darker the hall became. Flowstone lamps provided anemic, orange light. Sivi sniffed at them, recalling her failure to ignite *Predator* with such a lamp. Teynel tried to adjust one for more light. Instead of getting brighter, it went out.

"Let's get out of here," Garnan said suddenly.

"We can't abandon Eladamri," said Teynel.

"You're getting spooked," Medd suggested. "So a light burns out. So what? There's no real danger yet. Let's go on."

Teynel and Sivi were going on regardless. An open door partly blocked the passage in front of them. Teynel waved for everyone to stop. A low, steady light shone from the open door. With hand signals he indicated he wanted Garnan and Medd to stay in the corridor. He and Sivi would investigate the room.

Teynel peered around the heavy door. The cell was set up as a torture chamber—manacles on the wall, pans of hot coals, and all kinds of hideous tools were laid out on a table in the center of the room. A stout chair sat with its back to the open door. Someone was in the chair.

Teynel drew his sword. He slipped in, and Sivi ghosted in behind him, toten-vec in her hand. He carefully circled to the left around the chair while Sivi circled right. More and more of the sitter's face came into view.

"Eladamri!"

Teynel rushed to the chair. The elf was tied hand and foot to the massive chair. His head hung down. Teynel put a hand to his chest and felt a strong heartbeat.

"He lives!" he announced joyfully. Sivi knelt and began cutting the bonds on his legs with the blade of her toten-vec. Teynel used his sword to free Eladamri's hands.

"Water," Teynel said. Sivi brought the clay pitcher from the table. Teynel gently splashed some on the elf's face. Eladamri stirred.

"You came," he said weakly.

"I'm sorry, brother. There's been trouble," Teynel said.

"The airship?"

"I tried to destroy it, O Eladamri," Sivi said. "I failed."

Teynel poured water into the elf's cupped hands. Eladamri drank. "Can you stand?" Teynel asked. "We should get out of here as soon as possible."

"Give me a moment."

Sivi leaned her hip on the table. When she did, something cracked under her feet. Flecks of broken pottery . . . she picked one up. The shard was yellow boneware with a red glaze on it, just like the water pitcher Teynel held. Someone must have broken an identical jug.

There were sounds of movement in the hall, the scrape of metal on stone.

Medd cried out, "Soldiers coming! Teynel, hurry!"

In a flash Sivi was at the door. She looked past the two Dal fighters and saw at least fifteen palace guards coming down the passage.

"Time to go!"

"Time indeed." Eladamri rose swiftly from the chair, without a trace of pain or injury. Teynel, still kneeling beside the chair, stared in amazement.

"I was beginning to think they'd never get here," the elf said.

"What are you talking about, brother?" said Teynel.

"Your doom, rebel fool."

Teynel stood up, sword in hand. He'd spent many days with Eladamri, and they'd always been of similar height—Teynel was about a hair taller, in fact. The Eladamri with him now was more than six inches taller. Even as he gazed in horror at the familiar face, the bruises and burns were fading from view.

"By the gods," he said. "It can't be!"

"What is it?" Sivi said. To her horror, she saw Teynel raise his sword to strike Eladamri. The surprisingly strong elf caught Teynel's wrist, and with a brutal motion he broke the Dal fighter's arm. Teynel's sword fell to the floor.

Already the two rebels in the corridor were hotly engaged with Citadel guards. The too narrow hall didn't allow the Rathi troops to exploit their superior numbers, giving the rebels a small chance.

The impostor Eladamri, still holding Teynel by the arm, stooped to retrieve the rebel's sword. He examined the hilt briefly, nodded, then with his left hand thrust the blade through Teynel's chest. The Dal rebel gasped.

"Bastard!" Sivi yelled. She flung the toten-vec at the impostor. He tried to dodge, but he was hampered by the dying Teynel. The iron blade caught him on the side of the neck. He snarled with rage and hurled Teynel's lifeless body at the Vec warrior woman. Tearing the blade from his neck, the impostor seemed to swell even larger, distorting his false elven features grotesquely.

Sivi recovered the toten-vec and lunged for the door.

Medd and Garnan were holding off the guards, who seemed strangely reluctant to press their attack. Sivi stood back to back with Medd, watching the door of the interrogation cell. She expected the misshapen Eladamri to emerge, but instead, Greven *il*-Vec stepped into the hall. She knew it was the same man by the neck wound she'd given him.

"Dread Lord," called the captain of the guards. "Are you all right?"

"Quite all right. Watch out for the pretty one. Her little toy can sting."

"What's happening back there?" Garnan said, desperately parrying concerted sword thrusts.

"Never mind! Keep your eyes front and fight!" Sivi cried.

The Greven impostor did not attack either. He backed away, always keeping his eyes on Sivi. At the first door beyond the open cell, he stopped and put a key in the flowbot lock. Greven stepped farther back, opening the door as he went.

"I'd love to remain and watch the fight, but I have an appointment with Lord Crovax," he said. "In my place I leave you a gellerac."

From the black cell door a single red tentacle writhed out, seeking something to grab. It found its liberator's leg and tried to coil around it, but Greven brought his heel down sharply on the leathery appendage. It retracted a foot or two and changed direction. Two more tentacles appeared, followed by a fat, wallowing torso covered in the same dark red leathery hide.

"Friends," said Sivi. "We're in trouble."

The rebels and the guards stopped fighting to gaze at the monster. More and more of the gellerac oozed out the door. A bulbous upper appendage reached the light. The top was covered with a mass of white miniature tentacles that wriggled and flexed in faster imitation of the lower tentacles. Midway between the thing's neck and animate "hair" was what might be a mouth—an obscene star-shaped orifice rimmed with oily gray skin and drooling pink saliva. The palace guards muttered among themselves and fell back.

"You have only to keep the rebels from escaping," Greven told his troops. "Otherwise you can leave them to the gellerac."

The beast filled the width of the passage, and there was no sign it had fully emerged from its cell. The tentacles gripped the door of the interrogation room, pushing it shut. Liin Sivi wondered if the monster would simply crush them with its disgusting, ponderous bulk. As if in answer, the vile mouth erupted outward, inverting the wet skin to reveal row upon row of conical teeth.

She lashed at the creature four times in quick succession. The blade of her weapon scored deep gashes in the monster's blubbery flesh, but it hardly seemed to notice. A blood-red limb as thick as her arm wrapped around her ankle and jerked her to the floor. The gellerac, moving with astonishing speed, hurled its toothy lips at her.

Medd stepped in and drove his sword through the creature's mouth. Blackish blood poured from the wound, and the gellerac vibrated with pain. It heaved Medd off his feet and threw him against the wall. The respite gave Sivi time to slash the tentacle gripping her leg. It loosened, and she scrambled out of reach with help from Garnan.

The Rathi troops had withdrawn more than six yards.

Sivi got to her feet. "I don't think this monster knows friend from foe—let's see if it likes fighting them as well as us!"

They retreated to the point where the guards had stopped.

Sivi called out, "O Captain! Hear me!"

"What do you want, Rebel?"

"That beast has no eyes—I wonder if your men taste as good to it as mine do?"

"What's your point?"

"I'm just wondering what happens after we're dead? How're you going to stop it?"

More mutterings from the Rathi soldiers, made all the more urgent as the gellerac rolled rapidly down the passage after them. Sivi and comrades ran right at the guards, who lowered their sword points. The gellerac hit the line of guards and caught two in its tentacles. They yelled and hacked at the creature with their swords. Some of their comrades joined in. A few at the rear turned and fled.

"This is no warrior's fight," Sivi said. "Your master cares nothing about your lives!"

The Rathi captain watched, a loathsome look on his face. One of his men vanished underneath the gellerac, his screams muffled by flabby flesh.

"Fall back!" shouted the captain. "Fall back to the bridge!"

The Stronghold troops broke and ran. The captain tried to corral the rebels, but Sivi warned him off with lightning cracks of the toten-vec. The gellerac had slowed its advance while digesting its first catch.

Sivi, Medd, and Garnan backed down the left hand passage.

"You can't escape," the Rathi captain said. "Surrender to me, and I'll protect you from the monster!"

"You'd better worry about your own hide, O Captain," Sivi said. "We'll take our chances elsewhere!" She slapped Medd on the back and they ran down the open passage.

Halfway around the tower, they waited and listened. The heavy sliding noise of the gellerac wasn't evident.

"Liin, what happened to Teynel?" Garnan asked. In few words, she described the bizarre trap they'd fallen into, and Teynel's death. Garnan covered his face and wept quietly.

Medd looked to Sivi. "When did Greven il-Vec become a shapeshifter?"

"Why ask me? Anything seems possible in this mad fortress!" Soft scraping sounds filtered down the dim corridor. "Time to move on."

They arrived at the opposite side of the tower and noticed another gate. It was standing open, so they reconnoitered carefully before going through. There was no sign of Greven or anyone else.

Medd examined the gate. "This lock's been forced."

"Why would the Rathi force their own lock?" said Garnan.

Sivi narrowed her eyes. "They wouldn't. Come."

They burst onto the bridge. Two Rathi soldiers stood guard halfway along to the next tower. When Sivi, Garnan, and Medd appeared, the sentries drew swords and blocked the path.

"Wait," muttered Sivi under her breath. "We're still friendly soldiers until somebody tells them otherwise."

They approached slowly. The sentries had the visors down on their helmets.

At a distance of six paces, one of them shouted, "Halt!"

Sivi saluted sloppily. "Greetings."

"What's the watchword?" said the sentry.

"Eh?"

The sentry flung out his arm, pointing his sword at Sivi. "What is the watchword?"

Sivi glanced helplessly at Medd and Garnan. They dropped their hands to their sword hilts.

"Tell this stupid soldier the watchword!" the sentry barked.

The second sentry replied, "Tant Jova!"

Tant Jova? "Who are you?" Sivi demanded. Up went the visors. "Kireno! Shamus!"

There was much back slapping as the rebels were reunited at last. Sivi cut short the celebration.

"Teynel and the rest are dead, and our presence is known."

"We heard the alarm," Shamus said.

"We came to find Eladamri, but we didn't."

"He's with us," Kireno said. "He got himself out, and rescued another prisoner from the cells. They're hiding in the map room, yonder."

"Take me there," Sivi said. "I have much to tell him."

* * * * *

The hall filled with dignitaries, court functionaries, and idlers. The array of banners was still in place, but so great was the demand for space, the flags were pushed back to the walls by the steadily growing crowd.

Belbe stood on the dais beside the empty throne, watching people arrive. Still in her Phyrexian armor, she fixed the rococo emblem of the Hidden One in the plume holder of her helmet. She'd been unable to find Ertai all morning, and a cold clutch of fear gripped her inside. She could think of nothing else to do but hide the plasma discharger behind the vacant throne. A fresh powerstone glowed within it.

It was an hour past midday. The incoming crowd thinned. From beyond the open doors came the tramp of men marching in parade step. Onlookers scampered out of the way as a column of men in bright steel armor and white mantles, four abreast, marched straight into the convocation hall. It was the Corps of

Sergeants, two hundred strong. In accordance with tradition, their scabbards were empty, but Belbe knew the two hundred toughest men in the army of Rath didn't need swords to intimidate their opposition.

The leading sergeants, led by Nasser, halted the column at the foot of the throne. No orders were shouted, but the outer two files of men made quarter turns to the right and left respectively. The assembly shrank from the line of sergeants, who thus formed a glittering lane through the crowd.

Nasser bowed to Belbe. "Excellency, my lord Crovax is coming," he said. Belbe did not reply. She nudged the Phyrexian weapon with her toe and felt its reassuring weight.

A tall figure came walking across the antechamber. Belbe's pulse throbbed hard until she recognized the broad shoulders and towering height of Greven il-Vec. He bowed to her from the doorway, then tried to find a way outside the human aisle. In the end, he pushed his way through the crowd and took a place at the wall, on Belbe's right.

Someone else approached, a smaller person this time—too small to be Crovax. Belbe made out his face at a long distance. It was the Kor, Furah, garbed in gray leather. He moved with sinuous grace between the stern, unmoving sergeants. He took his place beside Greven and never took his eyes off the young emissary.

The timepiece behind Belbe silently flickered through some abstruse Phyrexian equation, then displayed Rathi time: one hour, one minute past midday.

She saw him a hundred yards away, striding confidently down the central corridor toward the antechamber. He was wearing his white ensemble again, the one Belbe would forever associate with the hostage massacre. Her recognition must have shown on her face, for the entire hall fell hushed long before Crovax reached the outer chamber.

His footsteps were loud against the hard walls. Belbe licked her lips and tried to swallow.

When Crovax reached the top of the steps, Nasser raised his right foot and stamped down hard.

Steel and stone rang together as he cried, "Lord Crovax!"

"Crovax!" shouted the sergeants.

With the skill of an actor, Crovax waited at the door until his men stopped cheering. Then, in utter silence, he ascended the aisle, his gold-trimmed mantle rippling with the wind of his passage. Greven switched his gaze to Crovax, but Belbe noticed Furah was still watching her. Crovax halted at the foot of the throne.

"Your Excellency sent for me?"

She nodded, slowly. Crovax turned and faced the hall.

"People of Rath," she began. "I, the emissary of the overlords, the Lens of Abcal-dro, the chosen representative of the Hidden One, greet you."

"All power to the Hidden One!" Crovax exclaimed.

"All power to the Hidden One," answered the crowd.

"Since arriving here, it has been my mission to find a new governor of Rath. I was charged by our masters to put the crown on the head of the strongest candidate, to insure the rule of Rath was given to the most powerful, most intelligent, and most loyal servant of the Hidden One."

Belbe lowered her hand behind the throne, feeling for the tip of the plasma discharger. She found the smooth prongs, but before she could finish her ritual declaration or pick up the weapon, a small disturbance broke out at the rear of the hall.

She stepped away from the throne. A small, bright object, about the size of an apple, flew into the room. People at the back shrank from it or swiped at it with their hats. In neither case did anyone touch it.

Crovax was livid. Without moving, he tried to snare the flying object with flowstone pincers called up from the floor or nearby columns. The spiny sphere easily dodged the clumsy claws, and the only ones caught by them were unfortunate courtiers near the center of the crowd.

The object danced down the aisle. The sergeants watched it, but they were unsure whether to break ranks and seize it or not. The ball flew past Crovax's head and hovered in front of Belbe.

"A friend of yours?" asked Crovax icily.

She held out her hand, charmed by the playful sphere. It ran its soft spikes gently over her palm, and she was seized with a desire to have this object and keep it with her always.

It darted away, and Belbe ran after it. The crowd dissolved in frantic gossip. Crovax grabbed Belbe's arm as she passed.

"Where do you think you're going?"

"I must have it . . ."

"What about the ceremony?"

"I'll come back—I will—as soon as I catch this thing."

He shook her, none too gently, saying, "You can't leave until you discharge your duty! Say the words, you stupid little—"

Greven interrupted. "She cannot say anything now, my lord. She's under a magical compulsion."

"What! Who dares—?" He must have answered his own question, and he shut his mouth. Releasing Belbe, he spoke in Nasser's ear. Crovax went to the steps leading up to the throne and sat down, casually crossing his legs.

Nasser shouted for quiet. "People of Rath!" he said. "There will be a minor delay in the ceremony. Lord Crovax has asked that no one leave the hall until the emissary returns."

To make sure of it, the sergeants locked arms to keep people away from the doors. Belbe ran out, chasing the glowing ball. Nasser spoke hastily to the seated Crovax, then hurried after her.

CHAPTER 19
Survival

The cavernous Map Room was the scene of a somber reunion. Sivi broke the melancholy news to Eladamri that they had failed to destroy *Predator*, and half their force, including Teynel, was lost. This was countered by Eladamri's survival and the addition of Takara to their group.

They shared their simple rations with Takara. She recovered her strength rapidly after eating and drinking, and willingly lent her knowledge of the Stronghold and its workings to the rebels' cause. Medd, who knew something of the healing arts, tended Eladamri's injuries. The rebel leader's left arm was broken at the wrist, so Medd made splints from seats in the Map Room, bound Eladamri's arm with them, and fitted him with a sling. His knee, though badly bruised, did not seem broken.

Sivi described Teynel's death to Eladamri. "The man in the torture chamber looked exactly like you, O Eladamri," she said. "It was only when he began to change that we suspected the truth."

257

"You say he turned into Greven?" asked Takara thoughtfully.

"Yes. I saw Greven *il*-Vec when we first arrived, and it was definitely him."

Eladamri studied Takara closely. "What does it mean? Is Greven a shapeshifter?"

"Not unless he's acquired the gift since I've been imprisoned."

"Then who killed Teynel?"

Takara traced a line on her face with a single finger, down her nose, across her lip to her chin. "There is a possibility . . ."

"Never mind that!" Garnan said. "We must get out of here!"

"Agreed," said Eladamri. "Takara, what's the best way? Takara?"

She looked up from her frowning daydream. "What? Out? Why, we have to go through the Citadel."

The young rebels groaned. "Can't we keep going in this direction?" said Shamus, pointing away from the fortress.

"That direction is the mogg warrens," Takara said. "A maze of tunnels, shafts, and mogg nests, infested with thousands of ugly, bad-tempered creatures. We wouldn't get a hundred yards inside before we were attacked, lost, or eaten."

The map room fell quiet.

At length Eladamri said, "We got in by stealth and disguise, so it's only natural we leave the same way."

"Our disguises are wearing a bit thin," Sivi said.

"We'll change them. If they're looking for an elf and five soldiers, we'll become something else."

"My face is known," said Takara.

"You could become a man," Sivi suggested.

Takara smiled thinly. "I don't think I could carry it off as well as you, My Dear."

Sivi reddened and was about to utter a sharp reply, but Eladamri cut her off.

"Our strength lies in staying together and going as quietly as we can. I've never run from a fight in my life, but there are some odds a wise warrior doesn't test. Seven of us against the entire Stronghold is not a battle, it's a prolonged execution."

They did what they could to change their appearance. Those in Rathi uniforms discarded their mantles and tore them into rags to polish their helmets and breastplates. Kireno, slimmest of the rebels, took off his breastplate and gave it to Eladamri, turning his backplate around to wear on his chest. Medd wrapped Eladamri's head in makeshift bandages to obscure his elven features.

Takara watched this with considerable amusement. "You should've been actors," she said. "You look like a touring company of bards."

Sivi reached across Garnan's waist and drew his knife. She advanced on Takara, holding the blade in a threatening manner.

"Call her off, Eladamri. I'm your valued guide, remember?"

"Liin Sivi—"

Sivi swung the knife in a wide arc. Takara tried to block by grabbing Sivi's knife hand. The Vec woman was far stronger, and Takara had to use both hands to hold off the knife. Sivi's free hand darted in. She snatched hold of Takara's long red ponytail and spun her around by tugging on it sharply. With her comrades shouting "No! No, Sivi!" she slashed Takara's hair off right where it was tied.

Sivi tossed the heavy hunk of hair on the floor and returned Garnan's knife.

Takara knelt by her shorn locks. "Why did you do that?"

"You need to change your appearance too, O Takara," Sivi said. "Without that hair and with a little dirt on your face, you can be a charwoman."

"Enough," said Eladamri sharply. "I won't have this bickering."

Medd was nearest Takara. She went to him and wordlessly demanded his knife. Sivi stood back and let the toten-vec drop from her hand. Medd wouldn't give the woman his knife, so she took it herself. Sivi flipped the lethal end of her weapon back and prepared to cast it.

Staring at the Vec woman with hollow eyes, Takara used Medd's knife to saw off even more of her hair. When he saw she didn't mean to attack Sivi, Medd gently took the knife away from Takara and offered to even up the horrid haircut.

"Your problem," Takara said to Sivi, "is that you don't go far enough."

Laughing, Sivi recoiled the toten-vec. "I'll try to remember that."

From being five soldiers, an elf, and an emaciated woman, they were now six reasonably tidy soldiers and a crop-haired, emaciated woman. They cleaned up the map room to hide the fact that they'd been there and left the tower by the upper bridge to avoid the gellerac still loose in the prison.

There were no new sentries on the bridge, so they hurried across.

"Don't like it," Sivi declared.

Takara pushed past her to take the lead. "They don't expect intruders between the Citadel and the mogg warrens," she said. "No one's that crazy."

"No one but us," Kireno said.

Medd and Shamus shrugged at each other and followed her. Kireno and Garnan went next, leaving Eladamri to shoo Sivi along.

"I don't know if I like that woman or hate her," Sivi muttered.

"Make up your own mind," replied Eladamri. "But until we're free of this place, don't turn your back on her."

* * * * *

Just inches to go.

Ertai could hardly see, his eyelids were so swollen, but with his mind's magical eye he could see the cube now extended over the edge of the furnace cone. In another twenty minutes, it would be over. His last hope, the retriever, apparently failed. Belbe had not come.

Facing death, he had the odd thought that he would be contributing to the composition of Rath in a very literal way. All bodies returned to the soil, but his would disintegrate in the furnace and be whirled into the flowstone matrix. His component atoms would mingle with the substance of Rath, pass through the factory, and be pumped onto the surface along with billions of pounds of flowstone. Would there be a little patch of Rath that was Ertai? He wondered if his consciousness would survive. If so, he hoped Crovax would walk over him someday. He'd be sure to trip him.

Ertai.

He recalled a book he'd read in one of the royal libraries

about the death pits of Rath. Past evincars had used the black tarry residue left over from the making of flowstone to fill in gaps in the Stronghold cavern. As it was poisonous and corrosive, some evincars had taken to tossing unwanted prisoners into this muck. As a result, the book claimed, the death pits had achieved a kind of collective sentience, melded from the souls of the people who died in it.

"Ertai!"

It was a real voice calling his name. He managed to open his right eye to a tiny slit.

"Belbe!"

The retriever worked after all! She looked splendid in her black diamond armor and Phyrexian headdress. She was tearing at the cube with her hands, but the surface was too hard and smooth. She could make no impression on it.

"Tube," he said. "Break the tube."

* * * * *

She jumped down and found the feeder tube on the back. No thicker than her little finger, she easily snapped it. Semi-liquid flowstone spilled across the platform until she crimped the tube shut. Tiny silver spheres danced around her feet.

She heard feet pounding on the ladder coming up the furnace cone. A man in bright armor appeared—Nasser. The narrow ledge between her and the ladder was speckled with spinning globules of flowstone, still not solidified. She guessed the radiance of the energy stream was keeping them liquid longer than normal.

"Excellency! Stay where you are! I am to bring you back to the coronation!" Nasser shouted above the crackling beam.

"I'll come back once Ertai is safe!"

"My orders are to bring you back immediately. Let the boy go!"

"No!"

He drew his sword. "You must. It is the will of Crovax."

Belbe slid her feet along to avoid stepping on the flowstone globules. She struck a fighting pose.

"You cannot compel me!"

Nasser saw the flowstone droplets and plainly understood the danger. He imitated Belbe's foot-sliding and inched close. The Rathi sergeant jabbed tentatively with his sword tip. Belbe swatted the flat of the blade away with her bare hands.

"This is senseless!" Nasser declared. "Come back with me and complete the ceremony. You can save the boy afterward!"

"I do not jump to Crovax's bidding! Go back and tell him I'll return when I choose!"

Belbe slid closer and unleashed a kick that caught Nasser at the waist. He was a strong man, and though the blow drove the wind from his chest, he kept his feet. He sheathed his sword and swung a mailed fist. Belbe blocked one punch, but the other hit her solidly on the cheek. She staggered back, slipping on bright silver pellets of flowstone. Only the weight of the cube behind her kept her from falling backward into the furnace.

"Had enough?" Nasser asked, lowering his hands.

From a sitting position she sprang three feet in the air, driven upward by the power of her fingers and toes alone. She spun, using the centrifugal force of her turn to make her feet into lethal weapons. Her left foot clipped the tip of Nasser's nose. Her right met his jaw, which shattered under the impact. His hands flew up, and he reeled away. Flowstone greased his tread, and he fell face down on the platform, on top of more silver globules. With a single deep scream, he slid feet first into the furnace.

Belbe wasn't much better off. Completely out of control, she too landed face down, but because she was astride the platform, she was able to grip the edges with her hands and feet, avoiding Nasser's fate. Even so, her right hand, forearm, leg, and calf were singed by the energy beam.

Pain was nothing. She carefully got up, brushing away the deadly droplets beneath her.

"Ertai!"

"You won," he said, vastly relieved. "Can you get me out of here?"

"I'll try."

She crouched beside the cube and blew on the scattered silver pellets. One by one the frictionless spheres skittered into the furnace. When the platform was clean, she put her shoulder against the cube and pushed it back from the edge. It was enormously heavy, but she shifted it back far enough that it wouldn't easily topple over the ledge.

Belbe rattled down the steps to the control dome. There were all sorts of implements there, and she found a cabinet of heavy tools meant for dealing with accidental spills or accretion problems. Belbe grabbed an ax, a wedge, and a sledgehammer with special flowstone cutting heads. She tucked these under her arm and ran back up the steps to Ertai.

Belbe put down the hammer and wedge and attacked the cube with the ax. Using both hands, she swung the heavy ax in a wide arc from behind her head. It struck the cube with a loud clang, cutting an inch deep gouge in the surface. Belbe swung again, and without realizing it, let out a hoarse, angry yell. The cube shifted slightly from the blow. She hit it again, and again. After eight terrific hits, the ax fell from her hands.

Her shoulders were dislocated. Wincing from the unsuppressed pain, Belbe climbed atop the cube. She crawled to Ertai, now resting his chin on the metal.

"I can't do it," she gasped. "Not with these tools. I'm sorry, Ertai."

"It's all right. I'm about gone anyway," he whispered.

"Don't you dare leave me," she said, grasping his cheeks in her hands. "You're my friend—my only friend! I won't let you go."

When he didn't answer, Belbe tried clawing the stone around his neck. He'd loosened it a bit with his own magic before fatigue had claimed him, so there was just enough room for her to hook her fingers inside and pull. Her shoulders burned, and her nervous system sent out insistent warnings for her to stop.

"Need help?"

She jerked around and spied Crovax on the furnace cone. A halo of residual energy was fading around him. He'd teleported from the coronation ceremony. The intense blue glare of the energy beam made his dark skin look gray, and his white garments glowed with reflected radiation.

"Don't taunt me, Crovax!" Belbe said. "I disposed of your man, and I can dispose of you!"

"Threats, Excellency? And here I came to offer my help."

She slid off the cube. Her arms were almost useless, hanging at her sides like dead weights.

"Release Ertai," she demanded.

"I will, on one condition."

"No conditions! Release him!"

Crovax folded his arms. "You know I can command the cube to squeeze him to jelly from where I stand," he said. "Or I can have it throw itself into the furnace."

Breathing hard, fighting the pain, Belbe glared hatefully at Crovax. She was beaten. As long as she cared what happened to Ertai, he had her.

"All right. Name your condition."

"I'll dissolve the cube and leave the boy here, if you return with me to the ceremony directly and do what you promised to do."

It was too simple.

"Is that all?" asked Belbe.

"That's all. Of course, whether or not the boy survives his close exposure to the energy beam is a matter out of my hands."

Belbe made two fists. The effort made her shiver. "I'll bring him with us!"

"No," said Crovax. "You must leave him here. That's my condition. Say yes now, or the offer will be withdrawn."

She lurched toward him and was gratified to see him step back.

"Why do you need me so much?" she said. "You have the power to rule Rath. Why are you so set on me proclaiming you evincar?"

"Stupid question. You're the emissary of the overlords. What I am, I owe to them, and I need their stamp of approval. I can rule Rath as I am now, but there are factions within the Stronghold that will not recognize me as evincar without your declaration.

"Time is short, Excellency. Our conjunction with Dominaria is just days away. I don't have time to suppress rebels, woo support from the local population, and prepare for the invasion of Dominaria all at the same time. Your announcement that I am the true evincar will save me much effort. Now come. There's no more time for banter. My crown awaits."

"Free Ertai."

Crovax nodded. The cube promptly began to melt, like a pat of butter on a hot griddle. Silver rivulets of flowstone spilled off the edge into the furnace. In seconds, Ertai's shoulders were visible. Belbe held onto him as the liquefied flowstone sluiced away.

She kissed him lightly on the forehead. He cracked his swollen eyes.

Ertai's voice was a hoarse whisper. "I heard what he said. Go. I'll be all right."

"I'll come back for you."

His head lolled to her shoulder. Ertai whispered in her ear, "Let's use your portal and escape."

Belbe lowered him carefully to the platform. "That may not be possible," she said.

"We must."

Strong arms pulled her away. Crovax put an arm around her waist and held her close. With her injured arms Belbe did not fight.

"I hate you, Crovax."

He smiled quite pleasantly. "Good. A strong ruler should be hated and feared. Now that I've achieved the one, I'll see what I can do about the other."

Before Belbe could respond, he teleported. Everything was blanked out in a fierce white flash—vision, hearing, all her senses. Even Belbe's hatred was extinguished for the duration of the trip.

* * * * *

The rebels reentered the Citadel easily enough, but fifty yards inside the palace they ran smack into a cordon manned by a large contingent of Rathi soldiers. Takara dropped back from her lead position to walk beside Eladamri.

"What are you going to do?" she asked.

"Bluff. What else can we do?" He whispered to the others. "I'm your captain—say nothing, but follow my lead."

A breastwork of boxes had been erected across the circular junction, and at least a hundred soldiers milled around behind the barrier. At the rebels' approach, the commander of the cordon came out and ordered them to stop.

"Identify yourselves!"

Eladamri stepped out from the ranks of his band.

"We were called to the prison a few hours ago," he said. "Something about a breakout. We caught this one walking around loose." He took Takara roughly by the arm and shoved her forward. "Some of Lord Volrath's creatures are free in there, too, so we had to clear out."

"There are rebels at large, disguised as royal army soldiers," said the commander. "See anyone suspicious?"

"Not a soul. There was some kind of trouble in the mogg warrens, though. We got as far as the Map Tower, and we heard a commotion from there."

The commander laughed harshly. "Ha! If the damned rebels went to Mogg Town, that's the end of them!" He braced a scrap of parchment against his knee and made some notes using a charcoal stick.

"What's your name, soldier?" he asked.

"Drannik. Captain Drannik," said Eladamri.

The commander, who was only a lieutenant, stiffened and threw a salute. "Sorry, sir! I didn't recognize your rank!"

"That's understandable. If you're through, Lieutenant, we have to take this wandering prisoner to Lord Greven."

"Let 'em through!" the officer shouted, and the barricade was opened for the rebels.

Takara regarded Eladamri sourly, but she allowed herself to be guided through the cordon. The rebels crossed the junction to the main corridor. Crates used to create the bulwark on the other side were pulled apart for them.

"Just a moment," called the lieutenant. "For my report, Captain Drannik—what company are you with?"

Garnan flashed the elf four fingers. Eladamri shook his head. They'd been claiming to be from the Fourth Company all along, and the Rathi troops were on to that ruse.

"We're from the Tenth Company."

The soldiers taking down the barrier for them suddenly stopped. The lieutenant's charcoal stick snapped and fell to the floor. His smudged hand went to his sword hilt.

"*We* are the Tenth Company . . . I've never seen you before. They're the rebels! Take them!"

Sivi and the men tore at their weapons. Eladamri pushed the bandage back from his eyes and snatched the Rathi sword from his hip. The way was open, but a hundred Rathi soldiers surrounded them.

Sivi parried a sword thrust with her stolen blade. The toten-vec was hidden behind her breastplate, and she needed a few free seconds to get it out. Medd dashed in front of her to ward off any fresh attacks.

Garnan, Shamus, and Kireno formed a triangle in front of Eladamri. With his injured hands, the elf was in no shape to fence with the enemy. The rebels held their own for several seconds, then Sivi got her toten-vec unleashed. In short order she struck down three Rathi soldiers, clearing a way to escape. Takara, unarmed and not fighting, took Eladamri's arm and drew him to the unguarded opening in the wall of crates. Once he was through, the other rebels slowly retreated. Sivi whipped her weapon back and forth, forcing the soldiers to maintain their distance. When they got too bold, the whistling blade of the toten-vec caught them in the face, throat, or leg. Sivi was the last rebel to leave the cordon. Medd shouted for her to hurry.

"I'll be there," she replied.

One of the crates used to block the way was poised atop another. Sivi retreated through the gap and buried the tip of her blade in the top of the crate. With a two handed pull, she toppled the box from its place, blocking the way.

"Yes!" Sivi flicked her wrist to recover the toten-vec. She tugged in vain. The iron blade was hopelessly pinned underneath the heavy crate.

Soldiers were scrambling over the barricade. Sivi glanced over her shoulder. Her friends were almost out of sight. She threw down the handle of the toten-vec and drew the less familiar sword. Four soldiers dropped to the floor and came at her. She parried the first, dodged the second man's attack, ran through the third man as he lowered his guard prematurely, and received the fourth soldier's sword point directly in the chest. It slid off her cuirass but got snagged in her belt, piercing her side just above her left hipbone. Sivi backhanded the man who'd wounded her, turned, and tried to run.

More men poured over the barricade. Bleeding profusely and

limping, Sivi managed to make it only a few feet before she was overtaken. She cut savagely at her attackers, but the sword was wrenched from her hand. The iron hilt of another connected solidly with her head, and she went down.

Takara and Kireno hastened Eladamri along. They'd changed direction twice to throw off pursuit, doubling back to a corridor running upward through the Citadel into the palace area. As they huddled beneath an archway shaped like a monstrous animal's ribcage, it became plain Liin Sivi was not going to catch up with them.

"We should go back," Medd said, moving away from the others.

"Stop!" Eladamri said. "You'll be taken as well."

"But Sivi—"

"He's right," said Takara. "She's already dead."

Silence ensued. Medd slammed a fist against the skeletal arch. "She stayed behind so we could escape!"

"It was her choice," Garnan said, putting a hand on his comrade's shoulder. "We should honor her sacrifice by staying together."

"It's my fault," said Eladamri. "I thought I was being clever by changing what regiment we came from. I didn't know we were in the midst of the Tenth Company."

"If you're all through taking blame, I suggest we move on," Takara scolded. "There are a lot of passages to cover, and now that we've been discovered, they'll flood the corridors with troops hunting for us."

Eladamri agreed. The direct route—around the factory and out the grand causeway—was likely to be thick with alert enemy soldiers. Takara suggested they ascend into the palace and go around the factory at a higher level.

"There are flowstone pipes and braces branching out from the factory to the crater wall," Takara said. "We can follow those."

"Are there openings to the outside?" asked Shamus.

"Oh, yes," she said. "There's all sorts of vents, blowholes, and exhaust channels perforating the crater."

With heavy hearts, the four rebels went on, climbing the circular ramp into the palace quarter.

Taking up the rear, Eladamri turned to Takara. "What do you think our chances are?"

She avoided his eyes. "Few or none. Frankly, it's astonishing we've gotten this far. There must be something else going on here, something vital and diverting."

Eladamri explained what he knew about Crovax and his claim to the throne. Takara actually smiled when she heard this.

"What's amusing?" he said.

"You speak of this Crovax as if his elevation were a foregone conclusion," she replied. "Nothing is certain, especially in the Stronghold."

Above and ahead, a clash of steel meant the rebels had encountered another hostile patrol.

Eladamri hurried as hard as his battered legs would take him. One whole turn of the ramp revealed the rebels hotly engaged with six palace guards. Takara hung back, flattening herself against the wall. Eladamri drew his sword and entered the fray.

Slipping in beside Shamus and Garnan, he awkwardly traded cuts with a heavily armored guardsmen. Shamus landed a telling blow to the man's shoulder, who dropped his spear. While stooping to retrieve it, Eladamri rapped him smartly on the face with his sword hilt. The guard rolled down the ramp, out cold. He slid to a stop near Takara. She tugged the ornate dagger from the guard's belt and with both hands shoved it through the unconscious man's throat. Eladamri saw her do it, and when she stood up, their eyes met. Takara shrugged.

Another guard fell, the victim of a stop thrust by Kireno. The remaining four began to withdraw, but the rebels kept the pressure on them. One man tried to run. Garnan sprang after him, but in his haste he forgot the guard's nearest compatriot. The Rathi guard swung his heavy spear sideways, the shaft taking Garnan in the gut. The Dal warrior doubled over, shocked by his sudden reverse, and the fleeing guard turned and speared him through the back. His triumph was as short lived as he was, for in the next instant Medd drove his sword through the guard's chin. The other guards were boxed in against the wall and cut down by the hard-fighting rebels.

Sweat pouring down his face, Eladamri knelt with Medd beside Garnan. Medd tried to find a pulse, and failing to find one, shook his head. Eladamri gently pulled his hand away.

"He was a gallant comrade," said the elf. "Now we must hide his body."

"Why?" said the anguished Medd.

"We can't let the Rathi know we're losing numbers. We couldn't help them taking Sivi, but we must disguise our losses so they don't know how few we are."

They dragged Garnan to the top of the ramp and pushed him into a small oval opening Takara identified as a warm-air duct from the flowstone factory. Kireno and Shamus carefully wiped away all traces of blood between the duct and the place where Garnan had fallen.

"Where are we?" Eladamri asked.

"Below the courtiers' apartments," Takara said. "Over there are the Dream Halls."

Reduced to just four, the rebels hurried on. The passages already echoed with the sound of massed soldiers. The sweat on Eladamri's neck began to go cold. This was the sort of end he feared most—hunted, dying by inches, like a beast at bay. Compared to this, even the torture chamber was preferable. He'd resigned himself to death the moment Greven and his moggs had chained him to the wall. That he survived was a great victory, and for a while he allowed himself to hope they might escape. Now the coils of Rathi power were slowly enveloping them. His brave fighters were dying one by one, and the end seemed inevitable.

Like an animate hedge of spears, a wall of guards blocked the passage in front of them. Refusing several calls to surrender, the rebels retraced their steps to the top of the spiral ramp. Even as they reached the landing, they could see a stream of armed men surging up the ramp from below.

"Not good, not good," Medd kept repeating.

"We need another place to go—now," said Kireno.

Takara pointed. "The only place left is the Dream Halls, but the doors are sealed, and only the evincar can open them!"

Eladamri urged his friends to follow. "If I'm to die, I'd rather do so in a place called the Dream Halls than in a common, crowded corridor like this."

Shamus, the fastest of the group, overtook the elf chieftain and reached the enormous double doors first. He slammed his shoulder against the right panel, and to his surprise, the door yielded.

Two hundred soldiers and guards pursued the rebels to the very doors of the Dream Halls. Some paused to cast spears at the fleeing party, but all missed. Kireno, Medd, Takara, and Eladamri slipped through the open door. When their leader was through, the warriors threw themselves against the door. When it was shut, Medd slammed the massive foot bolt into the floor, locking it. Shamus and Takara slid a huge horizontal bolt into place as well.

Kireno and Medd laughed at their near escape. Shamus paced back and forth in front of the doors. Takara slumped to the floor.

Eladamri alone walked deeper into the Dream Halls. The vast dimensions, the frowning pilasters decorated with busts of Volrath—it all somehow reminded him of a strange forest clearing lined with lofty black trees.

He fingered the wooden fetish hanging from his neck. His instincts were right again. This would be a good place to die.

CHAPTER 20
Trial

She vanished in the wink of an eye. Even against the constant stabbing brightness of the energy stream, the flash of Crovax's departure with Belbe was intense. Ertai felt the displaced air and excess power lap over him, a whisper against a roar.

He rolled onto his hands and knees and began to crawl. It was a long way from the edge of death to the theater of the living.

* * * * *

The crowd did not dare leave the convocation hall. Restless but also afraid of what might happen to them if they didn't bear witness to the ascension of Crovax, they remained in the hall, sweating and itching in their uncomfortable finery. An hour passed, then another, and a third was underway when a silent stroke of lightning blinded everyone, and a hot wind stirred the robes and gowns of the assembled court. Crovax had returned with Belbe in his arms.

The Corps of Sergeants, who had been at ease, snapped to attention. Courtiers old and young struggled to their feet or smoothed their heavy ceremonial robes. Without a word of explanation, Crovax sat down on the throne. The emissary of the overlords leaned on the arm of the great chair, a hand over her tightly shut eyes.

"Excellency, we're here," said Crovax. "Do your duty," he insisted.

She inhaled. "People of Rath," she began in a small voice. "I ask you all to forgive my weakness. The overlords set me the task of finding a new ruler for Rath, and with due diligence I tried to find the best candidate. I didn't realize until this moment the search was a sham, that the choice had already been made by the overlords even as I was being dispatched on my mission to Rath."

"Say what you came to say," said Crovax, growing impatient.

Belbe faced the audience. "I regret what I am compelled to say now. I give you the new evincar—"

"Stop!"

Crovax leaped to his feet. "Who dares interrupt?"

Two figures cleaved through the crowd—Greven *il*-Vec and the Kor chief, Furah.

"Greven, I'll have your head in an iron cage for this. I'll roast your brains over a slow fire, and even then I won't let you die—"

"Save your threats, my lord," said Greven. "There are more important matters to deal with."

The sergeants tried to bar his way, but Greven easily broke their linked arms apart. More of the Corps broke formation to box the hulking warrior in, but Crovax ordered them to let Greven and the Kor through.

"Why aren't you writhing on the floor?" Crovax demanded. "Your spine should be smoking by now."

"You're not the only one who commands the control rod," Greven said. "What you order, another can countermand."

"Nonsense! No one dares interfere with my will!"

Furah stepped forward. He bowed slightly and smiled, showing long, feline teeth.

"I've long looked forward to meeting you," he said. "Greven has told me of your activities."

"Who are you?" demanded Crovax.

"I am the one that chair belongs to. You, Crovax of Urborg, are a usurper."

Crovax lowered his head. The flowstone around Furah's feet

273

rippled in a series of tiny points, but none grew more than an inch, and none came close to harming him. The Kor chief, in his turn, spread his hands wide. A stream of flowstone balls, the size of Greven's head, burst from the walls and pounded Crovax. The last and largest ball struck him hard in the chest and drove Crovax backward over the arms of the throne. Belbe leaped aside, staring at Furah in utter disbelief.

The crowd jostled and elbowed each other for a better look at this unexpected challenge to Crovax. Those in front regretted their eagerness when the pavement beneath their feet erupted in a hedge of spikes. Dozens were impaled where they stood, and the ring of spikes completely walled off Furah and Greven from the rest of the room. Crovax appeared from behind the throne. Blood from a cut lip flecked his once spotless white tunic.

"You command flowstone well," Crovax said, descending the shallow steps. "Who are you?"

"I thought you would've guessed by now. Greven said you lacked imagination for anything but killing, but I'd hoped he was mistaken." He glanced at his giant companion. "Greven's a stout fighter, but he sometimes lacks discernment. Not in this case, it seems."

"Enough chatter. Explain yourself!" Crovax stared hatefully at the Kor man.

Rather than a spoken reply, Furah began to change. His shoulders expanded; his legs and arms lengthened. His skull widened, and his features swelled and disappeared.

In place of the pale, slender Kor now stood a man with a sculpted body of impossibly perfect proportions. Taller by a head than Crovax, he exuded grace and power. His face was carved in such a way as to suggest wisdom and strength.

The crowd spoke his name. "Volrath!"

Belbe was impressed. To simpler folk, Volrath might appear to be a god. Even as she thought this, many of the court went down on their knees and bowed their faces to the floor in abject reverence of their evincar.

"So, you've come back," Crovax said. "Why?"

"To reclaim what is mine," said Volrath.

"You forfeited the throne when you abandoned it. I am the new evincar." He turned to Belbe. "Tell him, Excellency."

Belbe lowered her eyes and said, "I am the emissary of the overlords of Phyrexia. I was sent here to appoint your successor."

"That is no longer necessary. I have returned," said Volrath.

"You've returned to your own death!" Crovax shouted.

The crowd cheered. "Volrath! Hail Volrath!"

Crovax spat out at the crowd. "The next mouth to hail this pretender will breathe its last!"

"You can slaughter them all, and it won't change the truth. I am Volrath. I am evincar."

"You're just a corpse that hasn't lain down yet!"

Crovax drew sword and dagger and advanced. Volrath, unarmed, reached out and drew Greven's oversized sword. As Belbe watched, Volrath enlarged himself to Greven's size.

"Stop it! Stop this at once!" she cried, charging between the would-be combatants.

Crovax tried to reach around her and cut at Volrath with his black-bladed sword. Belbe caught the blade with her hand. The sharp edge bit to her duralumin bone. Crovax tried to tug his sword free, but she held on.

Volrath whirled Greven's broadsword around his head as if it were a light stave. With Crovax encumbered by Belbe, he stepped sideways and thrust at the usurper. The emissary blocked his attack with her other hand. The blunt point of Greven's weapon bit deeply into her palm, but her metal hand closed tightly and would not let the sword go.

Volrath relaxed, letting go of his borrowed blade. Belbe tossed Greven's sword away. Crovax tried to wrench his weapon free, but Belbe turned and broke his sword blade in two with a single blow of her bleeding right hand.

"You're a formidable construction, but this intervention is ill-timed," said Volrath. "There can't be two evincars."

"I don't propose there be any more than one," Belbe said, throwing the end of Crovax's blade to the floor. The crowd pressed against the fence of flowstone spikes, trying to see what was happening.

Belbe, her hands bleeding copiously, mounted the steps and seated herself on the throne.

"This is my last act as emissary," she announced. "I will sit in judgment of a contest between Crovax and Volrath, and the winner shall be the sole, rightful governor of Rath."

Crovax hurled his sword hilt to the floor with a clang.

"Outrageous!" he roared. "I had your word I would be named evincar!"

"I also object," said Volrath more mildly. "I have been evincar for more years than this usurper has lived. Why should I submit to anyone's judgment or to some ridiculous contest?"

She addressed Volrath first. "It is true you were governor of this world, and during your reign the overlords were pleased with your rulership. However, when you abandoned your post to pursue a personal revenge against *Weatherlight* and her crew, you forfeited all credit with our Phyrexian masters. The Hidden One himself directed me to come here and find a replacement.

"Frankly, I am interpreting my orders liberally to even allow this contest, but I am sure our masters would approve," she said. Her head swam, and she tucked her bleeding, oil-streaked hands into her armpits. "Consider—consider it recognition of your past service that I allow you to clear your record of the stain of desertion."

It was impossible to read Volrath. His face was a living mask, alive, yet no more expressive than the statues in his private quarters.

Volrath pondered her words, then bowed. "Your Excellency is most generous. I accept your proposal."

Crovax was boiling with barely contained rage. The floor, the walls, the ceiling closest to him rippled and writhed under the force of his frustration. He turned his fearsome gaze from Belbe to Volrath, and his outward anger subsided.

"I see no problem," he said to Belbe. "This pathetic weakling presents no challenge to me. I will kill him, then I will kill you."

Greven, having already picked up his sword, stood at Belbe's right hand.

"For the duration of the contest, I will defend the emissary, so that no unfair advantage will be gained by threatening her," he said. So saying, he offered her a scrap of homespun bandanna. She regarded Greven's gift blankly until he tore the cloth in two and indicated she should use it to bind the wounds on her hands.

The doors of the convocation hall were opened, and the rearmost spectators were pushed out of the room by the Corps of

Sergeants. An open oval space was cleared of carpet, flags, and bystanders. Crovax's sergeants withdrew in a body to the right wall. The fence of flowstone spikes was dissolved, and those unlucky people slain by Crovax's initial fury were quickly removed.

Steel swords and shields of identical size and length were taken from two palace guards and provided to the combatants. Volrath pulled on a pair of scale-mail gauntlets. Seeing this, Crovax did the same. He dropped the gold-edged mantle from his shoulders. Neither man wore any other armor.

Volrath walked off a pace or two and started stretching and flexing his artfully carved muscles. Crovax called for wine and drank a goblet dry watching his opponent preen before the crowd.

Crovax dropped his goblet. "Time is short. Let's begin."

"I agree. What are the rules?" said Volrath.

Belbe folded her bandaged hands in her lap. "There's only one rule—win."

Crovax promptly lashed out with a wide sideways cut. Volrath threw himself back and brought up his shield. Sparks flew as the blade met the polished buckler. Crovax bored in, slashing and thrusting and using his shield to slam against Volrath's.

Volrath grew visibly taller even as Belbe watched. He moved so fast most people in the hall couldn't see his true motion, but Belbe's enhanced eyes followed every move. Volrath's arm elongated as he thrust it forward. The tip slid off the top of Crovax's shield and kept going. An ordinary fighter would have run out of arm by then, but Volrath's reach was preternatural. Crovax realized his danger and turned away just as the leading edge of Volrath's thrust clipped his left ear. He called on the floor to trip Volrath, but the flowstone waves broke over the former evincar's ankles like water and didn't impede him. In turn Volrath summoned another barrage of flowstone balls. Crovax was expecting them. Instead of liquefying them like his opponent, he batted them away with forceful commands. The skull-sized projectiles mowed down five onlookers.

Volrath retracted his arm to more normal proportions and advanced. He feigned an overhand attack, but again with amazing swiftness switched the line of his cut to an underhand thrust. Crovax blocked with his shield and struck out with his booted right foot. The hobnails connected with Volrath's leg below the knee.

"You're fast," Crovax said, grinning. "But you don't have a true killer's instinct."

"I've killed more people in one year as evincar than you have in your entire life, barbarian," Volrath retorted. "What you call 'killer instinct' is merely a lust for death. I am above such feelings."

They traded four hard cuts that left both their blades deeply nicked. For the first time, Belbe felt Volrath was concerned. He hadn't expected Crovax to last this long.

Emboldened, Crovax lowered his head and shouted sharply. He jabbed at his opponent's legs and stomach. Volrath gave ground grudgingly, backing up two steps, advancing one with a counter-thrust, then backing up two more.

Behind Crovax the floor humped up in a series of rounded semicircles. Crovax apparently didn't notice. Greven nodded approvingly.

Crovax's sword tip bounced off Volrath's shield. The latter executed a blinding pirouette, his blade coming edge-on at the side of Crovax's neck. He ducked, and his heel caught on the nearest hump. With an expression of utter surprise, Crovax fell. Volrath let out a triumphant laugh and leaped. He landed astride the fallen Crovax. Up went the bright sword—

Crovax vanished in a flare of white light. Volrath's blade went three inches into the floor. The flowstone softened, allowing him to recover, and his partisans in the crowd shouted warnings. He turned his head and saw Crovax materialize four feet in the air, directly behind him. There was no time to parry or dodge. Instead, Volrath shrank. He contracted his body by a fifth. Crovax's sword raked down Volrath's back, laying open his skin. Glistening oil spattered across the front of Crovax's white tunic.

Shrinking saved Volrath's life, but he had a painful wound from his left shoulder blade to his right hip. His dropped his hands to the floor and staggered forward on them. Grinning widely, Crovax tried trampling his foe into the floor. Flowstone splashed and flew as the men fought for control. Volrath rolled on his back. Crovax tried to overrun him and got a foot planted on his chest. The finely proportioned muscles in Volrath's leg uncoiled, hurling Crovax into the air. His feet didn't touch the ground for five yards, then he slammed into the tightly packed crowd.

He was up in a flash, hacking and slashing at anyone within reach of his blade. Courtiers and soldiers alike climbed over each other to get out of his way, but he slew at least ten before it became inconvenient to chase the others. Belbe knew this wasn't just pointless homicide; Crovax derived new strength from the death of others. He was refreshing himself in the midst of a duel by slaughtering innocent onlookers.

His back wet with glistening oil, Volrath went to the foot of the throne. Belbe could smell the crisp, electric odor of the fluid. Volrath's broad shoulders heaved. He looked to Greven *il*-Vec, standing with sword drawn at Belbe's side.

"How am I doing?" he asked wryly.

* * * * *

Ertai crawled all the way from the furnace mouth to the flow-bot lifts in the outer environs of the palace. Except for occasional patrols, he saw no one. Guards marched past him without stopping, the men idly watching his painful progress.

He reached the lifts and fell heavily into the closest one. It had been far too long since his last infusion. Without the dark energy to suppress them, his old injuries were slowly emerging again. The laboratory was a long way away. Despite his wounds old and new, his first thought was to find Belbe. Her life hung in the balance—he was certain Crovax would kill her once he'd been proclaimed evincar.

"Convocation hall," he said to the lift. The fleshstone flaps closed, and the flowbot sank through the floor.

The lift jerked to a stop. When the flaps lowered, he saw the antechamber was jammed with people. Everyone was craning their heads toward the open doors of the hall. Distantly he heard the sounds of combat, punctuated by shouts. Ertai grasped the leathery hide of the lift and dragged himself to his feet. If this was to be his last act, he wanted to enter standing and not on his knees.

He wormed his way through the mass of gawkers. Some shrank from his fearful, swollen visage and let him pass. Others regarded him with pity and stepped aside. When Ertai reached the inner edge of the crowd, the closely packed ranks of guards and courtiers parted to reveal a wan and worried Belbe, seated on the throne and guarded by the imposing Greven il-Vec. She was talking to another tall muscular fellow with an improbably handsome face—Volrath. Ertai recognized him from the statues around the Stronghold. He had an awful wound across his back. The flesh exposed was gray, not red. Ertai raised a hand in greeting.

Heedless of the danger, Belbe pushed past the tall, wounded swordsman and met the young sorcerer at the edge of the crowd.

"Have I missed much?" he whispered.

She lowered him to the floor. "You shouldn't have come. It isn't safe here."

"Where is one safe on Rath?"

Distracted, Volrath didn't see pinchers form out of the flowstone steps behind him. One pierced his right calf. He immediately banished them and, enraged, raised a wall of flowstone six feet high and one inch thick. He shouted so loudly the floor trembled, and the wall broke into a dense cloud of small pellets. Volrath flung his hands wide, and the mass of pellets hurled themselves at Crovax.

Up came the shield. With a sound like a thousand nails punching through a hundred tin plates, the pellets reduced Crovax's shield to a sieve. His tunic was shredded, and a score of pea-sized pellets buried themselves in his face.

Scored and blasted, Crovax threw down his ruined shield. He crossed his forearms, fists tightly clenched. A growl rose from his throat. It began low and guttural but grew louder and stronger as he focused his rage and pain. One by one, the flowstone pellets worked themselves out of his body, falling at his feet at a steady rate. Soon the floor around him was covered with hundreds of pellets.

Ertai tried to size up the situation. Volrath was an unknown quantity to him. He'd seen the ex-evincar's quarters, heard commentary from people in the Citadel who knew him. He was cruel, ruthless, shrewd, and a man of unusual appetites. Compared to him, Crovax was a machine—soulless, utterly devoid of guilt or feelings of humanity. Volrath would expect to win because of his superior skills; Crovax thought he could prevail through brute force and a willingness to do anything to win.

The battle would go on and on until sheer survival determined a winner. With his ability to renew himself with the lives of others, Crovax would ultimately win. Nothing Ertai could do would help Volrath. Once the former evincar was out of the way, retribution would inevitably fall on everyone else.

Crovax's two-handed stroke tore the shield from Volrath's grasp. The dented buckler caromed off the wall. Both fighters were reduced to swords alone.

Volrath assumed a sideways stance, the pose of a fencer rather than an infantry soldier. Crovax circled warily, trading occasional cuts and jabs. As he orbited outside of Volrath's reach, he glanced at Ertai and betrayed surprise as seeing the young sorcerer alive.

Volrath sidled forward a step when Crovax's attention strayed. His arm lengthened by two inches, and he carefully bent his elbow to hide the new growth. Volrath started his lunge. His arm straightened, and with the velocity of a striking viper, he drove his blade at the junction of Crovax's right arm and chest.

Crovax's eyes widened in alarm. He tried to backpedal out of danger, but his response was too slow. The nicked, dented blade flew at him. He brought his own sword up in a desperation parry, but the impetus of Volrath's lunge bore his hilt back against his own face. Thirty inches of tempered steel slid along Crovax's arm. Volrath's lunge had succeeded, and the startled usurper seemed paralyzed by the realization of his imminent defeat.

Time stretched out. The normal yellow gleam of the hall lanterns on the bright steel blade became purplish. Volrath's triumphant face fell. An unknown force was playing down the length of his onrushing blade. Someone was tampering with the fight, using old-fashioned magic to deflect his weapon. A horrified look on his face, Volrath watched the tip of his sword fall an inch, two inches, until it passed under Crovax's arm.

Everything came together with a crash. Volrath and Crovax collided chest to chest, Volrath's sword swinging uselessly behind Crovax's back. Crovax's own blade was bent backward over his shoulder by the force of Volrath's attack. He twisted, dumping the over-balanced Volrath and at the same time punching him hard in the face with his free hand. Volrath hit the floor. His sword bounced free and skittered away into the crowd.

Crovax threw himself on Volrath's back. He hooked his left arm around the man's chin and drew his head back, arching Volrath's back as if it were a longbow. The ragged edge of his sword came down to slice Volrath's taut throat. Volrath blocked the blade with his mailed hand.

The wall of courtiers and soldiers dissolved to reveal a captain of the palace guard, backed by a phalanx of his men. The captain's face was streaked with blood.

"My lords! The rebels!" he cried. "They've barricaded themselves in the Dream Halls!"

Belbe was on her feet. She flung a hand at the straining pair of fighters. "Hold!"

They continued to struggle. She appealed to Greven. The Vec warrior did not move.

"Declare a winner, or stand aside, Excellency," he said.

"You heard the captain," she said. "We must defend the Citadel!"

"That is the job of the evincar."

It all came down to this moment. Belbe looked from face to face, searching for an answer. Greven was impassive. Ertai smiled weakly, then sagged to the black pavement. Courtiers avoided her, soldiers pretended to be busy readying themselves to fight the rebels.

Finally, she looked down at Crovax. He had Volrath down, his head locked and his throat vulnerable. Only four mailed fingers prevented him from cutting Volrath's jugular.

"Do . . . your . . . duty!" Crovax gasped.

"Behold!" Belbe cried. "Behold, the Evincar of Rath! Crovax!"

The sergeants broke ranks and shouted their master's name. Most of the assembled notables joined in, though a good number quietly fled.

"Let him up," Belbe said above the roar of the crowd.

"He must die!" Crovax replied.

"He's lost. His life is forfeit, but your first duty is to quell the rebels in your own fortress."

Crovax agreed. He ordered his men to secure the former evincar and place him under close guard.

"Wrap him in chains of good steel," Crovax said. "Hang him by his feet so that no part of his body touches the structure of the Citadel. Seat ten men with bare swords around him. If the floor so much as trembles, strike off his head!"

Volrath was buried under a pile of sergeants. He didn't resist, but they pressed him hard to the floor and wound chains around his legs. His hands were wrenched behind his back and chained together. A hood was cinched over his head.

By the time Volrath was securely bound, the hall was almost empty. Guards and soldiers under Greven's command had already marched off. The sergeants bore Volrath away.

Crovax turned to Belbe. "Excellency! This is a great day!"

He dropped his sword and enfolded her roughly in his arms. Though she resisted, Crovax kissed her hard, smearing his sweat on her face as she stained him with glistening oil still oozing from her injured hands.

Alone, lying on the floor a few feet away, Ertai smiled.

CHAPTER 21
Reunion

Garnan pressed his ear to the door. "It's quiet out there," he whispered.

Shamus listened too. "They didn't just go away!"

"They're there," Takara said flatly. "A company was left to watch the door while the rest retrieve a battering ram."

Shamus blinked. "Battering ram?"

"Do you think they'll try to starve us out?"

Medd filled the relatively quiet moment by inspecting Eladamri's injuries. He dabbed salve on his burns and rewrapped them in strips of cloth torn from their army cloaks. Eladamri was sitting on the cold black floor, leaning against one of Volrath's monumental pilasters.

"Are you in much pain, Brother?" asked Medd.

"No."

"The burns are superficial. I fear some of your nails are lost and won't grow back." Eladamri nodded. Medd tied off the last bandage and set the elf's arm gently into a sling. "Do you think we'll leave here alive?"

Eladamri opened his eyes. "I don't know. Are you frightened?"

"Yes."

"I'm not. Live or die, I've made up my mind not to fall into their hands again. I do have regrets, though. So many unfinished tasks . . ."

Kireno returned from reconnoitering the Dream Halls. Everyone but Shamus gathered around Eladamri to hear the Vec warrior's scouting report.

"This place is huge, but it's basically one big room," Kireno said. "At the far end is a transom, all glass. There don't seem to be any other doors."

"What can you see from the transom?"

"The windows look down upon the prison and map tower, O Eladamri."

"Could we climb down?"

Kireno demolished his idea. "The Citadel is cut away under the Dream Halls, so there's no way to climb down. It would require hundreds of feet of rope just to reach the bridge to the prison tower we just left. To reach the floor of the crater would take thousands of feet."

"What about up?" asked Medd.

Takara snorted. "Climb hundreds of feet up the outside of the Citadel? Are you mad?" She shook her cropped head at the rebels' leader. "How is he going to climb any distance up or down with those ruined hands?"

"You've made your point," Eladamri said. "Do you have any useful suggestions, Takara?"

Her eyes glistened. "Write your wills."

From the doors Shamus called, "People coming—lots of them!"

The rebels rushed to the doors, weapons drawn. Takara slumped to the floor in the corner and covered her face with her hands.

The tramp of many feet was plain even through the massive panels. Muffled shouts were heard, and the floor vibrated under their feet.

"Stand back," Eladamri advised his men. He had hardly said so when a tremendous boom reverberated through the hall. The doors shook but remained solidly closed. The impact was repeated again and again.

The noise was punishing.

"If the doors don't break, the noise will break us!" Medd shouted.

After many hits, the battering ceased. More muffled voices, and the rebels could hear men scurrying away from the door.

"Take cover!"

Fire sprayed through the narrow space under the door panels and through the gaps at the top and sides. For a few terrifying seconds, the rebels waited to see if the tall doors would topple from their hinges, admitting a horde of Rathi soldiers. The doors stood firm.

"Ha!" Kireno said, slapping a thick black panel. "That's workmanship for you!"

"I guess Volrath didn't want anyone to disturb him in his sanctum," said Eladamri.

Buoyed by the doors' resistance, the rebels prepared for a siege. Medd got out his whetstone and sharpened their swords and knives. Kireno departed on another reconnaissance, this time searching for hidden doors or secret passages. Shamus continued his watch.

Eladamri rummaged through his garments. He found a slip of ragged paper and a blunt charcoal stick, once the property of the Rathi soldier whose uniform this had been. He sat down on the floor and began to write in slow, carefully formed letters. Shamus asked him what he was doing.

"Following Takara's advice," he said. "I'm writing my will."

* * * * *

Crovax left to lead the attack on the cornered rebels, but Belbe had to see to Ertai before she could join the Rathi forces outside the Dream Halls.

She managed to round up four terrified servants and ordered them to carry Ertai to Volrath's laboratory. The men were frightened to be abroad on their own. The whole Citadel was in an uproar, and the air was rife with tales of cut throats and stabs in the back. It was only by considerable bullying that Belbe was able to get them to carry Ertai to the infuser.

She left him on his makeshift stretcher. "These men will get you to the laboratory," she told him. "They know what will happen to them if they fail." The bearers shifted nervously until Belbe frowned them into stillness. "I will go to the rebels. I must speak to Eladamri again."

He took her hand. "And how are you?" he said, fingering her bandaged palm.

"I feel no pain."

"You're a liar."

Belbe slipped her hand free. "When your treatment is done, find someplace quiet to rest. Crovax will come looking for you."

"Speaking of that . . ." Ertai urged her to come closer. Belbe knelt beside the stretcher. "We must both escape! You have the means—"

"Shh." She covered his mouth with her hand. "When the time comes, the door will open. But there is a part I must play here."

She dismissed the servants and hurried to the Dream Halls. As she neared the entrance, she found the corridors clogged with tense, eager troops. What seemed like the entire garrison was crowded into the outlying passages, and it took some time for her to work her way through the mass of heavily-armed soldiers. By the time Belbe reached the foyer, she found Greven supervising the palace guards in setting up a battering ram. An iron double A-frame had been brought in, and a massive bronze-headed ram hung by chains from the frame.

Kneeling beside Greven was a captured rebel soldier, a young Vec with his arms pinioned behind his back, bleeding from untended side and scalp wounds. Crovax, still in his battle-soiled white outfit, stood nearby with a contingent of fifty guards, ready to storm the Dream Halls once the doors were breached.

At the count of three, the guards swung the battering ram back, then slammed it against the black doors. The ram bounced off, and the rebound threw the battering crew to the floor. Greven ground his teeth in disgust.

"Again!" he bellowed.

Twenty stout men grasped the handles on the ram and drew it back. Prepared for the shock this time, none of them fell down, but the ram made just as little impression on the door as last time.

"Keep going!"

While the guards vainly pounded, Belbe made her way to Greven's side.

In between the dull booming of the ram, she asked him, "What are the doors made of?"

"Some metal of Volrath's making."

"Flowstone?"

"No, Excellency. The lock mechanism is made of flowstone, but the rebels have barred the doors from the inside. Crovax tried to will the doors open, but they are impervious to his commands."

Twenty-six fruitless blows were struck, then Greven ordered the winded guardsmen to stand down. A fresh team formed to take their place, but Crovax had a different idea.

"Would Your Excellency have a go?" he said.

"I'm not strong enough to batter down those doors."

"No," he said, "but you're strong enough to use this."

A soldier passed him the Phyrexian plasma discharger she'd hidden behind the throne. He smiled ironically when she took the weapon from him. Belbe cradled the heavy gun in her arms.

Crovax fixed her with a stare. "It won't work on me, you know. I can absorb the energy of its blast. That's how I can handle the powerstones bare-handed."

Belbe swung around and fired the discharger at the doors. No one was ready, and the resulting explosion scattered troops in all directions. When the smoke cleared, the doors were not even marred. Crovax seemed impressed.

"A very useful substance," he said. "I wonder if Volrath could be persuaded to share the secret of its composition?"

Belbe tossed the discharger to him. She turned to Greven. "I want you to withdraw your men. Clear an area ten yards out from the doors. Leave the rebel prisoner with me."

He didn't question why she wanted this, he simply obeyed and ordered the soldiers back to the mouths of the converging corridors. The battering ram was dragged clear and abandoned. Belbe helped the semi-conscious Vec warrior to stand. A hard knock on the head had not only laid open his scalp, it dulled his wits.

"What's your name?" she asked.

"Sivi . . . Liin Sivi."

"Isn't that a female name?"

She raised her head slightly and peered at Belbe. "You're the first one to notice."

"That's all right. Liin Sivi, you'll soon be reunited with your friends."

Belbe ushered the dazed rebel fighter to Crovax. "Your Highness," she said, using his title for the first time. "Take your storming squad back, too."

"Why?"

"I mean to persuade the rebels to come out," she said. "I'll give them their wounded comrade as a token of trust. But they won't budge if they see your men poised to strike."

"You no longer command here."

Belbe smoothed the hair back from her face. Her arms felt leaden, her fingers were numb. Her healing capacity was reacting poorly to her many accumulated wounds.

"Do this, Crovax. It will cost you nothing. There's no way out of the Dream Halls, as you well know. This Vec woman will be just as much a prisoner inside as she is out here. If I can talk the rebels out, it will save lives and trouble."

He looked past her. "Lives are cheap fodder," he said. "But it would be a shame to ruin those fine doors before I can ask Volrath how they were made . . . all right, Belbe." He pointedly dropped her title. "You have my leave to try."

The storming squad faced about and marched back to the line of flowbot lifts. Crovax followed, the discharger hanging loosely from one hand.

Belbe and Sivi approached the imposing black doors cautiously. Belbe rapped quietly on an ornate panel.

* * * * *

On the other side, Shamus flinched at the unexpectedly civil knock.

"Brother!" he hissed. "Someone's knocking at the door!"

Eladamri shoved the paper scrap in his shirt. He stood close to the panel. "Who's there?"

"Belbe. The emissary."

He flushed with sudden emotion. "What do you want?"

"You're trapped in there. There's no way out. I've come to help you."

Medd, Shamus, and Eladamri exchanged startled expressions. Takara roused herself from her gloom and quietly joined the group at the door.

"Why should you help us?" Eladamri questioned.

"Wherever I come from, I'm flesh like you. I no longer believe in my masters' goals. The people of Rath deserve to live in freedom."

Eladamri clutched Shamus's arm. "Find Kireno," he hissed. "Get him here at once!" Shamus dashed away.

"Can you hear me? Did you hear what I said?"

"I heard you," said the elf. "What proof do you offer of your sincerity?"

"I've convinced Greven and Crovax to withdraw their men from the door. I have one of your comrades with me. She says her name is Sivi. If you open the door, only the two of us will enter."

There followed a frantic argument among Medd, Takara, and Eladamri. If it meant saving Liin Sivi, the Dal warrior wanted to take the chance the emissary was telling the truth. Takara would have none of it, and Eladamri said nothing but brooded over the face he knew was on the other side of the door.

"How will you save us?" Eladamri asked, once the arguments cooled. "If you're relying on safe conduct grants by Greven and Crovax, forget it. We're not trusting our lives to such faithless villains."

"Greven and Crovax know nothing of what I'm doing. Let me in, and I'll explain."

The rebel fighters came running to Eladamri. He hastily explained the situation.

"Do you trust this woman?" asked Kireno.

"No, but I intend to face her. There's something about her you should know. She's my daughter, you see. Or was."

"How did this happen?" asked Takara.

"I don't know. It's some awful ploy of Volrath's, I believe."

"Eladamri," Belbe called. "Time is short. Let me in."

He grasped the floor bolt. "Stand ready. There may be treachery."

* * * * *

The door opened a few inches. Ten yards away, Crovax leveled the discharger. He'd discovered that Belbe's story about it not firing for anyone but her was a lie. His earlier failure was simply a case of not knowing what button to push. He'd remedied his ignorance since then.

Eladamri's eye met Belbe's. "Send in Sivi."

Belbe steadied the Vec warrior and eased her into the gap.

"Now give me your hand," he said.

Belbe raised her right hand.

Crovax squinted through the sight pins at the back of Belbe's skull. Greven saw the evincar raise the weapon and take aim at her.

"Stop!" cried the warrior.

In one smooth motion, Eladamri jerked Belbe through. She stumbled, which was fortunate; in the next second a searing blast of plasma hit the door. The substance burst with a loud crackle, and glowing fragments showered in all directions. Yelling with alarm, Medd and Kireno shoved the door shut, and Shamus snapped the bolts back in place.

* * * * *

Belbe stumbled against Eladamri, but instead of catching her, he tripped her with his outstretched foot. She landed hard on her belly.

"I knew there'd be treachery," Eladamri said coldly. "Your marksman missed me."

Belbe got up, and the elf backhanded her. She fell again. Eladamri was about to repeat the blow when Takara stayed his hand.

"She may have no other value than as a hostage," said Takara. "But she's no use at all dead."

Belbe stood and shouted, "Why do you hate me so? Is it because I represent the overlords whom you fight?"

"I don't know your overlords," said Eladamri. "All I know is this world and the evil men who rule it. Those men decreed my family should be extinguished. I am the only one of my line who still lives.

291

"Perhaps you really don't know, but you were once my daughter. Her name was Avila. She was killed on the orders of Volrath and her body stolen. That was five weeks ago. How long have you been here?"

"I've been on Rath three weeks. Before that, on Phyrexia, two weeks . . ." Belbe looked at her hands, touched her own face. "Why would the overlords command Volrath to do such a thing?"

"It's very plain. By murdering my child, they hoped to terrorize me into submission. If that failed, they counted on me becoming unmanned by the sight of my dear daughter commanding the enemy host."

You are the instrument of our study. The words of Abcal-dro filled her with sudden loathing.

"I came to help you!" she said. "Volrath returned without warning. He fought Crovax and lost. Crovax is now evincar, and as long as he reigns, no one is safe—friend, foe, ally, or neutral."

"Tell them about Dominaria," said Takara. "Tell them what's going to happen when this world and that one join."

Belbe backed away from the rebels. "You know about the invasion?"

"Lady Takara was kind enough to explain it to us," Eladamri said. "I notice you didn't mention it."

"I've taken care of that! It won't happen so long as I remain on Rath!"

* * * * *

The elf drew his sword. His heart was pounding so loudly he thought they must be able to hear it. The enemy with his daughter's face edged away. He could not bear to see her like this, her mind empty of memories, her face mockingly free of a daughter's love. That she wore the colors of his blood foes, the livery of her own murderers, was the most unendurable fact of all.

"Wait, O Eladamri!" Kireno pleaded, trying to hold him back. He ignored him and raised his sword. Belbe turned and ran.

Thirty yards down the concourse, she stopped and faced the oncoming elf. His attack was clumsy, and she easily avoided it.

Belbe grasped Eladamri by his cuirass and threw him to the floor. She planted her foot on the wrist of his sword hand and plucked the weapon from his fingers. In one deft motion she snapped the blade over her knee and let the pieces clatter to the floor.

"The time for swords is past," she said. "I'm not your child, Eladamri. It's true I was made in the workshops of Phyrexia. I don't doubt I was made to resemble your lost child. It would suit my masters' purpose perfectly to use your loved one's face against you, but I had no choice in the matter, no more than you chose the face you were born with.

"I've come here to undo the cause for which I was created. I can get you out of here safely, if you want. That's all I'm offering."

He sat up stiffly. "On what conditions?"

"No conditions."

The rest of the rebels, including Sivi, leaning on Medd's shoulder, surrounded them.

"And how do you propose to get us out of here?" Takara asked, her voice dripping with venom.

"I have an emergency exit. Let me show you."

She slipped by Kireno and Takara and made her way to the fourth pilaster on the left side of the hall. The floor was littered with Volrath's shattered dreams, and Belbe's feet crushed the brittle shards to dust.

At the base of the half-column was a row of decorative studs. She pressed the third one from the left side, and a panel popped open, revealing a deep recess four feet high.

They crowded around. Two large boxes were stowed inside. Belbe dragged them out. The tall metal carton she tore open with her bare hands, exposing an intricately machined device three and a half feet tall and about ten inches thick. It had a square base, tall cylindrical sides ribbed with metal tubing, and a transparent dome on top.

"A weapon?" asked Kireno.

Takara's eyes shone. "No," she said, smiling. "It's a portal device."

"You've seen one before?" Belbe said.

"My father has used them in times past. This is quite a small one."

Belbe admitted it was. "It was provided to me for special purposes only. If any of *Weatherlight*'s crew or their equipment came into my hands, I was supposed to send them to Phyrexia for closer examination."

The other box contained a single powerstone. Belbe inserted it into the base of the unit, explaining it had just enough power to transmit four hundred pounds of material to another plane.

"Four hundred pounds!" Medd protested. "All of us together weigh a lot more than that!"

"I'm not going," Belbe explained. "As for the rest of you, you'll have to work out your own arrangements."

She took out the portal control unit from her belt and clicked the activator. The dome atop the portal device flickered to life.

"Stand back," she said. "It will throw the doorway across this axis."

The rebels watched in awe as the machine began to drone. The air between them and the far end of the Dream Halls shimmered and thickened, gradually losing its normal transparency. A square seven feet high slowly formed out of gray mist and flashes of light, like lightning in a fogbank. Medd went around the edge of the square. It was as thin as paper and opaque from both sides.

"Do we go now?" asked Kireno.

"It hasn't reached travel potential yet," Belbe said. "It may take another quarter hour before the door is open. Then I have to calibrate the transmitter."

"What?"

She smiled. "Choose your destination."

"Skyshroud!" Medd said. "Send us to the Eye of Korai!"

Belbe fiddled with the tiny dials on her control unit. Ripples of color sprayed across the gray square.

"You must understand," she said emphatically. "A portal is a transplanar connection only. I cannot send you elsewhere on Rath. You'll be going to another plane—another world."

She let this astonishing revelation sink in.

Sivi roused herself. "Will we ever be able to come back to Rath?"

"I don't know. What I do know is if you remain here you'll die, and the cause you've fought for will suffer a terrible loss."

"Whatever happens, Eladamri must go," Medd said. "Are we agreed on that?" Sivi, Kireno, and Shamus solemnly concurred. Takara chewed her lip and said nothing.

"I'll never be able to live with myself if I leave anyone behind," said the elf gravely. "Is there no other choice?"

"The unit will transmit four hundred pounds, no more," Belbe said. "Anything exceeding the power limit will not go through. The consequences for a living being would be disastrous."

"You mean, a person might arrive without their legs or head?" asked Shamus.

"Exactly so."

Belbe finished her power adjustments. The portal square was now brilliant blue, free of ripples or fog. She announced the portal was stable, and all she needed was a destination to align it with.

A long pause ensued. Finally Eladamri said, "Dominaria."

Takara's eyes widened in surprise. "Why there?"

"You told us our ancestors came from there. That means there are people there like us, including, I presume, elves. Dominaria is the target of Phyrexian aggression, and people there should be warned. I'll see to it they know what's coming."

He faced the azure square. "A strange woman told me things not long ago, things I didn't understand. Prophecies . . . I would be the savior of a world I'd never been to. A door would be offered to me, and I must enter it. I believe the Oracle *en*-Vec saw me going to Dominaria. So I will go."

Belbe set the coordinates for Rath's parallel world. The patient blue door began to flash and flicker again as the barrier between the planes was subverted.

* * * * *

Ertai jumped up from the infuser. He'd dialed in a double dose of dark energy, and got off the crystal platform bursting with newfound vigor. He'd had no time to warn the four servants who'd brought him to the laboratory. A silent wave of energy washed over them, transmuting them in minutes. They were now flapping around the room on fleshy wings or clinging to the walls with multiple pairs of legs. As he lay on the infuser and the dark glow flooded his anguished mind, the truth had burst upon him like a bolt from Belbe's plasma discharger.

She'd hidden her portal device in the Dream Halls. It was the perfect place to hide it. The ordinary inhabitants of the Citadel never went there, as they feared Volrath even in his absence. Crovax thought the halls were a vain, empty monument, so he never deigned to go there either. By luck, or fate, the rebels had chosen this room for their last stand—and Belbe was going in to "talk" to Eladamri. . . .

He had the good fortune to encounter Greven first. Crovax might have slain him on sight.

"Dread Lord!" he said, actually grasping the fearsome warrior by his broad shoulders. "Has Belbe gone into the Dream Halls yet?"

"Some time ago. It's been very quiet since."

Ertai was frantic. He could feel the weight of death or permanent exile on Rath settling over his shoulders. Fear, and perhaps too much decadent energy, warped his morals and loosened his tongue.

"We must do something, Dread Lord!" he said. "She has a portal device in there!" *Which I need to use!* was the part he dared not say out loud.

Greven shoved him away. "You'd better not be lying, Boy!"

"Why would I lie? We have to stop her!"

Greven roused his idle troops and had them stand to arms. "Come," he said, taking Ertai roughly by the collar. "We must report this to the evincar."

The stir among the soldiers spread ahead of Greven, and by the time he found Crovax sitting in an elaborate chair drawn from the flowstone, the new Evincar of Rath knew something was amiss. His expression hardened when he saw Ertai.

"What's this corpse doing here?" he said.

"Your Highness, the emissary brought a portal device with her from Phyrexia. According to the boy, she hid it in the Dream Halls," explained Greven.

Crovax bolted from the chair, which subsided into the floor. "A portal? Are you sure?"

"She told me so when we . . . I believe her," Ertai replied, his face burning.

"Would she use it to help Eladamri?" Crovax stopped himself. "It doesn't matter. Everyone in that room is hereby condemned to death," he announced. "Let's put an end to this game."

The chosen storming squad fell in step behind Crovax, Greven, and Ertai. The evincar strode to within a dozen paces of the locked doors.

"Will you summon them to surrender?" said Ertai.

"Why should I? They're dead as of this moment."

Crovax handed the plasma discharger to a guardsman, then pressed his palms together in an awful parody of prayer. He slowly raised his hands, spreading them wider as they rose.

A large hump appeared in the floor. Soldiers fell back as the cubic shape mounted higher. So much of the floor was drawn into the rising shape that the floor joists appeared as if shoals around the edges of the room. The summoned form took on the shape of a truncated pyramid fifteen feet high and twelve feet wide at the base.

"What's he—?" Ertai's question was cut off when the pyramid heaved itself forward and slammed against the doors. The entire Citadel quaked from the shock.

* * * * *

The sudden impact startled the rebels. "Crovax is tired of waiting," Eladamri said. "Is the portal ready?"

Belbe made some hasty calculations. "No, it's not fixed on the destination yet."

The massive ram hit the doors again. Loose dream catching machinery rained down, and for the first time the huge doors showed damage. The center was dented inward eight inches, and the gap at the top and bottom was admitting more of the bright light from outside.

"How much longer?" Takara asked anxiously.

"I don't know exactly—the unit's never been used before. It has no settings to compare to."

Eladamri grabbed Belbe by the hair and jerked her head back. "Hurry," he said. "If I find out you're delaying—"

"You're delaying me now," she said. He released her.

The remaining rebel fighters placed themselves between the

doors and the portal with drawn swords. Sivi tried to take her place beside Medd, but he gently pushed her away.

"I'm still good enough to fight with you!" she said. Her words were slurred and her movements shaky.

"You've had a hard knock on the head, Sivi," Medd replied. "You can hardly stand. Go with Eladamri. He needs someone to protect him."

"I won't leave you here to die!"

A third powerful impact caused more debris to shower down from the heights of the Dream Halls. The heavy shocks caused the portal unit to topple over. Belbe let out a yelp of horror.

She and Takara returned the device upright.

Takara was concerned. "Is it damaged?"

Belbe ran the test commands on two sides of her control unit. All the responses were normal. "No! But we'd better brace it—another fall could ruin everything."

* * * * *

Outside, Crovax was reeling. The battle with Volrath had depleted his strength, and the effort required to raise and move several tons of flowstone strained him to his limits. He gathered his power for a fourth attack, but he couldn't finish it. The giant battering ram froze inches from the doors when Crovax passed out. He pitched face down on the floor. No one attempted to catch him.

Greven closed the visor on his helmet. "Tenth Company, to the right! Sixth Company, on the left. At the double, charge!"

Hurrahing, the soldiers swarmed against the doors.

* * * * *

The feral shouting from the storming troops chilled Belbe's artificial blood. She tapped in the final coordinates, and the transplanar unit whined loudly. The portal locked onto a destination, and an image formed, filling the square top to bottom, side to side.

Weeping silently, Takara walked toward the portal. "Is that it? Is that Dominaria?"

The scene through the portal was of a verdant plain, green in the lush growth of summer. A few trees dotted the rolling savanna. The sky was blue—not so blue as the open portal, but a warm, living shade never seen in Rath's gray skies.

Eladamri was transfixed by the beauty of the view. "Is that it, Avila?"

Belbe didn't notice what he called her. "It should be."

Four hundred men pushed and pounded on the sagging doors. Medd, Kireno, and Shamus clasped hands. The interlaced hinges of the right-hand door began to squeal as the metal was torn apart.

Takara could stand it no longer. She pushed Eladamri aside and ran at the portal. Where she touched it, the image distorted in concentric ripples, like a pool of water after a pebble falls in. Then she was gone. Half a second later Belbe saw Takara's back as she ran through the chest high grass, away from the open portal. Away from Rath.

"Go, Eladamri," Belbe said.

"Not yet. I have something for you."

"What?"

The upper hinge gave way and crashed to the floor. The right hand door slowly fell, twisting the lower hinge as it went. Soldiers and guards, fired by their success, didn't wait for the door to fall, but clambered over it. Kireno shouted a Vec war cry and ran at them. Shamus followed, leaving Medd alone to ward off attackers trying to reach the portal.

Kireno stabbed two soldiers before they could leap clear of the door, but more poured over the sides, and he was soon enveloped in hostile blades. He traded cuts with foes on two fronts for several breathtaking seconds, then he was cut down from behind. A swarm of Rathi soldiers trampled the fallen rebel and overran Shamus. The nimble young Dal drew off at least forty guards as he retreated to the wall. He fought on, killing two and wounding four before the press became too great. He was impaled on no less than six swords at once and pinned to the wall. The soldiers drew back, leaving Shamus dead at the base of one of Volrath's pilasters.

"Eladamri, hurry!" Belbe cried. She wasn't armed, but she was prepared to use her considerable skills to safeguard his departure.

She watched the elf remove the wooden fetish from around his neck. It was a knobby little carving of a sprite, an ancestral spirit revered by elderly elves. Eladamri wasn't religious. The fetish had another purpose.

He snapped the figure's waist. The fetish was hollow. Inside the cavity was a small glass vial, closed with a cut glass plug and sealed with wax. It was the vial left in Avila's bed the night she died.

Medd shouted several words to Sivi, who was also unarmed but ready to defend the portal. She watched as Medd was engulfed in a storm of swords and shields. He died as she looked on, but he bought his leader a few more precious seconds.

Belbe backed away from the melee until she bumped into Eladamri. "What are you waiting for?" she cried. "Go! Will you go?"

"After you, Avila."

This time she heard him. She looked at him with genuine pity. "I can't go," she said.

He looked quite calm as he pulled the plug from the vial and flung the contents at her. There were only a few drops of death elixir in it. Most of it hit her armor harmlessly, but a single droplet landed on her cheek.

Belbe's hearing instantly failed. Her vision blurred, and when she wiped her eyes with her hands, she smeared the tiny droplet across her face. Her muscles locked, and searing pain shot through her entrails. An ordinary person would have died the moment the elixir touched her, but Belbe's powerful systems had more resistance. She was doomed, and she knew it. One by one her bodily functions folded up, ceasing to work. She was already deaf. Her vision was contracting to a narrow point.

Sivi lurched into her line of sight, and Belbe saw Eladamri push her backward into the portal. The bucolic scene of another world rippled, then settled to show Sivi on her back in the tall grass. She stared back through the portal at the two elves.

Belbe's knees failed. She slumped to the floor facing the portal. She shivered violently as her borrowed life fought with the toxin. Her lips parted to speak, but no sound came out.

"For the peace of my soul and yours, this had to be," Eladamri said. With a final knowing nod, he stepped through the waiting portal.

Greven and his soldiers had reached the transplanar device. One zealous guard tried to follow Eladamri by jumping into the portal, but there was not enough energy left to effect his transfer. Sixty pounds of the man landed in the grass beside Sivi—head, shoulders, one arm, helmet, part of a breastplate. The rest of him, a singed stump, fell back on the floor of the Dream Halls.

Its power exhausted, the portal shut down. The pristine image of the plain where Takara, Eladamri, and Sivi had escaped faded into murky gray mist. Belbe, pale as death and with tears streaming down her face, could just make out the words on Eladamri's lips.

"Farewell, Avila."

CODA
Memorial

When order was restored to the Dream Halls, Greven had his victorious soldiers line up by companies, facing each other. There they stood at attention until Crovax, recovered from his faint, entered the hall. The dead rebels were laid out for his inspection. Crovax gave them a cursory glance. Their souls were long departed, and so were not available to him.

Ertai skulked on Crovax's heels, anxiously searching for Belbe and the portal device. Looking past the evincar, he saw Belbe kneeling on the floor a few yards away, her head slumped to her chest. Disdaining the evincar's displeasure, he ran ahead of him.

"Belbe! Belbe!"

She didn't move and didn't answer. He touched the back of her neck and immediately knew why. Her skin was cold as ice.

"Belbe . . ." He knelt beside her. Her eyes were closed, her cheeks still wet. Ertai picked up her hand. Her fingertips were already turning black.

"Dead, is she?" asked Crovax. Ertai nodded dumbly. "How was it done? I don't see a wound. I didn't think a Phyrexian construct could be killed so easily."

Ertai blinked through his own tears and spotted a tiny glass vial on the floor. Seamed with cracks and empty, it smelled like newly mown hay.

Crovax took the vial from his hand. "I see. I'll have this analyzed. Potent poisons are useful things to have."

The evincar ordered Belbe's body removed, along with what remained of the portal machinery. Greven stood by awaiting his new master's pleasure.

"Eladamri is gone," Greven said.

"Where?" asked Crovax.

"No one survived to tell us, Your Highness. This device of the emissary's may provide information." He placed Belbe's portal control in Crovax's hand.

As soon as Crovax had the vital device, Greven was stricken with pounding waves of unimaginable pain. He bellowed and fell at Crovax's feet.

"This is just the beginning," he said. "I have years of pain in store for you. You impeded me, thwarted me, aided my enemy, and on top of all that, allowed the arch-rebel to escape."

Greven flailed helplessly, retching and beating his tormented face on the floor.

"The only reason I don't kill you is because you'll be needed in the coming war." He kicked Greven's head. "Besides, having Eladamri exiled to another plane is almost as helpful as having him dead—maybe more so. There will be no martyr's grave, no brave example for another generation of troublemakers."

He sent two guards to bring Ertai to him. They dragged the young sorcerer before Crovax and forced him to lie on his belly at the evincar's feet.

"Now, what shall I do with you?"

"I don't care."

Crovax drove a toe into Ertai's ribs. He moaned and doubled over.

"Don't play hero with me, Boy. I can make you care about anything." His tone relaxed. "But I do owe you, don't I?"

"Owe?" gasped Ertai.

"Don't you think I know you intervened in my duel with Volrath? I could see your childish spell weighing down his blade as easily as he could. No one else on Rath practices your brand of archaic magic. Why did you help me? I would've thought Volrath would have been more your sort of patron."

"I knew you'd win eventually. I thought if I helped, you'd spare Belbe and me."

"It's too late for the emissary. I suppose her rebel friends did her in." He frowned. "A waste of good Phyrexian technology, that girl. What were they thinking?"

He relented on Greven's punishment. The suffering warrior couldn't even stand after his treatment.

"As a reward for your unsolicited help, Ertai, I'll spare your life. In return, you will serve me. Do you agree?"

A faint spark of hope illuminated the profound darkness in Ertai's heart. "I have many talents, Your Highness. Perhaps I can demonstrate them to you."

"We'll see. In the meantime, I have use for your influence with the flowstone."

"My influence is nothing compared to yours, Sire."

Crovax smiled, and everyone in the vicinity flushed with fear. "For my purpose, your skills will be enough."

* * * * *

In a remote part of the Stronghold, the flowstone factory began a new day's production. The output accelerator and the flowstone gauge conferred, as was their designed custom, on the efficiency of the previous day's production.

"Yesterday's output was 648,922,765 tons," the accelerator said. "This is approximately fifty percent of our total capacity."

"It is one hundred percent," countered the gauge.

"Forty days ago we produced 1.2 billion tons of flowstone," said the accelerator. "That represented an effort of 108 percent of our capacity. How can 648,922,765 tons in the previous daily cycle be 100 percent?"

"It cannot," said the gauge. "Increase production to 1.1 billion tons in this cycle."

Lava input tubes at the very bottom of the Citadel were switched on. Prodded to full capacity, the factory rumbled into high gear. The pitch of production increased.

Nemesis

* * * * *

There were a lot of bodies to dispose of. The moggs dragged a heavy cart to the death pits and eased the bodies in one at a time to avoid splashing the deadly black tar on themselves. In went Dorlan il-Dal, former chamberlain of the palace. In went Tharvello, promising young sergeant. In went nine young men of the Dal and Vec, still clad in their borrowed Rathi uniforms.

The moggs hooted happily as the last of the bodies sank into the sable ooze. Though there were many bodies yet to dispose of, their shift was done. They had a half-day off. A holiday had been declared by the new evincar.

* * * * *

Tant Jova was dying. She was past one hundred-twenty years old, and all the skills of her clan's healers could no longer stave off the assault of old age. It was whispered in camp the real cause of her final illness was the fact that Eladamri and Liin Sivi never returned from their last raid.

Lying in her tent on a hummock in the Skyshroud Forest, Tant Jova called two people to her bedside, Darsett en-Dal and Gallan. The wealthy Dal merchant and the young elf warrior stood on either side of Jova's simple pallet.

"Long life to you, Tant Jova," said Darsett, pressing a hand to his chest.

"Rubbish," the old woman rasped. "My time left is measured in heartbeats. If I had a long life ahead of me, I wouldn't be lying here, would I?"

"What can we do, Tant Jova?" asked Gallan.

"I want you to pledge to continue the fight against the Stronghold. I know the night seems dark and long, but like all nights, it will end. Lead the free people of Rath into the morning."

"We'll keep the fight going," Darsett said. "Though I don't know what the point is now. We have a new evincar, worse than the last. The airship flies again, raining death on our people from above. The Stronghold seems mightier than ever, and we've lost Eladamri and many of our finest young warriors."

"The point is to fight, O Darsett," Tant Jova said, taking his broad hand. "Eladamri started his rebellion twenty years ago. You and I have been fighting just five months. If we can resist even when the enemy is strongest, we will prevail in time."

"Our agents report good progress recruiting in the Stronghold," Gallan said. "They haven't forgotten what Crovax did to their families."

The old Vec woman closed her eyes. "He dug his own grave that day," she whispered. "The time will come when all the righteous souls of the murdered will rise up and bring the tyrant Crovax to just retribution. . . ."

"Sleep now," Gallan urged. "Be at peace. Darsett and I will continue the battle."

Her sunken eyes closed. Gallan and Darsett slipped out, leaving the Vec matriarch to dream a last dream of freedom.

* * * * *

It was dusk. The two rebel leaders walked out from under the trees and looked up at the darkening sky.

"Have you noticed the odd colors in the sky at daybreak and dusk?" asked Darsett. "Sometimes the sky looks quite blue."

"It's strange," Gallan agreed. "But no stranger than some other tales I've heard. I'm in contact with elves in other parts of the forest, and with Vec nomads who range as far away as the Sawtooth Hills and the Weblands. They speak of phantom cities appearing on the plain at dusk, and ghostly forests and mountains visible just before daybreak."

"What does it mean?"

The young elf shook his head. "I'm no seer, but these signs must be portents of coming changes—changes that may alter Rath forever."

Darsett shoved his hands in his pockets. Loose coins jingled there. "I went to Eladamri's first meeting because I hated the high taxes Volrath made me pay," he mused. "Five months later, I find myself running a damned revolution and puzzling over mysterious omens. Does that make sense?"

Gallan couldn't tell him. At that moment, he saw the northern sky shot through with vivid blue. The low clouds were illuminated from some unknown source and glowed a sanguinary red. Such colors were unnatural on Rath, and their sudden, radical beauty left both Dal and elf speechless.

* * * * *

For reasons known only to himself, Crovax chose to give Belbe a sumptuous state funeral. The Stronghold was too confining for the spectacle Crovax planned, so the funeral pyre was erected outside the crater, on the smooth southern plain. The entire army of Rath was summoned to attend, each soldier with a new black mantle and black headbands tied around their helmets. Delegations from the Dal, Vec, and Kor were required to attend, and they did, clad in suitable mourning dress. The actual pyre was surrounded by over five thousand civilian onlookers. Many of the civilians wondered why a sturdy post had been set in the ground alongside the pyre and why it was fitted with heavy chains. Rumor had it an execution was going to be staged during the Phyrexian emissary's funeral.

The soldiers and civilians arrived at their designated places at the specified time, an hour before dusk. They waited and watched the causeway for signs of the funeral procession. To fill the long minutes, conversation turned to the strange colors people were seeing in the sky, and to the ghostly visions that appeared with increasing frequency at the start and end of each day.

It was unsettling, but then so was the new evincar. Unlike Volrath, Crovax made no pretense of royal manners. He was brisk and efficient, dispensing justice and injustice with equal facility. His first act after ordering Belbe's funeral was to purge over six hundred courtiers from the Citadel. They simply vanished without trial or trace.

The first visceral notes of a distant drumbeat filtered down the causeway. The restive crowd quieted, and the massed ranks of soldiers came to attention.

A column of palace guards appeared in full regalia, bearing flagstaffs instead of their usual polearms. Each staff carried a black oriflamme, hanging limply in the still air. Behind the guardsmen came a group of drummers, fifty strong, beating a steady rhythm. After the drummers came the torchbearers, sixty in all. They wore white tabards over black, and each carried a four-foot-long blazing brand.

On the heels of the torchbearers was the emissary herself, borne on a bier made of real wood. Belbe had been wrapped head to toe in sparkling white bandages. Only her pallid face was exposed. Her Phyrexian armor was piled at her feet. The entire bier weighed five hundred pounds and required eight stout guardsmen to carry it.

So far, the spectacle had been impressive but predictable. What followed Belbe's body made everyone gasp with surprise.

Volrath—alive and in chains.

Everyone assumed Volrath had been killed by Crovax soon after his defeat, yet here he was in all his lost glory. In the weeks since Crovax's ascension to the throne, technicians had been working on Volrath. They had removed—with varying degrees of success—most of his Phyrexian grafts and implants until all that was left was a shell of the godlike being Volrath had been. His beautiful body was gone, and Vuel's short, homely one was all that was left. Dressed only in a loin cloth, Volrath, properly called Vuel again, still managed to walk with glacial dignity, his head held high.

Some people bowed when he passed. Their names were taken by Crovax's police agents scattered through the crowd. Respect for the defeated was forbidden, and the punishment was death.

Next in the procession came the Corps of Sergeants in their bright armor, swords held rigidly in front of their stern faces. A hooded executioner walked in their wake, and a final contingent of palace guards brought up the rear. But where was Greven il-Vec? Where was the evincar?

The first company of guards dispersed to form a ring around the pyre and post. The drummers marched past the site and halted. A ring of fire encircled the funeral bed as the torchbearers spread out single file around it. The pallbearers entered the circle of fire with swaying step and carefully placed the bier atop the sturdy pyramid of kindling. They withdrew outside the cordon of guards.

Vuel entered the ring and paused for a moment at the foot of Belbe's bier. He bowed deeply, then walked to the post and snapped the manacles around his own hands.

The executioner took his place beside Vuel. He carried no ax or sword, just a small leather bag.

The final contingent of guards halted in the path, blocking it. The drummers carried on for a short while, then finished their march with a flourish of batons. Silence engulfed the scene.

Overhead, the drone of aerial engines announced the arrival of *Predator*. Greven was now accounted for. The airship emerged from the Stronghold and slowly circled the funeral site. The sky was unusually free of clouds, and no wind stirred the pewter dusk.

There was a flash near the pyre. Some of the spectators thought the fire had been lit, but it was Crovax's arrival. Most people had never seen him teleport before, and he was gratified by the awe rippling through the crowd. The evincar was resplendent in new white armor and helmet. Even his leather gloves were white.

"People of Rath!" he boomed. "This a solemn occasion. We are here to celebrate death—and celebrate we should, because death is as essential to life as food, warmth, or breath. Death is the great measuring rod against which we gauge our lives, and before us today are two whose lives have come to their end.

"The emissary of our overlords accomplished much in her short life. She should always be remembered for bridging the awkward and dangerous interregnum between my reign and that of the previous evincar."

He took a torch from the nearest bearer and raised it high. "Hail, Belbe! Emissary of the overlords!"

The guards repeated Crovax's cry, and the crowd took it up. Crovax thrust his flaming brand into the pyre, and the other torch bearers followed suit. The timbers had been soaked in volatile spirits and caught fire with great speed.

Crovax approached the executioner. "How are you, Ertai?" he asked.

Off came the hood. "Fine, sire. It is a magnificent evening."

The once cocky sorcerer had been changed. Modifications, not unlike Greven's, had made the man taller and wider. From under his heavy robe, Ertai produced not two but four arms! And his face was partially concealed from view by a metallic mask and shoulder plating. Only his forehead, eyes, and the bridge of his nose could be seen by members of the crowd. The upper end of the control rod implanted in Ertai's spine was also visible. The incision was still inflamed, but the yellow metal rod clearly showed through the boy's livid skin.

Crovax gave the order. "Prepare the injection."

Ertai knelt and opened the bag. There were two objects inside: a tall vial of silver liquid and a large metal syringe. He broke the seal on the vial and dipped the needle into the heavy liquid.

"This will take a few seconds," he said apologetically.

"Do the job right," Crovax said. He stood face to face with Vuel and said, "Any last words? Go ahead, speak your mind." He'd had Vuel's tongue cut out the night before. "Nothing to say? That's refreshing. Looking back at your reign, I have to say you talked entirely too much."

Ertai stood. "The preparation is ready, Sire."

"Proceed."

Ertai pushed the syringe plunger to expel any air. Silver droplets squirted from the needle. Where the droplets hit the ground, they formed tiny spheres that spun madly in place.

Vuel's eyes widened.

Ertai jabbed the needle into Vuel's carotid artery. The preparation was too dense to pump into an arm or leg vein. Vuel's bloodshot eyes bulged as Ertai forced the plunger down. He thrashed against his chains, to no avail. When the syringe was empty, Ertai jerked it out.

"Your Highness, it is done. Will you do the honors?"

Crovax folded his arms across his chest and inhaled deeply. "The task is yours. Carry out the sentence."

Ertai bowed. He stood by Vuel's side and formed the command in his mind. The former evincar trembled. His head snapped around, and he stared at Ertai in abject horror.

Vuel tore against his manacles as convulsions wracked his body. One by one his toenails and fingernails sloughed off. The skin of his extremities split, and red blood—no longer glistening oil—ran out on the gray ground. His joints disintegrated, nd as he watched, his fingers fell off, joint by joint.

Liquid flowstone coursed through his veins, obeying Ertai's ast command: *disassemble*. The nano-machines attacked Vuel rom the inside, dismantling his body at a cellular level. His knees dissolved and his lower legs dropped away, leaving the ormer master of Rath dangling by his manacled wrists. Then his wrists came off, and he fell to the ground.

* * * * *

Vuel landed face upward. As his ears and nose slid from his ace, as his teeth bubbled out of his mouth on the last breath rom his lungs, he saw the ever-gray sky of Rath change to per-ect, cloudless blue. It was the sky of Dominaria, and Vuel, son of Kondo, had returned home at last.

* * * * *

The fire burned out. Nothing but ashes remained of the flesh of Belbe.

The plain was empty. Vuel was gone. Not even bones were eft as the implacable flowstone disassembled him down to the ast gory mote. Ertai alone remained. He waited under a sky he knew for the fire to die. When the last small flames went out, he waded into the pile of cinders that had been Belbe's bier, needless of hot embers. Her metal skeleton was intact, though warped by the pyre's intense heat. He found her small skull, smudged and blackened but with bright alloy gleaming around the eye sockets. He tucked the warm skull under his arm.

His foot dislodged an unfamiliar object—a black sphere about four inches in diameter. He picked it up. It was cold to the touch, not hot, and not a speck of ash clung to it. The shiny sur-ace was seamless, unmarred. Phyrexian, no doubt. Belbe's "lens."

Even with a control rod in his spine, Ertai was terrified. He dropped the black orb and kicked it back into the ashes. All he wanted was the skull. He ran back to the Stronghold under the stars of Dominaria, praying the lens no longer worked.

MAGIC
The Gathering®

GET THE STORY BEHIND THE WORLD'S BEST-SELLING GAME.

The Artifacts Cycle

The Brothers' War
Book I
Jeff Grubb

In a battle that will sink continents and shake the skies, two brothers struggle for supremacy on the continent of Terisiare. Only one will survive.

Planeswalker
Book II
Lynn Abbey

Urza, survivor of The Brothers' War, feels the spark of a planeswalker ignite within him. As he strides between the planes, a loyal companion seeks to free him from an obsession that threatens to turn to madness.

Time Streams
Book III
J. Robert King

From a remote island in Dominaria Urza tries to right the wrongs he and his brother perpetrated against their homeland. Only a mighty weapon can turn the balance of history.

Bloodlines
Book IV
Loren Coleman

As the centuries slowly pass, Urza patiently perfects his weapon, waiting for the right moment(and the right heir. The heir to his legacy.

Lost Empires

n nooks and crannies of the FORGOTTEN REALMS® setting, explorers
search out hidden secrets of long-dead civilizations, secrets that bear
promises and perils for present-day Faerûn.

The Lost Library of Cormanthyr
Mel Odom

Is it just a myth? Or does it still stand somewhere in the most ancient
corners of Faerûn? An intrepid human explorer sets out to find the truth and
encounters an undying avenger, determined to protect the secrets of the
ancient elven empire of Cormanthyr.

Faces of Deception
Troy Denning

Hidden from his powerful family's enemies behind the hideous mask of his
own face, Atreus of Erlkazar seeks his salvation on an impossible mission.
Driven by the goddess of beauty to find a way past his own flesh, he must
travel to the ancient valleys of the enigmatic Utter East.

Star of Cursrah
Clayton Emery

The Protector crawls forth, the shade of a dead
city whose rulers refuse to die, and young
companions in two distant epochs learn of a
dreadful destiny they cannot escape.

THE SHADOW STONE
Richard Baker

Bullied by nobles, accused of a crime for which he bears no blame, Aeron seeks refuge in the forests of the Maerchwood. What he finds there will change his life and transform him into one of the most powerful mages in Faerûn.

THE GLASS PRISON
Monte Cook

Half-human, half-fiend. Torn between the darkness and the light. Vheod Runechild, a new kind of hero, travels the Realms to find the secrets of his past and future.

BEYOND THE HIGH ROAD
Troy Denning

The seer Alaundo prophesied that seven scourges would sweep Cormyr away in ruin. For centuries the royal family has stood watch against that day and devoted their lives to the protection of the realm. But in a time when their ancient guardians slumber and their most loyal servants disappear, who will protect King Azoun and his daughters?